LIGHTSPEED
The Quest

E. Douglas Ward &
Lonie Blackman Ward

Level 4 Press, Inc.
San Diego, CA

This is a work of fiction. All of the characters and events portrayed in this novel are either fictitious or used fictitiously.

This book is printed on acid-free paper.

Published by
Level 4 Press, Inc.
13518 Jamul Drive
Jamul, CA 91935
www.level4press.com

BISAC Subject Heading: FIC028020   FICTION / Science Fiction / High Tech
Library of Congress Control Number: 2006937611

ISBN: 978-1-933769-15-8

Printed in China

ACKNOWLEDGEMENTS

Intense collaboration while working on a project for years often brings out the best or worse of those involved. Authorship and writing a literary novel together are no exceptions. Thankfully, my husband, Doug and I complimented our joint life experiences, his as an Aeronautical Engineer (rocket engines) and CEO, mine as an Actress and Communicator. During our conception of "Light Speed," we worked as a team in bringing together our thoughts and inspiring the strengths of the other. Our collaboration was an intellectual journey, working as individuals, but philosophically and morally as a single entity. Thank you, my Doug, for your love, inspiration, vitality and courage to 'go beyond' a mere concept, and my pleasure of being a contributing part and co-author while working with your brilliant mind and vision.

Lonie Blackman Ward

Many years ago, as an engineer on ICBM's, among other large and small vehicle engines, all of us realized that chemical rockets would never be commercially practicable for entering deep space to planets and stars, particularly a manned voyage. I discussed my thoughts about an advanced propulsion system concept with my wonderful wife, Lonie. She urged me to write a fictional book and would work with me in imagination, editing, and most important — make the characters interesting, with individual personalities and talking as normal people. Without her, this book would have been just an engineering science-fiction novel, the reader never becoming intimate with the characters' minds, thoughts, goals and morals. Thank you, my Lonie, for your patience in hours of discussion, planning the plot, the numerous edits, and above all, your outstanding creativity. You are truly my soul mate and co-author. Above all, I love you "the bestest."

Edward Douglas Ward

DEDICATION

To the publisher,

William Roetzheim, Level 4 Press, Inc.

Bill, thank you for seeing the potential of our book. Your interest and enthusiasm, along with help where needed, was outstanding.

LIGHTSPEED

The world had changed drastically since the days of the first Moon landing and orbiting space stations. Highly advanced rocket transportation systems made civilization possible on both the Moon and Mars. Men, women, entire families, lived inside massive self-contained domed cities. These hemispherical communities were designed for everyday living, vacation spas and, most important, as work sites to extract minerals from the ground.

Also housed within these multiple confines were diverse manufacturing facilities. Taking advantage of the lower gravity, precision electronic equipment and rare alloys could be produced without the flaws so common when manufactured in Earth's gravity and oxygen atmosphere. Many metals, chemical compounds and products were processed and produced in gigantic space stations circling Earth, on the Moon and on Mars. Manned and unmanned cargo ships made regular runs to and from Earth, the space stations around Earth, the Moon and Mars. Around each of them, large space transports capable of carrying 50,000 metric tons of ore, supplies and materials, waited in orbit to be loaded with payload carried to them by smaller transport shuttles. Some of the orbiting ships were so large that they had to be assembled in orbit, never to land on Earth, the mother planet. From the asteroid belt between Mars and Jupiter, these gigantic vessels brought minerals and rare crystals to Mars for processing and, eventually, to Earth after further work on the Moon or one of the various space stations. Permanent space stations within the belt controlled robotics mining of the various asteroids.

Preprogrammed unmanned robot vessels still explored Venus, Mercury and the other solar system planets for minerals and gasses that would be economically worthwhile for use on Earth. Even Pluto, 5.9 billion kilometers from Earth, had been visited a few times. But the extreme temperature of almost absolute zero, or minus 273°C (centigrade), where all molecular activity ceases, had ruled out that planet for further exploration. Industry, on the advice of learned space scientists, had concluded that only Venus and Mercury might someday conceivably be worth the investment of domed cities even though their surface temperatures varied between -280°F and +910°F.

Other planets such as Uranus, Saturn, Jupiter and Neptune were also deemed too gaseous to provide a surface on which to build inhabited domed cities. Manned vehicles for the extraction of new minerals and gasses had surveyed a number of the larger satellites of these planets. Plans had been initiated to build domed cities on several of these selected satellites.

Vacation spas were so common on Mars and the Moon, that even the average family was able to spend a week or so on holiday, enjoying space trotting and jumping — particularly the children.

Earth transportation had evolved by the use of a rocket larger than anything ever envisioned during the original NASA Space Shuttle days. Gigantic Ground Orbit Transfer Vehicles, or mother ship lift rockets, carried up to 24 smaller reentry vehicles into orbit, each able to carry several hundred passengers. Every reentry vehicle was programmed to de-orbit and land in predetermined cities. The heavy Ground Orbit Transfer's entire function was to go to low Earth orbit, disgorge each reentry vehicle, and return to land half way around Earth to begin again the same operation. No place on Earth was more than two hours away from any major location. Short flights across continents used supersonic transports. City to city transportation was provided by HV 1000 trains, speeding along at 1,000 kilometers per hour.

The web of electric power lines from fossil and nuclear power stations was long gone, as were antiquated gasoline powered automobiles and the outdated gas stations that supplied them. Shielded radioactive isotope batteries, available at all stores, provided the necessary power for homes and the new automated cars and air-cars. Factories, mineral processing, and all other industries that required enormous power from fossil or central nuclear power stations now used self contained cold fusion power systems.

Home computers processed material at trillions of calculations per second. The power and speed of the immense twentieth century Cray super-computer, was now compressed into the size of a twentieth century laptop. Larger computers could even manipulate rapidly changing molecules in a fusion reaction or in molten metals.

Ground transportation had changed to the point where automobile accidents were a thing of the past. All vehicles were automated and administered by a central traffic control.

This was the world in which Arturo Newsome Diggs and his family lived.

Like all travelers throughout the ages, whether by stagecoach, train, airplane or space ship, Arturo was impatient to arrive at his destination. The Ground Orbit Transfer, or GOT, had been held up in New Delhi by heavy incoming sub orbital traffic. When the score or so of reentry vehicles, commonly referred to as REVs, were finally ejected, the arrival schedule in California was well over half an hour late.

During the flight, Arturo, like his seatmate, had noted the injected REVs sent into low orbit reentry to cities around the world.

"I don't know about you, but I'm ready to de-orbit and go home," the traveler next to him grumbled.

"According to my calculations," Arturo smiled, "unless we have to go around again because of traffic problems in San Diego, we should eject in about three minutes."

"Don't even mention delays," the man muttered in disgust, "if I have to sit in this REV one more minute than necessary..."

"...Know what you mean," Arturo cut in, "I had to get up at one a.m., California time, to catch this morning's GOT flight to New Delhi for a meeting."

"Wow! You've had a full day, all right," the traveler whistled through his teeth. "I'm like you, rather go for one day and get it over with. Don't like staying overnight. But it's a bitch to schedule daytime meetings in a twelve hour time-zone change."

"Well, for both our sakes, I hope we make it into San Diego on this orbit."

The man nodded and, enjoying the conversation, continued, "Have far to drive after we arrive at the REV port?"

"Yes," Arturo sighed, "that's the price I pay for living in a beautiful sanctuary 75 miles from downtown."

"Yeah, my wife and I tried that, too. But even with Central Traffic Control, just couldn't take it anymore. Damn, you can fly half way around the world in less time than it takes to get home from the REV port."

Arturo countered with a laugh, "So, what else is new?" His companion tapped his knuckles on the arm of the seat. "You know, it's a wonder more REVs don't run into each other."

Arturo thought for a moment before responding. "At least, only three or four hundred people are aboard a REV. If a GOT went in, four thousand might die in spite of the 'scape system". Even seasoned travelers did not want to delve too far into such possibilities; and so for a moment, there was silence between the two men. It was Arturo who resumed the conversation. "Well, in approximately ten seconds, we'll know if we're going to reenter on schedule or not."

Almost to the second, the automated reentry warning message flashed onto the scanning screen in front of them. "All passengers please re-tighten your safety net and check to see if your escape-pod is energized. We will deorbit in 30 seconds."

Automatically, Arturo pulled the body restraint around his torso, triggering a flashing purple light that signaled the 'scape pod was properly energized. He felt the GOT tilt slightly as the REV was disgorged. Glancing out the small window to his left, he saw the familiar orange glow of reentry into Earth's atmosphere. "Safe journey and landing in Texas, big GOT," he whispered to himself.

The San Diego landing was uneventful. Arturo stepped off the REV onto the automated walkway. He then pressed a code and was conveyed directly to his parked auto-car. Aligning his fingertips on the owner recognition bar, a green light flashed momentarily, allowing him to access the door. Entering the auto-car, he punched yet another set of automatic buttons to set the coordinates for his home, optimistic that he would get the shortest route instead of a lengthy detour around traffic. The auto-car computer automatically checked all routes with Central Traffic Control and fortunately chose the least congested direct route. Arturo impatiently waited for the message announcing how long it would take for an opening in the traffic pattern.

"Car 99342MXE, approximately ten minutes to entrance on silver ribbon track number A-2, thank you for waiting," came the robotics communiqué.

"You're welcome, as if I had a choice," Arturo mouthed back at the mechanical voice. "Home visi-phone," he ordered, with a sigh. The number was automatically dialed.

"Hello, Darling," he said, his tone belying fatigue, "I'm at the auto port, good trip, should be home in about forty minutes."

"Arturo!" his wife exclaimed excitedly, "I've been anxiously waiting your call. I know the GOT was late leaving India."

"Uneventful ride except for that, Jana, but I've got good news about the contract. Tell you when I get home."

"Can't wait to hear. Oh, by the way, I have a surprise for you. Mother and Father Diggs have stopped in for a visit and are insisting we go to their compound for dinner tonight."

"Great. About time mother got some work out of that new cook of hers."

"I refuse to repeat that message, Arturo. Shame on you," she teased.

7

"Just as well, mother's cooking is better anyway. Is Filip around? Tell him his dad wants to say hello."

"Oh darling, he's in town with his friend Bobby. Remember it's the weekend visit he's been looking forward to for weeks."

"Completely escaped my mind, sorry," Arturo shook his head, annoyed at his own forgetfulness. "Well, hope Bobby's parents won't regret having two boisterous ten year olds together for several days."

"No problem, they're both good kids and somehow bring out the best in one another."

"Ha! Spoken like a devoted mother."

"Arturo," she scolded, "Filip is a..."

A green light appeared, and the auto-car's electric engine began to purr quietly. "Just got the go-ahead, love, call you back if they reroute me. Love you"

"Love you, too, Arturo."

The car rolled out of the parking space onto the garage exit road. Then it automatically hooked onto the appropriate silver ribbon strip, one of thirty such ribbons that melded into the main road. On the assigned concourse, the auto-car's electric engine began to whine as it accelerated. It wasn't until it reached the stipulated 150 kilometers an hour that it settled back to a quiet hum.

Arturo set the comfortable seat to "recline" and lay back. He had hardly closed his eyes and started to relax when a shrill buzzer sounded from the instrument panel. The blinking red warning light indicated a malfunction on the concourse. Automatically, Arturo righted his seat and punched the query button. A schematic diagram showed that an auto-car had stalled on Arturo's designated route two kilometers ahead, and would have to be pulled out of the traffic flow. His auto-car, as did all others on the circuit, immediately decelerated until it came to a full stop. After a few seconds, the computerized readout displayed an alternate route around the disabled vehicle, indicating an extra twenty minutes would be required to bypass the obstruction.

"Some damn fool probably ran out of battery power," Arturo fumed, "no logical reason whatsoever for that to happen." He again barked at the computer, "Home visi-phone," and reached for the phone, pressed the button for his home number and almost barked again, "Jana, it'll be an additional twenty minutes before I roll into the garage. Some blasted auto-car stalled, and I've been rerouted."

"I'm so sorry, Darling," Jana replied.

"Damn it, Jana, an engine only needs a new isotope battery every 1,000 to 1,500 hours and the emergency auxiliary batteries are good for at least a 100 hours."

Knowing all too well how her otherwise composed husband could become irritable when tied up in a traffic jam, she responded, "Well if that's the problem, dear, I hope the idiot gets a heavy fine for going into traffic with faulty batteries."

"Particularly the auxiliary battery. Only takes a garage ten minutes to install new ones."

9

"As you've always told me, my love," and she chuckled, "there's simply no excuse for obstructing traffic because of a discharged battery."

"That's absolutely right, Jana," Arturo tersely agreed. "Isotope batteries are good for approximately 150,000 kilometers, not counting stops for route reprogramming."

Since all auto-cars were systematically inspected for proper maintenance and required a certification inserted into their Central Traffic Control access codes before they were allowed on any computer controlled roads, auto-car failures were kept to a minimum. Unfortunately, remaining battery life was not one of the checks monitored by Central Traffic.

Aside from Arturo's frustration at the delay, Jana wasn't the least bit worried about his safety in the auto-car. The computer controlled highways had so many safety features built into the system that a collision between cars had been unheard of for over twenty-five years. Automatic braking and restricted distances between auto-cars, along with the inability of a given car to swerve into another car on a separate silver ribbon path, made auto-car accidents truly a thing of the past.

"While you're in limbo, darling," Jana quickly changed the subject, "want to tell me a little about your trip?"

Arturo knew his wife's ploy was to get his mind off his boring detainment, and he smiled at her attempt. "Can't give any details on this unsecured line, dear," he cautioned, "except that it was highly productive."

"That's wonderful..." She started to say something, but was interrupted by a happy shout from Arturo.

"Hooray! Miracles never cease, Jana. Just got the message that the stall has been airlifted off the course. Won't be rerouted after all. See you on schedule. Bye!"

The auto-car smoothly accelerated to full speed, and Arturo leaned back in the cushioned seat, his thoughts centered on the fruitful Delhi trip.

The Indian tool company with whom he had met had agreed to purchase space on his company's Earth-to-Mars nuclear rocket transport. They, too, wanted more of that distant planet's fine-grain cobalt. The mineral mining endeavor on Mars had begun to produce various highly dense metals that could only be mined on Earth through extensive and prohibitively expensive processing.

Arturo was justly proud of the latest transport; and in reality, it was his work on the rocket propulsion that had made it all possible. After only one year of shuttling between Mars, the manned Moon-base and Earth, the transport had proven to be extremely reliable. Companies throughout the world were booking space for transportation of material to and from Mars, the Moon and the Mars-Jupiter Asteroid Belt. They would also use the transports to send their products to the manufacturing facilities on Mars. Each of the transports owned by the company Arturo worked for had a payload capacity of fifty million kilo's of material, almost ten times the payload of their largest competitor.

Engrossed in his thoughts, Arturo had not noticed his auto-car had turned off the main thoroughfare onto a side street. It was only when he heard the quiet deceleration of the engine, as it began making its way up the long winding hill to the cul-de-sac, that he realized he was almost home. The auto-car slowed to a crawl and then turned into the driveway. When it reached the designated space inside the garage, the electric engine stopped. Arturo flipped off the power switch, which also notified Central Traffic Control his destination had been reached and the car was no longer energized.

Jana was waiting at the door as Arturo got out of the auto-car. In the dim light of the front hall his lovely strawberry-blonde wife seemed to glow. Her smile gave an inviting welcome and her large green eyes glinted provocatively. He held open his arms to embrace her slender body. "Can't we slip upstairs for a few minutes?"

"We could, you sexy critter," Jana whispered, "but how about later tonight?" And she discreetly disengaged herself. "Mother and Father Diggs are waiting in the library. I'm sure they heard the property bell say that you're home."

"Damn," he rejoined and playfully patted her alluring posterior. "But I'll not forget about later"

"You'd better not!" Jana replied in mock shock.

Margarite and Thomas Newsome Diggs made a striking couple. Arturo's father was an exceptionally tall man; and even in his sixties, heavy dark brown hair still surmounted his craggy, handsome face. Margarite was almost her husband's height. She was uncommonly beautiful with a creamy complexion framed by hair as black as coal. Born in Toledo, Spain, to an aristocratic family, she had been schooled abroad, spoke several languages fluently and excelled in the arts.

Thomas and Margarite had met at the University of California in Berkeley while she was earning a master's degree in fine arts and he was completing his internship as a medical doctor. They were married shortly after Thomas hung up his shingle as a general practitioner.

Their only child, Arturo, carried the given name of his maternal grandfather, a famous Spanish diplomat, and the traditional middle name of Newsome. Margarite had almost memorized every passage in the Diggs' old family Bible, and had developed mystic esteem for her husband's distant ancestor, Ben Diggs.

Even after Arturo was born, Margarite pursued a career as an artist. She painted detailed miniature landscapes in the old romantic tradition of scrupulous depiction. No component of the whole was too minute to escape her precise eye.

Arturo's father had devoted his life's work to family medicine, even though in the age of specialization, the field was almost an anachronism. Thomas always found time for his avocation, astronomy; and though he did not have a degree in the science, he was held in esteem for his skilled papers on the subject.

When Arturo entered the library, Thomas and Margarite Diggs greeted their son ardently — his mother with a demonstrative hug and the customary European kiss on either cheek — his father with a vigorous handshake.

"Oh Arturo," Margarite erupted in her usual lively manner, "we're so glad you're home safe."

"Mom," Arturo laughed, putting his arm around her shoulder, "I was only gone a day."

"You know your mother, son – a day, a week, a month – it's all the same." Always forthright in his manner, Thomas asked, "Okay, how did the trip go?"

As the three stood together, there was no mistaking the family resemblance. Arturo had inherited traits from both parents. The maternal side was depicted in his dark hair, fair complexion, and zesty Spanish temperament, which he usually managed to keep in close check. The equally strong Diggs features were expressed in the rugged contours of his face, his sturdy build and thoughtful but penetrating eyes. His six foot four frame reflected both parents' stature.

"Excellent, Dad, excellent. I'll tell you over a drink."

"Is brandy okay, Arturo?" Margarite asked. Not waiting for an answer, she poured two brandies. "And one for Jana, too. She wouldn't have anything until you got here, but your father and I were not so patient."

As if on cue, Jana walked in the room. Margarite gave her a loving smile and handed her one of the two filled glasses.

"Thanks, Mother Diggs."

Margarite took a seat on the couch and watched Arturo and Jana clink their glasses together in a toast to each other.

"Come, Arturo, Jana sit down." Margarite patted two places on the curved sofa.

"Rather stand for a minute, Mother," Arturo replied, stifling a yawn. "Been on my rear for much of the last twenty-four hours."

Thomas waited for a moment and then again posed his question, "So, did you get the contract?"

"As a matter of fact," Arturo began, "the owner of the cobalt refining plant in India told me, confidentially of course, that Space Transport Corporation's price per pound to transport the cobalt from Mars to Earth, was less than 30% of our competitor's price."

"Congratulations! What's the time period?" his father probed.

"Five years, with an option to renew for up to 10 years."

"Oh, Arturo, that is wonderful news," his mother injected.

"I'm so pleased for you, dear," Jana said, squeezing his hand.

"GEO Transport," Thomas mused, shaking his head, "never was a reliable company anyway. Had too many accidents and made promises they couldn't keep."

"Dad, they're tough infighters," Arturo dissented. "GEO can still carry small loads to and from the Moon along with supplies to the space stations. Our space transports are geared for the heavy shipments." He took a sip of his drink and shrugged, "And that's where we want to concentrate. Let GEO have the other markets."

"Arturo, listen to me," Thomas walked over to his son, his voice intensifying. "Three years ago you became the chief engineer of Space Trans at the tender age of thirty-two. Don't be fooled into thinking that GEO Transport will be satisfied with only the small payloads. They'll move heaven and Earth to get your technology and build their own big nuclear rocket."

"Dad, we've been through this before." A slight note of exasperation colored his voice. "Only a handful of men understand how we were able to run the rocket exhaust at 30,000° C instead of the normal 4,000° C. Hell, it's my design, and I know how hard it would be to copy it."

"Arturo," Margarite cautioned, "heed what your father is saying. He knows of these GEO people through some of his patients."

"I know, Mother," Arturo overrode, "and I appreciate the concern, but..." and he turned back to face his father. "Remember how the old rockets were developed from 2035 technology? The only improvement made from then to 2075 was the amount of time between overhauls."

"I understand your reasoning, son," Thomas soberly conceded. "It took half a century to achieve the desired years between overhauls, instead of weeks. That was the difference that finally made space transportation a commercial reality."

Arturo restlessly waited for his father to finish before infusing his own reflections. "When the Space Transport Corporation began work on significantly improving the efficiency of a nuclear rocket in 2075, they studied hundreds of different methods during the next 35 years." Then more impassioned, "Millions were spent, but nothing really worked."

"And you, Arturo — right out of college in 2166 — were assigned to the group in charge of that project for Space Trans," Margarite added, proud of her son's brilliant accomplishments.

"Thanks for your vote of confidence, Mother," Arturo said with a polite bow in her direction, "but it took me six years until I hit on the idea of using the base rocket at its temperature of 4,000° C and employing, for the lack of a better term, a nuclear afterburner at 10 times the pressure."

"That had been thought of before, Arturo," Thomas said reflectively, then patted his son on the back, "but no one could keep the significantly higher temperature and pressure from destroying the thrust chamber."

"And that, Dad, is the key. We're operating at 30,000° C, at a speed of up to 600,000 kilometers per hour, an increase in efficiency of 300 percent."

Thomas' keen mind filled in the rest of the formula. "Which is only one half hundredth of a percent of the speed of light but allows for much higher payloads or, to steal a phrase from the far past," he chuckled, "more miles per gallon."

"Right again," and Arturo's voice became more rushed. "The continuous casting process of the thrust chamber's throat, as it melts and is replaced by its own cast off molecules, trapped in the closed loop process..."

"Stop right there, Arturo!" Thomas spoke sharply, holding up a cautionary hand and glancing warily around the room. Then in a whisper, "Who knows who may be listening with an eavesdropper? Don't say anymore."

Arturo looked reassuringly at his father. "Dad, the house is electronically swept. You know that. Anyway, what we're saying wouldn't make any difference. How to trap the molecules for rocket throat replacement is the closest kept secret at Space Transport. Only I and three others know how to program the onboard computer to tell the molecule 'getters' how and what."

"Arturo," Thomas solemnly admonished, "I still say the less said about it, the better."

"You're right. We'll change the subject." With a smile Arturo turned to the two women. "What does a man do around here to be fed?"

Immediately Margarite rose, a smile lighting her expressive face. "Señora y señores," she said, with a spacious gesture toward the door, "vamos a comer."

As Thomas took his wife's arm and escorted her from the room, he said over his shoulder, "Si, vamos a tu casa for food."

Concealed by high block walls, the adjacent Diggs family compounds were completely separate except for a covered walkway. Both Margarite and Thomas had contended, when building their home next to Arturo's, that privacy for each of the two families was of prime importance. Tonight, however, it had begun to rain heavily and the use of the covered walkway was much appreciated.

As the two couples walked over to the elder Diggs' home, a lively chatter went back and forth, except from Arturo. Even during dinner he was strangely quiet and reserved. He cordially answered when spoken to but he did not otherwise initiate any conversation. Several times, glances of concern passed between Margarite and Jana. It was only after the four were comfortably seated in the living room that Margarite decided to deal with his detachment.

"Arturo, my dear, you must be very tired. Would you rather get some sleep?" He seemed not to be listening and so she added, "Your father and I would certainly not be offended."

When he still did not respond, Jana gently prodded, "Arturo, your mother asked if..."

Arturo blinked a few times and tilted his head toward his wife as if he had not fully heard the question, "I'm sorry," he said, a frown creasing his brow, "were you talking to me?"

"Something is on your mind, Arturo," Margarite replied softly. "Would you care to talk about it? Or perhaps..."

"Yes, yes I would, Mother," and he spoke slowly and deliberately. "It's about the bequest."

There was a hushed pause as all waited for Arturo to continue.

"The bequest in the Diggs' old family Bible," Arturo haltingly resumed, "the one that my great-great — don't exactly recall how many 'greats' back — grandfather Benjamin Diggs, wrote in the twenty-first century."

Margarite could feel her heart pound and caught her breath. "I can see it in your face, Arturo," she spoke with prophetic emotion. "You want to build a rocket that can go to the stars."

Arturo gave a wan smile. "I don't know if I can or not, but I've got to try."

For a moment, Jana sat wide-eyed, looking at her husband; then she gently took his hand in hers. Alarmed by the chill of his fingers she held his hand tightly, to hopefully impart some warmth. "Grandfather Ben Diggs said that one of his descendants would try to reach the stars," she encouraged. "Arturo, maybe you are the one."

Nodding absentmindedly, he withdrew his fingers and patted his wife's hand. Like a man trying to come to grips with his own awareness, he slowly rose and began methodically pacing the room. It was some time before he spoke. "I had a serious discussion last week with Mohammed Nahal, Chief Executive of

Space Transportation," he paused and then continued. "Mohammed agreed, if we landed the order from India," suddenly he spun around, and grinned at his listeners, "to let me spend twenty-five percent of my time on just such a project — building a rocket to the stars."

"Thomas, Jana, Arturo," Margarite excitedly clapped her hands, "I have read and re-read all the writing in the Diggs' Bible. I have studied all the recording of births and deaths, all the way back to the founder of your branch of the Diggs family, the one you men almost reverently refer to as 'Old Newsome'."

Thomas started to speak, but Margarite shook her head at him. Her words almost ran together in her enthusiasm, "And yes, Arturo is the one to carry on Ben's work. He is the first since Ben, to be really interested in outer space. All the other Diggs have been doctors, musicians, writers, lawyers, sportsmen, and there was even a poet. None have been interested in space as a profession." Impulsively tweaking her husband's check, she added, "Not even you, Thomas, my darling." Margarite paused only long enough to take a deep breath before proceeding. "I cannot explain, but I do know there is something more to why Arturo must pursue Grandfather Ben's work. I can feel it," and she crossed her hands over her chest as if perceiving the assertion from within her very soul. "Thomas," giving her husband a meaningful stare, "you know I have had premonitions before."

Thomas nodded agreement, but it was Jana's composed voice that surprised everyone.

"Margarite's right, my darling. I've felt that for years." Her tone conveyed firmness. "You must go ahead with Grandfather Ben's work. But I think you've known that since you first read his bequest as a boy."

"I agree, Arturo," Thomas concurred. "Pursue your dream. Create a new space drive system for transportation to the stars."

Margarite walked over to Arturo and engulfed him in a tender embrace. For a timeless moment, mother and son stood in each other's arms. It was Margarite who gently pulled away to link her hand through Arturo's arm.

"Come, Son. We must take the old Bible out of the case. It's time we again read it together."

They walked across the room to what appeared to be only a paneled wall. Margarite lightly tapped twice on a particular spot in the fine-grained wood. The partition parted, and the vertical tambour door slowly slid back into the wall and exposed a large cupboard set inside. In this recess was a square container made of darkened glass. Margarite ran her fingernail down the edge of this receptacle until she came to a slight indentation. She pressed the notch, which instantly flooded the case with light. Inside the humidified glass box was the worn Diggs Bible.

As on the many other occasions when Arturo and Margarite had been through this same ritual, they felt their pulses quicken at the sight of the grand old leather bound volume. Arturo tapped the corner of the case to trigger a concealed lock that opened the front

22

glass panel. He carefully lifted the heavy book from its resting-place and carried it across the room.

Thomas and Jana had drawn chairs up to a small round table and were already seated. Margarite and Arturo took their places; and with loving care, she opened the book to the back pages that were filled with names, dates and places. Each of the family took turns reading aloud Newsome's first recordings and initial bequest, Ben Diggs and his bequest, through to the present and latest entries. After they finished, Margarite closed the Bible face down and ran her fingertips over the frayed leather back cover. Suddenly she removed her hand but, in deep concentration, continued staring down at the Bible.

"Mother Diggs," Jana inquired with concern, "do you feel all right?"

"No...not really," came the hesitant reply.

"Would you like some water?" Arturo offered.

But Margarite only gave a slight shake of her head with her eyes still on the Bible.

Jana followed her mother-in-law's intent stare and then quietly rose from her chair to move around the table. She placed her hand on the back cover to feel the threadbare binding. Impulsively, she gently opened the back cover and ran her hand over the frayed deerskin lining. Margarite watched and then placed her own hand on the inside liner. Both women rubbed their fingers softly over the fabric.

"Arturo," Jana called out excitedly, "there's something under this covering!"

"Yes," Margarite concurred, her eyes ablaze with elation. "If you look closely, there's a slight imprint of something round."

"Are you sure?" Arturo asked incredulously.

"Absolutely," Jana confirmed, and both women nodded in unison.

"See, Arturo, Thomas..." and Margarite pointed to the minute lump under the lining, "it looks to be about a half centimeter in diameter."

Arturo squinted down to where his mother and Jana's fingers indicated, shaking his head in disbelief. "I've looked at this Bible for years and sure never noticed that before."

Thomas put on his glasses and peered over his wife's shoulder. "Nor I. But I sure as hell see it now."

Arturo bent down and carefully began untying the leather lacing which bound the lining to the heavy, leather back. He then lifted up the backing to reveal a small round glistening object.

"It's imbedded in the deer skin. What is it, Arturo?" Jana questioned.

Though both men immediately identified the minuscule silver trinket, Thomas was the first to speak. "It's a computer chip, Jana. The likes of which I haven't seen anywhere, except in museums. Looks to be from the early twenty-first century."

"There's something more, my dears." Gingerly Margarite pulled two folded, yellowed, pieces of paper from between the binding and the cover.

24

"What are they, Mother?" Arturo asked in an electrified voice.

She unfolded the top paper and scanned it. Then with tears welling in her eyes, she handed it to Arturo.

"Darling, I think you should read this." Her voice was barely a whisper, "Although not addressed to you, I believe it was written for you."

Arturo took the handwritten page and read it to himself. When he at last looked up, his face was ashen, but his eyes radiated exhilaration. "I think everyone should hear Grandfather Benjamin Newsome Diggs' legacy," and with voice choked with emotion, he began reading aloud.

> This is my legacy to the right Diggs descendent, left in the same manner as old Newsome Diggs left his legacy to me. When you read his legacy, you will wonder as I have wondered: who he was and where he came from. Irrespective, all Diggs' descendents who read this must follow Newsome's legacy the same as I have.
>
> I have examined all available sources of energy that could possibly lead to a manned space ship traveling at light speed and beyond. I am now convinced that all who have studied this problem have been on the wrong paths and have overlooked the obvious solu-

tion. Since photons travel at the speed of light, the key is to use them for rocket propulsion. Yes, use what is thought of today as a weightless particle without dimensions and with zero rest mass. To obtain the energy required, you must develop a method of splitting the photon. The resultant energy released must be harnessed and used to push a manned rocket to the stars. Don't let scientific naysayers tell you that energy will not be released. It will occur in the same way that energy was released by the gamma-photon during the formation of the universe. The photon is made up of particles yet to be discovered and will not be discovered until the above is accomplished.

During the rejoining of the split photons, you will have accomplished the same effect as the elusive 'antimatter versus matter' effect that has long been sought but without success.

I have not solved the problems postulated by the Special Relativity theories of Lorentz and Einstein, which are currently accepted as fact. That is, mass or weight of a person or space ship will increase to infinity as the velocity of a space ship approaches light speed of 186,281 miles per second. Therefore, infinite energy will be required. The corollary theory of time slowing with increased speed and subsequent zero aging at the speed of light also remains to be answered.

These problems can be solved, but I leave that for a Diggs descendent. As a start, reevaluate how all things are relative to each other in terms of acceleration, time and physical surroundings. Therein, I believe is the answer.

How to exceed light speed is still another issue to be solved. I believe that a 'leap frog' approach is the key to the solution.

Nor have I solved old Newsome Diggs' riddle of his '∞ **Beginning**', and I don't understand his warning about people with the diamond shaped birthmark. I hope you will have a better understanding than I.

This then is the summary of all my worthwhile studies and conclusions. All my research is recorded on the computer chip. I only wish I could compare my work to the discoveries in your time. Use the foregoing wisely and lead mankind to the stars.

By My Hand:
Benjamin Newsome Diggs
San Francisco, California
United States of America
1931-2015

When Arturo had finished reading, the room vibrated with emotion, although it was still as a tomb.

"My God!" Arturo finally managed to exhale, "So that was what Grandfather Ben was working on and what he meant about hoping a descendent would follow in his footsteps."

Thomas picked up the computer chip, holding it thoughtfully between his fingers. "Probably about eight to ten thousand pages here," he estimated.

Jana handed her husband the other piece of paper found in the Bible. "This must be the legacy that Grandfather Ben mentioned, the original one from Newsome Diggs."

Arturo unfolded the page, alarmed as the centuries-old sheet of paper almost came apart in his hands. Laying it flat on the table, he shook his head in wonder.

"I'll take this in to the antiquity document lab tomorrow and have it treated and preserved."

"And Grandfather Ben's, too, darling," Jana added.

Arturo nodded and in a subdued and reverent tone began audibly recounting Newsome's concise legacy. He read every word clearly, his voice gaining in both awe and volume. When he had concluded, he slowly straightened, shaking his head in mystification.

"This is more than a legacy; it's a prophecy." He glanced at the faces of his family, studying their amazed expressions. "Do you realize that when Old Newsome died in 1888, man had not yet understood the term, 'light-years'?" He again scanned the paper, quoting aloud, "...*achieving the ability to approach and go beyond the speed of light, and exceed it by a ratio approaching infinity. Then and only then can mankind know the universe.*"

"Are you suggesting," Thomas inquired, a cynical glint in his eyes, "that this was not written by Newsome, but placed in the family Bible at a later date?"

"No, Dad," Arturo emphatically disclaimed, "all I asked was, how did he know about things that hadn't even been discovered in his time?"

Thomas gave a bemused scowl as he spoke haltingly. "My understanding, all these years, was that Old Newsome was not an educated man. So I'll echo your own question, where did he get the knowledge, hate to say it, and intelligence, to write such a message?"

A disturbed frown bridged Jana's sensitive features. She placed her hand lightly on Arturo's arm. "I believe you two gentlemen are pondering the wrong issue." She spoke so emphatically that both men turned to face her. "Does it matter where or how Newsome Diggs arrived at his education?" she persisted.

"Well, it's just that it seems improbable that..." Thomas began arguing.

"No, it's not 'improbable'," Jana broke in. "Perhaps you didn't hear one of Newsome's admonitions," and bending over, read aloud from the legacy, "...*Where I came from and who I was is not important. The important thing is: My chosen descendent must pass on his knowledge as I have this legacy, and to his chosen descendent and to his chosen descendant until space and time are one.*"

"Jana is right," Margarite nodded in agreement. "Come, I will show you." They all watched as she carefully turned the pages of the Bible to Newsome's original entries. "You see that distinct handwriting in the Bible?" She waited until all agreed and then indicated the legacy; "With your naked eye it is obvious that both were written by the same hand."

"They do look identical," Thomas conceded, "but there's one way we can immediately verify it." He strode to a desk, opened a drawer and withdrew a small scientific instrument. "This optiscope comparator will either authenticate or repudiate the handwritings."

"Thomas, my Thomas," Margarite chided, "if you can't reduce something to a computer equation, you think it's not true. Well, you will see," she resignedly sighed, "go ahead, use your fancy gadget."

Arturo watched his father hold the optiscope comparator over the pages, and systematically scan first the aged single page legacy and then Newsome's earliest handwriting in the Bible.

"Now we'll find out." Thomas murmured, handing the comparator to his son. Both men solemnly looked at the other and then Arturo walked over to a compact computer sitting on the desk. He switched on the set, plugged in the comparator, and began to input commands. Instantly the display terminal began the comparison between the two documents. In seconds, the readout confirmed that they were indisputably, written by the same person.

Even with this undeniable proof, Thomas had difficulty accepting the truth. Peering at the screen, he mumbled, "The same handwriting...no doubt about it...I just don't understand. How do you account for the improper English and sentence structure written in the Bible, versus the articulate wording in the legacy?"

"Thomas," Margarite put her arm around his shoulder, "my doubting Thomas..."

"All right, I give," Thomas sighed as he switched off the computer. Then with one last ounce of resistance, "But who was Newsome Diggs? Not just one of our ancestors from the mountains of Tennessee, I bet."

"Dad, if he'd wanted us to know, he would have said," Arturo asserted. "What we do know is that he left enough clues for us to determine that he was far ahead of all science in his time."

"Arturo," Jana questioned, her voice reflecting an uneasiness that she did not fully understand, "if Grandfather Ben didn't know what Newsome meant about a *'diamond birthmark'*, do you have any idea?"

"Not the slightest, darling," Arturo admitted with a shrug, "nor do I understand what

Newsome meant by '∞ **Beginning'** following his signature."

"Well, my dears," Margarite injected, "I hope you all accept the fact that Ben Diggs was Newsome's chosen descendent and that..." and she held up an outstretched palm to Jana.

"...Arturo is Ben's chosen descendent!" Jana jubilantly finished the sentence.

"And, remember, my son," Margarite softly predicted, "the legacies are to continue until mankind reaches the stars."

Thomas had taken a seat at the table, absorbed in his reading of Ben's legacy. A look of bewilderment began churning on his face, and shaking his head several times, he motioned toward Arturo.

"What's the matter, Dad?"

"Look at this, Son," and he held his finger above a single paragraph on the page. "Grandfather Ben thought that splitting the photon would provide enough energy — once harnessed — to achieve the speed of light." He then looked inquiringly at his son, "Isn't it true that a normal light beam photon doesn't have any appreciable energy?"

Arturo started to answer, but he realized that his father was not yet finished.

"Perhaps a gamma photon could possibly be harnessed," and he looked at Arturo for clarification, "but after the formation of the universe, haven't gamma photons all but disappeared?"

Arturo looked down at the rug and quickly calculated, "Whatever the type photon...it would have to contain something like an energy of 10^{17} eV...or spelled out, 100 quadrillion electron volts."

Thomas, with his knowledge of astronomy, astutely focused on mega-par-secs and light-years, and shook his head. "Arturo, it just doesn't make sense. There is no photon that..."

"Thomas, there you go again," Margarite scolded. "If you don't understand it, my love, then it must not be true or it can't be done." A laugh rose from her throat and she put her arms around his neck. "I love you anyway," and again she referred to him as, "my doubting Thomas."

Jana and Arturo didn't even attempt to suppress their chuckle. Even Thomas' face gave a slight grin. "Okay, I give in, my pretty Spanish doll. As usual you win," he good-naturedly replied.

"Arturo," Jana asked, "what do you think about the possibility of using photons for spaceship travel?"

"I honestly don't know, darling," he replied truthfully. "Maybe after I study Grandfather Ben's research data I'll have a better idea."

There was a slight cough from Thomas' direction. "Son, I have some spare time," he began humbly. "Would you like some assistance in obtaining the data on Ben's computer chip?"

An immediate grin covered Arturo's face. "Couldn't do it without you, Dad."

Thomas started to reach toward the archaic computer chip on the table, but he was stopped by Margarite's determined voice, "You're not going to begin tonight." Margarite spoke so forcefully that even Jana was startled.

"Have no fear of that, my dear," Thomas retaliated, his tone more fitting of an old country doctor soothing a delirious patient, "I'm just putting the chip away in safe storage."

Humming under his breath, Thomas unobtrusively put the silver chip in his pocket. Being careful that Margarite didn't catch his glance, he winked at his son and said, "The two legacies will be taken to Document Restoration tomorrow and then returned to the Bible — between the linings."

"Arturo, if you will, please put the Bible back in the case, so we can find it tomorrow."

Before dawn had fully broken the following morning, Arturo slipped downstairs to his study. In his concern not to awaken Jana, he hadn't even bothered to dress. Just as he turned on the main computer, there was a repeated tap on the sliding glass doors. In the dim daybreak light, he could barely make out the form standing outside. Walking across the room, he stifled a snicker at the sight of his father, also still attired in pajamas and robe. Arturo opened the glass door and his father strode into the room.

"Thought you might be up," Thomas placidly started the conversation, "but you couldn't get started without this," and he reached into his pocket to hand over Ben's small computer chip.

"Thanks, Dad." Humorously glancing at his father's clothing, "I take it you were in a hurry to get over here."

"No more than you were to get down-stairs," Thomas retorted. "You probably didn't even take time to make us both some coffee," he grumbled. "Well, activate the conversion program to extract the data from Ben's chip, I'll do the morning chores." He turned and padded bare-footed to the kitchen.

Arturo affectionately watched his father's retreating figure. Then with a sigh, turned back to the computer and began energizing the series of codes necessary to modify the antiquated computer language to current twenty-second century readout technology. It took concentration to give precise commands to the sophisticated demands of the program processor, and so he was too engrossed to hear the approaching footsteps.

"Well, well, well," Jana cooed, "I haven't had a pajama party since I was a little girl."

Startled, Arturo turned. He broke out laughing when he saw his wife and mother, both clad in their morning robes, bearing trays of coffee cups and sweet rolls.

"They beat me to it, Arturo," Thomas chuckled from behind them. He was carrying a silver coffee urn. "And worse yet," he said, "they were both giggling about it in the kitchen."

"Now really, Thomas," Margarite chastised, "did you men actually think that we didn't know you'd be up at the break of dawn to..."

Arturo rose and took the tray from Jana, saying as he did so, "You both know us too well, and thank you for the coffee and rolls."

Just then the computer issued a repetitive buzz to signal that an action must be taken. Thomas and Arturo turned, their full attention focused on the computer screen.

"Converting this little piece of antiquity is going to take longer than I anticipated, Dad."

Thomas pulled up a chair alongside his son. "Are you using the modulate or the alter procedures to regain the program?"

"I've got a faster technique, it combines then modifies..." at the sound of a high-pitched squeal, Arturo promptly set in the proper codes... "see, it's latching onto the data now."

The two men stared intently at the rapidly scrolling screen, oblivious to anything or anyone else in the room.

Jana poured two steaming mugs of coffee and set them and a plate of rolls on a nearby side table. Her mouth opened as if to speak and she started to place her hand on Arturo's shoulder, but then she thought better of it. For a long moment she seemed to be obsessed by the back of Arturo's head, and the corners of her eyes narrowed into apprehensive crinkles.

Her mother-in-law came over to her and whispered, "Would you join me in the kitchen for a minute?"

Jana had noticed Margarite's troubled expression. Without a word, she followed the older woman from the room and quietly closed the door behind them.

They had only walked a few paces down the hallway when Margarite placed her hand on Jana's arm. "I need to talk to you privately."

Jana merely nodded. Neither spoke until they reached the breakfast room and were seated at the table.

"There have been some unusual and un-explained 'incidents'," Margarite began in a hushed tone, "that have affected almost every generation of the Diggs family. We must find a correlation between these events."

"Mother Diggs," Jana shook her head, "I've had the opportunity to read every word that Diggs descendants wrote in the Bible, but..." she stopped in confusion.

Margarite hastily interrupted, "There are accounts in the old Diggs Bible and records about unexplained deaths and accidents, some sicknesses not diagnosed," there was a slight catch to her breath as she added, "and even two unexplained suicides..."

Jana waited for a moment before responding. "Perhaps it's just coincidental. There are many unforeseen — sometimes disastrous — events that befall families over generations."

"I have never accepted that these incidents were just 'accidents'." As if she might be overheard, she leaned closer, her voice a bare whisper, "Also, the many boxes in our underground storage vault are filled with newspaper clippings, pictures, documents, letters and albums — all concerning Diggs history."

"Those records are countless, Mother Diggs. It would take months, no," she corrected herself, "years to go through them in detail. Even then, do you believe any of your foreboding could be verified?" Jana saw that Margarite was trembling and quickly rose to engulf her mother-in-law in her arms.

"I'm all right now, my dear," but Margarite uttered the words with a deep sigh. "It's a burden on the soul to retain such harrowing thoughts for so many years and never express them."

Jana had always looked to Margarite as an unshakable pillar of strength; but now, her entire countenance was one of complete weariness. "Don't say anymore, Mother Diggs," Jana consoled, "I, too, sometimes get carried away with emotion, and mostly it turns out to be unsubstantiated worries."

Margarite managed a meager smile. "Thomas always examines me with unconcealed skepticism whenever I have spoken to him of these fears, and Arturo's analytical mind demands proven facts. Si, mi hija, " unconsciously using the familiar term for daughter, "perhaps you're right; my imagination works overtime."

Jana seemed visibly relieved at Margarite's conclusion. She gently placed her hand over the older woman's clasped fingers. "We all have choices: to worry ourselves senseless about what has or could happen or to be mindful that there is always peril in everyone's lives, not just ours...and to be aware of that certainty."

Margarite pulled back and though there was a look of disquiet in her eyes, her voice was matter-of-fact. "That's all I could ever ask, Jana. Thank you."

It had taken months to retrieve all the data on Ben's computer chip and to pore over printouts, and at the same time, digest the complex physics and equations. Arturo had worked late into the evenings as well as every weekend; and with Thomas' assistance, had assimilated the data pertinent to Ben's postulate of photon splitting and the hoped for energy release. Ben's research would save Arturo invaluable time that would be lost in pursuing futile courses.

Both Arturo and Thomas had been hunched in front of the computer for hours, but neither had any thought of time. Arturo rubbed his weary eyes as he scrolled for a particular piece of data. "Here it is, Dad," he motioned excitedly, "Ben's experiments conducted at the Texas Accelerator. This one explores focused high energy laser light beams directed at a small and exceedingly bright light source."

Thomas corroborated the coded number blinking on the screen with a raft of printouts on the desk in front of him.

"Got it," but there was disappointment in his voice as he read aloud Ben's qualitative analysis notation, "'although never scientifically proven, I believe the small light source changed composition as a result of the bombardment of unlike lasers. I also believe that this variance was the result of a photon having mass, and thus particles, but yet undiscovered'."

Arturo merely nodded and deftly struck the appropriate keys to bring up another document on the screen. "All right, my calculations indicate that if a photon could be split, it has to be done with another, but different light source, or sources."

Thomas glowered skeptically. "Irrespective, Arturo, all scientific research still indicates that a photon has no weight, mass and certainly no dimensions."

Ignoring his father's negative observation, Arturo replied, "Not if one chooses to pursue the theory that energy can be released when a photon is split."

"But if you, or any scientist for that matter," Thomas began lecturing, "still doesn't know the composition of a photon, then how in the hell can..."

"I refuse to accede to that train of thought," Arturo briskly interrupted, "I prefer to simply accept that photons do possess a heretofore hidden source of energy."

Thomas was ripe for a debate. "Ah ha, you're telling me that 'blind faith'," he loudly guffawed while slapping his fist on the table for emphasis, "is going to lead you to devise a method of splitting a photon and measure the resultant energy release?"

"If you elect to put it that way, then yes, that's exactly what I intend to do." Glancing at his father's reddened cheeks, he couldn't help adding, "That genre of energy, if harnessed, could possibly power a manned rocket to the stars at the speed of light."

Now he felt he had ammunition to win his point and Thomas spoke his words in enthusiastic triumph. "Ignoring, I take it, Einstein's increasing mass and slowing of time with the increasing speed theory."

Not about to be trapped, Arturo smiled. "As a matter of record, Dad, although none have yet been able to disprove Einstein, there are those who do question." To stretch his fatigued muscles, he stood up; his mouth gaped in a wide yawn.

Thomas jumped at the opportunity to renew the battle, "But as yet, no regarded scientist has publicly challenged the theory."

"You're right," Arturo amiably agreed, "but one way or the other, I'm not going to worry about it. My objective is to take just one step at a time."

Patting his father on the shoulder, he cheerfully winked down at the older man, "How about taking a breather? Don't know about you, but a tall, cool lemonade would set fine with me right now."

Thomas resisted the temptation to prolong the argument, but with characteristic aplomb, he knew when he'd been bested. Pushing himself up from the chair, he gave a placid sigh, "Sounds good to me, too, son." Then he quipped, "You buying?"

Margarite had not remained convinced of possible 'mere coincidences' regarding past Diggs' problems and continued looking for months for any speck of a clue, until she too had to concede to the inevitable. But she persisted in having the final word. "I feel strongly, Jana, that our men, especially Arturo, and one day, maybe Filip, are in great danger if the diamond birthmark ever shows up."

> *"Can he be the one and..."*
> *"It may well be, but...*
> *"If not, more will..."*
> *"Nothing before its time..."*

As majority owner of GEO Transport Company, at least on paper, and holding joint titles of Chairman of the Board and Chief Executive, Joal Lowe appeared to have the world at his feet. Such was the impression he was trying to preserve, even under the adverse conditions the company was now facing.

If the orders for cargo shipments to Mars and the Moon continued dropping, Joal Lowe did not hold himself responsible for GEO Transport possibly being forced out of business in a few years. Nor did he personally assume liability for failure of two GEO rockets with the loss of all payloads. The rescue of his crews by his competitor, Space Transport, was of only passing concern, and only then because of their being rescued by a competitor. He never considered assuming the blame for his initial failure to pursue development of a new rocket as Space Transport had done so successfully. Nor did he consider it his fault that he had lavished money on less productive ventures than on research to develop a larger rocket. To Joal Lowe, these failures were caused by a fluke or bad luck. The blame lay with the financial community, which did not grant the needed funds to compete with Space Transport.

Joal Lowe condemned the bankers for his failure to generate the loans required to create larger rockets. He did not accept their reasoning that Space Transport, with the introduction of their own gigantic-payload rockets, had an unblemished success of deliveries, without an accident or problem. In fact, those despised "bean counters," had announced their intentions to invest additional capital in Space Transport. They had rejected his offer to put up his own GEO stock as collateral and almost laughed in his face, calling it "paper money" that was already borrowed to the hilt.

These were only a part of the problems that faced Joal this afternoon. The most pressing was the cancellation notification he held crumbled in his stubby hands. Because of the loss of the two transports and all payload, he had been informed that the insurance coverage would not be renewed; without which, GEO could not operate.

"Damn them. Damn Space Transport. And damn that fuckin' Diggs!" He slammed his fist so vehemently on the desk, that he bruised his knuckles. The visual intercom blinked and advised him that a communiqué was on the screen. Joal let it flicker several times before growling, "Yeah?"

The scared face of his assistant appeared on screen, "I'm sorry to disturb you, Mr. Lowe," the voice trembled slightly, "but the directors are just going into the board room now."

"Let the bastards wait," he growled back.

"Shouldn't I let them know you're on your way, Mr. Lowe?" he persisted, his tone barely a whisper.

"Oh, shit!" He angrily flipped off the transmission.

For several minutes, Joal leaned back in his tufted swivel chair, his eyes closed. Gradually his outward features began a novel transformation. The fleshy face lost some of the coarseness, and his flushed cheeks subsided to a pinkish glow. The scowl that blanketed his forehead subtly changed into narrow permanent ridges. His pouting lips were now firmer. When he opened his eyes, the lids did not seem so puffy, nor the faded blue eyes, so hostile. Even his nose ceased to flare. Nothing about Joal Lowe, by any stretch of the imagination, could be faintly called comely, but he now had taken on the appearance of a prosperous plumpness. He picked up a portfolio and slowly walked from the room.

"Ladies and gentlemen," Joal announced to the assembled board members, "since we met last quarter, I only have a few statements. You have the minutes of the previous meeting and a summary of the past three months."

"Mr. Chairman," a busy director proposed, "I make a motion the minutes be accepted as presented."

Immediately the motion was seconded and carried.

"Just a minute, Joal," one of the more outspoken and forceful directors spoke up. "This summary shows that we are continuing

to obtain contracts for shipments to the Moon.
I understood that Space Transport had taken
much of our action. What's going on?"

Joal shook his head, as if astonished at
the remark, "Mr. Maxwell! Your perception is
wrong. GEO continues to obtain contracts, in
spite of Space Trans' new rockets." A smooth
smile curved his full mouth. "Our customers
remain loyal and are booking business with
us." No one, except Joal and his chief financial
officer, whom he had coerced into falsifying the
company's financial statements, knew the ex-
tent of the contracts that had been lost to
Space Transport.

"Well, what about our insurance coverage
after the loss of the two transports and payload? " the inquisitive Maxwell continued. "Will
the carrier still insure us?"

"Of course." Joal looked stricken that
such a question would even be raised. "They
have stated they will continue to insure us."

Maxwell stood, and in a piercing voice
demanded, "I'd like to see a copy of that letter,
if you please."

Joal lowered his eyelids to conceal the
canny look in his eyes and shook his head
back and forth sadly. His sigh echoed throughout the room as he slowly reached inside his
breast pocket and withdrew a folded sheet of
paper. He raised his eyes to focus a guileless
stare on his accuser. "Since you doubt my
word, read it for yourself, Mr. Maxwell." And he
handed over an expertly forged insurance company document.

As Maxwell scanned the single page, a chagrined look flushed his face, and he said simply, "I'll be damned." He passed the letter back to Joal and, obviously embarrassed, resumed his seat.

All eyes in the room were carefully averted from either the seemingly brash director or the chairman. Nonchalantly replacing the bogus paper in his pocket, Joal let the directors squirm in their chairs for a few moments.

"Now, ladies and gentlemen, as we were saying..." he began in a self-assured voice.

The meeting continued with an inconsequential agenda. The insurance problem had been adroitly swept under the rug by Joal's falsified documents. To the relief of the majority of the directors, the meeting was about to adjourn when Maxwell again requested the floor. "Mr. Chairman, ladies and gentlemen. No matter what we have been led to believe, GEO's position in the marketplace is tenuous at best." He looked around at the other directors for support, but most avoided his eyes. "It is my opinion that it's only a matter of time before Space Transport drives us out of business through better service and lower prices."

Silence greeted his words and, suspecting that his views were contrary to the prevailing consensus, he waved the summary papers that had been presented to each of the directors. "These are nothing more than mere cursory outlines. We need to set our sights on delivering more and more cargo to Mars and the Moon. What's required is a radical plan of action to get this company back on its feet."

"I suggest, Mr. Maxwell," Joal interjected, "that, if you have such a plan, it be now submitted." To play his trump card, he slightly lowered his voice. "Or we can proceed with the strategy that I have initiated."

"But you have not presented any strategy to the board," Maxwell countered.

"I have not, for a definite reason." A few eyebrows raised at this statement, but Joal chose not to notice. "It is patently apparent that in the past," he paused for emphasis, "there have been security leaks that could have come from no other source than this room." As was his intent, muffled gasps were heard from the directors. "For whatever reasons, a director, or directors, has passed information to Space Transport that resulted in our losing contracts through no fault of our own."

"By God, if you're insinuating," Maxwell's voice was an impassioned bellow, "that I..."

Joal's steely eyes stared at the director but said nothing.

"...that I was responsible..." Maxwell roared, "I emphatically deny..." but the questioning looks that confronted him from around the table chilled his bluster. Maxwell slammed his portfolio on the table. "I will not sit here and take these insults. Mr. Chairman, I tender my resignation."

"Accepted, Mr. Maxwell," Joal instantly approved. "Will the secretary please note," and he looked at his watch, "that at 2:45 p.m., Mr. Maxwell formally submitted his resignation from the GEO board." Before anyone could object, he held up his hand for order, "All in favor say aye."

There was a slight confused murmur from the other directors, and Joal banged the gavel, "Motion carried. Goodbye, Mr. Maxwell. Ladies and gentlemen, the meeting is adjourned."

Not waiting for the directors to stand, Joal gathered up his prepared documents, pulled his bulky frame from the chair, and stalked from the room. His still frightened assistant held out a bundle of messages, but Joal whisked by as if he were invisible. He slammed the door to his office with such force that the pictures on the walls tilted.

"Maxwell, you son of a bitch," he screamed in frenzy, "who the fuck you think you are taking me on like that...shittin' bastard!"

Throwing his portfolio toward a chair, he strode to a locked cabinet behind his desk, opened it and withdrew a thick file. He pitched it on the desk and then collapsed into his chair. Beads of perspiration began pouring down his round face, and he mopped the salty droplets with the back of his hand. Flicking on the visual intercom, he snarled, "Turn down the fuckin' climate control..."

"But Mr. Lowe," the assistant protested, "it's already set at maximum cold. I can't..."

He switched off the picture phone before he had finished, cursing under his breath, "Stupid ass!" Then mimicking his voice, "'It's already set at maximum cold'...asinine prick..."

The outburst seemed to relieve his tension and removing his jacket, he spread open the bulky file on his desk and began sorting out the separate dossiers. Each contained confidential and personal information on every key employee at Space Transport. He had spent months trying to expose any individual weakness, which could be exploited and then used to obtain data pertinent to the well-kept secret of their high performance rockets. But his concentration was focused on one file in particular, whose cover sheet read, "Arturo Newsome Diggs."

"You fuckin' bastard!" His face turned into a grotesque knot of pure hate. "Every fuckin' Diggs that ever lived has tried to obstruct or destroy us. But not this time! Not with Joal Lowe, you won't!"

His lips curled into a misshapen grimace as he recalled the countless stories that had been passed down through generations about how his kin had vented their hate and revenge on the Diggs family through unsolved maiming and murders. Anyone who dared cross a Lowe was destined to have revenge wreaked on themselves, in particular the Diggs family. Like his ancestors Joal felt no remorse about inflicting pain on anyone who stood in the way of his desires.

He smiled with self-satisfaction at the thought of one of his many vindictive retaliations. He never regretted the millions he spent to drive an electronics company into bankruptcy. The beautiful daughter of the owner had no right to refuse his advances, and she never should have laughed in his face and told him, "I wouldn't let you touch me if you were the last man on Earth." After the 'accident,' no man would ever want to touch her. The exquisite features and the body that Joal had so lusted after were beyond reconstruction.

"The money spent," he gloated, "was well worth it."

Joal reclined in the cushioned chair and rested his feet on the desk. It was some minutes before he resumed an upright position. Closing his eyes, he searched his memory for a specific number. When he had recalled the correct sequence, he gave the code for a secure line before voicing some digits into the visiphone.

No image came on screen, just a curt voice that said, "Your name and message."

Impatiently Joal answered, "Lowe. The time is now."

The screen remained blank, but the muffled voice gave forth a terse command. "Two hours. Have the payment with you." No sooner had the words been spoken than the transmission was abruptly broken.

Joal was waiting at the appointed meeting site before the designated two hours. On the ground, tightly clamped between his legs, was a heavy, nondescript briefcase. Although the locale seemed deserted, his eyes swept the area with a distrustful scrutiny. From time to time, Joal looked at his watch. It was exactly at the designated hour when he felt a presence behind him.

"Herr Lowe."

The suddenness of the voice so startled Joal that he tried to spin around, but the unwieldy case hindered his movement.

"Horst?" The question was underlined with a note of foreboding.

"Yes, Herr Lowe."

There was nothing remarkable about the short-cropped blond haired man who stepped around to face Joal, except his piercing blue eyes. He was of medium height but of inordinately muscular build. His taunt square face showed no lines, a sign that the eyes and mouth rarely smiled. It was difficult to surmise his age. Only by the mature, well-modulated voice, could one judge that he was not as young as he appeared.

"God damn you, Horst. Why the hell did you sneak up..." Joal started to rant.

"Herr Lowe," his lips curled, "I have been standing here for some minutes."

Joal's fleshy eyelids lowered into pulpy slits. He had no use for this man and his insolence, but he forced his hostility aside. Reaching in his pocket he withdrew a folded note and handed it to Horst.

"These are your orders," and he motioned toward the case at his feet, "and the advance payment of six kilos of gold."

Horst did not even glance at the briefcase on the ground but opened the letter to read the instructions.

"If you succeed," Joal hissed, "five times this amount will be deposited in your name in a vault."

Horst was not concerned by the proposition that he would be paid later at an unnamed location. There had already been many jobs performed for Joal and he had always been compensated as promised. Besides he had incriminating records of all prior services for his own protection.

"No, Herr Lowe," knowing how Joal was irritated by that salutation, "the price for this assignment is double that offer."

For a split second Horst saw the loathing on his employer's face. He, in return, did not like anything about Joal; but business was business, and so he stood his ground to wait the predictable decision.

"All right," Joal conceded, "I agree, but as usual, no record of human involvement is to be found — ever!"

Sentiment, in a distasteful job was for amateurs, and Horst was a professional. He did not need to be reminded that any assignment with which he was involved was to leave no evidence of human participation. All commissions were done with the expertise that blamed the results on an accident, a coincidence, or "acts of God."

"No problem, Herr Lowe," he shrugged. "It will be done as you require. Now I will take my leave."

Effortlessly Horst picked up the briefcase and as covertly as he had arrived, disappeared.

Three tedious months had elapsed, and Arturo was still no closer to a theoretical method of splitting the photon. Every spare minute of his time had been spent working at his home computer. Wearily he rubbed his strained eyes, welcoming the sound of Jana's footsteps and the interruption.

"Hello love, I'm back." Inwardly she winced at the fatigued expression on her husband's face. Putting down her packages, she asked, "And what great accomplishments have you made while I was out spending all your hard earned money?"

"Not a blessed thing," he replied crossly. "Still trying to figure out how to obtain the elusive energy from photons." With a dispirited shrug, he rose and walked to the window. "It's my fault, Jana, the answer's there. I just can't seem to find it. Every time I think I'm close, some damn complication comes along."

"You're being short tempered to yourself, my darling." It was said softly and not as a reprimand.

Arturo turned, a chagrined smile on his face, "Come to think of it, my fuse has gotten shorter."

Reaching out, he drew her unresistingly toward him until their mouths and bodies met.

"It's about time you came up for air," Jana finally whispered in his ear, "and smelled the flowers."

"What say," he proposed, a glint in his eyes, "that we run away together for a few days."

"Arturo," Jana asked suspiciously, "have you been eavesdropping?"

"I don't think so," he retorted innocently.

Taking his hand, she led him to the sofa and perched on his lap. "What say you to a second honeymoon?"

Arturo nibbled at her earlobe, and in a husky voice he murmured, "I'm ready, right now."

Jana made no attempt to draw away. "That's all right too, my love," she teased, "but I was also suggesting a little trip to the Twilight Resort. If you remember the spot, it's on the Moon, just at the light and darkness border."

"Uh huh," he mumbled while nuzzling at her neck.

"Arturo," her voice sounded piqued, "did you hear what I said?"

"Uh huh," he repeated, then in a laughing tone, "If my memory is correct, that's the place where the water recycle system went out and the reserves were used up before anyone caught it. We only had wine to drink for two whole days, and then we cursed them when the system was finally fixed."

Jana was about to remonstrate when Arturo again laughed. "It was also where we spent our honeymoon. If I remember, you were held captive in the room and..."

"...all my clothes and nightgowns were hidden," Jana took his face in her hands. "In any event, darling, your parents are planning a trip to Twilight Resort, and I thought we'd join them."

Arturo pulled back, a look of disbelief on his face. "Wait a minute, I adore my parents, but..."

It was Jana's turn to laugh, "We would have separate rooms, you know."

"Them or us?" He mockingly retorted. "I will consider it, but only if I can hide your clothes again and take you captive."

"Knowing your parents, I think they will be discreet and not bother to ask if we suddenly disappear for a time."

"Under those conditions, then, it should be fun."

"Besides, my darling, you need a break. We haven't taken a vacation in two years; not since you read Ben's and Newsome's legacies." Excitedly she began setting forth the plans. "Filip is going to spend the time with friends in San Diego. And your mother and I have already contacted the travel agency and checked on Moon shuttle bookings and reservations at the Twilight Resort."

Arturo listened and then shook his head. "No. Don't book the commercial Moon shuttle. Better yet, I'll make arrangements for all of us to go on one of Space Transport's cargo ships. The captain's lounge will be more than adequate."

"But what about transportation to the resort and luggage transfer?"

"You mean we're taking luggage...with clothes in them?" he asked incredulously, his voice filled with mock disillusion. "I thought this was going to be just another rollicking honeymoon."

"Oh, Arturo!" Jana playfully scolded.

"Transfer to the resort is no problem, believe me," he said in a more serious tone. "Besides, I've been looking for an excuse to ride in our new transport. The initial shake down run, around the Moon and back will take place next week, and then it'll be ready for service. I'm not expecting any problems, so you can plan on hitching a ride on the first official cargo trip, in two weeks."

Jana had ridden with Arturo on several previous Space Transport cargo flights, and she didn't quite know why she even asked the question. "Sure that the company won't mind our tagging along?"

Arturo dismissed the query with a laugh, "You're kidding, honey." Then a faraway look invaded his face, "This ship has improvements in the engine that I'd like to see first hand, especially since each of them are my brainchildren."

Any trace of foreboding immediately passed, and Jana replied brightly, "All right, sounds great. Now I want to call Margarite and firm up plans to go. She's going to make the resort reservations."

Even Arturo was becoming enthusiastic about the planned holiday. "Knowing Mother, she'll get the best accommodations in the place. Didn't the owner, can't recall his name off hand, buy some of her paintings for the enclosed dome lobby?"

"Sure did, but I don't remember his name either."

Arturo took a small Space Transport schedule from his pocket, "As to when to leave, exactly...two weeks from today, on May 15 at 0900 hours."

An obscure, uneasy feeling swept over Jana. "Arturo, no fair backing out," she began hesitantly, "I really think we need this vacation."

"Don't worry, you're going to be stuck," he slyly winked, "with me..."

Teasingly she poked at his chest. "If you thought our honeymoon was great, I've got years of experience with you now," and in a sultry whisper, "we don't even have to leave the suite, unless we want to. Remember what can happen in one-third gravity?"

"Now you're talking my language, Mrs. Diggs." He began unbuttoning her blouse.

"Not now you over-sexed monster," Jana murmured, suddenly jumping off his lap, "but just you wait until I get you in bed tonight."

"Look who's talking about over- sexed! I remember when..."

Jana shushed him and started for the door.

Arturo lunged for her, but she adroitly shut the door before he could grab her.

For several minutes he just stood, absorbed in pleasurable hedonistic thoughts. It was with a sigh that he returned to the computer and began work on the elusive solution to the photon problem, losing himself in deep concentration.

The pinhead size eavesdropper, embedded a month ago in the miniature portrait, had done its work well. Margarite had painted the exquisite canvas, a likeness of Arturo's paternal grandmother many years ago. The "dropper," — as it was referred to by the technician who had

been covertly hired to plant it — had been surreptitiously placed within the right eye of the
miniature. No one had questioned the uniformed serviceman who arrived at the appointed time to clean the carpets. The job had
been arranged so masterfully, that Arturo and
Jana were not at all suspicious that from their
study a scrambled signal was being sent to a
communications satellite and then retransmit-
ted to a computer on Earth's surface. Any
word, noise, conversation or movement was being recorded. They would never be aware of its
presence; the "dropper" possessed a short life
and was programmed to disintegrate, leaving
not a speck or trace that it had ever existed.

The following week, as Arturo had predicted, the new transport space vehicle was
primed for its maiden flight. Systems had been
checked and rechecked by the hundreds of
Space Transport technicians and by the manufacturer's own technicians. Each system was
certified to be operating as required; and a detailed log of each unit was kept and checked off
by the appropriate supervisor. Arturo himself
inspected the specific upgrades to the ship's
engines.

"Mr. Diggs," the senior engine service
technician inquired, "have you verified the engine computer program and certified it as operating properly?"

"Affirmative, Dorn," Arturo responded.
"Each function has been played back and
routed through the engine control system.
Every component is working as required."

"As I understand it, Mr. Diggs," Dorn studied his portable computer readout, "the upgrading of the engine for additional performance depends on modifying your computer software. Isn't this the first major modification since your original program in our new generation of ships?"

"That's right, but we've been working on it for almost a year. When it was tested with the engine on the static stand, it passed with flying colors. Normally, we'd have to make minor adjustments, but not this time." And there was a justifiable note of pride when he added, "All the computer and lab work paid off."

"Yeah, Mr. Diggs, I saw you in the lab and tech room at all hours of the night." Dorn was a long time employee and dedicated technician and he knew the work that went into a successful program.

Arturo grinned, "Well, we crammed a two year job into just over eleven months, and to do it, we had to burn some midnight oil."

"Well, if you did it, it'll be okay. We wouldn't have these new ships if it hadn't been for you. My God, we own the transport routes." The comment was said admiringly. "I'm still amazed at the way the engine throat melts and is reformed through your molecule getter. Must take some software program to control the system, since all are interrelated back to the fusion reactor."

"It is some program. Took me four years to develop it." Because he had known Dorn for so many years and thought he'd be interested, Arturo volunteered, "The key was management of the fusion reaction with the molecule getter without causing a bootstrapping loss of the core, which could, of course, cause a catastrophe."

Dorn nodded, removed a pen from behind his ear, and handed Arturo the computer and logs. "Okay Mr. Diggs, we're all set. If you'll sign off on the final approvals of the engine and computer program checkout logs, we'll call it a day." The senior tech handed Arturo the cipher for his signature approval.

Arturo jotted his initials on the instrument and handed it back to Dorn, who stifled a yawn as he scanned the report. "Looks good to me, Mr. Diggs. Going to be good to get home early for a change."

"That's for sure." With a chuckle, he cuffed Dorn on the shoulder. "I'm leaving for my air-car right now. You behind me?"

"Sure am, Mr. Diggs." He watched until Arturo left the control panel area and then announced over the intercom to the waiting engine technicians, "You heard the boss. The checkouts are finished and we can go home. I'll clean up. No use everyone staying around." No more dismissal was needed, and it was only seconds until the techs had picked up their equipment and hurriedly left.

Humming under his breath, Dorn started stowing pieces of checkout gear and picking up the cables, transmitters and portable readout equipment. He strolled to the restricted zone entry, shut the door, and locked it from the inside.

He breezily called out, "I'm closing up the joint, anyone still here?"

Satisfied that he was alone, he walked over to an elevator on the port side of the stationary freighter transport, and pushed the lift control. Entering the ship through the open cargo door, he immediately went to the main computer housing, disengaged the security seal, and pulled off the front panel. For a long minute he stared intently at the mass of wiring and gauges. He took a small red marking pen from his trouser pocket and placed an almost imperceptible dot on one of the cables connected to the computer. After he studied the exact location of the red dot, a smile of relief crossed his face. Reattaching the front panel, he replaced the green seal and punched in the appropriate codes, signifying the panel was secure.

It was still a mystery to him why anyone would pay so much money for the identification of the cable connecting the engine computer to the molecule getter. He quickly dismissed any uneasiness by replaying in his mind the speculation, which he had clung to from the start of his accepting the assignment. "So they want to know how the system works. Big deal. Revealing which cable connects them doesn't make sense. But, the big money they offered will sure come in handy; and Lord knows, the family needs it with four kids approaching college age." He roused himself from his thoughts and left the transport ship.

He was guilelessly humming an indistinct tune as he nodded to the security guard at the outer gate and caught the jitney for his auto-car.

The following day, the manned shakedown cruise around the Moon and back to the hanger, was performed without a flaw. Arturo, from the control tower, had monitored the recordings of each engine function of the mighty rocket. When the flight and checkout crew emerged from the huge transporter, there was much cheering and clapping.

"Great job, Captain."

"Excellent flight."

"Performed exactly as predicted, Arturo."

"A 20% payload increase."

The Chairman and CEO, Mohammed Nahal, gave a brief speech about what the upgraded transporter meant to the corporation, heaping praise on Arturo and his engineering team. "Had it not been for Mr. Diggs and his team, we wouldn't have had the first new generation transports, much less this upgrade which will increase payload by another 20%. I would like to announce that effective today, Mr. Arturo Diggs is invited to join the board of directors of Space Transport. Further..."

This was a most welcome surprise to Arturo. He was well aware that directors were entitled to healthy shares of Space Transport stock, just to sit on the board. The honor also meant that he would never have to be concerned about income for the rest of his life. If something happened to him, Jana and Filip would be well taken care of.

The senior technician, Dorn, enthusiastically clapped and cheered along with the others when Arturo's board invitation was announced. He liked and respected his boss, particularly admiring the way Arturo rolled up his sleeves and went to work with the techs and, when necessary, became one of them.

At the conclusion of the speeches, Dorn was one of the first to leave the building and hurry to his auto-car. He had ceased to wonder why he was being paid to have placed the red dot on the computer cable. "What the hell," blocking all guilt from his mind, "it's their damn money, and besides, there was no harm done".

It was dark when he arrived at the appointed meeting place. When an auto-car pulled in beside him, he did not think it odd that it was manually driven. As had been pre-arranged, he was to get out of his car and into the one alongside.

"I placed the red dot on the cable with the pen you gave me," Dorn spoke rapidly, almost short of breath, "but I still don't understand it."

"You are not being paid to think or ask questions."

The bluntness of the answer made Dorn squirm uncomfortably. He quickly sized up the blond-haired man, with the piercing blue eyes, seated beside him. He was sure he outweighed his adversary by fifty pounds and that alone bolstered his resolve to ask, "How do you know I even did as you requested?"

A knowing laugh preceded the harsh reply, "Because, we taped you removing the secured panel, placing the dot, reattaching the panel and falsifying the security seal."

The tech froze, his bravado reduced to pure fear. "How? Why?"

"To assure ourselves that you would perform your task and not take our money without doing what we asked. As to how we have you on tape during your clandestine operation," he gave a shrug, "that's our business."

"I don't believe it!" Dorn almost shouted, then in panic, challenged, "You're lying...show me."

As if anticipating this situation, the blond man reached over and switched on a small portable viewer. Mesmerized with terror, Dorn watched the accurate screening of Arturo leaving the control room and his own dismissal of the other techs, replacing the equipment, locking the control room door, even his voice clearly calling out, "I'm locking up the joint, anyone still here?" His every movement was recorded, even the placing of the small red dot, which was barely discernable on the tape, but monstrous in Dorn's terrified realization.

The tech paled; his voice was barely audible, "If anyone saw this, it would mean my job, my career..."

"No problem," came the brusque response, "no one will ever see this tape, except you and me. Here is the money we promised. You may count it if you wish."

"I don't want your money," and he frantically lunged for the viewer, "I want the tape."

"You certainly may have this one. But I should warn you that there are other copies."

"But why? What do you want of me?" and Dorn could even smell the fear that his sweating body was secreting.

In a soothing voice, as if to convince a child that it is all right to take that first step, the blond man reassured his anxious companion. "We want nothing that will be of an injurious nature."

"I won't..." the tech protested, "I won't do anything that might hurt the new transporter or anyone in it."

"Here, take your money," as he handed over more currency than the tech had ever seen at one time. "You did a good job. You have earned your payment."

As Dorn clasped the cash with both hands, greed overrode any other thought. As if the pack of large denomination bills might disappear, he rapidly stuffed them in his pocket.

To watch a man grovel, while renouncing all his moral ethics for the sake of a mere pittance, was the only aspect of his work that Horst scorned. He had put more formidable men than this proud technician in such compromising positions, and they all had eventually succumbed. One way or another, it was his job to find their weakness — and their price.

Horst gave a semblance of a smile; his penetrating eyes locked on Dorn, but his voice was smooth and reassuring. "We want you to do one more small job for us. There will be much more money, enough to enable you to retire and, if you choose, never work again."

"And...no one will get hurt and the ship will not be damaged?" the tech countered, trying to justify himself. He desperately tried to ignore the trap in which he knew he was caught.

"You have my word," Horst uttered with absolute sincerity.

The special marking pen and the placement of the red dot, had only been Dorn's trial test. Horst had carefully orchestrated the taping of the deed; for nothing more than blackmail would assure that the tech would perform the ultimate task.

"You are to take this," Horst continued, handing over a small black object about five millimeters in diameter and barely a half-millimeter thick. "Before the next flight of the transport, this is to be positioned directly atop the red dot you made with the marker. Then, as before, you will properly affix the final security seal."

The tiny round button shaped device lay in the palm of Dorn's hand like a flattened mole on the skin. He looked down it at with distrust. "What is this thing? What will it do?"

"It is simply a recorder to monitor the signals in the cable," Horst answered, a truthful ring in his voice.

Dorn was familiar with the workings of industrial espionage. He had been well briefed at numerable company security lectures. As a senior technician, he also knew that signals from the subject cable would be of no help to anyone desiring the secret of the engine-computer program, that being only one small part of the total controller system. He frowned warily. Surely, he thought, no one was stupid enough to pay so much money for such a limited piece of data. "Then all you want are the signals from the computer program?" he blurted out. "That's it! That's all?"

"You're smart, Dorn," Horst complimented. "That's why you're a chief technician. Yes, we want the signals. They will be transmitted to our recorder; and after the flight returns to the Earth base, you can remove the device and destroy it." Then in his most persuasive tone, "No one will ever know. You will have the money, and you'll never hear from us again."

The tech studied the minuscule signal transmitter, trying to shake off his misgivings. "Are you positive that this will not cause any problem to the transport?"

"None whatsoever," Horst replied reassuringly. "Here, I'll even show you."

Picking up the device from Dorn's sweaty palm, he affixed it to the cable leading to the visi-phone. He then pushed a concealed button to expose a miniature visual recorder beside the seat and trained it on the visi-phone. Deftly he dialed a number and, while adjusting a frequency dial on the visual recorder, began transmitting his voice.

"This is a visi-phone check, thank you."

The readily identifiable signal of the visi-phone was instantly displayed on the screen. When he adjusted another dial, his words were automatically projected. "As I said, this is nothing more than a signal transmitter." His tone was non-threatening and friendly. "Nothing dangerous about it."

Dorn's acquaintance with both the visi-recorder and the signal transmitter was enough to show him that neither could present danger to the transport or anyone aboard. He thrust from his mind the twinge of remorse for doing anything that was clearly a violation of all Space Transportation's regulations. The uppermost thought was of the huge amount of money destined to be his.

"All right," Dorn impulsively agreed, "I'll do it, but..." then he tried not to stumble over his words, "...but...you have...to pay up front!"

Without any change of expression, Horst congenially accepted, "Of course. If that's the way you want it. Absolutely no problem." He feigned reaching toward a briefcase lying on the back seat, then stopped and turned to the tech with a steely look. "Perhaps it would be better, for all concerned, if payment were made after the completion of your duty."

"No...no...I want my money now." The tech's voice rose an octave in pitch.

Frantically, Dorn grabbed for the case, but a vicious blow to his wrist made him shrink back in pain. "What the hell," he screamed, holding his bruised hand. "What do you want of me?"

"You are to place," and Horst forced the small signal transmitter back in his hand, "this device on the transport before the next flight. If you do not do as ordered," he indicated the incriminating taped evidence in the portable viewer, "a copy of your activities will be given to

Space Transportation." To clinch his argument, he shook his head, and added in a meaningful voice, "Think what that would do to your family."

This was the ultimate shock, as Horst had intended; and he watched with satisfaction as Dorn flinched and then obediently deposited the black button-like object in his shirt pocket.

An involuntary shiver ran the length of the tech's spine, and he did not look up when he asked, "When do I get paid?"

"On May fifteenth, the day the transport leaves on its first official voyage to the Moon." Horst's face had relaxed, and his voice actually sounded friendly, but underneath that composed exterior was a seething contempt for the tech's gullibility. It was so easy to get people to do one's bidding, when a Sword of Damocles was held over their head, and enough money offered.

"Where..." Dorn nervously questioned, "...do I get my money?"

"You will be informed. Now go to your auto-car and stay there until I leave."

The tech didn't wait for another directive. In his haste, he half ran, half stumbled to his vehicle.

Horst put his auto-car in manual drive and did not follow the customary silver ribbon route. Pulling away, he glanced back in the mirror to see that Dorn had obeyed instructions. He then muttered disdainfully under his breath, "Sniveling swine."

A full twenty-four hours had passed, and Arturo was still feeling the euphoria of the successful maiden voyage of the transport and his nomination as a director of Space Transport. When a call from the Space Trans manager of Traffic Operations came through, his mood was jovial. "Yes, Brian, what can I do for you?"

"Arturo, sorry to bother you, but I've just received word from Mars that they've got a serious crisis with the engine computer on the transporter that just landed. The crew can't get it to checkout during pre-flight."

"What seems to be the problem?"

"They don't know. The ship is all loaded and ready for launch. And, Arturo, this one has a penalty for late delivery of the product to the European Community of Nations. If we don't deliver by the deadline, it'll cost us dearly."

"Did they run the on board reprogram system?" Arturo mentally started an automatic checklist of possible abnormalities.

"Yes, and they've functioned the computer through the base station system as well. It keeps showing a 'reprogram' code. Seems to be stuck on that." The manager sounded exasperated.

"Can they use the spare computer?"

"No. The security system on that program prevents unauthorized entry, removal or theft." His strained tone exhibited the futility of the situation.

"Tell them to override it. They have the override codes."

"Tried that, but the computer won't accept them," he emphatically stated. "Only thing they could do is cut the cables and remove the unit. But then, they'd never get the new computer wired up in time to make the deadline."

"What about reschedule of another transporter to take the load?"

"My first thought, Arturo. This baby is the largest in our fleet, and it's loaded to the gills. It'd take two of the smaller transports to carry the shipment, and there isn't even one that's immediately available for that kind of turnaround."

"I'll get someone up there right away to take a look," and Arturo switched off the communication.

There were only two people beside himself, who could possibly break or override the security program code and effect the repairs. He barked into the visi-phone, "Get Levy and Murph up to my office immediately. We have a problem on Mars."

"Hey, Boss," his assistant apologized, "no can do. Levy's on vacation in the Alaska wilderness and won't be in contact until the seventeenth of May."

"Then send, Murph!" Arturo impatiently interrupted.

"That's what I'm trying to tell you. Remember, Murph went in the hospital for a right lung transplant and is completely out of action. He's still in recovery."

"I forgot," Arturo said sheepishly and immediately asked, "how is he?"

"He's doing fine. Sorry, Boss," the assistant looked sorrowful. "Is there anyone..."

"No. No one else." Forcing a smile, he added, "It's not your fault, Jake. I didn't mean to take it out on you."

The assistant nodded, and Arturo shut off the intercom. For a long moment he just sat there looking blankly into space; then, shaking his head, knowing there was no other alternative, he called home.

"Jana, I'm afraid I've got some bad news, lover." He explained the situation in detail.

She tried very hard not to show her disappointment and attempted to be philosophical, "There will be another time, dear. The Moon's going to be there for a while. We'll just plan another trip, later."

Arturo knew his wife too well, and an inspiration hit him. "Look Jana, Mars is close to Earth right now, and if I take one of our hotshot shuttles to Mars this afternoon, it'll only take me five days to get there. Once I solve the problem, we can still have our vacation."

"But we're scheduled to leave in less than two weeks. How would you make it back in time?"

"Here's my idea. Why don't you go with Mother and Dad on the fifteenth as planned? I should be able to join you shortly after that. And tell you what, I'll arrange to stay for another few days to make up for not being there initially."

A bright smile lit her face. "Oh, Arturo, that would be wonderful. But, can you fix the problem that quickly?"

"To be able to join you and have a second honeymoon, you bet."

"What time this afternoon will the shuttle leave for Mars?"

"In about two hours."

"Oh, Arturo, I won't get to see you before you leave," Jana said disconsolately, then quickly added, "Yes, I will. Filip and I are leaving right now for the base to see you off."

"That's too much trouble Jana," Arturo said, secretly pleased that she was coming.

"See you, love," and the visi-phone abruptly disconnected.

The Mars shuttle was scheduled to leave in 20 minutes. Arturo impatiently checked the time again; perhaps Jana and Filip had run into a detour with jammed traffic and would miss his departure. For some reason he felt it urgent to see her before leaving for Mars. After fifteen more minutes, he was just about to board the lift for the shuttle, when he spied a Space Transport air-jitney racing across the field.

"Darling, we were held up in horrid traffic," Jana cried out breathlessly, "and I had to declare an emergency to central control to make it here."

Filip raced his mother to his father's waiting arms and received an immediate bear hug. But it was barely a moment before he squirmed away, finding more interest in watching the other planes, transports and aircars.

Jana let herself be enveloped by Arturo's outstretched arms and held tightly. He tenderly stroked her hair, and she burrowed her head into his shoulder.

"Get the darn thing fixed, darling, and come back to me as soon as you can," Jana implored.

"I will my love. We'll meet at the resort and wow...what a time we'll have."

The ship's third officer coughed politely and said, "I'm afraid we have to go, Mr. Diggs."

Arturo hugged Jana tighter, his kiss passionate. With a sorrowful sigh, she disentangled herself from Arturo's arms, kissed him gently on the ear, and whispered, "I'll be waiting."

Giving his son's hair a final ruffle, Arturo boarded the lift for the shuttle. Just before entering the cabin, he looked back and saw Jana and Filip waving. He returned the salutation, but an odd thought struck him, "Funny, Jana hasn't seen me off on a Mars trip for some years. And bringing Filip...?"

When Arturo had disappeared into the shuttle, Jana took Filip's hand and started to head for the main entrance of the port.

"Hey," a man's voice greeted, "Mrs. Diggs, Filip..."

She turned and immediately recognized the handsome young face of one of Arturo's flight engineers.

"Hello, Conrad," she replied warmly, "haven't seen you in ages."

"I'm on my way up to control tower. Would you both like to go up with me and watch the shuttle blast off?"

"Yeah," Filip excitedly responded, "can we, Mom?" Jana's nod of approval was all the boy needed, and he darted after the engineer.

As Jana stood by the window in the control tower, she felt a desperate loneliness. Trying to brush off the strange feeling, she tried to concentrate on the reality that she and her husband would be together again in a few weeks, but it didn't seem to work. Suddenly she felt a hand on her arm, and she broke her reverie.

"Mrs. Diggs," one of the air controllers had pulled up a chair by the window, "why don't you have a seat, there's going to be a slight delay in the takeoff of the shuttle."

An instant look of panic crossed her face, "Is there a problem?"

"Just a holdup on the ground, Ma'am. Nothing to worry about," he reassured. "Be about thirty minutes." But the concern on her face prompted him to expand, "An orbiting GOT just ejected a Los Angeles bound REV, but the main space port can't accommodate them because of an emergency landing. They've diverted the REV to us."

"Thank you for letting me know," Jana smiled, starting to take the proffered chair, but before she was seated, a queer feeling gripped her. Impulsively, she asked, "Would it be possible to contact the captain of my husband's shuttle and request, if it's not too late, that he take two more passengers?"

"No ma'am, there's plenty of time."

"Thank you," and she rewarded him with a beautiful smile.

The controller immediately radioed the captain of the shuttle, who, when told that the passengers would be Mrs. Diggs and her son, straightway approved the request. It never occurred to anyone to ask why they had not come aboard with Arturo. All at Space Transport — who knew the Diggs — were aware of their closeness.

"Lift them aboard," was all the shuttle captain spoke into the visi-communicator.

Arturo was engrossed in a thick report relating to the troubled transport stuck on Mars when the door to his cabin opened. With absolute surprise and amazement, all he could say was, "Jana, Filip, what are you doing here? Is something wrong?"

"Nothing now, my darling. We just decided to join you."

He looked speechlessly at his wife and son.

Jana lowered her lashes, and asked, "You're not cross with us are you?"

"Heavens no," he managed to finally sputter, "but what about Filip's school...and..."

"He'll be fine," Jana assured her husband. "He'll learn more in these next few weeks than he ever could in a classroom." She tossed her head and gave him a beaming smile and turned to her son. "Darling, why don't you go with the captain, he'll show you your quarters with the relief crew."

"What a fabulous surprise," was all Arturo could rally.

"And, darling, now we can have this room all to ourselves. By the way, we have to send a message to your Mom and Dad," Jana went on in a matter-of-fact voice, "that all three of us will join them at the Twilight Resort on our way back from Mars." Jana then took his face in her hands and kicked the door closed with the heel of her shoe.

On precise schedule, the shuttle arrived at the Mars base. After a short stop at the guest housing, Jana and Filip went directly to the shopping complex to renew their meager stock of borrowed crew clothing and toiletries.

Arturo proceeded to the problem transport, which was quartered in the mile-wide enclosed dome. As the automatic personnel mover propelled him through the myriad passageways connecting all transport launching pads, his mind was racing over the computer security problem of the freighter. He had already resolved that it had to be something simple.

As many times as he had been to Mars, Arturo still had trouble adjusting to its 38% of Earth's gravity. He found that the legibility of his writing was somewhat lacking. Using simple tools many times resulted in over tightening of connectors and consequent damage. He always managed to acclimate eventually, but until then, he needed a technician with him for any task involving precise handwork.

One compensation was that the transport flight deck had its own atmosphere, and he wasn't required to wear the space suit, with its life giving oxygen. He smiled when he thought of the 96% CO_2 atmosphere. No danger ever of fire in un-pressurized areas. When transport work involved any danger whatsoever of fire, it was de-pressurized and the Mars atmosphere was allowed to enter.

Within a few hours he had studied all the previous printouts of the pre-flight procedures and verified that the security program was causing the computer to issue re-calibrate messages. He purposely had designed the security program to direct the computer to issue false messages if someone tried either to enter the program or remove the actual computer from its installed location.

He issued his personal code, the only one possible to override the security system. Under normal circumstances, this procedure should have penetrated the security software, but instead the computer flashed the standard 're-program' message. He repeated the process innumerable times, using different methods of input, but it was all to no avail.

"Sometimes one can overdo things," he muttered angrily to himself. "Damn, it'll take time to break into the security design. Too quick or too sudden, it could crash and take the computer with it."

Arturo called the base manager, "Karl, I need to set up a test to duplicate the problem here. Do you have more than one spare engine controller that I can use to check out my codes?"

"Sure do, Arturo. Where do you want it?"

"In your computer maintenance lab, as soon as possible," then almost as an afterthought, "and I'll need a couple of your techs to assist."

"No problem. Just holler for anything you need."

By the time Arturo arrived at the lab, security guards armed with laser pistols were delivering the test controller. With the assistance of the experienced technicians, Arturo reprogrammed the security system on the spare computer with the identical readings as the defunct computer in the transport.

"Well, people, it's worth another try."

Again he inserted his personal override codes and intently watched the readouts. There was still no entry into the security software, but also no damage showed to the flight computer.

"Damn it all! Have to start from scratch. Okay, everyone, back to square one," Arturo grumbled.

After four more days of hard work and frustrating failure, Arturo devised a completely different approach to reproducing the problem. This time, he was convinced he had succeeded in duplicating the flight computer symptoms. As the techs prepared for the test, Arturo idly looked at his watch. It read May 15 at 0200 hours in the morning, Earth time. He frowned, for in seven hours his parents would be boarding the new Space Transport freighter leaving for the Moon. "This bloody approach better work," he thought to himself, "or we can forget about joining them."

Carefully, he input his personal codes to enter the security system. With crossed fingers and a look skyward, he hopefully commented, "Once again everyone. Let's hope they work without damage to the computer."

The security system flashed a bright red light three times, which was replaced by a green flashing light.

"That's it, men! We've done it!" Arturo shouted jubilantly. "Entering the transport flight computer system should be no problem. Now we know what to fix."

They left the lab and rushed back to the troubled transport. This time Arturo entered his access codes with confidence, and when the security system flashed a bright red light three times, then the flashing green light, everyone breathed a sigh of relief.

"Now you troublesome son-of-a-bitch," Arturo muttered out loud, more to himself than to anyone in particular, "let's see what your problems are."

It was several more hours of meticulous work before the actual problem was discovered. Holding a newly developed galliumite chip between his forefinger and thumb, Arturo shook his head in exasperation. "This is the little bastard that allowed the programmed codes to inter-link," he explained to the service techs. "During the checkout procedure the computer thought an unauthorized entry was underway and thus displayed erroneous signals and readouts."

"We've been using those galliumite chips for almost two years now, Mr. Diggs — no problems before."

"Well, I'm not taking a chance, I'm putting the use of galliumite chips on hold until the manufacturer can fix the inter-linking of input codes." Then with a relieved smile at having discovered and fixed the problem, "Replace this, but use one of our old and proven chips."

"We'll take it from here, Mr. Diggs, and thanks."

As Arturo started to leave the transport, he glanced at his watch. It was exactly 0900 hours, Earth time.

"Well folks, have a good trip," he said aloud. "See you in a few days."

One of the techs ran up, concerned that he had perhaps missed an order. "Sorry, Mr. Diggs, did you say something?"

"No," and for the first time in several days, he laughed. "Just talking to myself. My folks are on their way to the Twilight Resort on the Moon. We'd be with them now if it hadn't been for this damned security system problem."

The tech nodded and returned his smile, "Great vacation spa." Then trying to be helpful, he added, "By the way, I think there's a transport leaving at 1500 hours, Earth time. It's stopping on the Moon to pick up some more cargo," and he winked. "Bet you and the family can hitch a ride."

"Thanks. I'll go over to the general manager's office and brief him. Maybe Karl can fit us on that 1500 transport."

"Hell, Mr. Diggs, he'd off load cargo to make room for you and your family. You saved his bacon."

"Sorry it took so long and thanks again for all your help," he said, with a wave of his hand.

On the way to the manager's office, Arturo stopped to brief the transport captain and first officer. They had more questions than he'd anticipated, and so it was a full hour before he walked lighthearted into Karl's base control area.

His detached thoughts were still on the successful repair of the transport and the impeding vacation, and he paid scant attention to the grim look on the manager's face and disregarded the one-sided phone communication.

"Yes, I understand the message. Please put it in my computer immediately. Yes, he's here now."

Karl's features were ashen, and his hands were shaking as he hung up the visiphone. "We just received a message from the Space Transport Chairman for you, Arturo," his voice barely audible.

"He must have sent it about 8 or 9 minutes ago, since it takes that long to receive messages from Earth. What did he have to say, Karl?"

It was not at all unusual that the chairman personally sent messages to him when he was in space, and Arturo fleetingly wondered what had so upset his friend Karl.

Karl had brought up the chairman's image on the holographic viewer and motioned Arturo to come over. Arturo immediately noticed that the chairman was not behind his desk. He was seated uncharacteristically in one of the side chairs in his office. Normally, messages were either transmitted verbally or in writing. For the message to be transmitted by the chairman from a side chair was most curious. Suddenly, Arturo felt a sense of foreboding as he walked towards the hologram image of the chairman. He stopped, and the chairman's image began to speak.

"Arturo, I don't know how to tell you, but..." he faltered and began again, "our flight to the Moon this morning has had a problem and..."

For the first time, Arturo realized that this was more than a routine call. Arturo felt a lump knot his stomach. "My God, my parents are on that flight. What do you mean a problem?" he said out loud as if the chairman could hear him.

"I'm afraid, Arturo," and the answer was slow in coming, "that our tracking system and the international tracking system reported a catastrophic explosion in the transporter at L-5, where the Earth's gravity and the Moon's gravity are zero and..."

"Exploded, that's impossible!" Arturo said loudly, unaware of the tears pouring down his cheeks. "You don't have all the facts. It can't be..."

The voice from the hologram image continued with the known details, and Mohammed Nahal's voice again faltered before he continued with, "Arturo, there's no question now," and there was a pause before he continued, "the transporter was a total loss."

"But what about the 'scape systems? They couldn't have just vanished!" Arturo yelled out in complete denial of the facts, as if the chairman's image could hear him.

As if anticipating Arturo's questions, the image continued, "No signals of 'scape systems being energized were recorded. One minute the ship was there, and the next minute it was gone in an explosion that went off the monitoring scales of the satellites in synchronous orbit. It could only have been an explosion of the fusion reactor."

Arturo thought to himself, "But that can't happen to that system. There are too many safeguards...it can't happen... the crew... Mother... Dad..."

The chairman waited a moment, as if he could feel the anguish Arturo was feeling and then continued. "We'll hold the Mars transport you just fixed until you're ready to leave. Get on it and come home. There's nothing you can do. By the time you get here, we'll have a handle on the telemetry data."

There was a long hesitation, and the chairman's message concluded with, "Karl, at their convenience, get Arturo, Jana and Filip on the transport. We'll handle everything here until they return."

Only with concentrated effort, did Arturo regain a semblance of composure. But his voice betrayed his anguish. "Karl, I need to talk to Jana now. We'll be on the transport to Earth as soon as it's ready to leave." Without another word and with inner fortitude holding him erect, he walked swiftly from the room.

At exactly 1000 hours on May 15th, Dorn punched in the coordinates for the appointed meeting place that would propel his brand new auto-car along the silver ribbon. He smiled broadly as he sat relaxed and content in the costly vehicle. It was loaded with every possible extra: visi-phone, visi-corder, long life battery and wheels, satellite reception, the latest directional computer, shade-changing glass and a lavish interior.

Dorn had watched the Moon transport lift off without incident. He still had a slight concern regarding the reason for placing the black chip on the cable, but the apprehension was quickly dissipated by the thought of the money he was about to receive. With satisfaction, he turned on his new visi-corder and leaned back to listen to his favorite music station. The plans to leave Space Transport and see the world during a three-year leisurely trip with the family had already been made, even to the hiring of a tutor for the kids. Then they'd buy a house on the California coast, on a cliff overlooking the ocean, and use it as their base home. Maybe they'd buy condos or apartments in other cities to use when they traveled. After all, he thought, "There's more money than we'll ever need and we can do just about anything we want."

Dorn's reverie was broken when a voice intruded the comforting music.

"We interrupt to bring you an important announcement. A transport belonging to Space Transportation Corporation, en route to the Moon, has apparently exploded during flight. We have no further details regarding possible survivors, or of the explosion. This tragic news item comes from our source at International Tracking."

Dorn sat upright and feverishly punched in the all-news satellite broadcast. The report was the same. An explosion, and no word of survivors.

"Oh my God, our first accident. An explosion...that can't happen. The fusion reactor can't blow up...it has too many safety systems...impossible." He began shouting, "The reports are wrong. An explosion...can only happen if...over-pressure of the reactor. It can't be... unless...the getter went crazy...which would..."

Dorn had not noticed that the auto-car had stopped and he had arrived at the predetermined coordinates. He sat baffled; listening to the repeated news broadcast and racked his brain about what could possibly cause an explosion.

"Lord God Almighty," he screamed in horror, his mind instantly focusing on the black chip he had placed on the engine controller and getter cable, "am I responsible?" In agony, he threw his hands up to cover his face, unaware of the auto-car that had pulled along side.

It was not until he heard a rapping on the window and saw Horst motioning him to open the door, that the full impact hit him. Mechanically, he flipped the lock open and, before the blond man was even seated, burst out, "Did I cause the explosion of the Moon transport this morning?" Not even waiting for a reply, he repeated the fearful plea, "Please tell me I didn't! No...no...no...I didn't do it!"

Horst took his time getting into the car without answering or even looking at the sobbing man. Dorn suddenly felt a terrible sense of foreboding.

"Please, please tell me I had nothing to do with it," Dorn cried out. "The black chip I placed was for signal monitoring only...please tell me!" He pleaded for exoneration.

"As you wish," Horst spoke with no trace of emotion in his voice, and Dorn did not notice the expression of contempt in his eyes. "You did not cause this morning's accident of the Moon transport."

"Thank God," the tech gasped with relief. "I thought that possibly the black chip might have interfered with the signal processing of the reactor engine controller and the molecule getter. If the controller were to..." but Dorn stopped in mid-sentence. The full truth became apparent. "If the signal were to be overridden causing a complete failure of the..." When the reality struck, his fear turned to anger. "You son-of-a-bitch. You said no harm would come to the transport. You caused it! You caused it!" Dorn screamed.

"No, Dorn. You caused the accident." The level tone and the bluntness of the accusation made the larger man cringe. Horst matter-of-factly placed a briefcase on Dorn's lap. "Here's your money. It was a job well done."

In revulsion and terror, Dorn shoved the case to the floor. "I'll kill you!" he screamed. "I don't want your blood money," and he lunged at Horst's throat to throttle him.

Dorn didn't feel the small needle prick his wrist. He was only aware of being gripped by a pair of hands like steel clamps as his fingers were wrenched from Horst's throat.

"Just relax, Dorn. It's almost over."

Suddenly, the tech felt such a piercing throb in his chest, he involuntarily cried out with pain. He felt his heart was pounding so violently, it seemed about to explode. Instinctively, he knew he was dying, but he managed to gasp, "Why?"

"Hate and envy," the professional assassin answered truthfully without any emotion. There was no reason to lie now. The answer he gave was not the cause of the explosion, but the motivation of his employer.

Dorn felt as if his heart and chest were in the grip of a giant vise. The pain was so severe that he passed out before his heart exploded.

Horst placed the dead man's right hand over his still heart, and his left hand reaching out for the Central Traffic Control distress alarm button. He had never intended to leave a witness. The deceased had only been an instrument, and Horst felt no remorse. Emotion and sentiment were reserved for amateurs. An autopsy, if performed, would disclose only that Dorn died of a massive heart attack.

Grabbing the briefcase, which was filled only with wadded paper, Horst got into his car. He purposely did not notify central traffic control and drove leisurely away.

The memorial service for the crew and passengers of the ill-fated Space Transport freighter was deferred until Arturo, Jana and Filip returned from Mars. The devastating destruction was still thought to have been caused by the complete failure of the fusion reactor. It had happened so suddenly that the escape modules didn't have the necessary one-second to be energized and thrust away from the transport.

Arturo had insisted, over the objections of the chairman, on returning to work immediately. He had personally gone over all the available telemetry data and had not been able to discover anything more than his engineers had. His assistant and chief engineer, Bo Jacobs, was currently working with him on the latest recounts, again exploring every facet of the telemetry tapes.

"All we know for sure is that everything is normal until the record traces stop. Pressure recordings of the crew's atmosphere peg suddenly. Obviously the result of the..." The engineer refrained from uttering the word "explosion."

"Were there any traces of...?" Arturo couldn't bring himself to ask if pieces of human remains had been recovered.

Bo quickly answered, "No, not that we know of. We picked up all the transport pieces we could find. They were scattered all over space, but we should be able to reconstruct some of the ship and hopefully see where the problem started. Unfortunately, a large part of the ship was vaporized." There was a note of resignation in his voice. "But we may not glean much information from the reconstruction, and the recovered parts have traces of radioactivity."

"Let's go down to the hanger, Bo. We've got work to do."

The few recovered fragments from the transport had been carefully laid out behind radiation shields. One look and Arturo knew without question there had been an explosion.

"Tell the rest of the engineers to assemble in the data analysis center in fifteen minutes." Bo nodded and started to follow orders, but was stopped by Arturo. "You meet me there, as soon as you can."

Arturo was studying the flight telemetry records, when his chief engineer joined him.

"Here's exactly when the crew cabin atmospheric pressure monitor pegged." Arturo pointed to a specific blip on the diagram. "And here's an expanded graph of the reactor pressure. Everything was normal until then, Bo, then a 100 milliseconds before the explosion," and he turned, his face a mask of a stony hardness, "and it was an explosion, the engine pressure began rising steeply from the normal 10,000 psi to 25,000 psi. The temperature only increased slightly over the normal 30,000° C design point."

"Then we can rule out the impossible situation of the fusion reactor becoming a bomb and blowing up?"

"Yes, it looks as if pressure in the engine had a rapid increase for some reason yet unexplained."

Arturo's engineering crew had quietly assembled in the room. They did not interrupt, but listened intently to the conversation.

"What's the speed of this trace?" Arturo asked, indicating the pressure tracking.

"We blew it up to a 100 times normal, sir," one of the junior engineers volunteered. The trace, which normally occupied only a tenth of a millimeter of paper, was enlarged to cover a full centimeter from start to end.

"Let's blow it up to 10,000 times," Arturo ordered. "That will give us a trace of a full meter from beginning to end, and maybe we can see any anomalies that occurred."

The printer began spitting out the 10,000 x trace, and Arturo started scrutinizing it before the long paper completely emerged from the machine. When the printer stopped and ejected the copy, the engineers clustered around him, all examining the pressure curve, looking for any clue that could determine what went wrong, what caused the engine reactor over-pressure.

"There seems to be a pattern of oscillation here at the beginning that is repeated over and over," the chief engineer said, as he continued to look even more closely for repetition of the event.

"Okay, now we know where to look. This oscillation," and Arturo pointed to a particular area at the beginning of the pressure curve, "here, it's the same as the normal reactor oscillation. But if you look at how it changes as the milliseconds go by, you'll see that it's being influenced by something else."

"It's almost as if the engine controller tries to correct for the over-pressure, and something is telling it to continue whatever it's doing. The controller is trying to return to normal operation, but something is directing it to..." another engineer observed.

Arturo stopped him in mid-sentence, "My God, the engine controller tells the reactor to identify the positive and negative particles going into the getter, which replaces the throat of the engine as it is melted away. Simply stated if it says 'negative', fewer particles are replaced. If it says 'positive,' more particles are replaced."

Arturo's mind was racing. The throat of the engine was the key to the force that drove the rocket and thus pushed the transporter through space. If the throat was too big, the force or thrust went down and the engine was inefficient. If the throat was too small, the pressure became too high and the engine again became inefficient. The throat of the engine had to be held close to the desired design. But if the throat was closed off, like a stopper in a sink, and the reactor continued its normal operation of pumping super-heated enriched beryllium hydrogen for exhaust through the engine throat, the pressure would go up and an over-pressure explosion of the reactor would occur — but not a nuclear fission explosion.

The engine controller software had built in redundant safety to prevent such an event. As Arturo studied the pressure trace, it was obvious that the "controller" was trying to correct for the positive particles continuing to build up in the throat, which ultimately acted as a stopper in a sink. The difference was the "water in the sink" simply stopped draining. In the fusion rocket engine, it continued to supply the enriched beryllium hydrogen to the throat. Since it had no place to go the pressure increased until the reactor blew apart. When it blew, the enriched beryllium hydrogen exploded, resulting in the entire transport being blown apart in a mighty blast not unlike a nuclear explosion.

Arturo hurriedly began explaining his conclusion to the assembled engineers. He also defined how the engine controller had continually tried to correct the problem but, for reasons unknown to him, had failed.

"Mr. Diggs, could it be that the software that tells the updated and redesigned engine controller had a bug or a cross link in it, which caused the controller to hunt for correction and ultimately fail?" another engineer hypothesized.

"Certainly, anything is possible." Arturo conceded, "However, as we all know, the system was tested and retested for cross links and possible bugs. Plus the test flight around the Moon was flawless."

"In fact, during that test flight," the chief engineer expanded, "the crew sent signals to induce all possible failure modes conceivable, and the controller responded perfectly. We even had a signal induced to only let the getter gather positive molecules, which would have resulted in the same thing, a complete closure of the acceleration engine throat."

"And the controller shut down the reactor as programmed," one of the engineers responsible for that phase of the procedure, quickly added.

"But, Mr. Diggs, if the controller was trying to correct the problem, as you said, the traces show that it was trying to shut down the fusion reactor, but it didn't. Doesn't that show that the program controlling the engine had a flaw and that it continued to drive the reactor to destruction?"

Another senior engineer begrudgingly inquired, "You're the only one that knows the complete program. Is it possible there was a latent defect that we all missed, that actually caused the explosion?"

"No it isn't. You're drawing conclusions that have no basis in fact," the chief engineer tersely defended.

The senior engineer, chastised by his direct superior, only smiled and nodded his head. But Arturo was dumbstruck with the possibility that the assertion could be true.

The following day the San Diego Electronic Herald had blatant headlines on all news viewers throughout Southern California, which in turn were picked up and transmitted throughout the world:

TRANSPORTER EXPLOSION CAUSED BY ENGINEERING ERROR

The story went on to say the fusion reactor exploded because of a faulty design in the software that drove the engine controller. It covered the loss of life and pointed out that

Arturo Newsome Diggs, his wife and son were not on the flight, but his mother and father were. One news analyst pointed out that it must have been Providence that kept Mr. Diggs and his immediate family off the same flight.

Newsmen stationed themselves outside Arturo's home and office and bombarded him with the typical news questions, designed to obtain some sensational disclosure.

"Did you suspect a flaw in your calculations of the engine controller?"

"Is that why you didn't go with your parents?"

"Mr. Diggs, how do you feel about the loss of your parents?"

"Do you think you pushed technology too far?"

"Did you and your parents get along?"

"How can we prevent this terrible and tragic event from occurring in the future?"

"Why did your wife and son decide to join you at the last minute? Did she suspect something?"

"How does your wife feel about this, Mr. Diggs?"

There was one question that Arturo responded to, but not to the press, "Since you're responsible for the death of your parents, what are your plans, Mr. Diggs?"

Arturo called the chairman, Mohammed Nahal, and tendered his resignation from the board of Space Transport, Inc. and as vice-president and chief engineer of the corporation.

Mohammed tried to talk him out of his decision. "It'll all blow over, and the media will find something else to follow. Don't resign."

"I have to resign. It will never be the same. I couldn't face the people who trusted me. They followed everything I did in complete faith that my designs and calculations were always right. I must resign."

After many in-depth conversations, Mohammed finally agreed to Arturo's resignation as an officer, but only under the conditions that his Space Transport stock options would remain in effect and that he stay on as a full time consultant. This was not altruism on the part of the chairman, but rather a shrewd business proposition. Arturo would continue his private explorations on achieving the speed of light. All his research would remain classified, known only by him and the chairman. Whatever his findings, Arturo deemed it only fair, that they would ultimately be signed over to Space Transport.

Arturo and Jana decided not to sell either of the adjoining houses and move to another location. Instead Arturo redesigned his parent's home into a vast office containing high tech tape machines, computers, and equipment — most of which — were quietly supplied by Mohammed and the company.

Horst's meeting with Joal Lowe to collect the final payment for his services had been set far away from inquiring eyes. They met at a secluded resort in the desert, almost a hundred miles from San Diego.

"It's too damn bad that you didn't get the entire family," Joal growled. "Of course I'll deduct 25% of the agreed-upon payment, since Arturo Diggs and his family escaped." He stared into Horst's eyes for any sign of agreement.

"Hardly, Herr Lowe." Horst's tone was steely. He was not the least intimidated by the arrogant bluff. "There will not be anything deducted. You were informed that Diggs, his wife and child would not be on the Moon transport." He then mimicked Joal's high-pitched nasal voice, "Part of a loaf is better than none, go ahead with the plan." As he locked eyes with his employer, he merely shrugged his shoulders.

Joal sensed that he, himself, might be in some danger. This meeting place had not been arranged by him. Besides, it was not in his interest to antagonize such a man as this. More importantly, he might need similar services again.

"Okay, I agree," he said with a sigh. "Just wanted to see if you were on your toes. My auto-car is open. Go take your gold; it's in the back seat."

As Horst went after the gold, Joal's eyes narrowed, and he automatically rubbed his left forearm, a gesture, which Horst had seen him do when perplexed. Then the flabby lips parted as if to say something, but instead, a shrieking sound issued like that of an animal in pain. If Horst hadn't known better, he would have sworn the man was in agony. But the insane screech had occurred before, and always after untraceable assignments for Joal had been completed.

"You know, Horst, maybe it's better that Diggs is still alive." Joal's voice reeked with hate. "He's held in disgrace by his peers and his superiors." Then he almost cackled, "They think he killed his parents, not to mention the crew and passengers of the transport. He'll never be a force to be reckoned with again. Yeah, this way is better." Again the bizarre cackle erupted from his throat, "but still, all of them would have been preferable and…"

Horst averted his eyes in disgust, and did not listen to the remainder of Joal's ravings. He had already decided that if any future jobs were accepted, the payment would be "gold in advance." Horst was an astute professional, and he knew that anyone who had so much hate bottled up was not to be trusted in the business of "untraceable events."

LIGHTSPEED

THE BREAKTHROUGH

The rented air-car was in sight of the immense laser test facility. When Arturo Newsome Diggs looked down, the huge round torus shaped building always gave him the impression of a monstrous skinny donut.

Situated on the plains of eastern Colorado, the site had been built by a consortium of companies in a joint venture with the government, Space Transport being one of the major private participants. The overall "donut" was one hundred and eighty kilometers in diameter, with a circumference of five hundred and sixty-five kilometers. The torus cross-section was a hundred meters in diameter. It was an outstanding scientific achievement in design and construction and much in demand by industry, institutions and governments. Here, researchers and corporations came from all parts of the world to test lasers, electron guns, particle accelerators and other equipment in the gigantic mirrored enclosure.

This was the same facility in which Arturo, two years earlier had succeeded in splitting photons. He had spent a considerable amount of time analyzing equipment before deciding to use a small 5,000-watt fusion reactor, which could produce a concentrated light source, heavy with photons. For the energy to split photons from the reactor, he chose the newly developed 5,000-watt rubyionium gas laser electron gun. Each piece of equipment could vary the diameter of their beams from one micron, or 1/10,000 of a centimeter, to a full centimeter. By placing both pieces of equipment in a vacuum, he aimed the laser gun beam at a right angle to the fusion reactor beam. His calculations had indicated the rubyionium electron emission from the laser gun would split the reactor beam photons.

For over a year there had been no success, until he discovered that pulsing the laser gun beam at a particular nanosecond rate split the single fusion beam into two beams. The rubyionium electron beam no longer simply passed through the fusion beam but was absorbed by the split beams. Careful measurements found that the split beams were exactly 90 degrees apart and that the bright one was charged positively and the black one negatively. He named the bright beam, Posafon, and the black beam, Negafon, for the assumed particles they contained.

Elated over his discovery, Arturo attempted to measure the hoped for energy release as a result of the photons being split. Much to his dismay, absolutely no energy release was measured even though the equipment could measure fractions of an electron volt. He continued trying varying pulse rates, different beam diameters, and angles of impingement. Though frustrated at not finding the desired energy release from his split photons, he never gave up his quest.

The recorded voice of security jolted Arturo back to the present. "Please enter appropriate voice code for entrance to Laser Test Facility."

"Arturo N. Diggs, request permission to land," he responded.

"Thank you Mr. Diggs. You are cleared," came back the authorization. "Test area 314 is expecting you."

Arturo spent the day using the facility's recently installed measuring equipment, but all his attempts in bombarding focused light from the fusion reactor with the rubyionium laser electron gun were again to no avail. Even with the minutest calibrations, no increase in energy could be detected.

"Sorry, Mr. Diggs," the assigned technician shook his head, "we've re-calibrated as you requested, but..."

"Not your fault, Todd," Arturo gave a wan smile of dissatisfaction with himself. "I was just so sure that today would..."

"Wish we could continue," the tech apologized, "but we're already over your allotted time."

"Thanks, for your patience, Todd. I appreciate it." He began gathering up his papers, belatedly remembering to be courteous, "and thank the rest of the crew for me."

"Sure, Mr. Diggs, maybe next time, huh?"

Arturo cuffed the tech on the shoulder. "Sure, Todd, maybe next time." He turned on his heel to leave the test area, but halted when he spotted a white coated, squat figure briskly walking towards him.

"Well, Mister Diggs," a voice boomed from across the room, "I see you've failed again to find energy." There was a tone of ridicule in the voice as he added, "In your, so called, photon split."

Even though preoccupied with his thoughts, Arturo instantly recognized the voice and face but chose to give no outward indication of acknowledgement.

"I'm Dr. Rollie," the chalk faced man pompously introduced himself. "Doctor" and he emphasized his title, "Carlyle Rollie."

"Yes, Dr. Rollie," Arturo nodded, "I remember. We met in England."

"That's right, Mister Diggs. When I heard your paper in London about the experiment, it was obvious that you were chasing a dream."

Arturo's first inclination was to retaliate, but he forced himself to hold his tongue. He knew of Rollie's reputation all too well. Rollie was a spellbinding speaker who could lecture on practically any scientific subject. His favorite caper was to debate other scientists or theoreticians, usually with the idea of discrediting them.

"In fact, Mr. Diggs, if memory serves me," Rollie snickered sarcastically, "you even had little call names for the particles." He wiggled his forefinger toward Arturo's face, "Ah yes, little posey-fons and neggy-fons."

"The split photons were labeled Posafon and Negafon," Arturo said quietly as he struggled to keep his temper.

Undaunted, his well-modulated voice rising, Rollie continued, "As you surely remember, Mr. Diggs, from the floor of the conference I told you that photons have no inherent energy release."

"Dr. Rollie, you have spent your career in research," Arturo rebutted, "but never have I heard any of your theories being developed."

"Ah, but I still obtain large grants for the application of my work," Rollie smugly countered.

"If you'll excuse me," Arturo said stiffly, "I have business to attend to."

Rollie put his hand on Arturo's arm, "My dear boy, how can a photon be split, something that has no mass or dimensions? Seems to me you've simply redirected the light beams, same as any good prism would do. Waste of time."

"Please remove your hand," Arturo snapped. He realized almost too late how close he was to losing his calm.

With an offended look, Rollie retracted his hand but then moved directly in front of Arturo. "Well, well, aren't we touchy?" he taunted. "Just because your theories can't be proved and..."

Arturo made a sudden movement directly towards his tormentor and in a husky voice challenged, "Get the hell out of my way or so help me I'll walk over the top of you."

"Well, what I've heard about your temper must certainly be true," Rollie mocked, but he quickly stepped aside.

The embarrassed technicians, overhearing the entire confrontation, turned their backs when Rollie bellowed, "I'm glad I had witnesses! I swear that man was about to strike me."

Arturo was seething as he rapidly strode out of the high intensity laser lab.

"Mr. Diggs!" A bass voice called out, "I say, will you stop for a minute?"

Impatiently, Arturo turned. Coming towards him was a tall gangly man, looking to be in his early seventies. A raincoat was thrown around his shoulders as if to disguise his rumpled clothing. A mop of tousled rusty brown hair, speckled with gray, connected with the Lincolnesque beard that covered much of his dark brown face. In the midst, were a prominent hooked nose, animated dark eyes and a sensitive mouth that flashed white teeth.

"Mr. Diggs, they told me inside that I might find you on the way to your air-car and that..." his voice came in short huffs. "Whew...took me a while to catch up...not used to walking so fast. Rather out of shape, I'm afraid. "

Arturo was in no mood to talk to anyone. But the man held out a proffered hand, and Arturo found his own hand in a firm grip being vigorously pumped up and down.

"Mr. Diggs, I'm Marshall Bernside. I wonder if I could have a minute of your time. You see, I heard your paper on photon research, and it was most impressive."

Arturo, taken aback, could only stammer, "The Marshall Bernside of Northwestern University? Dr. Bernside, the father of modern sub-sub-atomic particle research?"

"Yes, I'm afraid so," the older man modestly conceded, releasing his tight grip on Arturo's hand, "but then, whether I'm the father of the research you mentioned, depends on to whom you're talking to at the time and whether or not they agree or disagree with my findings."

"How may I help you, Dr. Bernside?" Arturo's manner revealed his respectful admiration.

"First of all, my friends call me Marsh. Only my students, or enemies, call me Doctor. I want you to consider calling me Marsh, and I would be honored if I may call you Arturo."

Both men smiled and again shook hands as Arturo said, "Okay, Marsh it is, and it's my honor to have you call me Arturo."

"Now, about your paper on photons. I say, do you think we could sit down some place and talk."

"Of course," and Arturo quickly pointed his finger at the foyer, "we can use the VIP lounge just inside that entrance." Taking the older man's arm, he led the way.

When they were seated and both taken advantage of the excellent beverage service, Marsh gave a satisfied sigh, and sipped from his glass before speaking.

"Mr. Diggs," Marsh started formally, then with a dazzling smile, "Arturo, I was most impressed with your speech to the Royal College of Astronomy in London. I wanted to speak to you then," and he diplomatically coughed, "but you left rather abruptly."

Arturo snorted, "When you found me today rushing from the building, it was under similar circumstances. I had another verbal run-in with the infamous Dr. Rollie in the test lab."

"That pompous overeducated, self-aggrandizing old fool," Marsh blurted. "The London committee chairman should have been horsewhipped for letting him harass you about your theory."

"Honestly, Marsh, I've given this some thought. I just wonder if his remarks were pre-arranged."

Marsh absently stroked, more caressed, his bushy beard, a habit to which Arturo was to become very familiar over the years. "Interesting observation, yes, very interesting." His electric black eyes flashed. "To harass the presenter into a withdrawal of his theory, or at the minimum, have those present concede that 'perhaps Dr. Rollie has a point'. "

"Especially when the press is present."

"Ah, good point, my boy," and Marsh tapped Arturo with his forefinger. "How often have we read the media's latest quotes or questions by, 'the esteemed, Dr. Rollie'?" A grim frown wrinkled his brow. "Unfortunately, Rollie's method is to throw out unanswerable challenges to a hardworking scientist and thereby cause many worthwhile theories to be discarded."

"I've heard it expressed, privately, of course, that there are those in the scientific community that consider him to be nothing more than the equivalent of a 'gadfly' at a stockholder's meeting."

"Don't ever fall into that trap, Arturo," Marsh cautioned. "A 'gadfly' is generally harmless, but this is not the case with bad-dog, Collie Rollie."

Arturo's mouth fell open and, he exclaimed, "What did you call him?"

"Don't tell me that you've never heard..." and Bernside broke into a hearty guffaw, "heard him referred to as, 'Bad-Dog-Rollie'?"

"Can't say that I have," and Arturo smiled, "but it sure fits."

"There are those, for whatever their reasons, hang onto his every word, hoping to be included into his inept little world."

Arturo pursed his mouth in consternation. "I had truly hoped, when I made my presentation to the Royal Academy, to find others who could understand my theory and possibly offer additional information, or at least advice."

"That's why I'm here, Arturo, not to offer advice, but to learn." Marsh clapped his hand on Arturo's shoulder.

"To learn, Marsh?" he replied in surprise. "Why, I've read all your books. You were writing and investigating sub-sub-atomic particles before I was born. Your theories are accepted as gospel everywhere in the world."

"Bear with me for a minute. I may be approaching 80, but I haven't taken leave of my senses. Yes, my theories are, for the most part, universally accepted. But there is one man, whom I admire, who does not accept all of them."

Arturo's back straightened as he challenged, "Who may I ask is that?"

"You, Arturo, you!" Marsh emphasized his point by wiggling a long bony finger almost in Arturo's face.

Taken aback, Arturo emphatically denied the accusation. "I don't know what you're talking about."

"Your theory that photons have energy. Yes, yes, I know you believe you have succeeded in splitting photons, even to the point of giving the presumed particles names and..."

"Damn it, Dr. Bernside, I did split photons, and yes, I did name them." Arturo could feel his blood rush in anger, "Posafon for the positive charged one and Negafon for the negatively charged one. And I don't appreciate you inferring, Dr. Bernside..."

"Now hold on young man," Marsh interrupted, holding both palms up in protest, "you do have a passion about those things you really believe in." Smiling broadly, he smacked his hands together. "I like that in a man! Shows spirit! Shows mettle! Call me Marsh!"

"What's your point?" Arturo's voice had a distrustful coldness.

"First, I believe your theories. They make sense, common sense that is. Second, many of my unsolved mysteries of particle research are now solvable. Others I deduced as being right, I now know are wrong. Somehow, I've known for years that some of my popular theories were really not based on firm ground." He gave a wry grin. "One starts to believe one's own press clippings, I suppose."

Arturo felt his indignation slowly subsiding. "I don't quite follow your reasoning."

"Simple, my young friend. The rational that photons have energy that can be harnessed, proves many of my postulates relating to why particles behave as they do." He paused, searching for just the right word, "well, at least explain."

"For example?"

"Take the furon particle I discovered 20 years ago. Although it is a sub-sub-particle of the neutron, I have never been able to explain why it didn't give off energy when excited by an electron. Now it's apparent that any photon in the vicinity nullifies the energy release though..."

Arturo's imaginative mind was racing, and he interrupted, "Yes, I see what you mean. The potential positive and negative charges internal to the photon are canceled and thus cancel the furon charge."

"Now you're beginning to understand what your theories really mean to sub-sub-atomic particle research." He shook his head, "Unfortunately, there will be naysayers, doubters and disbelievers. But I, Marsh Bernside," and he puffed out his chest, "choose to agree with you."

The two scientists continued talking and comparing theories for several hours. The discussion produced many sketches of particle movement and behavior penciled on rumpled napkins, none of which could have been understood by anyone but them.

Marsh eagerly accepted Arturo's invitation to join him for dinner. During the meal, neither man actually realized what he was eating. They only picked at their food, using their forks and knives to emphasize various points.

"My God, it's almost midnight." Marsh seemed shocked at the lateness of the hour. "I have a six o'clock experiment in the morning."

"It has been a great afternoon and evening, Marsh." Arturo held out his hand, which was promptly taken. "Don't know when I've had a discussion so thought provoking."

"But, you were the teacher. All I did was use your thoughts to put some of my own into perspective. In return, I hope I helped put some of your ideas into a different light."

Arturo beamed. He felt a warm affection for the elderly black man seated across from him. "Look, why don't you come out to San Diego and visit Jana and me. We could continue the discussion. I need some new ideas for detecting energy from split photons."

"Excellent. I accept. Let me get a few things straightened out at Northwestern, and I'll give you a call." Marsh placed his hands on the table and started to rise. Then he hesitated, a scowl on his face. In a hushed tone, he admonished, "Arturo, I suggest you keep working on your theories, but don't reveal the results. No sense in wasting time defending yourself against a bunch of jealous and self-appointed scientific fools!"

Arturo had called Jana when he decided to take the 1,000-kilometer per hour overhead train back to San Diego instead of the air shuttle. The trip through the Rocky Mountains, the desert and into Southern California was full of beautiful scenery. Besides, he wanted to think about the previous night's provoking conversation.

The HV1000 train was analogous to the old twentieth century subways of New York City, except for three things. First, the train was above ground, and rode on a magnetic repulsive cushion between its U-shaped carriage and the rail below it. Second, the tube encasing the train was fabricated from a high strength clear plastic. The overhead platform was thirty meters above ground, which gave an outstanding view except when tunneling through the mountains. And last, the train was pressurized like an orbiting vehicle because the plastic tube had all air removed. The almost perfect vacuum offered no resistance to the train speeding along at 1,000 kilometers per hour. Vibration was nonexistent. The super-cooled magnetic motors were silent, and the only sounds heard aboard were those of other passengers.

"I'm jealous," Jana teased, as they walked out of the train station, "one of my favorite trips is on the HV1000."

"The scenery is always beautiful, any time of the year," Arturo agreed. "Too early to see the desert cactus flowers in bloom, but breath taking anyway." As an afterthought he added, "Yes, a very relaxing ride."

To her practiced eye, her husband looked distracted and weary, anything but relaxed. He had mentioned that the experiment had not produced any evidence of energy release, and she attributed his preoccupation to disappointment.

"Don't give up Arturo. You'll find the answer," she encouraged. "When we get home," and it was seductively whispered, "I'll make you forget everything but me and the family."

Jana saw his strained face brighten, and her heart ached for him. "Oh, I almost forgot," she said hastily. "Todd, the senior tech from the laser test facility called just after you left Denver this morning."

Arturo raised an eyebrow. "Did he leave a message?"

"Just to return the call when you got home, or tomorrow morning, if you arrived after 5:00 o'clock."

"Probably found something I forgot to sign before leaving," And he casually dismissed the message from his mind.

When Jana and Arturo were inside their auto-car, the coordinates for the trip home were input to the computer. As the car started to roll out onto the silver strip, both fell into each other's arms. "Arturo, you know that it is against Central Traffic Control law to make love while an auto-car is moving and..." As Arturo hushed her with a kiss, Jana flipped the switch that turned on the one-way windows.

The next morning, Arturo was in his study, doodling with three-dimensional vectors of split photons while waiting for Todd to answer his visi-phone call.

"Laser Facility, Test Area 314," the senior technician automatically responded. Then he saw Arturo's visual image flash on the screen. "Oh, Hello, Mr. Diggs," he smiled broadly, "have a good trip back to San Diego?"

"Yes thanks, I did. What did I forget to sign, Todd?"

"Oh, nothing, sir. You're pretty good about marking off on the logs." Then there was a slight pause. "I'm not sure it means anything, Mr. Diggs, concerning your experiment to measure photon energy," and he frowned, "but at kilometer coordinate 285.21, one of our energy measuring systems registered an almost imperceptible increase in voltage."

"That's interesting," Arturo kept his face expressionless as he asked, "how much increase did you measure and for how long?"

"The time was very short, approximately a nanosecond, but the energy was there." Todd hesitated and then added emphatically, "And there's no question about that, sir, the trace is very visible on the measuring chip."

"Yes, I understand, but what was the energy rise?" Arturo tried not to sound excited.

"Almost a thousand electron volts. An almost imperceptible amount, but definitely measurable. Does that mean anything to your experiment?" Todd looked hopeful. "All of us here hope so."

"Anything is possible, Todd," Arturo smiled, "but don't hold your breath."

"Mr. Diggs," Todd averted his eyes from direct contact with the visi-phone, "we all heard Dr. Rollie's remarks about your experiment... and, well, we don't care for that pompous old prick." Once he had gone that far, the tech abandoned all restraint. "He's continually complaining when his tests fail that it's our fault. Frankly Mr. Diggs, he's a pain in the 'you know what'." The tech looked embarrassed by his spontaneous statements and quickly added, "Please don't quote me, Mr. Diggs, but that's the way all the techs feel."

"Never fear, Todd. You're not alone in your assessment." With a reassuring grin, Arturo could not resist adding, "I wonder if he has had an original thought in his miserable life."

Todd almost choked as he attempted to hide his laughter.

"By the way," and Arturo tried to sound casual, "Todd, do you think you could bootleg a copy of that energy trace to me? I'd like to take a look at it."

"Hell, Mr. Diggs, if you want I'll send the location report right now," Todd offered, "and I'll get you the measuring chip itself if you wish. Just keep it to yourself."

"Both would be great, Todd. I really appreciate it. I'm not sure what it means, but I have to follow every lead."

"I've got the trace and the location report right here. I'll transmit it immediately." He ran a scanner over the reports and Arturo's receiver began printing them out.

"Was this the only sign of increased energy?"

"Yes sir. We ran the 'finder' over the entire record and that one blip is the only increase measured. The interesting thing is the increase was measured 285.21 kilometers around the torus from your experiment. I assure you there was absolutely no indication of increased energy anywhere else around the entire 565 kilometers of the torus. Something caused it. What, I don't know."

Todd watched as Arturo studied the trace. "It may mean nothing, Mr. Diggs. Ordinarily we wouldn't have paid any attention to such a small blip, but all of us know how hard you've worked to prove your theory and really hope that this means something."

"Todd, at the moment, I just don't know. But in any event, I want to thank you and all the others for finding the blip and thinking of me. I won't forget it. Oh, one more thing, can you send the chip to me, as you suggested, without getting into trouble?"

"Yes sir, can do. As you know these sensitive chips are only good for one measurement and no one will ever miss it," the tech answered with conviction. "We destroy them by the hundreds after the data is recorded and sent to archive storage."

"Gotcha," Arturo laughed, "and data in the archives never sees the light of day again, does it?"

"Only by those who know what to ask for," Todd said with a sly smile.

"One last favor, Todd, if you can without getting yourself or anyone else into hot water." Arturo knew he was pushing, but he had to make the request, "Would you simply classify this blip as miscellaneous energy increase, without reference to my experiment — just until I can figure out what it means. I know that the normal test results must be documented in the computer Test Results Register."

"Already done Mr. Diggs. The actual chip will be sent tonight. Hope it helps."

"Todd, I owe you. Again, I don't know what it means, but I intend to find out. Thanks so much. Next time I'm there, I'm taking you and the crew out for one hellava dinner." Todd started to protest, but Arturo merely waved and turned off the visi-phone.

Arturo pored over the blip on the energy trace, trying to figure out what it actually denoted. He was sure of its importance, but exactly what it was had him stymied. The trace looked normal and definitely registered an energy increase, albeit an insignificant amount. "Why," he thought, "one thousand electron volts was less than a trillionth of a normal electrical watt." He'd have to calculate the exact amount sometime. "Still an energy rise was an energy rise and that meant something. One thousand electron volts measured, but I need billions of kilowatts, not minuscule electron volts. Yet, it is something, and I better get cracking on understanding it."

"Arturo, you've been at this for a week now," Jana tried to keep from scolding.

"I know darling, but the answer is here. I just can't find it," he admitted with dissatisfaction.

"And that's not the only thing I'm upset about, you big lug!" And Arturo was startled by her irate tone. "You forgot to tell me about meeting the famous Dr. Marshall Bernside."

"Oh my God. I'm sorry, Jana," he apologized. "What about Marsh?"

"So...it's Marsh, is it?" Jana shot back with a laugh. "Well, he called this morning to accept your invitation to dinner, the one you forgot to mention."

"My love, when I got home from Denver," a devilish look spread over his face, "there were more important things on both our minds than mere talking — about either Marsh or business."

Jana gave a throaty laugh, "I forgive you, darling." She brushed the hair back from Arturo's forehead. "I honored your invitation. Marsh, as he also asked me to call him, will be here tomorrow."

Arturo pulled his wife down on his lap and hugged her. "Thanks, my love. You'll like Marsh. He's not only a nice guy..." and he kissed her cheek, "but just as important, he believes in my work."

"That's what he told me, and so I immediately put him on the 'good guy' list. I asked him if he could make it by mid-afternoon so we could have plenty of time to talk before dinner." Jana got up from Arturo's lap and started to leave the room.

"What did I ever do to deserve you, Mrs. Diggs," Arturo beamed at his wife.

Jana stopped to give him a dazzling smile.

"Maybe Marsh can shed some light on this damn energy trace blip." Arturo broke the spell with a sigh, "I sure as hell can't find its meaning."

"I hope so, darling." She kissed her husband. "I'll let you get back to work."

Jana had not even left the room before Arturo was already bent over his computer, barking equations into the voice translator.

Punctually at four o'clock the following afternoon, the property entry signal buzzed. Arturo glanced at the monitor screen and saw Marsh getting out of the taxi auto-car and walk towards the house. He found Jana in the front entryway and together they opened the door.

"Welcome, Marsh." Arturo greeted their guest with genuine pleasure. "Come in, come in."

"Thank you, Arturo." All but ignoring his host, Marsh beamed at Jana. "And you are Mrs. Diggs. Though Arturo told me all about you, I fear that he was much too modest in your praise. You are all he said and more so. Forgive an old man, but I seldom have the opportunity to meet so lovely a woman."

"Dr. Bernside," Jana reciprocated with her own flattery, "and Arturo didn't begin to tell me what a charming and handsome gentleman you are."

"Ah, my dear, your words are a pleasure to my old ears." He winked and bent his lanky form in a bow, "I hope that Arturo is just a little bit jealous of me. That would make my whole year." Marsh then roared in laughter.

Spontaneously, Jana held out her hands, and Marsh grasped them in his. "Jana, my dear," and Marsh planted a kiss on each of her cheeks, "so good to meet you."

"Marsh," Jana responded by kissing both sides of his face, "it is my pleasure."

"Okay, you two," Arturo interjected good-naturedly, "it's obvious that no further introductions are needed."

Arturo took Marsh's arm and Jana the other, "Come on in, Marsh, and I'll get you a glass of wine. We'll talk about the way the world should be as opposed to how it really is."

Two hours of intense conversation had passed before Arturo got around to mentioning the energy blip Todd had measured during the photon splitting test. "Marsh, here's an energy trace that has me completely baffled. What do you make of it?" He handed over the trace and location report.

The elderly scientist glanced at the data for a few seconds. "However small, it's obvious something happened that resulted in an energy increase."

"The measured increase was 285.21 kilometers from where I had the photon test set up," Arturo asserted, "and there was absolutely no increase measured when the photons split into Posafon and Negafon beams."

"Doesn't make sense; however, I believe as you do, this insignificant energy increase definitely has something to do with your theory of obtaining energy from splitting photons." Marsh then added with conviction, "It's just too coincidental that the increase was measured during your test."

"I agree, but during a steady three hour testing period, only one blip and no others?"

Marsh cupped his hand around his chin and began stroking his beard. "That facility is designed to measure the effectiveness and efficiency of lasers, from surgical to welders to communication signal carriers to..." he stopped with uncertainly, not sure exactly where his pondering thoughts were leading.

Intuitively Arturo elected to emulate the same line of concentration. "The torus is truly a scientific achievement, Marsh. Just think of it. The torus is so big in diameter that the magnetic fields allow the laser beams to travel around without touching the mirrored surfaces."

"It is a triumph, particularly since it was proved, over 250 years ago, that light rays will bend when in the vicinity of a high gravity force such as the sun. Then in 2158 Chan Loc discovered that a much less force would be required to bend light rays if a large enough facility such as the Colorado one were built with mirrored surfaces of RMS 4."

"It was a hell of a discovery, even if it does take 10,000 megawatts to power the super-cooled magnets that simulate gravitational force and cause the laser beams to curve

122

around the facility. It's amazing how they travel around the entire 565 kilometers and arrive back where they started less than two milliseconds later and within less than a thousandth of a millimeter of where they originated," Arturo mused.

Jana had been standing at the door listening for some minutes, waiting for an opportunity to change the subject. "Hey guys! It's time to stop for a while. Dinner is about to be served."

Both men courteously stood, and Jana offered her arm to Marsh, who straightaway started to escort his hostess to the dining room.

Following Jana and Marsh down the long hallway, Arturo glanced absently at the imposing gilt-framed mirror hanging across from the hall window. In the twilight of evening, the large single windowpane reflected back into the mirror, making the window itself almost a perfect mirror. Arturo moved back and forth counting the reflections from the window and, in turn, the mirror, until each disappeared.

"Marsh, come here, quick," Arturo called out in excitement.

"What is it, Arturo?" Marsh answered and dropped Jana's arm.

"Stand right here and look at this mirror." In his enthusiasm, he pushed Marsh into the same spot where he had been standing. "Look at the reflections of the mirror and the window. Look how they go back and forth."

"I see them, Arturo, but what..." the older man asked, a baffled note to his voice.

"It's the answer!" Arturo whooped. "The Posafon and Negafon beams split into right angles to each other — or 45 degrees from the original photon beam. They each bounced off the mirrored walls and traveled around the torus continuing to bounce off the walls the entire 565 kilometer distance."

Exhilarated, Arturo madly waved his arms up and down in an attempt to describe the event. "See, if the Posafons and Negafons bounce off the mirrored walls, they form a chain of diamond shaped light beams, one after the other. Each diamond is really a square with 90 degrees at the corners, and..."

Marsh quickly interrupted, "And these diamonds lay point to point in the chain around the entire torus and..."

"And since the mirrored walls are not really completely perfect and some breakup of the beams occurs when the beams are reflected from the walls," Arturo continued the concept, "the particles may or may not collide."

"Yes," Marsh reflected, "but, if by chance they do happen to collide somewhere around the torus, perhaps an energy release occurs?"

"You bet. The chances of the photon particles initially splitting, colliding and creating energy is very small in my original test setup."

"Arturo, Marsh," Jana gently broke in, "I can keep dinner warm, if you prefer to..."

"No darling, no need, but," placing his arm around her shoulder, "thank you for asking. We'll need to work some detailed calculations out on the computer, but only after we eat." He turned to Marsh, "Did I mention, that not only is my wife beautiful, a renowned published author, but also a fabulous chef? Follow me, good Doctor. I'll prove it."

After dinner in Arturo's study, Marsh was calculating the chances of colliding particles while Arturo sketched intricate diagrams. Both men were independently working toward a common goal. After a few minutes, Marsh handed Arturo an equation, which he immediately transcripted to the computer.

They watched the screen as Arturo read aloud the instantaneous answer. "Almost 4 times ten to the ninth power or 4 billion to one. That's the random probability based on the mirror imperfections of the torus."

"Exactly my calculation," Marsh nodded.

Arturo leaned back in the chair, talking more to himself than to Marsh. "I've been looking at energy release to occur during the original split of the photon, the same as splitting the atom." Suddenly his expression changed and his words rushed out with excitement. "Marsh, that's not where the energy is. It's in the recombination, or more accurately stated, the colliding of the split photon particles. And further, I'll bet, that if the Posafon and Negafon were to collide as soon as possible after splitting, the energy release would be much higher."

Marsh did not even bother to acknowledge; instead, he began to expand Arturo's hypothesis. "All right, if I assume that each bounce or reflection of the two beams was 80 meters measured diagonally and the point of energy release was 285.21 kilometers away," he muttered under his breath, furiously jotting equations, "then there are approximately 2,522 links in the diamond chain. Assuming an energy loss from each reflection of..."

He handed the scribbling to Arturo, "Here, input that into the computer."

With great deliberation Arturo spoke to the computer. Both men waited expectantly for the response.

"Here it is," and a happy smile spread over Arturo's face, "if they were to collide at the end point of the first diamond, the energy given off would increase from the measured one thousand electron volts to a million billion electron volts."

"My God, Arturo," Marsh replied in awe, "do you realize that is almost as much energy as the original gamma photons had when the universe was formed?"

"Since our calculations are based on assumed losses of each reflected bounce of the photon particles," Arturo went on, "do you think the Posafon and Negafon collisions could actually release as much energy as the initial gamma photon?"

"Let's see. If we assume the energy release is the same as a gamma photon...10^{17} eV, then..." Marsh scrawled a quick calculation and then methodically stroked his beard before continuing, "...each collision is the equivalent of approximately .016 watts, which translates to...let's see now...which, in layman language translates to needing collisions of almost 50 billion particles per second to generate 1,000,000 horse power."

The men were speechless as they contemplated the sheer magnitude of their premise.

"Lordy, Lordy, Arturo," Marsh exulted, "depending on the density of the original photon beam, the power available is unlimited and..." he stopped abruptly as Arturo slapped his hands together in mirth. "What are you laughing at?"

"At you, Marsh. Here is the distinguished Doctor Bernside, using horsepower to measure a quantum of potential energy and..." Arturo was laughing too hard to continue.

Marsh grinned and conceded a slight chuckle as he looked at Arturo. "At least horsepower is something everyone understands. People don't have to stop and think about conversion factors and what they all mean." He then pointed a finger at Arturo. "If more of my students had boiled down their high-sounding theories to simple terms, perhaps they would have discovered more keys to success. Take yourself, Arturo." His tone was almost accusing, "You, my maverick young genius, broke the code of what the energy rise in the torus meant by looking in a mirror."

Arturo got the point immediately. "Touché, Professor, touché." He patted his colleague on the back, "I concede to the more senior scientist."

Marsh sniffed and tried to look insulted, but the twinkle in his eyes gave him away. "It would indeed appear that the right track has opened up, Arturo." Then in a somewhat pensive tone, he added, "Perhaps, we need to be more certain as to the repeatability."

"I agree wholeheartedly." The enormity of this new theory suddenly became overwhelming, and Arturo stood up. With his hands clasped behind his back, he began pacing the floor. "A whole new test setup will have to be designed, one that will precisely focus the beams at the first diamond collision point. Perfect reflector mirrors, as an example, will be needed to direct the initial split beams of Posafons and Negafons to the exact desired location."

"Go on, go on," Marsh encouraged, but when there was no response, he took the initiative to keep the conversation moving, "I agree that additional tests are needed. Beyond that, have you given consideration to the harnessing of this newly discovered power source?"

"Yes, I have," Arturo responded quietly, his eyes glistening, "but considerable more thought needs to go into controlling the energy release for its use as a propulsive force which will push a space vehicle up to the speed of light."

The elder scientist's jaw fell slack and then widened into a grin. "Ah ha! So that's what you're working on." Belying his years, he swiftly sprung to his feet and grasped Arturo's shoulders with his slender hands. "Here I thought you were simply looking for a new source of energy. The speed of light, you say. Hell of a goal, Arturo. About time someone attacks that problem. Never did believe that Einstein's theory couldn't be broken."

"Marsh," and Arturo's eyes had a faraway look; "the Diggs family has been considering this problem for nearly 300 years. If man is to attain the speed of light, I believe light or photons must be used as the propulsive medium."

"The hell, you say!" Marsh stifled his urge to probe further in deference to Arturo. He then dropped his hands and said tactfully, "Well, I won't ask any more questions, but you make sense to me. The less I know about the details, the better. But, if you will allow me, I offer any and all assistance."

"I accept!" A relieved smile of appreciation appeared on Arturo's face as he held out his hand. "Your offer is most appreciated, Marsh. Most appreciated. There are so many other problems to solve." For a brief second, he seemed overwhelmed at the immensity of his task, "So many."

"One problem at a time, my boy, one at a time." Marsh took Arturo's arm, and steered him back to the computer. "Now let's get to work on the equipment you'll need for the new tests."

For six grueling months, Arturo worked on the design of the test equipment and procedures that would be needed to focus Negafon and Posafon photon beams precisely to maximize the chances of particle collisions. The final piece of intricate equipment had been sent to the Colorado Laser Test Facility.

Marshall Bernside, true to his word, had not only stayed in contact but had been of invaluable support in resolving many of the complicated calculations and design problems.

To keep all distractions away from Arturo, Jana served most of his meals in the study. As she laid down the tray for the evening meal, she glanced at her husband's pale face. His tanned features had faded into a colorless hue, speaking months of strain. Walking over, she placed a hand on his shoulder and, maintaining a cheery voice, asked, "When do you plan to leave for Colorado, darling?"

Much to her delight, he swiveled around in the chair and took both her hands in his. "The day after tomorrow, assuming Todd and his techs get all the gear set up in time. They've double checked the installation, and made sure it's going to be ready for use on the allotted date."

"Is Marsh joining you?"

"You're kidding," he said laughingly and pulled her unresistingly closer. "Wild horses couldn't keep him away. Don't know what I'd have done without Marsh. Not only did he expedite the design calculations, but he helped me inspect the equipment at the fabricators."

"How long do you think the experiment will take, lover?"

"I should be gone just overnight. It won't take that long to run the test and examine the data." Arturo looked at his wife with adoration. "Jana, none of this would have been possible without you. You have been my biggest support, and..." The sentence was left unfinished as Jana's mouth pressed on his.

The atmosphere was optimistic as the test setup was being completed. Marsh executed the final adjustment of the laser electron gun as Arturo carefully set the pulsing rate for the exact cycles per second that had previously resulted in successfully splitting the cold fusion reactor photons.

"We're ready when you are, Mr. Diggs," Todd announced over the intercom.

Marsh and Arturo gave the thumbs up signal.

"Here we go, Mr. Diggs." Todd stepped to the console, to explain the test pattern, "This time I've placed duplicate instruments around the entire torus, not just at the predicted point of particle impact. If any energy increase occurs, we'll measure it, sir."

"Go, Todd." Arturo smiled confidently.

The senior tech held up two split fingers in a victory sign and then flipped a switch to bring a one-micron beam from the fusion reactor in a normal straight line.

"Now for the rubyionium laser electron gun, Mr. Diggs," and Todd threw the appropriate switch. "Mr. Diggs, Dr. Bernside, better watch your display screen!" he said. "We're measuring a terrific amount of energy. Wow!"

Marsh, stretching out his long legs, reached the data display just before Arturo but then politely stepped back. "Arturo?" With palms up, he ushered his younger colleague ahead. "You must have the first look."

Arturo stared in disbelief at the readout. "Marsh," he whispered, "it's reading as you predicted, 1600 watts."

Marsh diplomatically elbowed Arturo aside to ascertain the data for himself. "Arturo, look!" Marsh shouted in elation, "Look, I say!"

"I see! I see!" Arturo smiled.

At the point where the Posafon and Nega-fon beams impacted at right angles to each other, a soft glow appeared. Emanating from the radiance was a thin dark line that disappeared into the distance.

"Well, one point six kilowatts it is," Marsh muttered, satisfied. "Let's see if our calculations are correct, there must be about 100,000 particles per second colliding."

The men looked at each other, then with wide grins shook hands and fell into a bear hug. They continued to follow the instantaneous data, and with relief found no change in the experiment. The energy release was constant and unvarying for over an hour. No other energy blips were found anywhere else around the huge torus. It was obvious to both Arturo and Marsh that the beams were impinging precisely at the intersection point and no photons had gone astray to bounce around the torus.

"Todd," Arturo spoke into the intercom, "can you increase the fusion reactor beam from one micron to 10 microns in diameter and the rubyionium laser electron gun the same amount?" To Marsh he confided, "The energy should go up proportionally to the area increase or 100 times as much."

"Sure, Mr. Diggs." Todd replied. "Just a minute while I shut down both beams." In a moment, the tech's voice was back, "Okay, Mr. Diggs, here we go, both set at 10 x increase.

Here's the fusion reactor beam and... now... laser beam."

The experiment performed exactly the same except for a greater energy measurement and a larger soft glow around the impact point of the split beams. Arturo and Marsh silently monitored the energy demonstration.

"You were right, Arturo," Marsh whispered. "It's reading 160,000 watts, or 160 kilowatts."

"Should we see how high we can go?" Arturo asked eagerly.

"I'd be careful, Arturo," Marsh's tone was wary. "That amount of energy has to go somewhere in spite of the energy absorbers downstream."

"Good point. Good point, Marsh." Arturo agreed and then spoke into the intercom. "Todd, can you increase the diameters of the beams 10 microns at a time, but be careful to monitor any potential problems?"

"No problem, Mr. Diggs. But don't worry; the facility has automatic shutdowns of all equipment if anything goes wrong. Have to have those safety features, some of the big laser tests are powerful and sometimes..." He stopped abruptly, realizing he was treading on other companies' confidential tests. Arturo admired Todd for that trait; he knew that his own test results would neither be broadcast or revealed.

Each successive test proved as predicted. As the beam was increased in diameter, the resultant energy release was increased proportionally to the square of the micron diameter ratios. After a test at 100 microns and the resulting energy of 16,000 kW, Todd stopped the test to await Arturo's further directions.

"Todd, will you now increase the diameter of the beams by 100 microns, and if everything goes okay, increase by 1,000 microns at a time?" Arturo requested.

"Sure thing, Mr. Diggs. Give me a second to change the adjustments."

At a 10,000-micron diameter, the one-centimeter split beams broke up suddenly and the measured 160,000,000-kilowatt energy release went to zero. The reactor and laser beams ceased at the same time.

"What happened, Todd?" Arturo asked worriedly.

"Automatic shutdown, Mr. Diggs. I don't know what transpired, but we'll know in short order."

True to his word the problem was soon found. One of the mirrors Arturo had designed to reflect the split beams to the intersection point of the Posafons and Negafons had a one-centimeter hole burned completely through it. Thus, the automatic shutdown, to prevent damage to the torus' mirrored walls.

"I should have thought of that," Marsh muttered. "Too much concentrated heat. That's a problem, but one that's solvable."

"In any event, Marsh," said Arturo buoyantly, despite his disappointment at the unforeseen suspension of the test, "we now know our theories are correct."

"Your theories, Arturo," the older scientist promptly corrected. "I'm only a helpmate.

You have done a magnificent job. My God, do you realize what this means?"

"Yes," he happily concurred, but with some reservation, "however, a lot of work still remains."

Marsh caught his note of apprehension. "Look at it this way, Arturo," he said, "that small fusion reactor has a capability of only five kilowatts. The energy release of one centimeter diameter beams was over a 160,000,000 kilowatts of potential power..." he paused, a devilish grin exposing two rows of gleaming white teeth, "...or as much as 214,000,000 horsepower!"

Arturo had been listening intently, but he was jolted into laughter by his friend's last sentence. "I give! Horsepower it is, so even scientists like me can understand. Thanks Professor."

Both men turned when they heard Todd's voice behind them. "Looks like your test was a success, Mr. Diggs. Congratulations!" He held out his hand.

"Thanks, Todd," Arturo modestly accepted the tribute, "and thanks to your techs." Putting his hand on Marsh's arm, he kept his voice casual. "Was the speed of the photon beam recombination measured before the shutdown?"

"Yes, it was, Mr. Diggs. C equaled three hundred million meters per second, the exact speed of light. By the way, the energy absorbers can only handle 100,000 kW per second, but they didn't show any absorption. None at all.

Yet the energy measured was very high. Where did it go and how did it dissipate?"

"Well, that does bring up a valid question." Arturo's fingers were deliberately digging into the elderly man's arm. "Marsh, guess our next phase is to figure out how the energy dissipates."

Marsh started to interject a theory, but then coughed to cover his lapse. "Yes, yes, Arturo, I agree...our next phase."

Todd seemingly did not catch the discreet by-play. He only nodded politely as he turned away. When the tech was well out of earshot, Arturo pulled Marsh aside and whispered, "I think I know how the energy dissipates, but let's not discuss it now. Remember the absorbers are 500 meters downstream of the test."

"That does make things somewhat more complicated," Marsh replied. "In any event, how do you intend to harness this power into a space vehicle propulsion system?"

But Arturo was staring into the distance, deep in concentration. It was almost as an aside when he replied, "One step at a time, Marsh. One step at a time." Breaking his concentration on the test results, he said, "Now, I had better call Jana to tell her the results and that I'll be gone one more night. We have to take these guys to dinner this evening."

Good to his word, Arturo extended a dinner invitation to all the engineers and technicians who had worked on his experiments. There, one and all toasted him for his success. All knew what he had done, but none knew what his plans were for the newly found energy. The energy dissipation was not mentioned, only the measured energy release.

It was well past midnight when Arturo and Marsh left the restaurant. Both were feeling a mellow exhaustion as they walked in silence the few blocks to their hotel. Suddenly Arturo stopped short and asked, "What did you say Marsh? Sorry, I was day dreaming."

"I didn't say anything Arturo, you must be hearing things," Marsh replied sleepily and then gave a mighty yawn.

Arturo was almost positive he'd heard a voice, but he shrugged it off. He was tired. It had been a long but rewarding day.

> *"Finally, one of the keys has been inserted..."*
> *"Another lock opened..."*
> *"But so many more yet to..."*
> *"Nothing before its time..."*

Joal Lowe had left strict orders not to be disturbed by anyone, irrespective of who it was. His anger had been spiraling for weeks. Today especially, he was making no effort of pretense, in either word or action. During the past few years Geo Transport had shrunk to one twentieth of its former size. Competition from his archrival, Space Transport Corporation, had driven him close to bankruptcy, and consequently, he had been forced to reduce his business to serving customers who needed only small cargos delivered to the orbiting space stations.

"At least," he said to himself, "the bastards left me that."

The handful of investors he had enticed to put additional money into his company for the purpose of upgrading rocket transports had long since withdrawn. As justification, they had used Joal's inability to obtain rights to Space Transport's propulsion system — the system originally designed by Arturo Diggs in 2175.

Joal's pudgy hand quivered in rage as he again reached for the electronic newspaper printouts. As if to taunt him, the bold head-lines shrieked out:

"Photon Split Results in Energy Release"

"New breakthrough: Noted Scientist Dis-covers Photon Energy"

"Arturo Diggs Hailed for Remarkable En-ergy Findings."

Bitterly, he reread the articles, his face contorted into a grimace of violent hatred. Suddenly, he began tearing the papers into shreds. With a snarl he wadded the pieces into a tight ball and threw it across the room. The emotional exertion left his pulse racing and his breath hurrying in short gasps. The blood ves-sels pounded in his thick neck, and beads of perspiration trickled down his flushed face. Reaching into his pocket, he withdrew a cap-sule, popped it into his mouth and washed it down with the open bottle of whiskey on the desk. Out of habit, he unconsciously rubbed his left forearm, as if stroking the diamond shaped birthmark would speed the passing of his anger. As he regained a semblance of com-posure, he wiped his brow with his handker-chief and then voiced a number into the visi-phone.

The screen remained blank but a terse voice answered in a single syllable, "Speak."

"It's Joal Lowe."

Horst's face came on the visi-phone; his piercing blue eyes riveted on Joal. Though the short blond hair was now graying at the tem-ples, the square face had not aged and the aus-tere features were the same.

"You look older, Horst," Joal observed. "Perhaps your line of work has become too strenuous for you."

Not rising to the bait, Horst's steely stare never left Joal. "What service do you want, Herr Lowe?"

Joal's hands tightened into fists, but his round face had a banal smile. "Do you remember, Arturo Diggs?"

Horst did not reply, only gave a curt nod of affirmation.

"Then I have two tasks for you to perform immediately." His voice was autocratic. "We will meet at our usual place – today!"

The glaring blue eyes narrowed, the thin mouth tightened, and Horst's tone was level and caustic. "Before I agree to a meeting, payment must be in advance and also I must know the exact nature of the assignments you wish me to undertake."

Joal's first impulse was to slam back, "We'll meet when I say, you miserable son-of-a-bitch." Instead, he held his temper and forced a mock smile, "I see you haven't changed." He paused for a moment, but did not lose his smile. "All right. Have it your way. I want you to get..."

It took Joal several minutes to summarize the assignment, before he finally asked, "Can you do it?"

Without a blink Horst replied, "It will take time and considerable money."

"How much time and how much money?"

"The time depends on the amount of money. Arrangements will have to be made with many people."

"I think you have read the articles published about Diggs over the past few months," Joal stated, satisfied that Horst would again carry out his wishes.

"I always keep up with previous jobs," the professional replied bluntly.

"Then we meet today?" The eagerness in Joal's voice emphasized the ruthlessness of his plot.

"My payment will be forty kilos of gold, in advance, to begin the arrangements. All other expenses will be due and payable at need. Success determination is a different matter."

"What do you mean, 'a different matter'?" Joal's face scowled in displeasure.

"In this case, Herr Lowe, I shall be the judge of success – not you. Those are my conditions." The words were uttered with frigid finality.

There was no choice but to accept the terms, but Joal's jowls quivered with his wrath and he ground his teeth as he replied, "I agree. Three o'clock this afternoon at the usual place."

The visi-phone screen went blank, and for a long moment Joal just glared. "You mother fuckin' bastard," he finally screamed, picking up the whiskey bottle and smashing it into the now empty projector screen.

Arturo Diggs had driven himself ceaselessly during the past year. Many important breakthroughs, with the advice and assistance of

Marshall Bernside, had been accomplished, and today the culmination of their test theories was scheduled to begin at the Colorado Laser Test Facilities.

Todd and his crew were making the final adjustments to the test setup as Arturo and Marsh stood talking out of earshot. "Marsh, if our theories are right," Arturo whispered, "this test should reveal a new particle."

The elderly scientist nodded optimistically, his eyes ablaze with anticipation, "Yes, my boy, regarding Einstein's theory..." stopping abruptly as one of the engineers moved into hearing distance.

Arturo took Marsh's arm and discreetly led him from prying ears to continue their cryptic discussion. "Todd was good enough to install the personal recorder and preset pulsating laser gun I brought along. If all goes well, and nobody asks questions, I'll be able to take the findings with me instead of having them accessible to others in the lab's data banks."

Marsh started to reply but was interrupted by Todd's voice over the speaker, "Ready when you are, Mr. Diggs."

Arturo winked at Marsh, and held up two crossed fingers. "Okay, Todd," he called back, "let her rip."

The test lasted 20 minutes. When Todd approached the two men, he had a dejected look. "Sorry, Mr. Diggs, changing the diameters of the fusion reactor and laser beams to vary the energy release didn't work. The beams only perform when using the same diameter."

"Todd, you also ran a test with both beams the same diameter?" Arturo questioned.

"Sure did, Mr. Diggs," consulting his log to verify the findings, "both before and after we varied the two beams." Then reading from the record, "With both beams at 10 microns in diameter the energy release was 160 kilowatts." A warm smile crossed his face as he handed Arturo a copy of the readout, "When the beams are the same diameter, sir, it's repeatable, just like the previous tests."

Arturo gave a noncommittal shrug as he folded the readout and stuck it in his pocket. "Well, that finishes it for this test, Todd. As usual it was a great job. Many thanks to you and the crew."

Todd acknowledged the praise with a slight wave before turning to press the switch for the lab intercom. "Okay fellows, good job," he announced over the loudspeaker. "That's it for now. We'll take a fifteen minute break before our next setup."

The senior tech made imaginary notes in the log until he was sure the crew had cleared the lab. Only then did he shift his attention back to Arturo and Marsh. "Mr. Diggs," Todd's voice was low and secretive, "if you'll come with me, I'll retrieve your personal recorder and laser gun from the torus." Then almost as an afterthought, "Sure you don't want me to have it downloaded into our main computer?"

"No, but thanks anyway, Todd," Arturo replied evenly. "It's just duplicate data of the test. Means I don't have to log on to your mainframe from my home." Then with a chuckle he

144

added, "As you well know, it sometimes takes hours before I can plug into the lab's computer."

"I hear you, Mr. Diggs," Todd replied with a smile. It only took a few moments for him to detach the recorder and laser gun from the outside perimeter of the torus shell. "Here you are, sir." As he handed Arturo the two vital pieces of equipment, he frowned. "You know, we don't usually allow personal instruments to be used in the lab..."

Holding an outstretched hand, Arturo quickly cut in reassuringly, "I understand, Todd. You have my sincere appreciation." If Todd had a moment of reservation, it passed as he handed over the mechanisms to Arturo.

"But just one more question, Mr. Diggs, I still don't understand where the energy went. It was there all right," and he shook his head in bewilderment, "but the energy absorbers don't register any measurement."

This was the specific question that Arturo fervently wanted to avoid, but he knew he would arouse suspicion if he did not give a response. "Well Todd, I guess we don't have an answer." He turned his attention to the recorder and laser gun, which he was putting in the fitted case. "Suffice to say that we know energy is released." With a smile, he clapped Todd on the shoulder. "Where it goes remains to be seen. Anyway, I've taken enough of your time for today. Thanks again for another great job."

Only when Arturo and Marsh were outside the building, and strapped into the auto-car seats, did Marsh finally burst out laughing.

"Arturo, you old pretender, we both knew that varying the input beams differently wouldn't work. Now tell me, what exactly were you really testing for?"

"Remember your theory of particle conversion? How this was much like the old materialization theory of transformation of energy into particles with a mass?"

"Yes, photons passing close to the nucleus of an atom."

"Well, I applied the same theory to Posafons and Negafons and, guess what?" Arturo's voice was jubilant. "If it proves out, we have a new particle, although probably a very short lived one."

"And your portable recorder will measure the mass and speed of the particles in full color. Although they can do the same thing at the laser facility," here Marsh grinned devilishly, "you didn't want the data in the mainframe computer banks."

"My God, Marsh, the older you get — the smarter!" Arturo joshed back.

"Lordy, boy, come on, let's read the data." His long bony fingers reached anxiously toward the recorder.

"Not so fast, sir," Arturo gave Marsh a tap on the knuckles, "I've got a power pack and a remote enlarging monitor in the room. We can take our time and read the data there."

"Well, what the hell are you waiting for, boy?" Marsh quickly voiced the hotel coordinates and gave an undignified whoop, "Let's go."

When the recorder and remote monitor screen were connected, the men drew up chairs and rapidly scrolled through the automatically magnified data.

"Look at that soft bluish haze," Marsh excitedly pointed, "in the diamond shaped area where the photons first split and then bounce off at forty-five degree angles and meet again."

"I see! I see!" Arturo pushed a switch to rerun the data in slow motion.

"Okay, Marsh, here's when the test begins. The fusion and laser gun beams are the thin white lines. Now, at the first photon split, as they go off at right angles and bounce off the two mirrors into a diamond shape, the Posafon is the red line, and the black streak is the Negafon."

"Can you slow it down even more Arturo?" Marsh scooted his chair closer to the monitor screen. "That's it! Oh my God, right there, at the impact point where the Posafon and Negafon next meet, there's a swollen soft purple sphere."

In his enthusiasm, Marsh rose from his chair, his body completely blocking the remote monitor. Without turning he shouted in agitation, "Arturo, why don't you say something?" Not waiting for a reply he exclaimed, "Now look; the sphere then forms a paraboloid, which is a purplish black haze. My God, there are two distinct...no, three areas. Beyond the initial bluish haze, there's a purplish black paraboloid, then another paraboloid, oriented in the same direction, but from which a normal looking pink photon beam appears from the center."

When there was still no word from Arturo, he spryly whirled around. "For God's sake, man!" There was an accusing tone to his voice, "Don't you have any comment?"

"You're standing in front of the screen, Marsh." Arturo retorted. "I haven't been able to see one damn thing you're talking about."

Marsh moved aside and hung his head in mock apology. "Oh...sorry, my boy."

For a few moments both men stared silently at the screen. Marsh resumed his chair as Arturo began brisk commands to download the various data. Each man then began to voice his observations as the data appeared sequentially on the screen.

"Negatively charged particles are evident in the black area for a distance of 30 meters..."

"Particle speed in the black area is c, 300 million meters per second, speed of light..."

"Particles have a life of 100 nanoseconds, or a ten-millionth of a second..."

"Bluish particles are positively charged..."

"Bluish particles appear to be a plasma – and pinkish beam is nothing other than a normal photon beam, no charge..."

"The mass of purplish black particles are almost one gram each..." Marsh started to recount, but could stand it no longer, and jumped up slapping Arturo on the back. "My God, Arturo. Do you realize what you've just done? You've discovered a particle with mass traveling at the speed of light. That breaks Einstein's principle that nothing with mass can travel at the speed of light. If those particles can travel at c, a space ship can."

"I know, Marsh, I know. Almost like blasphemy isn't it? Your previous work made this possible, my friend. If you hadn't discussed the sub-sub-atomic particle theory and discovered the particle you named furon, I never would have deduced that this was possible."

"Thank you for those words, my boy. But, I only thought about it. You did something about it. That's what counts."

"It took both of us, Marsh. Both of us." Arturo spoke fervidly. He wanted to award credit where it was due.

"Thank you, son," was all Marsh could muster. Touched by the tribute, he turned away, dabbing self-consciously at his eyes. For a moment, he just stood, embarrassed by his sentimentality and then grumbled, "We've got work to do, young man. Enough of this idle yammering."

Marsh whipped out his new generation hand-held computer and began to input commands. As the readout results flashed on the minute screen, he placed his glasses atop his nose and glared down until he was satisfied with the answers. "Depending on how it's harnessed," Marsh lectured in his finest professorial style, "a beam one centimeter in diameter would produce particles at the rate of ten-trillion per second. A mass of one gram each would produce an expelled flow rate of ten-billion kilograms per second, at the speed of light."

Arturo started to input similar calculations into his own equally hi-tech small computer, his head nodding in absolute agreement.

"Lordy, Arturo," Marsh bellowed, his dark face glowing with the exhilaration of the moment, "at a momentum exchange ratio of 75%, you've got enough propulsive force here to accelerate a huge ship at 1,000 times the force of gravity to the speed of light in about eight and a half hours. And the amazing thing is, particles give up their mass after traveling about 30 meters and return to a normal photon beam. Amazing! Fantastic!" He almost crushed his computer as he clapped his hands in excitement. "You've got your propulsion system, Arturo, my boy."

"Many would say that we created energy, Marsh, and obviously deduce that it's not possible."

"That's the beauty, Arturo, you didn't create energy, you simply converted existing photon energy to something usable — an energy that obviously was there all along just waiting to be released. Now it makes sense."

For several more hours, the two scientists continued to discuss all the ramifications of the exhilarating data test results.

"It's obvious the blue haze is comprised of positively charged furon particles," Arturo said as they once more viewed the replay from the recorder, "which repel the negatively charged purplish black particles in the paraboloid."

"And the impact of the Posafons and Negafons create the new purplish black particles in the paraboloid," Marsh recited for seemingly the hundredth time.

"Yeah, and the blue haze is analogous to a force field, allowing the purplish black particles created at the impact point to flow smoothly away at c, the speed of light."

"Just one more point that we haven't fully addressed." Marsh spoke slowly. "With the huge force of the purplish black particles moving at the speed of light, why didn't they destroy the torus?"

"It was a chance I took, Marsh, and thank God my calculations were reasonably accurate. Since the torus was open behind the cold fusion reactor and the test setup, the bluish negatively charged particles, or plasma, nullified the force of the purplish black particles."

Marsh pursed his mouth and methodically stroked his beard. "Sort of like letting loose of a blown up balloon with openings in each end. The balloon stays in one place instead of flying around the room as it would if it had only one opening for the air to escape."

Arturo couldn't help but chuckle at the precise analogy, though his eyes widened in mock-shock. "A balloon, Marsh. Isn't that correlation a bit elementary for a scientist of your renown?"

Tapping his nails rhythmically on the arm of the chair, Marsh uttered a resonant sniff as Arturo roared with laughter at his friend's piqued facade. "But Marsh, you're exactly right, just like a double opening in a blown up balloon — that's where the energy went."

Marsh managed to keep a straight face. "Thank you. Now if the 'pupil' will allow me to finish my dissertation?"

Arturo smiled affectionately at his friend.

Marsh cleared his throat with a grumble. "As I was saying, the plasma dissipated around the torus in the opposite direction from the Posafon and Negafon beams, and the mass of purplish black particles had nothing to push against."

"Right! Now all we have to do is place a barrier behind the reactor to seal up one end. Your famous 'balloon theory' comes into play and, voila, we've got a rocket propulsion system powered by the force of the exiting mass of purplish black particles."

"Beautiful. Thank God your calcs were correct, my boy. Otherwise..." and he gave an involuntary shudder, "the whole laser test facility could have been destroyed by the terrific force of the purplish black particles."

"I allowed for that, Marsh," Arturo replied. "I knew the particles didn't have anything to push against." There was a quiver in his voice as he continued. "However, if I had been wrong..."

"One gram particles at the speed of light would have destroyed anything in their path. $E=MC^2$, you know." Marsh coughed nervously and dismissed the bleak thought. "No matter, you were correct as usual." He walked over and poured himself a stiff drink. Motioning to the bottle, he lifted another glass toward Arturo, but the younger man shook his head.

"Well, my young friend," and he raised his glass, "since the huge purplish black photon mass is traveling at the speed of light, your space ship should also reach the speed of light. Remember your first physics theorem, Arturo?" Marsh teased. "For every action, there is an equal and opposite reaction."

At the mention of the simple theorem, Arturo guffawed. "On second thought, Professor, I will join you in that drink, while you define that 'complicated' physics theorem of action versus reaction."

Relieved to be free from the long months of tension leading up to this latest successful test — which produced results as yet only known to them — they continued discussing the data until after the witching hour.

"But what about Einstein's theory regarding mass getting heavier and smaller in size?" Marsh yawned and stretched his arms outright to relieve his weary muscles. "And time becoming shorter as the speed of light is approached?" But Arturo's frown made him recant, "I know, I know. Your decree is, 'one thing at a time'."

"It's late Marsh," Arturo smiled, trying to stifle his fatigue. "You're right though, one thing at a time. We'll get into that later."

"I'm having too much fun to go to sleep," but another giant yawn overtook him. "I'm afraid I must admit, these 80 plus-year-old bones don't hold up as well as they used to." With effort, he pushed himself from the chair, but halfway up, another thought struck him and he slumped back in the seat. "Why was the energy release continuous, Arturo? Why didn't the Posafons, Negafons, fusion reactor and laser beams disturbed by the plasma of furon particles cease to split the photons? My own theory is that in some way, the particles with mass and the furon particles alternate while being formed." Marsh stopped and looked at Arturo. "But, I'd like to hear yours."

"You are not far from what actually happens, Marsh. I only discovered the answer today. I didn't know what would happen when I found that the laser had to be pulsed to enable the photons to be split. After finding that energy was released upon collision of the split beams, I had only theorized that new particles would be formed."

"Yes, exactly my hypothesis," Marsh said. "But it couldn't be proven until your portable recorder registered the actual particle movement — visually that is."

"When the laser is turned on, the energy release is building the furon plasma, which immediately converts the furons into the purplish black mass of particles we see on the color monitor. Then the laser is turned off, and the plasma and resultant particles dissipate in a 100 nanoseconds, at which time the laser is turned on again to start the process anew."

"That's it then," Marsh exclaimed, slamming a closed fist into his palm, "You're pulsing the laser at rates of half the particle life, or 50 nanosecond intervals."

"As I said, Marsh, I only figured out the exact sequence of events today. Obviously, the pulse rate is only known to the two of us. I supplied the preset laser gun to the test facility — and only I really knew the pulse rate — and now you. Fortunately, Todd didn't monitor the pulse rate on his instrumentation."

"But how did you know to use a 50 nanosecond pulse rate?" In sudden understanding of what really happened, Marsh hit his forehead with the heel of his hand. "Wait a minute, I told you the life of a furon was 100 nanoseconds. That's how you knew!" All his fatigue was gone. "How did you know the energy would produce furons?" he asked.

"Whoa, Marsh," Arturo held up his hand. "From our discussions, my erudite friend, and from reading your books, I theorized and calculated what would happen. Also, in one of your original books, you had a couple of furon calculations based on work performed by Alan Aspect in 1982, of the University of Paris. He found that by changing the polarity of one photon, another one would have the opposite polarity – and it happened at a speed greater than c. And that, my great friend, led me to the Posifon and Negafon theory. Thus the furon."

For a brief moment, Marsh looked overwhelmed. "I'm proud that my simple theories helped, Arturo, and you were able to put them to practical use."

"Simple, my ass," Arturo countered. "If it hadn't been for you, Dr. Marshall Bernside, who knows how long it would have taken to do what we've done."

"Again, thank you for those kind words, my boy." Marsh smiled and rose wearily to his feet. "With that, it really is my bedtime." He waved in Arturo's direction and, without even a goodnight, left the room.

No sooner had the door shut, than Arturo switched on the recorder and remote monitor. Bleary eyed, he continued to study the data on the screen and evaluate it with the notes and calculations he and Marsh had made during the long evening hours. He leaned back in his chair, unaware that he had closed his eyes. It was several hours later when he awoke. His body was in an unnatural position, and an aching charley horse was in the calf of one leg.

Painfully hobbling around the room to work out the cramp, he staggered over to the table for support. His finger accidentally hit the fast forward button on the personal recorder, setting the remote monitor into motion. The photon test began replaying, but the increased speed gave the impression of a whirling wagon-wheel.

His sleep-laden eyes were not quite in focus and his vision blurred. The spiraling vision emanating from the monitor caught him unawares. Then something about the pattern stimulated the nucleus of an idea in his racing brain. Overwhelmed by the revelation that formed, he could only mumble, "Oh, my God," as he sunk back into the chair. Placing his palms together against his forehead, he fell into a deep meditation, and it was several minutes before his tightened jaw turned to an elated smile. He switched on the visi-phone and excitedly gave a number.

Marsh's drowsy voice came over the speaker, but the screen was blank. "Yes, operator, is it time for my wake-up call already?"

"Marsh, it's Arturo."

There was a pause before Marsh responded. "My God, boy!" His tone was just short of hostile. "Are you mad? Do you know what time it is?"

"The hour is of no importance," Arturo shot back, "just put your robe on and come over to my room."

Marsh's blurry-eyed face filled the screen. "What is the matter with you? It's not even dawn."

"It won't matter when you hear what I've just discovered. Please, come on over." Arturo heard a distinct grumble of protest.

While waiting for Marsh to arrive, Arturo jotted down some calculations and reset the recorder. He was humming under his breath when the door opened, and Marsh, barefoot, clad in pajamas and robe, stumbled inside.

Obviously out of sorts, the gray-bearded scientist marched over to the bed and sat down on the edge. "You woke an old man from a sound sleep," he complained. "This better be important, or I swear..." and he shook his fist at his colleague.

Pulling up a chair in front of his friend, Arturo ignored Marsh's ill humor. "Here's where we left off," he began seriously. "Envision being able to vary the energy release from the collisions of the Posafons and Negafons by controlling the rate of flow of the negatively charged Negafons."

Marsh's scowl was contradicted by a sudden gleam in his eyes.

Arturo leaned closer and spoke precisely. "Imagine two counter discs, made from bands of carbon, rotating at high speed. They would absorb the Negafons. Here, I'll show you an example."

Using a remote switch he activated the recorder. The photon test, preset at an accelerated speed, began whirling across the monitor screen.

Marsh's eyes were riveted on the display. He put on his glasses, walked over to the monitor, and studied the whirling picture before turning slowly to face Arturo.

"If you will grant me a small metaphor," Marsh said, "the principle you foresee is much like an old wagon-wheel, comprised of a series of open spokes. If the 'wagon-wheel' was stopped, the Negafon stream would then pass between the spokes."

Arturo nodded. As he opened his mouth he had trouble finding the right words. "Well, Marsh..." he paused for a few seconds, "simplistically speaking, that's exactly the rationale, except your 'wagon-wheels' are dual rotating bands of carbon."

The venerable old eyes glistened. "I'm pleased that you grasped my rudimentary analogy." Then his tone became businesslike. "In other words, full power could be obtained, or energy release completely stopped through the coupled carbon spokes. The amount of the opening is what would allow the massed stream to pass, and be infinitely varied from zero to full power."

Arturo banged his hands on the arms of his chair. "That's the concept, my brilliant friend."

"And what, may I ask, are you naming these new particles from derived photons?"

"I hadn't really thought about it before," Arturo admitted hesitantly.

"Well, you have Posafons and Negafons producing a particle with mass..." Marsh volunteered.

"That's it! You've just come up with the ideal epithet — Massafon. The new particle will be named, Massafon," Arturo concluded.

"So now, with the wagon-wheels coupled with the reactor beam, the laser beam, the two mirrors and a large diameter tube to hold all of the contraptions, you've got a light speed rocket engine that has variable thrust!"

"Yes, and we'll name it the Massafon Engine," Arturo said.

After issuing the press release on the photon energy split, Arturo was inundated with interviews. When the secured line on his visi-phone buzzed, he cursed under his breath. "Damn, now they're coming through on this line." His impulse was not to answer, but the insistent whir was more annoying than a talk with another reporter. But he smiled widely as Marsh's image appeared on the screen.

"Sorry, Arturo," he began apologetically, "did I break you away from something important?"

"Hell, Marsh, you're a breath of sunshine after all those damned media types who have been badgering me the past several weeks."

"I assume, my boy," and a bright smile flashed on the screen, "that is meant as a compliment."

They chatted a few moments, until Marsh abruptly changed the subject. "Arturo, everyone is asking me to get you to be the main speaker at the upcoming meeting of the Chicago Branch of the Royal Astronomical Society." Noting Arturo's glower, he added, "Not only the board of governors, but the full membership."

"Sorry, Marsh, but I just..."

In his best style, the elder statesman began his pitch. "Now I know that all the latest results of the photon split are privy, but there are aspects that are public knowledge. Your work can be used to develop an unlimited energy supply for Earth use, not to mention orbiting space station power."

"Marsh, I couldn't give a tinker's damn what others want to use my results for," Arturo began. "Moreover, my research wouldn't be accepted as practical, that body of 'higher thinkers' are a bunch of naysayers."

"Say no more, my friend, I understand." There was a sad note in his voice. "Well, it was nice talking to you, Arturo, and please give my love to Jana."

"Wait a minute, Marsh," Arturo recanted, "When is the meeting? I accept your invitation to be a guest speaker."

"Arturo, don't do this just for me," and there was an appalled look on the dark brown face. "I couldn't stand the thought of it."

"You know that I'd never do that, nor would you ask me to." Arturo was rather ashamed of himself. "You're right though, my research is a source of unleashed power, and it would be good for mankind — though I do have two conditions."

"Which are?"

"First: I won't make any mention of the Massafon particle, only the energy release from the Posafons and Negafons. Second: If my presentation is well received you will receive equal credit."

"I thoroughly agree with the first point. As for the second item, damn it boy, I don't need accolades. I've acquired all any honest man should ever receive in a thousand years." Suddenly, Marsh sounded alarmed. "But, what if you're right, and it isn't well received?"

"Then it's on my shoulders."

"No way, son! Absolutely, no way!" Marsh adamantly retorted. "Hell, Arturo I've jousted with the best of them, including that lightweight bastard, Collie Rollie." He chuckled, "Why, do you know he won't even say hello to me anymore."

"Can't blame him," Arturo laughed. "The last time he took you on, you shoved it up his ass."

There was no use of further discussion. Dr. Marshall Bernside was a respected giant among research scientists, and had triumphantly survived the onslaughts of the nadirs for decades. Arturo's only concern was he simply didn't want Marsh discredited or hurt by the new generations of dissidents.

"Send the schedule, Marsh. I'll be there," and the visi-phone went blank.

Jana had been standing by the door to Arturo's office. "So you're going to accept the invitation?"

"I may as well, Jana." Shaking his head, he muttered, almost to himself, "But, I still don't understand why all of a sudden it seems so important to the Academy. They've known about this work for a couple of years. After my presentation in London last year, I didn't think they were really interested."

Jana laid her hand on his shoulder. "It's obvious that they want to explore how the energy can be harnessed for various new power sources. It is a great scientific breakthrough, you know, Arturo."

"Thanks, my love," his mouth brushed her fingers, "but as far as I'm concerned, this 'great discovery' only means one thing to me — build a space vehicle which will achieve and even exceed the speed of light."

"I assume you have no intention of telling them that or mentioning the new Massafon particle."

"No way! Let others harness and use the energy as they wish."

The electronic message center intruded on their conversation with its rhythmic humming. Jana reached over and glanced at the cover page. "It's from Space Transportation, darling, from Mohammed Nahal, and it's marked Confidential, 'your eyes only'."

"Remember, I told you I talked with Mohammed last week about building an unmanned prototype and testing the ship in space?"

Jana only nodded and handed the transmission to her husband.

Arturo scanned the paper, "Listen to this, Jana," he beamed, "they're ready when I am. It'll be built at the research center model shop up in Montana and you can bet," he added, "under the tightest security the company has ever known."

"Darling, that's wonderful. When will you be ready to start work?"

"Probably about a year. I've got to design the engine and finish the various calculations. In the meantime, they're going to place an order for the fusion reactor and rubyionium gas laser electron gun."

"Oh, by the way, Arturo," Jana injected, "I'm going to Chicago with you. I wouldn't miss your speech for anything." Then she tapped him on the head, "Besides, I promised Marsh that we'd have dinner together every night."

Grabbing her wrist, he playfully pulled her toward him. "I've been set up by two masterful con artists. And what if I'd refused to give the speech?"

She ignored the comment and nipped at his ear lobe. "We'll make it a short vacation. Maybe we'll even take Marsh along with us on an overnight cruise on Lake Michigan."

That he'd been skillfully maneuvered into speaking at the Academy did not really phase Arturo, but he jokingly retaliated, "I don't know that I trust that conniving old man on a romantic cruise with my beautiful wife."

"Oh, we'll be very, very proper," was Jana's wide-eyed reply.

At the plush suite at the Chicago Palace Hotel, Arturo, Jana and Marsh were each finishing a late evening cappuccino.

"My boy, the attendance tomorrow will be overflowing." Marsh's face was animated. "From all reports, this will be the largest meeting the Chicago Branch of the Society has ever had. Scientists from branches all over the world have come just to hear your speech."

"Ah, modesty becomes you, Marsh," Jana said. "With you as the introducing dignitary, it would be my humble guess they came to hear the famous Dr. Marshall Bernside."

"Jana, my lovely girl, if I were thirty years younger, no even twenty," and he reached for her hand, "I'd take you away from Arturo and bask in your every word."

"Damned if I don't believe that, Marsh," Arturo tried to look jealous. "Fact is, I worry some about it."

"Oh yes, I see you're alarmed." Marsh joked back. "Good! Makes my whole day — no, my whole month — would you believe, year?"

"Well, while you two Romeos fight over me," Jana said, and gave Marsh a gentle kiss on his forehead, "I'm going to get some sleep."

Marsh chivalrously got to his feet. "Never, my dear, have I been dismissed so graciously. No need to show me to the door, Arturo." Then he added, while waving over his shoulder, "Goodnight, my friends, see you in the morning."

There was standing room only for Arturo's presentation. To accommodate the overflow, the Academy had been required to install sound and visual equipment in several other ballrooms in the hotel.

Arturo's discourse was greeted with attentive response. There were some slight murmurs but more than a dozen rounds of applause. He personally felt the speech was being well received, and was preparing to conclude when he glanced at Marsh, who immediately gave him a thumb's up sign.

"In summary, ladies and gentlemen, here are the results of our tests to date. Beams from a 5,000-watt fusion reactor and a 5,000-watt laser electron gun produced particles we named Posafons and Negafons. When these two particles collide, they produce an energy of 10^{17} electron volts."

Arturo paused, more for effect than to give the audience a moment to jot down notes.

"The result, as you all know, is the equivalent to the energy of the original gamma photon that was a part of the original formation of the universe."

There was a shocked intake of breath around the room. Arturo took a sip of water from the glass on the podium. "A one centimeter beam," he continued, "at a collision rate of 10 trillion particles per second, the continuous energy release is 160,000,000 kilowatts..." Purposefully not looking at Marsh, "...or as some might prefer to say, a potential horsepower of approximately 214,000,000 — continuous."

There was a trickle of grunts from the audience at his use of the archaic word, "horsepower." He waited until the room was again silent. "This translates to the equivalent of over a 100 of the old nuclear power plants of the early twenty-first century. With 10,000 watts input, an efficiency of 1.6 billion percent is realized. Of course, there is no radiation danger, and correspondingly, no resulting waste products to be disposed of."

Arturo scanned the auditorium of faces. Many were smiling while others had disbelieving frowns.

"Before leaving the podium, I would like to give credit where credit is due. Had it not been for a man all of you know, the gentleman I'm honored to call my close friend and mentor, Dr. Marshall Bernside, energy from photons might have taken many more years to obtain than it did — if ever."

With that final statement, Arturo stepped back and allowed Marsh to take the podium.

Leaning forward with a stern glare, the aged scientist growled into the speaker system, "Don't you believe all that balderdash about my help." Then in his deep resonant voice, he continued, "But do conclude that I also am honored to call Mr. Arturo Diggs, my close friend...and that goes double for his lovely wife, Jana."

Amid the applause, Marsh, with a deep bend of his lanky frame, bowed toward Jana. Then his manner switched to that of an austere authoritarian. "Enough of that." He motioned for Arturo to join him at the podium. "Mr. Diggs has kindly consented to answer questions from the floor."

The questions were routine and readily answerable; then the infamous Dr. Carlyle Rollie held up his hand. Though he would have preferred to ignore him, Marsh could not deny the gadfly's request, and so he begrudgingly acknowledged Rollie.

"Thank you Mr. Chairman." Rollie stood, basking in the attention riveted on him while he cleared his throat. As if on cue, a battery of lights spotlighted him and the whir of recording began capturing his every word and gesture.

"Mr. Diggs, the energy release of each particle collision, presumed release, that is," Rollie's voice had a note of patient reasonableness, "you claim is equivalent to the gamma photon, which as we all know played a key roll in the original formation of the universe. But those particles were consumed or nearly all consumed during the formation. Are you saying you have reestablished the original gamma photon?" Rollie questioned while raising his hands in mock incredulity and then continued, "...'The photon', which science has tried to find in quantity for centuries without success?"

There was a flurry of murmurs and nods from the audience, but Rollie remained standing and kept his eyes on Arturo.

"No, Dr. Rollie. I'm not saying the elusive gamma photon has been found or recreated," Arturo answered calmly. "The test results simply indicate that the energy release is comparable to the original gamma photon."

Before anyone else could be recognized from the podium, Rollie staunchly continued, "So we really can't prove that each collision will duplicate the gamma photon energy." He then tipped back his head for emphasis. "Mr. Diggs, how do you know that one centimeter beams of your self-named, what were they, oh yes, Posafons and Negafons, can produce 10 trillion particles per second, assuming they are particles?" Rollie turned to face the rest of the audience. "Seems to be an incredible amount of particles, doesn't it? And the amount of kilowatts appears terribly high."

Arturo was irritated by the obvious affront. "As I covered in my speech, that number is from the measured test results from 5,000 micron beams. The amount of particles are calculated from extrapolation and..."

But he was overpowered by Rollie's booming voice. "Then, Mr. Diggs, I suppose we have no choice but to accept your calculations and extrapolations, although..." he reached down and lifted up a book, opening it to a marked page, "...according to one of our esteemed scientists, Dr. Marshall Bernside, his early theories tend to refute your data." A slight smile parted his lips. "Could it be possible, Mr.

Diggs, that you might have made a miscalculation?"

"No, I did not make a miscalculation, Dr. Rollie," Arturo icily refuted.

Blandly shrugging, Rollie resumed his seat. Others were recognized, and the questioning from the floor continued. Many queries seemed posed intentionally to evoke negative answers. One energetic young man began debating Arturo by going into a lengthy dissertation, which led nowhere.

Marsh finally interrupted, "If you actually have a point, young man," he snapped, "would you please make it."

Chagrined by the gruff rebuff, the young man stuttered, "My colleague, Dr. Rollie has found..." and he motioned toward the doctor, "that such claims as Mr. Diggs has made are only figments of an incomplete hypothesis."

There was a surge of disbelieving gasps at the stunning indictment. Only Marsh's repeated banging of the gavel on the podium finally brought order.

"I don't know who you are, sir," Marsh growled, pointing an admonishing finger at the brash young man, "nor do I believe I wish to know. But, if any more such frivolous and unwarranted comments are made," and his menacing scowl left no doubt of his words, "that person will be censured by this academy. Now are there any further valid questions from the floor?"

A few more provisional inquiries were raised, which were quickly and smoothly answered by Arturo. Then, from the rear of the room a man's husky voice rose above the others, "Mr. Diggs, I believe Dr. Rollie is correct in his assumption that none of us can actually refute your findings, since we're not privy to the calculations. But, even if true, what are the practical applications?"

Before Arturo could reply, another dissident voice cut in, "I agree. As far as a new source of power, why? Our cold fusion reactors are clean. They have excellent efficiencies and supply all the power we can ever envision needing, either on Earth or in space."

The statement was barely out of his mouth when another negative voice began addressing the audience. "That's correct. The cold fusion reactors, along with the transportable isotope power packs, dispense more energy than we anticipated, and it's delivered simply, cheaply, safely and reliably." As if by pre-arrangement, he motioned toward Dr. Carlyle Rollie, "What are your expert observations on this, Dr. Rollie?"

As before, Rollie was swiftly bathed in beams of electronic media spotlight. Seemingly reluctant to take the floor, he modestly waved his hand in protest but amidst a sparse round of applause he slowly rose.

Arturo and Marsh glanced at each other. Something was definitely amiss. Glancing at his watch, Marsh held up his hand. "Ladies and gentlemen, if questions from the floor are finished, we will draw this session to a close."

"If you please, Dr. Bernside," Rollie amiably requested, "academy colleagues have posed some engaging remarks. I would appreciate just one more moment to set the record straight."

All attention converged on the speaker as he guilelessly smiled and looked around the room for sanction to continue. As heads bobbed in approval, there was nothing either Marsh or Arturo could say that would not create a scene.

"Thank you, Dr. Bernside," and he gave a half-stilted bow toward Marsh before turning to face his audience. "It has taken well over a century," Rollie was truly a compelling orator, and his voice rose and fell with a captivating intensity, "to rid our Earth of the multitude of central nuclear, fossil and water power generating stations with their electricity transmission lines."

For full effect, he rolled his eyes skyward and raised his palms in gratitude. "Our planet is now blessed with bountiful energy, transmitted in part by laser transmission towers and beaming satellites." Suddenly he twirled around and faced the podium, "So I ask you, Mr. Diggs, what good is your new energy source, other than an interesting scientific toy?"

"Dr. Rollie," Arturo succeeded in keeping his voice even, although it had a steely edge to it. "I leave that in your good hands and the others here to evaluate the usefulness of this energy source."

"Mr. Diggs," and Rollie's tone was deceptive, "the laser test facility energy absorbers didn't record any energy absorption, is it possible that..."

Marsh held up both arms. "Dr. Rollie, you've had your say."

Rollie's eyes innocently widened with dismay. "But we need to understand if a possible charade is being..."

"I told you, Collie Rollie, you've had your say!" Marsh's dusky brown face grew even darker with anger. "Now shut up, or so help me I'll shut you up myself."

A flurry of nervous undertones and edgy coughs ran rampant around the room. "Ladies and gentlemen, I apologize for my outburst," but Marsh's tone did not sound remorseful. "To see and hear a supposed Academy colleague act as we have just witnessed," and he glared at the now seated Rollie, "particularly one that has never had a practical application for any of his damn fool theories is more than I can take."

Taking a deep breath, he turned to Arturo. "Mr. Diggs, on behalf of the Academy I also apologize to you. I hope you will accept. This meeting is now adjourned."

The audience sat for a moment in stunned silence then noisily began chattering. A few came up to the podium to congratulate Arturo on his work, but most only gave him furtive glances as they hastily left the room.

That evening, the Chicago Electronic Sentinel broadcast an article written by the senior science editor about the Academy symposium.

NEW ENERGY SOURCE REFUTED
"World famous scientist, Dr. Carlyle Rollie, during today's global

symposium at the Chicago Branch of the Royal Astronomical Society of London, refuted the practicality of a so-called new energy source presumably discovered by a Mr. Arturo Diggs of San Diego, California. Dr. Rollie, among many other distinguished scholars, also questioned the validity of Mr. Diggs' test results as being overly optimistic about the amount of energy to be gained from photons. He also questioned the validity of the quoted energy releases from the presumed splitting of a massless and dimensionless photon."

The article repeated each and everything of Rollie's direct quotes, both during the meeting and at a subsequent press interview. When questioned about Dr. Marsh Bernside's explosion to him, Rollie was quoted as saying:

"Dr. Bernside was one of the world's great resources and has done innumerable good for the world's scientific community, but after all, the man is well into his eighties. Even though age does take its toll, I'm sure he had the best of intentions."

Beside himself with anger at the media account of Arturo's presentation, and especially of Rollie's remarks, Marsh paced his hotel room in a rage. "By God, I'm going to call the Sentinel's science editor, along with every scientific journal and electronic news media station and give them hell for this coverage." He banged the wadded printout on the desk. "He practically accuses me of being senile. Senile, my ass, I'm personally going to knock that bastard's teeth out."

Jana fidgeted with her nails and then opened her mouth to say something, but Arturo's comforting glance and smile allayed her qualms. He walked over to his aggrieved friend and put his arm around Marsh's shoulders.

"Marsh, let it go. Rollie's comments will die away and be forgotten." His voice was reassuring, "Don't lower yourself to his standards. Besides, as we discussed, I'm only interested in one thing for the new energy form — light speed, and that's all. If someone else wants to develop the system for power, let them."

"I hear you, Arturo," Marsh conceded, but his anger bubbled back. "But that shallow son-of-a-bitch insulted you, and me too, for that matter."

"You've been through this many times." Arturo tried to cool Marsh's indignation. "Remember the furor over your first sub-sub-atomic particle publication? Took 10 years and a lot of flack before it was finally accepted as gospel." Arturo laughed softly, "Let it go, Marsh."

"Arturo, I love you like a son and normally I'd take your advice. But not this time."

With clenched fists, he began prancing around the room shadow-boxing an unseen adversary. "I'll nail that cockroach, Collie Rollie, if it's the last thing I do."

Under any other circumstances the scene would have appeared comical, but neither Jana nor Arturo were inclined to laugh. Marsh straightened and abruptly stopped his pugilistic shenanigans. The keen old eyes held a perceptive gleam, and his no-nonsense tone was unfeigned. "My dear friends, don't you both realize by now that this entire media coverage with Dr. Rollie and his stooges was nothing more than a pure setup?"

Jana and Arturo had privately discussed such a possibility but had been at a loss to understand any motive for discrediting either Arturo or Marsh. With a sigh, Arturo nodded to his wife. Now that Marsh had brought it out in the open, there was no way that he would be deterred or put off from his objective.

"All right Marsh, we agree. I'll help in whatever you plan to do."

"So, you two had already come to a conspiracy conclusion?" His tone was accusatory, but his eyes twinkled, "Were you trying to shield 'a senile old man' from getting into a scrape?"

"Not exactly to shield you, Marsh," Jana began. "It's just that we haven't any proof."

"Thank you my dear, I understand." Then turning, he thumped a finger against Arturo's chest, "And you, young man, I don't want distracted by anything, anything at all. You must concentrate on getting the prototype space propulsion system built. That's the important thing now. Leave Collie Rollie and his cronies to me."

"Marsh is right, Arturo. Your goal is to achieve a light speed engine and fulfill your part of the Diggs legacy, or at the very least, enough of it to pass on to the next chosen Diggs descendant."

"Atta girl, Jana," Marsh said gruffly. "You tell him!" Admiringly he winked at Arturo. "She's not only got beauty but brains. Now you listen to the two of us. I'll handle it," he commanded, closing the subject.

"All right. All right, I give," Arturo capitulated, "but on one condition." Marsh raised a skeptical eyebrow, "Promise me if you need my help, you'll call immediately."

Marsh grasped each of their hands in his, binding the promise, "Done and done, my children," he beamed and then gruffly scowled, "Now I'm going to bed to get some much-needed sleep."

2190
UNEXPECTED PAYOFF

True to his word, Marsh hammered away at "nailing" Dr. Carlyle Rollie to the wall. In the beginning, a few journals accurately reported his opposition to Rollie, but then they were silent. What was baffling, were the instances when Marsh publicly exposed Rollie for his basic scientific errors and gross exaggerations, which even an undergraduate student wouldn't make, but none were published or reported in either the media or scientific journals.

Many Electronic News reports began with, "Dr. Rollie's 'Charisma'," and used it as if it was a deserved title — when that noun came too repetitive others were substituted, such as 'Brilliance' and 'Insight' — the spin masters of the century had not lost their command of hyperbole on the innocent public. Dr. Carlyle Rollie had become the most quoted scientist on record. His negative views about anything and everything were accepted as gospel.

As Rollie gained strength, Marsh began losing his esteemed position in scientific academia. The media constantly alluded to "his advanced age" with unflattering referrals:

"Dr. Bernside was a great man, responsible for modern day sub-sub-atomic particle theory, but it is necessary to note that the elderly scientist has not published any new theories in many years."

Time after time, Arturo had come to Marsh's defense, but to no avail. In truth, even though his data from the laser facility data spoke for itself, it was not accepted for practical application in scientific quarters. Others had duplicated his results, but they were not able to harness the energy releases that were considered worthwhile to receive financing for continued research. Rollie and his cohorts of "learned" scientists continually sneered at the use of photon energy until its use was finally thought of as an interesting but impractical potential energy source.

Arturo Newsome Diggs became, persona non grata, except at Space Transportation Corporation. They alone believed and understood — the Chief Executive Officer — Mohammed Nahal, in particular.

The past two years had physically, but not mentally, taken its toll on Marsh Bernside. The interminable discussion of his age had increased his resolve but not dulled his sharp intellect. A noted journalist had agreed to interview him that very afternoon, and he was determined to make one more stab at undermining the detested Collie Rollie if nothing more than for his own personal satisfaction.

Looking out the window of his apartment, he marveled at the frozen beauty of Lake Michigan. "Lordy me," he said aloud, pure awe in his voice, "I wish Arturo and Jana were here to share this sight with me."

His meditation upon the fresh snow reflecting off the lake was broken by the shrill sound of the visi-phone. He commanded the screen on; a young man's face appeared.

"Dr. Bernside?" His voice wavered slightly and he seemed embarrassed.

"Yes, this is Bernside."

"I'm sorry to inform you so close to your appointment, but I'm Ms. Darrin's assistant..." the rest of the message was hastily rattled off. "She asked me to tell you that her interview with you for the Scientific Gazette is canceled."

"When does she wish to reschedule the interview?"

The young man momentarily averted his eyes, "She just said," and he fumbled for words, "the interview was canceled."

"I see. Thank you for calling."

As the visi-phone went blank, Marsh felt a crushing pain in his chest. He grasped for the chair and slumped down into it. With supreme effort he said, "Visi-phone on. Arturo." The call was immediately put through.

Jana and Arturo stood waiting anxiously in the corridor of the intensive care unit. The doctor's diagnosis of Marsh's stroke had been encouraging, but he also warned that it had left him without the ability to walk. Although his speech was somewhat still slurred, he was mentally alert and was expected to regain full use of his voice.

"Arturo, let's bring Marsh back with us to San Diego. We have plenty of room and besides, with Filip in college and you spending so much time in Montana, he'll be a welcome guest." Then she frowned, "The only thing is, will he go with us?"

"He'll come," Arturo replied softly. "I'll see to it."

Over his strenuous objections of being a bother, Marsh finally consented to let Jana and Arturo talk him into living with them. The motorized prosthetics permitted him some freedom of movement, but he would allow neither Jana nor the full time nurse to help him unless it was absolutely necessary. Though his enunciation was not yet up to par, he was able to get all of his points across. He insisted on keeping himself busy by writing or punching in commands on his portable computer concerning all of Arturo's work and research.

As Marsh sat in the study with Arturo, intently watching the screen and listening to the voice reports, he could tell that Arturo was having trouble working out a stubborn problem involving energy control. After jabbing some calculations into his own hand held computer, Marsh handed it to Arturo. On the screen was a derived formula and Arturo only stared at it for a moment before smiling broadly to give Marsh a

180

thumbs-up sign. The formula went directly into the master computer and immediately supplied the answer for which Arturo had been fruitlessly searching. After that, Arturo hooked Marsh's portable computer to his own so that the elder scientist could follow everything firsthand. Marsh was never treated as an invalid but as a valued member of the family.

Even with Arturo working 18 hours a day on the prototype light speed rocket, he always made time to talk with Filip and Marsh. With Jana, he was the same as he had always been, loving and ready to sit down and listen to her say, "Come on big boy, let's do something together."

During the past two years, Dr. Carlyle Rollie's scientific reputation grew enormously. His continued attacks on Arturo Diggs and the frail Dr. Marshall Bernside, had given him the prestige of a scholar who could take on anyone in the scientific community and win. He had more requests for keynote speaking engagements than he could possibly handle even though he had quadrupled his fee. Most of his speeches were about the futility of harnessing the photon for energy.

Many a young scientist fawned over him and several of the older ones simply accepted or ignored him without comment. They had learned quickly that to oppose Dr. Rollie was the "kiss of death". Rollie actually believed that it was his superior knowledge and intellect that had brought him to his current level of fame and fortune. He also knew that on occasion, he did make small errors, but none he felt were of enough significance to alter his inevitable summarized remarks at the end of each speech. He was too smart to draw final conclusions or make recommendations about other work or research. Rather, he presented questions that were always designed to evoke negative responses or plant seeds of doubt for harvesting at a later time. In this manner, he could never be proved wrong.

He was proud of his accomplishments and never ceased to remind his audience that, "We scientists must always be on guard for research charlatans who would waste the world's time and energy pursuing pipe dreams. We must always question until the truth be known about new scientific theories." Anyone who took issue with him was finally forced to admit that, "Perhaps, Dr. Rollie has a point." He was amazed at how the news media had embraced him and quoted, word for word, his speeches regarding energy from photons. "Interesting," he thought. "The small media portion that dared publish disparaging or questioning articles about my speeches had either stopped or were no longer around." Most gratifying of all, the hated name "Collie Rollie" was not voiced aloud anymore — by anyone.

One evening, Rollie sat contentedly in his plush Miami apartment reading a review of his latest oratory, reveling in the glowing praise. When the visi-phone buzzed, he almost refused to respond. But whoever wished to reach him was being very persistent, and so he finally answered. When he saw that it was the gray-haired man he knew only as Mr. Smith, he commanded the visi-phone to accept the call.

"Dr. Rollie," Mr. Smith ordered, "an auto-car will pick you up in 30 minutes in front of your complex."

"After two years not hearing from you, you expect me to simply jump like some damned puppet." Rollie's face was a picture of indignation. "I've got other things scheduled for tonight." His evening was actually free, but he simply had to exercise his newly found authority.

"Dr. Rollie, I know you're a busy man, but I would like to bestow a further reward for your outstanding work," Smith replied with a chilly smile.

Rollie preened himself at Smith's praise, but he decided to push his new power. "Just drop it in the mail. I can't be bothered tonight."

"It would be my honor to deliver it in person and shake your hand. I trust you will permit me this last request. You have done well." The smile was now a bit wider.

Rollie let a few seconds pass and then glanced at his timepiece, "Well, if you insist. I suppose a few hours can be spared."

"Excellent. I look forward to seeing you again."

As promised, an auto-car was waiting outside the complex at the exact appointed time. What surprised Rollie was that it was his own personal vehicle. Unlike their first and only meeting two years ago, the destination program was locked in and Rollie saw that he was going to a different roadside rest area from that of the previous rendezvous.

As the auto-car sped along, Rollie mused about the "further reward." He had been paid in full for all his work. Each month, for two years, there was a package with no address, just his name, sitting on his desk. At first, he was uneasy about how it came to his office since there was no record of entry on the security system. After the first few packages, which contained generous amounts of money, he simply stopped worrying. The income from his speeches and the packages had enabled him to live exceedingly well.

He had never understood what actually prompted the media to praise him so for his attacks upon Arturo Diggs and Dr. Bernside. What he didn't know was that money and other rewards had been carefully placed in the right hands. He had developed sufficient conceit to believe it was his outstanding mind and scientific wisdom that had attracted such support.

As the auto-car gave a slight lurch off the main road, Rollie noticed a sign reading "Rest Area Closed." Another auto-car followed him in from the other direction and stopped along side. There was no other vehicle in the area. The man Rollie recognized as Mr. Smith opened the door to Rollie's car and seated himself.

"It's good to see you again, Dr. Rollie."

"After dragging me away from important business this evening, you had better make it worthwhile." Rollie's voice sounded annoyed.

"It will be, Dr. Rollie. You performed well, but the job is now finished."

Rollie smiled smugly, "Yes, and you damn well know I achieved the desired results. Diggs and Bernside will never again be able to hold their heads up in scientific research."

"True. Now let me shake your hand for your excellent performance." He stretched out his hand to grasp Rollie's, "You were successful in complete character assassination."

The gadfly scientist winced at the choice of words; but just as he took the proffered hand he couldn't resist asking, "Tell me, what exactly was behind your request? Why were their reputations so important?"

Smith's left hand encircled Rollie's right wrist in a friendly manner as he still lightly pumped the other man's hand. "Hate and envy; the same reason you had, Dr. Rollie — hate and envy."

Rollie didn't feel the slight pinprick on his wrist. Though he thought it strange that his hand was still being shaken. Suddenly he felt his heart pounding as if it would explode. Pulling his hand away and trying to grasp his chest, he only had time to say one word, "Why?"

"Your job is over," was the simple answer. Horst had only contempt for Rollie and his kind; however, his occupation denied him a show of feelings.

As was his practice, he placed Rollie's right hand on his heart, and arranged his left arm as if it were reaching for the Central Traffic Control distress alarm button.

The reports of Rollie's death were the featured articles of most of the various news media:

"FAMED SCIENTIST DIES OF HEART ATTACK"

His career was outlined, along with his diatribes against photon energy and his attacks against Arturo Diggs and Dr. Marshall Bernside. The day after the first news release, few spoke about his death; and after three days, he had been forgotten.

Dr. Marsh Bernside responded with a shrug when Arturo and Jana read him the reports. The man's name was never again spoken in their home.

Joal Lowe was to meet Horst at the usual place where they normally transacted their business. Horst, always the professional, had arrived early to make sure that the area was secure. He never took the chance that he would have the same fate he himself had dispensed so many times. When Joal arrived at the appointed time, he stepped out of his auto-car and entered Lowe's vehicle.

"As usual," Joal briskly started the conversation, "you'll find the remainder of the agreed-upon amount in the briefcase behind you." He made no mention of his satisfaction or dissatisfaction with the disgracing of Arturo Diggs and Dr. Marshall Bernside, or of the demise of Rollie.

Silently, Horst took the briefcase, opened it, and then nodded to Lowe. The business completed, he opened the door and began walking away, eyes alert for signs of any unforeseen danger.

As Horst reached his auto-car, he heard a maniacal laugh, like an animal screaming in pain. It was the same sound he'd heard Lowe give before. The hairs on the back of his neck bristled. Without turning, Horst entered his auto-car and commanded a destination. As his vehicle carried him past Lowe's auto-car, he could not help seeing the look of insane hatred on Joal's face. The sounds even penetrated through the closed windows. He ignored Lowe's shrieks. Were they of pleasure, agony or a vendetta, that covered him like a cloud? Horst didn't know which and cared less — he was a professional assassin without emotions.

Mohammed Nahal was waiting at his private elevator door to greet Arturo. The partition had barely slid open when the Chairman's arm was cordially draped around Arturo's shoulder. "Welcome back to Space Transport," he boomed, "and God's Country."

"Don't you mean," Arturo wryly corrected, giving his friend a friendly slap on the back, "Allah's country, Mohammed? Besides, the natives of Montana would surely take issue with calling San Diego God's Country."

"All the same thing, my boy, all the same thing," he replied as he ushered Arturo into his office. "And thank you for taking the time to stop by and brief me instead of going straight home."

Since their early days of working together, this friendly banter was typical.

Grimacing toward the visi-phone, Mohammed waved Arturo to a chair. "I'll be with you in a moment, my friend, one of the company directors believes he needs a word with me."

Arturo tactfully hid his impatience at the interruption. The prolonged junket to the Space Transport Research Laboratory in Montana had taken longer than expected, and he was anxious to be going home to Jana, Filip and Marsh. Instead of accepting the proffered chair, he sauntered over to the window. Taking a deep breath, he then expelled his momentary agitation. He really was eager to give Mohammed a summary of his progress with the demonstration space vehicle. The chairman's support in providing whatever he asked for and ensuring the full cooperation of Space Transport's research and model shop technicians was a godsend. Arturo, as in all his dealings with Mohammed, had again been given a free rein.

Between the skyline of the city and Coronado, Arturo absently observed the specks of white sails winding their way through the harbor. His reflections gradually drifted back to his first years with the company. Mohammed was then chief engineer of Space Transport and had taken the then young Mr. Diggs under his direct tutelage. When he was promoted to President, Mohammed personally saw to it that Arturo was offered his old job. But their friendship was truly tested when Arturo presented his work to the Space Trans Board, requesting their approval for the necessary funds to develop a new rocket engine. The incumbent Chairman of Space Transport was hesitant to commit so much money, and Mohammed had threatened to resign if the funds were not approved. It was only after much haggling that the aged chairman finally allowed a vote. And to his surprise, an overwhelming majority of the board approved the expenditures. Immediately after the meeting, Mohammed authorized Arturo's work on the new high temperature nuclear rocket. This was the research that catapulted Space Transport to being the unchallenged leader in the industry, leading to a 100% market share for Mars and Asteroid-Belt heavy loads. Shortly after, Mohammed was appointed chairman. The rest was history.

Arturo and Mohammed had the highest respect for each other's judgement and ideas. Securing money for Arturo's latest work on the Massafon engine was no problem. Space Transport's profit was beyond even Mohammed's wildest dreams.

Deep in his reflections, Arturo was startled to feel a sharp tap on his arm. "Now, my friend," Mohammed joshed, as he led Arturo towards an overstuffed settee, "bring your thoughts back into this room and tell me about the computer model of the photon engine."

"Caught me day dreaming, huh, Mohammed?" he grinned, but his mind instantly focused on the issues at hand.

As Mohammed settled into the comfortable couch and put his feet up on a hassock, Arturo choose a straight-back chair.

"It looks good, Mohammed," and he leaned forward, "the unmanned, emergency supply vehicle we adapted for the demonstration will be ready in a couple of months for the engine."

"I understand," the chairman casually commented, "but there are still a couple of problems."

"The main one is finding a material for the mirrors that reflect the Posafons and Negafons to the precise impact point for energy release without burn-through," Arturo stated matter-of-factly. "The other problem is the demonstration of full light speed will require leaving the solar system. The latter issue we can discuss later, after I've plotted a course."

"Can you demonstrate the engine at reduced beam diameters? That is, say at 5,000 micron diameter beams instead of the full one centimeter?"

"Yes," Arturo responded, then qualified, "but the space frame will of necessity require corresponding less weight. And although the principle will be demonstrated, the later usefulness of the vehicle will be severely limited."

Mohammed half-closed his eyes. "Same argument you gave when developing the high temperature nuclear engine. 'Do it right the first time and make it full scale'. I remember it well." He closed his eyes and smiled as he lifted his face skyward, "Allah help us, we sure had our necks stuck out on that one." Slapping his knee, he bellowed, "Okay, I agree! Go for it! But, I suggest that if a suitable material can't be found in time to meet your schedule, you go to a smaller beam."

"Are you concerned about the expenditures?" Arturo asked with concern.

"Hell, no!" Mohammed's deep voice boomed out. "We've got more money than Mars

192

has sand. No, Arturo, my interest is not money or any schedule. I'm funding this out of my discretionary funds and haven't told the board a damn thing about it."

Although Arturo had suspected that the chairman had not been completely open with the directors, this frank admission of concealment took him by surprise.

"Arturo, don't look so shocked," Mohammed gruffly chided. "The board has too many loose and wagging tongues to suit me."

"I understand, but..."

Mohammed brushed away his objections with a wave of his hand, "No, buts, it's just the way life is." In a swift move his feet hit the floor, and he was standing over Arturo. "No, my commitment is seeing your work proven. Both you and Marsh Bernside suffered because of that bastard Collie Rollie." He made no attempt to conceal the vehemence of his words. "The world is a better place now that Rollie's gone. Never did understand what that creep was actually up to, and why the press wouldn't let go."

Arturo started to say something, but the scowl on the chairman's face stopped him. "I'll bet our security people could have gotten to the reason for his attacks," and Mohammed turned away, sighing, "if I had not honored your request that we drop it."

Arturo had initially pondered the same question but had come to the conclusion that he'd made the right decision. He was about to repeat that dictum when Mohammed chuckled, "I'm rambling, Arturo, but whatever path you decide to follow, I'll back it." There was no doubt that Mohammed meant what he said; and within the events he could personally control, his word was his bond.

Arturo withdrew the portable computer from his breast pocket and thoughtfully input some data. "Your recommendation about a smaller beam, if I can't find a material in time for the full one-centimeter beams..." he handed the readout to Mohammed, "my calcs indicate that we could use 5,000-micron diameter beams without mirror burn-through."

"What about using one of the Moon emergency personnel vehicles? It's about the right size and could be modified much quicker than the larger one. What would you estimate, probably two months?"

Arturo thought for a minute and then nodded his assent. "Assuming it works, and I'm sure it would, the vehicle could be used for limited personnel hotshot trips to Mars, the Moon or the asteroids." Recognizing the wisdom of Mohammed's suggestion, he pushed himself from his chair. "Fine, if I can't find a suitable mirror reflector material by the time the two vehicles are ready for launch, we'll go with the smaller version."

"Good! One thing about you and me, Arturo, we can talk without either of us worrying about the other's motives. God willing, we..." Mohammed stopped and grinned, "In-shállah, infidel." He stuck out his hand and indicated without saying that their meeting was concluded.

"Thank you, Mohammed," Arturo warmly grasped his mentor's hand, "I'll keep you informed."

"Love to Jana, Filip and Marsh. By the way," and he tapped his forehead, as he remembered to relay the almost forgotten message from his wife, "Elma wants all of you over for dinner when you have time. We'll leave the date up to you."

Arturo was almost at the door when Mohammed directed, "Use the company air-car, my friend, it will be a faster trip home. My chauffeur will bring it back."

Apparently no one heard the arrival announcement when Arturo walked up the sidewalk and let himself in the front door. There was conversation coming from the library, and the deep pile of the Oriental rug muffled his footsteps. His intention was not to eavesdrop, but as he walked down the hallway, he could not help but overhear the discussion.

"Mother, Dad doesn't need anything else on his mind right now," Filip was saying in a fervent voice. "He's up to his armpits trying to design and build the first demonstration model to prove his propulsion system. Besides, it's his only night home in a month. Let's tell him after he's had a chance to wind down. It's better to hit him with it when he's relaxed."

"What do you think, Marsh?" Jana asked. "How do you think Arturo will react?"

Never having regained absolute control of his voice after the stroke, Marsh answered haltingly, "It's hard to say, but one thing I do suggest, Filip is the one to tell him."

A guilty feeling engulfed Arturo as he surreptitiously listened to the conversation, but his curiosity had been aroused. "What could be so bad," he thought, "that Filip hesitated to reveal it to me?" He started to enter the library, when his son's voice made him halt.

"You and Dr. Bernside are right, Mother. I'll tell Dad as soon as he gets home." His tone was firm and laced with a grown man's determination.

"No, Filip," Jana scolded. "Not until I've had first crack at welcoming him home. That's the ritual you know and…"

But before she could finish, both Marsh and Filip guffawed. They knew that Arturo and Jana would spend the first few minutes alone, irrespective of who was present in the house. Arturo tiptoed back down the hallway, reopened the front door and quietly closed it. Then he pressed the entry button and reappeared inside to call out in a thunderous voice, "I'm home. Where's my greeting committee?"

Jana came from the library to welcome him. Filip and Marsh chose to stay in the library; they knew this was Arturo and Jana's time. Their love of each other had not ebbed over the years. "Come on, let's go find a private place," Arturo whispered.

"Later, big boy," Jana said as she kissed him again. "Later."

Ordinarily, Arturo and Jana wouldn't have worried about "the family." But he knew tonight was different and simply said, "Later it is, lover."

"Filip and Marsh are in the library, darling," Jana said as she took his arm. "Come on in and join them."

After an enthusiastic greeting and small talk about progress with the propulsion system, Arturo was acutely aware of a prevailing uneasiness.

Filip, his handsome face looking unusually tense, finally broke the ice, "Dad, there's something I need to discuss with you."

Arturo merely looked surprised. "Sure Son, go ahead, what is it?"

Looking first at his mother, then at Marsh, Filip began the explanation with self-conscious composure.

"Dad, I've finished all my required courses for the Ph.D. in planetary geology, and my advisors have offered me an associate position at the university to teach the Mars courses." The dark blazing eyes and the sudden rush of words attested to his enthusiasm. "My thesis is underway, but I don't want to spend time in laboratories or in classrooms. I need to do something..."

Holding up his hand, Arturo gently admonished, "Whoa, son, take your time. We've got all evening."

Taking a deep breath, Filip absently ran his fingers through his crop of thick dark hair. "Dad, the bottom line is," and once he'd undertaken the explanation, the words began to flow more easily, "I've been contacted by the Robot Mining Corporation regarding taking a position with them as an associate geologist responsible for analyzing new minerals."

"What about finishing your doctoral thesis?" That was the one point that Filip feared would be his father's response. "You can't receive your degree until it's accepted, and once you go to work," Arturo advised, "the job will require more time than you think."

"That's just it, Dad," undaunted, he launched into his prepared rebuttal, "you see, the job is on one of their permanent space stations in the asteroid belt between Mars and Jupiter." Filip tried to read his father's reaction, but Arturo's face remained noncommittal.

"Don't you have to sign on for a year's tour on the station?" Arturo offhandedly inquired.

"That's just it, Dad..." he paused, expecting an objection, but when none was forthcoming, Filip continued, "the firsthand experience I'll get can never be obtained in the classroom. Although robots do all the mining, some trips to the asteroids are necessary to study the various mineral formations. As an example, when the sensors signal that other minerals are combined within the matrix of the minerals being mined, someone must provide direction as to how to proceed and..." he paused, again anticipating strenuous disapproval; but when his father said nothing, the silence was deafening. There was a lull before Filip continued his unfinished sentence, "...it takes a trained person to ascertain whether or not another mineral should be first removed, either to eliminate the danger of it being rendered useless due to breakage or being pulverized in the separators. And, Dad, new heretofore unknown minerals are being discovered all the time. My primary job will be to analyze and classify them for possible use."

Arturo studied his son before replying, "Filip, you understand that you can only leave the space station every three months and then only for a week on Mars, which for the most part is for a physical checkup."

"I understand." The young man's voice was positive and decisive. "But, the chance to do this, when I'm only 22 years old, is something I can't pass up." His tone reflected the pride he felt, "Out of nearly a thousand applications received for the twelve open positions, I was the only graduate student chosen."

"Filip," Arturo gave his son a searching look and then held out his hand, "I think it's a great idea." A warm smile lifted the corners of his mouth, "And may I say, I'm very proud of you."

Filip responded to his father's blessing with a heartfelt hug. He then put an arm around his mother's shoulders and the three stood in a silent embrace, broken only when Marsh tapped on the arm of his wheelchair.

"Best damn thing that ever happened." And he extended his arms to Filip. "Congratulations, my boy."

It was difficult for Filip to restrain his emotions at the outpouring of warmth. He bent down and gently locked his arms around Marsh.

"Now hear this, all of you," the old man prophesied, his bearded chin resting on the firm young shoulder, "I predict that Filip's year on the asteroid belt will be more worthwhile than any of us know."

"With mentors like you three," Filip said, rising and giving each a flourishing wave, "how could I not do something worthwhile?"

Mothers have always had the innate ability to get to the heart of their feelings, and Jana was no exception. "When would you have to leave, Filip?"

"Since my classes are over and the first replacement geologists to arrive at the asteroids will get their pick of which one to work on," he hastily replied, trying not to upset his mother, "as soon as possible."

"And when is, 'as soon as possible', young man?" Marsh bluntly probed.

"The first vehicle is leaving in three days. The next one is in two weeks. I'd like to be among the first there."

When Jana's support had been enlisted, she had agreed with Filip's aspirations; but her misgivings were not the thought of her son now being a man and leaving the nest, but of the unknown perils of the asteroid job. The permanent space stations, components and subassemblies, which had been built on Earth and Mars and assembled on location, were certainly not the safest havens. She had read about the various hazards people stationed on the asteroid's surfaces constantly faced, and there were always the distinct possibilities of life support system malfunctions.

Filip saw what was running through his mother's thoughts. "Mom," taking her delicate fingers in his, he was alarmed by the coldness of her touch, "there are risks one has to take, whether here on Earth or on an asteroid. Please don't dwell on the downside of life. It's not like you." He brushed her forehead with his lips.

"My goodness," her long lashes damp with tears, "was it that obvious?"

Reaching in a pocket for a handkerchief, she quickly dabbed at her downcast eyes. She had not intended to show her concern. With a pounding heart, she mustered the courage to put aside her own feelings of apprehension, raised her head with poised dignity, and flashed a smile. "My darling son, you're a man, capable of making your own decisions regarding your destiny. For that I'm so proud." Her face changed to one of calm. "But only three days before you leave. Come on. You, no we, have a lot to do!"

Filip hugged his mother and effortlessly lifted her off her feet, accompanied by roars of encouragement from Arturo and Marsh.

Six busy, productive months had elapsed since Filip left for the space station in the Mars and Jupiter asteroid belt. Mohammed Nahal had insisted that he be sent to his new assignment aboard one of the Space Transport freighters with the nuclear engine his father had designed two decades ago. It was not uncommon for family members to be granted space, when available, since the ship made regular runs from Earth to the Moon and Mars, carrying supplies, equipment and human cargo on to the permanent Asteroid-Belt space stations. On the return trip its payload was vast tons of ore to be processed into ingots on Mars. Other ingots and minerals were sent for further refinement to the Moon and Earth to eventually become finished goods.

During this same period, Arturo had made countless trips between the large laser test facilities in Colorado and Montana. He had immersed himself in testing countless materials for the reflective mirrors that would withstand Posafon and Negafon beams at one centimeter in diameter without burn-through. He had every conceivable appropriate substance being ground into mirrors at the Space Transportation labs in Montana; none would pass the magic one-centimeter diameter beam threshold without suffering burn-through. In desperation, he even tried highly polished two-carat diamonds. Although they had longer endurance, even the costly diamond mirrors eventually disintegrated. When both the large and smaller demonstration vehicles were ready for final propulsion system installation, he had to make the decision whether to continue searching for a superior substance or go with the original material that would withstand 5,000 micron beams.

Mohammed Nahal sat comfortably in Arturo's home office, his feet propped up amongst the stacks of prints, computer analysis and reports.

"Reminds me of the days," the chairman indulgently reminisced, "of those many years ago, when I was but an insignificant chief engineer working on a new transport design that I thought would revolutionize space travel." A faraway look crept into his dark eyes. "You had just come to work for me and were the only one that made any sense about the engine temperature problem."

"Yeah, those were fun days, Mohammed. You taught me about the practicality of business," Arturo replied, "instead of keeping my head in the clouds."

"A little practicality never hurt anyone, Arturo," he answered jovially, "but common sense coupled with a grasp of theoretical applications — that's the rare item." Mohammed was waxing philosophical, "Ah, but when the two are wed, something miraculous happens and practical applications emerge."

"You and Marsh should team up, Mohammed. You'd be a hellava pair, since you both espouse the same philosophy. 'If it ain't broke, don't fix it', is a bunch of crap, because nothing would ever be improved."

"Hell, Arturo," Mohammed planted his feet on the floor, "if I didn't have the discretionary funds for this work of yours, can you imagine the song and dance I'd have to go through with the board?"

He began mimicking one of the more nervous members in a falsetto voice. "'But Chairman Nahal, we now control all the solar system. Why do we need another propulsion system?'" Then in a nasal whine, "Mr. Chair-

203

man, if I may have the floor, this technology of Mr. Diggs' has been questioned by scholars and respected scientists. Maybe we need more research," he puffed his cheeks and spoke through puckered lips, "before committing ourselves to another flight vehicle..."

Arturo laughed uncontrollably. "Stop it, Mohammed, please, you're killing me."

"All right, that's a fair reason." He glanced at the ornate grandfather clock across the room and seemed amazed at the hour. "Anyway, I've got to leave soon, and I want a quick briefing on where we stand and your plans."

The short briefing by Arturo was expanding into its second hour, protracted by Mohammed's numerous questions regarding various computer model projections and vehicle hardware design. The chairman was particularly interested in why the "molecule getter," Arturo developed prior to 2180 and the heart of Space Trans transport vehicle propulsion system, couldn't be used to replenish the reflective mirrors that were currently such a problem.

"It seems to me," Mohammed said, "that the molecule getters serve as a continuous casting process. They keep the engine thrust chamber throat on our current freighters from being destroyed by the 30,000° C temperature by catching the gaseous molecules and redepositing them in the throat."

Arturo was ready with the answer. "Except, the molecule getters won't replace the mirror with the exact smoothness required for precise aiming of the Posafon and Negafon beams to their collision point."

He grabbed a tablet and began scratching out detailed pencil marks on the paper. "Here, you can see that the aiming of the mirrors has to be continually adjusted. That's because of slight deformation, or movements caused by temperature changes, or stresses on the vehicle and propulsion system structure. But I've used the control part of the molecule getter computer program, to keep the mirrors in alignment."

"I'm also intrigued by your method of varying the thrust or force of the propulsion engine through the wagon wheels."

Mohammed had affection for nicknames, and so he proposed that Arturo's new invention of the "wagon-wheel," be named just that. He liked it because of its simplicity: two counter rotating wagon wheels that allowed for controlling the flow of the Negafons prior to the impact point. Thus, allowing full flow of the Posafons and controlling the Negafons from zero to full flow could infinitely vary the energy release.

"All right, Arturo, let's go through the summarization together, one last time."

Both men had a printout of the detailed procedures and began alternately reading summaries aloud.

"The smaller vehicle, 10 meters diameter by 80 meters long, will be used for the demonstration test..."

"The redesigned and upgraded lithium-11 pentaride-bumper shield on the front of the vehicle for protection from space dust at high velocity was adapted from the freighters..."

"The diameter of the Posafon and Nega-fon beams in the Massafon engine will be 2,000 microns or 20% of the burnout diameter at one centimeter. This assumes, of course, a momentum transfer of 75% efficiency..." and Mohammed paused and frowned.

"I can't readily test the engine," Arturo broke in, "and so the flight will serve for both engine and flight tests."

The chairman nodded and proceeded with the checklist of the impending test flight.

"Since the emitted Massafons have a life of 100 nanoseconds and only travel 30 meters before reverting to photons again, the engine exhaust is 31 meters long to ensure the particles don't hit the space station during launch and damage it..."

"The light blue plasma force field which converts into Massafons will push against a barrier located just behind the cold fusion reactor and the Massafons will push against the plasma, thus propelling the vehicle from momentum exchange..."

"The vehicle is programmed to travel in a straight line, away from all known meteors, asteroids and space dust concentrations..."

Arturo took a deep breath, before saying with satisfaction, "I personally will man the telemetry signals to the vehicle from the Space Trans space lab if any are required..."

"On board computers will record everything that occurs..."

"The vehicle is programmed to come back to the Space Trans orbiting station..."

Looking up from the printout, Arturo stared past Mohammed. "I have two concerns: the communications signal time lag, and what will happen at light speed. Einstein's accepted theory is that mass becomes infinite, among other issues. But the Massafons travel at c, light speed, and they don't seem to have a problem..."

Mohammed was fully aware of this issue and so he candidly inquired, "What do you propose to do?"

"First, if something goes wrong at c, any command I may send will never catch the vehicle, since as you know, communication signals travel at the same speed, c. For that matter, as the vehicle goes faster and faster, the communication time increases proportionally to the vehicle speed."

"And secondly?"

"In so far as the increased mass problem, time and vehicle size shrinking, I believe they're relative to an observer only and not to the vehicle or any inhabitants. We'll just have to wait and see."

"And that completes a summary of the program status and plans for the demonstration test," Mohammed finalized.

"One item I didn't mention, Mr. Chairman, nor is it in the printout."

"And what is that?"

"The rubyionium laser gun pulse rate is the key to splitting the cold fusion reactor beam into Posafons and Negafons."

"So that's why no one has been able to duplicate your work at the laser test facility in Colorado," he shrewdly smiled. "I knew it had to be something different."

"I have never divulged the rate to anyone, Mohammed." Arturo gave a lopsided grin. "Although Dr. Marsh Bernside is privy to how I arrived at the rate, he refused to have me identify the exact pulse. But, Mohammed, certainly if anyone deserves to know the rate of pulsing, it's you." Arturo averted his eyes; his voice was somber. "That is, in case something should happen to me."

"No. No, I don't need to know. That little secret stays with you. I ask only that if something did befall you, the pulse rate could be recovered for later use on further photon engines."

"It's all taken care of, Mohammed. If that unforeseen event happens, you'll receive a computer chip that will program the laser gun to the accurate rate." He then waggled his forefinger at his friend. "A word of caution. If anyone attempts to break the code to determine the rate of pulsing contained in the chip, it will automatically be wiped clean and all programming lost."

"Can the programming on the original chip be copied for use on another rubyionium laser gun?"

"Yes, as many times as one wishes." Arturo had a pang of second thoughts, "But I still think that you should be aware of the rate, Mohammed."

"No, Arturo. It's better only you know for the time being. Maybe later, when we're replacing all our ships' nuclear engines with your new Massafon engine. Maybe then I'll need to know."

The great clock on the wall chimed the hour, interrupting their flow of conversation. Abruptly Mohammed rose to leave. "Great job, Arturo. Keep me informed. If you need anything, just let me know." It was as though there was another matter he wished to discuss, but instead, almost as an afterthought, inquired, "When do you plan to conduct the first test?"

"In two weeks. The final check out of the controls and the computer program will take place next week."

Mohammed nodded, but he still had something on his mind. He averted his glance, hoping that Arturo would understand his reticence, but his hesitancy exposed his anxiety. "Arturo, there is another point," he cleared his throat. "Have you taken into account that the computer could, if a problem occurred on the return voyage, keep the vehicle from impact with a planet or space station? At light speed...well, a force of such magnitude..." but he broke off the remark in mid-sentence.

This was certainly a possibility that Arturo had seriously considered, and he had made preparations for all imaginable eventualities. "Yes, Mohammed, that indeed would be crisis. That's why I've programmed the vehicle to travel away from all planets and the sun, by going at right angles to their orbital paths."

A look of relief flushed the Chairman's high cheekbones, and he gave a deep sigh. "It was an issue that had to be addressed," and he patted Arturo on the shoulder, "although I knew that..."

"In fact, Mohammed," Arturo interrupted, "if a vehicle, weighing 300,000 kilograms, traveling at light speed, did crash, the energy release would be the equivalent of three trillion tons of nitroglycerin."

"Allah, in heaven!" Mohammed's eyes widened and then he mentally calculated the comparable release of energy. "That's more than, let's see...that's more than 50,000 of the old twentieth century fifty megaton hydrogen bombs."

"That's right. Enough energy to destroy all life on Earth, and most likely Earth itself — not to mention other planets. There could be chaos in our solar system and..."

Shaking his head, Mohammed waved off further discussion. "Enough. You've given this serious thought my young friend. What you're saying is that even if the vehicle did go astray the chances of hitting a planet, Earth or the Moon..."

Finishing the sentence, Arturo supplied the calculated odds, "...is over a billion to one."

"Good odds," he nodded approvingly and repeated emphatically, "very good odds." Then he quickly moved to another subject. "Are you sure that the vehicle can be taken to our space station without anyone knowing what is going on?"

"Every possible security precaution has been taken. The vehicle is being crated and labeled as a new hotshot personnel shuttle for use on the Moon."

"Who else is involved?"

"Only myself and three highly trained technicians who worked on the project will be needed for the launch. These same people will receive the tracking data for performance and communicate any required signals for control in case the preprogrammed flight path needs tweaking."

"Be careful, Arturo." The chairman seemed almost apologetic about making the warning.

Closely scrutinizing the chairman's face, Arturo felt compelled to ask, "What are you worried about, Mohammed? You seem very concerned."

"As you know, Arturo," and his words were spoken low but with meaning, "we've continued the inquiry into the catastrophic explosion of the transport that..." but he couldn't or wouldn't say more.

Momentarily gripping the back of the chair, Arturo's face paled at the mention of the tragic death of his parents. Painful as the memory still was after all these years, he controlled himself and asked simply, "Have you found out anything new?"

"No, we haven't and we've been unable to duplicate the problem under the best of laboratory conditions. I'll never believe that the engine controller failed. Someone and something..." Mohammed paused. He did not wish to continue voicing the negative, especially so near the new launch. "Just be careful, Arturo."

"I will, Mohammed," he earnestly promised. "I will."

Two weeks later, when Arturo and Jana were in the library talking about the impending test of the new propulsion engine, Marsh wheeled himself into the room in his motorized chair.

Neither Jana nor Arturo had to be told that his frail body was failing almost daily. His mind was still sharply honed, as was his ever-present wry humor. A profusion of Santa Claus like white hair and a manicured beard framed his dark brown craggy face like newly fallen snow.

Marsh intuitively pieced together their shared glances and startled them with a loud comment. "Hell Jana, Arturo, waiting to see how the Massafon engine works is the only reason I haven't let go, and gone on to my just reward." He pointedly looked down at the floor, but then shook his head. "Sorry, wrong way." His eyes fluttered toward the ceiling as he smiled.

The mere thought of Marsh not being with them sent an involuntary shiver through his friends, and they tried to hide their apprehension with cheerful smiles.

"All right, Arturo, my bright young friend, when do you push the button to launch the test vehicle? As scheduled I hope, 'cause I want to still be around to hear about the results."

Arturo winced. "The final vehicle checkouts have all been completed. Everything looks good." Arturo kept talking, trying to maintain a breezy tone. "I'm taking the flight controls computer program up to the space station tomorrow. Assuming no problems in integration of the program with the Massafon engine, we should be able to launch within hours."

"Are you satisfied with the controls that keep the reflective mirrors at the proper angles to ensure collision of the Posafon and Negafon beams?" Marsh pumped for more information, his keen mind always on the lookout for small technicalities.

"That, Marsh, as you well know, has been the most ticklish problem of all, other than trying to find a mirror material that will hold up under beams a centimeter in diameter," Arturo answered ruefully.

"Refresh my memory," Marsh persisted, "what success did you have with inserting the larger mirrors?"

"It's just another precaution, Marsh. I installed slightly concave mirrors that will readjust the beams to another area if a burn-through does occur. My calculations indicate that these larger mirrors will accommodate four burn-throughs before the Massafon engine is inoperable."

"It'll work my boy," he assured, "it'll work. And when it does, we'll drink a toast."

"Dr. Bernside," the firm voice of his private nurse rang from the doorway, "it's past your bedtime." Before he could protest, the nurse began guiding his chair from the room, "Now be pleasant and say goodnight."

"Goodnight, Marsh," Jana and Arturo called in unison but only heard back a loud snort that sounded more like "goddamn" than a good night salutation.

When their friend was well out of ear-shot, Jana looked at her husband. "Darling, I agree with Marsh. Your engine will work. Finally your dream of light speed will come true. I'm so proud of you and all you've done," and she leaned over to kiss him. As he drew his wife closer, her eyes widened in chagrin, "Oh darling, how could I have forgotten? We received a short message from Filip today."

"About time! Haven't heard from him for several weeks. What did he have to say?"

"He wished us luck on 'the project'. Said he'd been to the surface of some of the larger asteroids. He's really enjoying his work, even though twelve and sixteen-hour days are not uncommon," she recited. "He was sorry we weren't able to join him on Mars last month during his week's rest and relaxation. Of course he knew that you'd be busy with the new vehicle test; that's about all."

"When this is over," Arturo promised, a yawn smothering his words, "we'll make it a point to join him on his next Mars R & R."

He started to settle into a comfortable position on the couch, but Jana leaned over her husband, just low enough to expose the cleavage of her enticing firm breasts. She took his hands in hers and led him unresisting down the hallway to their bedroom.

Jana walked to the center of the taste-fully decorated master suite and kicked off her shoes. She turned and began to unfasten the tiny round buttons that secured the front of her flowered silk blouse. Arturo stood quietly. She preened for him without any trace of primness and slipped off the filmy material.

Arturo followed silently when she walked softly toward the antique Queen Anne dressing table, with its beveled mirror reflecting back their two images. He entwined strands of her silky hair between his fingers and spontaneously picked up a sterling handled brush. With strokes from years of practice, he began brushing her long hair — slowly and quietly.

Their unabashed intimacy had grown through caring and perfecting the art of sexual expressions, one to the other. As Arturo continued brushing, their bodies ached for physical contact. However, both dallied and preferred to revel in their closeness.

Jana's face flushed in anticipation as her husband's practiced hands began to roam over her now quivering body. She guided his fingers behind her back to unlatch her bra. She stood up and took off the ruff of frilly panties and stepped back.

The tilt of her head beckoned Arturo to follow. She bypassed the four-posted bed and stretched out her nude form on the down filled chaise lounge. As he kneeled beside his wife while removing his shirt, he gazed at her and said, "You are the most beautiful woman in the world." A gasp caught in his throat as her practiced hands caressed his bare chest.

"And you, my Arturo, my lover..." but his mouth pressed against hers. They fondled, played and delighted in every touch and stroke until the moment of their ultimate final delight.

Arturo awoke and propped himself up on one elbow and marveled at the pure tranquility in Jana's beautiful face. He gently brushed a damp curl from her brow and bent over to kiss her closed eyelids.

A muffled, contented moan escaped from her half open lips and for a moment Arturo thought he'd awakened her, but her steady breathing reassured him. He gently lifted her from the couch and carried her to their bed. Jana didn't stir when he placed her head on the fluffy pillow and tucked the sheet around her shoulders. Their love of each other always seemed to be a miracle of joy fulfilled. Making love before an important milestone in their lives had become a ritual.

She awoke as they automatically inter-twined their legs and gave a deep sigh of satisfaction, their arms pulling each other closer. Within seconds, they fell into a deep slumber.

The elevator leading to the hotshot personnel shuttle glided open. Arturo and Jana emerged hand in hand. Even though it was time for Arturo to go to the space station for the launch, they squeezed out every last minute.

"I waited until the last minute, Jana." Arturo reluctantly dropped her hand and opened his briefcase. "Thought you might like a souvenir." He took out a portable hologram and turned it on. The test vehicle appeared as he handed it to her. "For luck," he said.

"Oh Arturo, she's beautiful!" As she turned the small hologram over to see the vehicle from all angles, Jana noted, "I see you named her." She peered at the name painted just behind the round nose cone, "but I can't quite make it out." Then she joyously exclaimed, "You named her the *Jana*! I'm thrilled." She threw her arms around Arturo and enthusiastically kissed him. "Thank you, my darling."

"She had to have your name to grace her bow, love, and not just for luck. Since neither of us can go on the mission," he softly whispered, "at least my wonderful wife's name can accompany her through space."

Arturo hugged Jana one last time, then entered the elevator. As she had done so many times before, Jana went to the control tower to watch the small shuttle rise slowly from the ground, pickup speed, and disappear quickly into the clear blue sky on the way to the floating space station and the awaiting test vehicle.

All was in readiness for Arturo's arrival. He carefully checked the status of the *Jana*; and, satisfied that all was in order, began the final briefing with the three Space Transport technicians. Proud to be chosen as the elite team, which would try to achieve the speed of light, the techs listened closely as Arturo outlined the flight plan programmed into the ship's computer.

"The outward bound flight profile is to accelerate the *Jana* to light speed in a calculated time of 8.5 hours. The Massafon engine

217

will shut off and she'll coast for an hour at c, during which the ion guidance engines will turn her around. At that time, the Massafon Engine will be restarted, firing backwards for 8.5 hours to decelerate and slow her down. At zero velocity she'll re-accelerate and head for home. That's the summary of the outbound journey. She'll reverse the sequence coming back to the space station."

Sally, the senior tech and sole female member, commented, "So on the way back she'll achieve light speed in another 8.5 hours, coast for an hour, fire backwards for another 8.5 hours to slow down and dock at the space station."

Another tech mentally calculated aloud, "The round trip time adds up to 36 hours."

"Exactly," Arturo nodded, ratifying his calculation, "one way there of 18 hours and 18 hours back to the station."

"Mr. Diggs," the third and youngest of the techs requested, "summarize again the particulars of the mission profile and the vehicle parameters."

"Okay, good point. The *Jana* weighs 300,000 kilograms. At a maximum 1,000 g's acceleration for which she's designed, the 30 million kilograms of thrust available should take the vehicle to 300,000 kilometers per second, or light speed, in 8.5 hours. Since she'll be 4.6 billion kilometers from Earth at that point, it will take 4.25 hours for her voice computer and data to let us know her status, since communication signals in space only travel at the speed of light."

"So we won't know whether or not c has been achieved for 8.5 plus 4.25 hours, a total of 12.75 hours."

"You're exactly right, Sally," Arturo agreed, but he held up a cautionary finger. "By the time her signal tells us c has been reached, she will have finished the coast phase of 1.1 billion kilometers and traveled another 3.3 billion kilometers in the deceleration phase." With their full attention focused on him, Arturo reminded, "As you know however, we will be receiving and monitoring data continually throughout the flight."

Punching in the statistics, the senior tech quickly read out the results. "So she will have another 1.3 billion kilometers to complete the outward bound journey, slow down to zero and start back."

"Correct. The vehicle will go outside the limits of our solar system, beyond the distance of the planet Pluto by 4.4 billion kilometers, but by the time we get the signal that she's heading back, she'll really have finished her return coast phase and turned around again."

"And will have fired the Massafon Engine in reverse again to slow down and dock back here at the space station," the youngest tech volunteered.

"Right on," Arturo concurred with a nod of his head. "Maybe we should also review the times we'll receive all the key messages of the *Jana's* flight plan after the scheduled launch of 1100 hours."

"We have all the times on the computer, but if you agree, I'd like to post the major times beside the master clock, sir," Sally requested.

"Good idea. But remember that when we receive the messages regarding vehicle status, she will really have traveled to a different location. For example, when she's at the end of the one way trip, she'll be 10.3 billion kilometers from Earth and it will take 9.5 hours to receive her message from there. In the meantime, she will have traveled 5.7 billion kilometers back towards Earth and the space station," Arturo cautioned.

"Understood Mr. Diggs." Sally was a perfectionist. She wanted to be sure that every detail be in order. "Now let's review the times of the key messages to be received."

Complying with the request, Arturo quickly launched into the particulars and rattled off the data in rapid order.

"Assuming launch this morning at 1100 hours, we will receive the reaching light speed message exactly twelve and three quarter hours later." He glanced at the large round precision clock on the wall, "That will be at 2345 hours tonight."

"...At the end of the one hour coast period, her message will be received 2 hours later. That would make it 0145 hours early morning of tomorrow..."

"...When she has decelerated to zero velocity at the maximum distance, another twelve and three-quarter hours will have elapsed and her message received at 1430 hours tomorrow afternoon..."

"...When she starts her coast period again, that message will travel at the same speed as she does, both at c. Therefore the message for deceleration to return to the space station and the coast message will be received at the same time. Another four and a quarter hours will have passed and both messages will be received at 1845 hours..."

"...She will dock here at the station four and a quarter hours after that at 2300 hours for a total trip time of 36 hours..."

"The round trip time will be 36 hours for a total distance of 20.6 billion kilometers traveled at an average speed of 159,000 kilometers per second..."

While Arturo related the statistics, the senior had made, in large print, a chart of the times when the key messages would be received, stapling it on the wall under the master clock.

1. 1100 hours - launch
2. 2345 hours - light speed at 300,000 km/sec
3. 0145 hours - begin deceleration at the end of the coast period
4. 1430 hours - reach zero velocity and start home
5. 1845 hours - start the return coast period after achieving light speed again and the homeward deceleration signal
6. 2300 hours - dock at the space station

"Am I correct in the chart times, sir?" the senior tech questioned while examining her handiwork.

"Absolutely, Sally! And it's an excellent idea to have a visual chart," Arturo complimented. "Also, the hologram simulator of the solar system and the *Jana's* flight path will give us a visual indication of progress. The planets are not to exact scale of course, but at least we have an indication of the *Jana's* position relative to the solar system."

The stationary hologram of the solar system that seemed suspended in the middle of the room was a beautiful three-dimensional representation of the planets imperceptibly rotating around the sun in their normal orbits. The flight path was depicted as a perpendicular dashed line at right angles to the saucer shaped solar system and its planets. As the *Jana* traveled, the line would become solid. Larger dots on the dashed line represented the key events of reaching light speed, coast period, deceleration and the return flight.

Arturo walked around the colorful hologram and admired its beauty and technological achievement. To the technicians he commented, "You all did a great job setting this up. I only wish that the flight path were in real time. Bloody communication time delays. At least, when the mission is finished, we'll have a record that can be played for others to see and enjoy."

The techs smiled in appreciation; Sally said simply, "Thank you." Then with a droll

grin, "Sort of reminds one of our hologram receivers at home, doesn't it?"

"Well, sort of," Arturo humorously countered, "but much more meaningful than some
of the programs broadcast for 'entertainment'."
His face became serious, and his tone all business. "Is the Massafon Engine hologram set
up?"

"Yes, it is Mr. Diggs. Let me turn it on."
Sally softly said the code and a three dimen-
sional representation of the engine compartment sprung into view. The reactor and laser
beams were explicitly imaged, along with the
Posafon and Negafon beams, even the reflective
mirrors were clearly visible.

"All engine data is also fed to the hologram, Mr. Diggs, so we can see a representation of what is going on as the data is received."

Reassured that all was in readiness,
Arturo primed himself for the task at hand.

"One other question, Mr. Diggs," Sally
asked, still reviewing the chart, "if we left the
engine on during the coast phase, would the
Jana exceed the speed of light?"

"No, she wouldn't." Arturo replied. The
three quizzical expressions made a further explanation necessary. "You see, the ship can't go
faster than the Massafon particles, which by
their very nature travel at 300,000 kilometers
per second and no more, no less."

"So the speed of light is the maximum
the engine will ever achieve?"

"Yes," he answered directly, not wishing
to go into the possibilities of how to exceed the
speed of light. "One thing at a time, one thing

at a time. Right now our goal is to achieve the speed of light." With thumbs up, and a broad smile, Arturo commanded, "All right team, let's go to work."

All checkouts of the *Jana* had been completed and the mirrors meticulously installed. Arturo began voice entering the final check sheet summary into the computer records.

"Cold fusion reactor operating normally..."

"Rubyionium gas laser electron gun charged and normal..."

"Posafon and Negafon mirrors set for optimum null positions..."

"Computer and feedback program to null the mirrors within one thousandth of a micron set and tested..."

"Wagon-wheels operating normally at zero and programmed five second increments of .1% each to 1% and then 1% steps to the maximum of 40% power required for the vehicle to reach light speed..."

"Initial power levels set at one-tenth percent..."

"Telemetry and computer recorders operating to requirements..."

"All auxiliary power supplies fully charged..."

"Vector control ion engines sequence normal..."

"Flight profile computer checked and sequenced..."

"Shutdown and safety systems engaged..."

"Vehicle signal receivers and antenna engaged..."

"History of the vehicle, *Jana*, and her origin in the safety box..."

Arturo paused at the last voice log. He had taken the precaution of enclosing a history of the *Jana* and her planet and solar system origin in a fireproof and practically indestructible container. He had also placed glass photographs, 3-D holograms of items he deemed important and computer chips of scientific equations. The final item placed in the box was a hologram of him, standing along side the *Jana*. Just before he closed the container, a thought struck him. Also included was a hologram of Jana, Filip, Marsh and himself standing in front of their house. If the *Jana* went astray and was discovered in another solar system or even in a galaxy other than their own Milky Way, the origin and Earth's civilization could hopefully be understood.

The check sheet summary was finished and the *Jana* was ready for flight test.

"Station Control, this is Arturo Diggs at Jana Control. All checkouts are complete on the *Jana*. She's ready for flight test."

"Roger, Jana Control. We confirm your launch window of 1100 hours in exactly five hours and forty minutes. Will you be ready by then?" Station Control inquired.

"Roger. That's affirmative, Station Control. We'll use the remote arm to position her."

"That's a roger, Jana Control. Good luck on the new hotshot personnel shuttle. We need all we can get. Be sure she's floating free before engine initiation. Otherwise if she's still connected to the remote arm, the center tube will spin like a top," Station Control cautioned.

"That's a big roger, Station Control. We'll make sure that she's free before ignition." Arturo winked at his three techs and got back a cocky thumbs-up sign.

"Good luck, Mr. Diggs," Control said in an unemotional voice.

The remaining time to launch went quickly as all monitoring recorders and the *Jana's* various power supplies were integrated and fired up. The remote arm was engaged just as Arturo and the three technicians had executed so many times in rehearsal. A final dry run sequence of events was conducted. All equipment showed green lights. The onboard artificial intelligence computer had voice capability, which would announce key events as they happened. Arturo had programmed the voice as a time saving backup to the voluminous data that would be recorded on the many recording chips. Routine key points would be transmitted immediately and, most importantly, if any problem occurred, the AI computer would immediately announce the same. This would allow for extra split seconds of time to respond instead of having to discern the problem and take corrective action from the monitored and recorded telemetry data.

Arturo watched through the view port, as the remote arm swung the *Jana* into position away from the space station. The lead technician released the arm's grip and the *Jana* was floating free. Quickly re-engaging the arm, the ship once again was held captive. Arturo thought, "She wants to fly. I can feel it. God, after all these years — the moment of truth."

"Five minutes and counting," the senior tech intoned.

Thoughts were racing through Arturo's mind, many which had nothing to do with the impending launch of the *Jana*. He remembered the 304-year-old legacy of old Newsome. Arturo could recite the entire legacy, word for word. Mentally he recalled a part to himself.

> *"Trips within our solar system will be child's play compared to the conquest of the stars and galaxies of stars which are many light years away, indeed hundreds, thousands, millions and even billions of light years beyond Earth. My chosen descendent will leave another legacy for his descendants to follow: the means for achieving and going beyond the speed of light, and thereby exceed it by a ratio approaching infinity. Then and only then can mankind know the universe."*

Then Ben's legacy ran through his mind. In particular he remembered the part about photon energy.

> **"Since photons travel at the speed of light, the key is to use them for rocket propulsion. Yes, use what is thought of to-**

day as a weightless particle without dimensions, with zero rest mass. To obtain the energy required, you must develop a method of splitting the photon. The resultant energy released must be harnessed and used to push a manned rocket to the stars. Don't let scientific naysayers tell you that energy will not be released. It will occur; in the same way that energy was released by the gamma photon during the formation of the universe. The photon is made up of particles yet to be discovered and will not be discovered until the above is accomplished."

Arturo knew he had misunderstood the rejoining of the Posafons and Negafons to obtain energy release and had pursued the wrong path for too long a time. He mentally recalled more of Ben's legacy.

"During the rejoining of the split photons, you will have accomplished the same effect as the elusive 'antimatter versus matter' effect that has long been sought but without success."

Arturo smiled as the legacies of his ancestors raced through his memory. He almost laughed when he remembered that he expected the energy release from splitting photons, instead of the rejoining them through collisions. Old Ben had been on the right track, but he could not carry out the experiments with what, to Arturo, was archaic equipment. It wasn't Ben's fault. He suggested the rejoining of the photons, but didn't understand what the results would be. No matter, Arturo himself had discovered the energy release through the accidental collision at the laser facility. Thoughts of how those great men had prophesied the speed of light and how to achieve it ran through his head. And now it was in his hands and his alone.

He was abruptly interrupted in his reverie.

"Thirty seconds and counting, Mr. Diggs," the senior tech announced, her voice precise and calm.

Out of habitual custom, Arturo's hands immediately reached toward the console and the switch for the voice command computer. He watched the seconds tick off on the counter in front of him. When the counter registered zero he gave a loud and firm command. "Initiate engine sequence! 2146379 alpha omega." The latter numbers and words were solely known by him, and had to be uttered in his precise voice wave, before the computer would accept the "initiate" command. Alpha omega, "the beginning and the end" had seemed fitting when he chose the codes.

The remote arm released its grip on the *Jana* and swung out of the way, leaving the ship floating free in space. He automatically began calling out the sequence of events registering on the monitor screens.

"Reactor and laser energized…"

"Wagon-wheels at zero opening and spinning normally..."

"Massafon level is zero, normal..."

"All data parameters normal and the Massafon Engine is stabilized at zero thrust..."

Convinced that everything was operating as required and that the moment of truth was at hand, Arturo gave the final command necessary to begin flight of the *Jana*.

"One tenth per cent power on my mark," he said softly to the relay computer. With a final check of all the operating parameters, he called out, "Now!"

The master clock on the wall read 1100 hours.

Arturo's "now" command allowed the counter rotating wagon wheels to open slightly and allow one tenth percent of the Negafon beam to pass and collide with the Posafon beam. The remaining Negafon particles were absorbed harmlessly in the black part of the spokes in the wheel.

In spite of his concentration while watching the *Jana* slowly move away, he had a fleeting thought regarding how old Newsome had signed his legacy: "*Newsome Diggs, ∞ Beginning 1800-1888*," with "*∞ Beginning*," underlined with a flourish on each end. "Infinite Beginning," he thought, "what did it mean?" Pushing the thought from his head, his eyes were riveted on the vehicle as it picked up speed and went out of his sight.

Along with the three technicians, Arturo began monitoring the recorders and listening to the onboard computer monotone voice as it announced key events.

"Massafon Engine now at full power. Vehicle continuing to accelerate. Posafon and Negafon beam diameters maximum at 2,000 microns."

"Speed 10,000 kilometers per hour and accelerating. All systems normal."

"Speed 100,000 kilometers per hour and accelerating. All systems normal."

"Speed 500,000 kilometers per hour and accelerating. All systems normal."

"Speed 1,100,000 kilometers per hour and accelerating."

Arturo was fully aware that the computer voice he heard was delayed more and more as the Jana went further and further away from the space station. Just over five minutes later, the computer voice began again.

"Massafon Engine operating normally at a speed of 3000 kilometers per second and accelerating."

Arturo had programmed the computer to announce speed in kilometers per second after reaching 10 million kilometers per hour. Fifty minutes later the voice began again.

"Speed 30,000 kilometers per second and accelerating."

The unemotional computer voice relayed messages of increasing speed and vehicle status. Time between the voice transmissions continued to increase from minutes to hours, as the Jana went further and further away from the space station.

A few minutes over 12 hours later the voice resumed.

"Speed 285,000 kilometers per second and accelerating. All systems normal."

The moment of truth. Would the *Jana* reach the speed of light, c, of 300,000 kilometers per second?

Arturo appreciated that to reach c, the *Jana* didn't depend as much on power level, as on the time required at a constant propulsive force pushing a given vehicle weight. He and the technicians were carefully monitoring the speed increases versus time. After all, the Massafon Engine had primary benefit only in the solar system. Even at the speed of light, it would take 4.3 years to reach Proxima Centauri, the nearest star, a round trip time of almost 8.6 years. It was not a practical travel time but one that mankind would eventually endure. But tomorrow, that was a different story. Tomorrow, he'd exceed light speed to reach the stars more quickly. His only concern was, "When was tomorrow?"

The computer voice droned on. "Speed 298,000 kilometers per second and accelerating. All systems normal." Two and a half minutes passed before the transmissions began again at 10-second intervals.

"Speed 299,500 kilometers per second."
"Speed 299,600..."
"Speed 299,700..."
"Speed 299,800..."
"Speed 299,900..."

Arturo watched the instruments, knowing in his own mind that if light speed had been reached, it had happened four hours and fifteen minutes ago because of the signal transmission time to reach the space station. The computer had already instructed the Massafon Engine to shutdown and to begin the coast period and turnaround for the deceleration phase. He scrutinized the hours old data, listening with guarded anticipation for the computer voice to resume. Ten seconds later the systematic voice rewarded him.

"Light speed achieved. Speed 300,000 kilometers per second. All systems normal. No observed change in the vehicle, vehicle components or the beryllium test bar. Visual atomic clock running normal and indicating elapsed time to c of 8 hours, 30 minutes and 45 seconds. Massafon Engine shut down per program. Initiating turnaround of the vehicle and one hour coast period at c."

The master clock on the wall read 2345 hours. The hologram representation of the flight showed a solid line to the first large dot.

Arturo gave a loud war whoop, shouting, "We did it. We did it."

The three technicians all shook his hand, and there was general jubilation in the control room as the realization of the momentous event actually sunk in. Arturo's exhilaration never overrode his anxiety to hear the next computer voice report of the *Jana* being turned around from her headlong flight path and begin slowing down from light speed to start the trip back to the space station.

After watching the instruments and listening for the onboard computer voice for almost 13 hours, Arturo suddenly felt drained.

Two hours later the computer voice returned.

"Coast period at 300,000 kilometers per second is completed and the vehicle has been turned around."

"Massafon Engine engaged at full power to terminate forward light speed velocity. Expected time to zero velocity is 8.5 hours. All systems functioning normally."

The master clock read 0145 hours. The hologram representation of the flight showed a solid line to the second large dot.

"I can't wait to read the data. What an achievement you've made Mr. Diggs," one of technicians said with a happy smile on his normally serious face.

"She's not home yet. We've got another twelve and three quarter hours before hearing that the vehicle is on the way home. Let's save our celebration until the *Jana* is safely docked and secured by the remote arm. Then we'll really have a party, the like of which..." Arturo stopped in mid-sentence as the onboard computer voice recommenced.

"Malfunction. Malfunction of the Posafon mirror. Beam is passing through mirror and impinging on the carbon trap..."

The pronouncement, coming from the static unemotional voice, sounded all the more awesome. Arturo and the technicians physically blanched.

"Initiating Massafon Engine shutdown..."

"Reorienting Posafon mirror to valid reflective area..."

All their faces showed apprehension at what would or could possibly be the next message. The seconds seemed like hours as they vainly waited for the computer voice to proceed.

Nervously, Arturo darted to the data readout of the mirror position and, with relief saw that the orientation was being automatically adjusted. Quickly transferring the incoming information to the hologram model of the Massafon Engine, he anxiously watched as the mirror was moved to allow the simulated Posafon and Negafon beams to again impinge. At that moment the computer voice resumed its monotone.

"Posafon mirror reset to new reflective area..."

"Initiating Massafon Engine restart..."

The two or three seconds that passed seemed an eternity to Arturo as he anxiously watched the hologram model and the data.

"Massafon Engine at full power and operating normally..."

"Speed 295,000 kilometers per second and decreasing..."

"All systems normal..."

Arturo wiped the beads of perspiration from his forehead while studying the incoming data. Knotting his brow, he scrutinized the hologram and saw that the Massafon Engine was again operating as predicted.

With a heartened half-smile, he commented to the silent technicians, "Well, folks, we have two more positions available on the Posafon mirror. Let's hope we don't need them."

Data continued to be recorded on the portable chips that Arturo intended to take back to his own computer to be thoroughly analyzed after the mission. There was nothing that either Arturo or the technicians could do now but wait. As they sat patiently in front of their data consoles, lack of sleep and tension made their eyes blurry and heads drop forward in exhaustion. Though they all tried not to give in to their weariness, it was only when an arresting piece of data was received that they stirred from their catnapping to take note.

Exactly eleven and three quarter hours later, Sally, while monitoring the visual readout, excitedly called out, "Mr. Diggs, the vehicle has slowed to zero forward velocity."

At that moment, the computer monotone voice began speaking.

"Forward velocity is zero. Distance traveled 10.3 billion kilometers..."

"Turning vehicle and preparing for the return trip..."

"Massafon Engine engaged and operating at full power..."

It was the vital message all had been waiting, and cause for a loud cheer from everyone.

The master clock read 1430 hours in the afternoon. The hologram representation of the flight showed a solid line to the third and last large dot.

"She's on the way home. Congratulations again, Mr. Diggs." And Sally made a ceremony

236

of proudly crossing off the 1430 hours time on the chart. Turning to the small group, she announced, "Next key message on the chart will be at 1845 hours, which means that she's been through the coast phase at c and beginning the deceleration phase for home."

Wearily rising from his chair, Arturo held up his hand in counsel, "Remember now, the *Jana's* real position is at the final deceleration point not at the initial deceleration point."

But the techs were not to be denied their euphoria at hearing the *Jana* was on the way home. They all but ignored Arturo's words of wariness.

Half an hour passed and the mood was still elated until the computer voice boomed out another dire message.

"Malfunction. Malfunction of the Posafon mirror. Beam is passing through mirror and..."

"Initiating Massafon Engine shutdown... "

"Posafon mirror reset to new reflective area..."

"One more area available..."

"Initiating Massafon Engine restart..."

An eternity seemed to pass as Arturo anxiously watched the hologram model while the technicians monitored the incoming data, nervously awaiting the subsequent missive from the computer voice.

"Massafon Engine at full power and operating normally..."

"Speed 17,676 kilometers per second and increasing..."

"All systems normal..."

Arturo shouted into the hologram, "Quick, enlarge the Posafon mirror representation."

When the holographic image of the mirror reached a meter in diameter, he shouted, "Stop. Hold it right there." His eyes narrowed in scrutiny at the floating but stationary mirror facsimile. Two small holes surrounded by blackened crinkled material were all too apparent. It was obvious that if the mirror suffered another burn-through, it might not be able to be repositioned again to a clean reflective area. The blackened area was larger than Arturo had anticipated. In desperation he began furiously reworking the positioning program, in the eventuality it would be needed. Completing the necessary adjustments, he began rapidly giving commands to the computer to instruct it to transmit his revised program to the *Jana*.

For the next four hours, the technicians completely forgot about their lack of sleep as they anxiously monitored the never-ending stream of data. Arturo tried to predict every conceivable contingency as his eyes riveted, almost hypnotically, to the hologram of the Massafon Engine.

The computer voice began relaying information in such a rapid sequence, that the words almost ran together. "Speed 300,000 kilometers per second. All systems normal, entering coast phase. Massafon Engine shut down as per program. Vehicle turned around for slow down and docking program..."

This was the message sent at the start of the coast phase after attaining c and would travel the same speed as the vehicle. Now the deceleration message would be received at almost the same time.

"Coast phase complete, energizing Massafon Engine for deceleration phase..."

"Massafon Engine operating at full power..."

"Speed decreasing..."

"All systems normal..."

The master clock read 1845 hours. The hologram representation of the flight showed the return trip as a parallel solid line from the last large dot to the second and third large dots.

Arturo's entire focus was sealed on the holographic representation of the Posafon mirror. The Posafon beam shown clearly, radiating back in the third reflective clean area. Moving his mouth wordlessly, he tried to impose by sheer will that the mirror operate without burning out. More than three hours had passed since the computer voice had reported, and when a short crackle emanated from the speaker, everyone in the room turned in anticipation.

"Malfunction. Malfunction of the Posafon mirror..."

"Resetting mirror to new position using updated program..."

"Engaging engine..."

With a pounding heart, Arturo watched the Posafon beam reflect on the mirror, but only partially impinge on the Negafon beam. It

239

was all too obvious that the required full impingement was simply not occurring. Powerless to make an adjustment, his hands clenched helplessly; then his eyes widened in alarm as he detected a barely discernible shift of the mirror. Any movement of the mirror, even negligible, could only mean one thing; the vehicle had changed its course, be it ever so slight. At that precise moment he saw the Posafon beam breakup on the mirror and, instead of a solid beam, the reflection scattered. The computer voice, in its annoying monotone, came through the speaker.

"Posafon beam has broken up. Shutting down Massafon Engine..."

"Speed is one-half light at 150,000 kilometers per second..."

The tech monitoring the flight path data and hologram, called out, "Mr. Diggs, the flight path has been altered, not much, but definitely altered, sir."

Arturo didn't waste a second and issued terse commands. "Quickly, plug in the current data to the hologram. Bring up the prevailing flight path on the large monitor screen. Cross reference all the displays." Then more to himself than the others, he said grimly, "At the current speed of the *Jana*, she'll pass the solar system planetary orbits in an hour."

The technicians rapidly began their assignments, checking the data and ordering the computers to plot the new course. The altered route change was in the thousands of a second of arc, but even such a small variation could drastically vary the intended flyby distances from the orbiting planets. There was possible danger. Although the odds against impacting a planet was practically astronomical, Arturo's mood was still of concern as he studied the hologram mirror and gave commands to the computer. From the incoming data, he hastily calculated that it would take approximately 35 minutes for his reprogrammed mirror positioning to contact the *Jana.* If the vehicle continued at her present speed of half c, she'd reach Earth's orbit in just over 50 minutes. He now had only 15 minutes in which to find a position on the mirror, which would allow the Massafon Engine to operate and slow down the vehicle for docking at the space station.

"Mr. Diggs," Sally had to almost shout to be heard above all the activity, "the flight path appears to be on a direct collision course with the Moon!"

Arturo's mind jumped at the fateful announcement. The mere possibility of the *Jana* hitting the Moon shattered his concentration. The force on impact, at even half-light speed, would be the equivalent of over 25,000 of 50-megaton hydrogen bombs. The Moon would undoubtedly break up in a violent explosion and inflict mass devastation on Earth and its population. Momentarily, he stood seized in a waking nightmare, envisioning massive Moon chunks hurtling through the atmosphere and hitting Earth with explosive forces which were heretofore undreamed. Even if Earth were not hit, the breakup of the Moon could change Earth's north south tilt, or even its orbit around the sun. Life was so very fragile, delicately balanced between temperature extremes and gravity. The impact of such a catastrophe struck him with such force that tears welled in his eyes at the thought.

Forcibly thrusting this horrendous possibility from his mind, he regained his composure and returned to issuing rapid commands to the computer. Unless the Massafon Engine was engaged, there was no way he could change the flight path. Any thought of returning the *Jana* to the intended space station had vanished. His only objective now was to again get the engine operational and correct the course.

Concentrating his full attention on the holographic mirror image, he decided to input three different positions, trying each in order, with the full knowledge that he only had one chance for success. Arturo had no idea which one would work, if any. Time now was of the essence. He had done all he could do in the remaining minutes. Taking a deep breath, he forced himself to calmly begin instructing the computer to relay the three positioning programs to the *Jana's* main computer and to the backup computer. His final command was the flight path deviation so the *Jana* would pass far from Earth, the Moon and all planets orbiting the sun.

Forty-five tense minutes elapsed before the monotone of the computer voice began its announcements to the hushed and waiting group.

"New positioning program received and on line..."

"New position of the Posafon mirror achieved..."

"Engaging Massafon Engine..."

Arturo watched the holographic mirror image intently as the Posafon beam reflected off the mirror. The still blackened area began to grow until it was in the beam's primary reflective area. The beam instantly broke up as the computer voice began relaying the results.

"Massafon Engine shut down..."

There was an anxious pause before the voice resumed.

"Mirror repositioned to second area of choice..."

"Engaging Massafon Engine..."

To Arturo's dismay, the Posafon beam briefly reflected from the holographic mirror image, then scattered. The computer voice relayed the results.

"Massafon Engine shut down..."

"Flight path on collision course with the Moon..."

The senior tech, with undisguised alarm in her voice, shouted, "The vehicle will impact the Moon in two minutes and 18 seconds. There is now no question about it. The *Jana* is on a direct flight path to the Moon and..." She looked to Arturo for any direction or action that could avert the impending disaster.

Before Arturo could reply or even gather his frantic thoughts, the computer voice interrupted.

"Speed 149,486 kilometers per second..."

"Mirror repositioned to the third area of choice..."

"Engaging Massafon Engine..."

"Vehicle slowing..."

"Engaging directional control engines..."

"Course changed by five degrees as directed...

"Neither the Moon nor any other planet now on direct collision course..."

"Vehicle continuing to decelerate..."

The master clock read 2157 hours. The hologram representation of the flight displayed a solid line passing close to the last large dot representing Earth and the space station.
The room echoed with sighs of relief.

The unemotional computer voice again began broadcasting.

"Speed 147,644 kilometers per second and decelerating..."

"Passing the space station and Earth..."

Though the four knew they would not be able to actually glimpse the *Jana,* since she was traveling at almost half light speed, human reflex made each of them instinctively look out the view port. There was nothing save the blackness of space and the shine of distant stars. As each person contemplated the terrible disaster that could have occurred, there was an eerie silence in the room.

"Mr. Diggs," Sally finally broke the silence, "the world will never know just how close it came to possible oblivion." She stopped and turned to look at Arturo. "And how it was your last minute work that diverted the *Jana* to a new course. I suggest that none of us ever discuss what happened, to anyone, not even our families."

Taken aback, Arturo stared blankly at his senior technician. It took him a moment before he could answer. "It wouldn't be proper to conceal such an event, Sally." He hesitated, and the three techs respectfully waited for him to continue. "But, I do have a grave concern. Public reaction to such a potential catastrophe could possibly destroy any future trials for operational space vehicles at light speed."

"We know that, Mr. Diggs," the younger of the techs spoke up. "We know that," he repeated with conviction, as his coworkers nodded their heads in agreement. "You see, working with you to achieve the speed of light has been the most gratifying task any of us has ever undertaken. We're a part of helping achieve success."

"If word gets out," Sally injected with determination, "it won't be from us. We want to see your work, and our work, succeed. We didn't design the vehicle. But, we did build it and test it."

The elder of the male techs purposefully cleared his throat. "Don't you see, Mr. Diggs? The *Jana* and future *Janas* are as much a part of us as they are of you." Feeling perhaps he'd overstepped his bounds, he quickly added, "In different ways of course but, nevertheless, a part."

When Arturo didn't respond, Sally added with passion in her voice, "If you don't say anything, we won't."

Moved by the spontaneous outpouring of support, Arturo stood silent as each technician nodded approval. Then one by one they rose, holding out their right hands to seal the bargain of silence. Wordlessly taking each outstretched hand in turn between both of his, the agreement was validated. No word or discussion would ever be spoken by these three techs regarding the averted catastrophe.

None of the crewmembers wanted to be the first to break the solemn mood, and so it was up to Arturo to take the lead. "Okay, everyone, let's get cracking and plot new flight paths to return the Jana home after she comes to a complete stop."

Immediately everyone reverted back to his or her duties as if nothing had happened. The entire group knew that it would take just under four hours and fifteen minutes for the Jana to again reach zero forward velocity. If the Posafon mirror didn't burn out, the vehicle could be turned and headed back to the space station. As the three techs worked on their assigned functions, Arturo preoccupied himself with the holographic representation of the Posafon mirror. The more he analyzed the burned-out areas and the reflected Posafon beam, the more he realized what his decision would ultimately have to be.

Time seemed to pass slowly for the technicians as they chatted and monitored the Jana's deceleration; but Arturo, deep in thought and mental calculations, didn't seem to notice. It was only when he walked over to them with a somber expression on his face that their chatter abruptly came to a halt.

"Since all of you, as you said," pointedly repeating their words, "'are as much a part of

246

the *Jana* as I,' it's only right that you should be a part of a decision, or if you will, a recommendation I have to make."

The technicians swiveled around in their chairs to give Arturo full concentration.

"I don't believe we can take the chance of trying to bring the Jana back to the space station at velocities reaching 75,000 kilometers per second."

A look of disbelief crossed each face, and Sally opened her mouth as if to protest. Arturo held up his hand for silence. "If the mirror burns through again at that velocity, we won't have another chance at repositioning. If the *Jana* hit Earth or anything else, such as the space station, at that velocity the energy release would be over 3,000 of 50-megaton hydrogen bombs. We can't take that chance. She would again have an uncontrollable flight path."

The techs shot furtive glances at each other; the acute disappointment was obvious on their faces. "For the past hour I've studied the mirror image and there simply isn't an area left that can be depended upon to reflect the Posafon beam properly." Arturo moved to a small worktable, motioning them to join him as he sat down.

The chief technician walked over to the hologram of the engine and examined the mirror closely. With a resigned sigh, she glanced back at her coworkers; her head nodded in agreement.

"What do you wish to do, Mr. Diggs?" the youngest tech inquired.

"When the *Jana* decelerates fully and stops her forward velocity, she'll be just over a billion kilometers from Earth. If the Massafon Engine is set for a max velocity of 40 kilometers per second, or 144,000 kilometers per hour, she'll reach Earth in just under 11 months and we could pick her up."

The techs had braced themselves for the worst scenario, but this was a much more positive solution than they had envisioned.

Encouraged by their reception of his plan, Arturo quickly elaborated. "If she did have a flight path towards something like a space station, we'd have time to move it out of the way or use the guidance thrusters to change her flight path, which would work at that low velocity."

He stopped to give them a chance to comprehend the proposal, then looking squarely at each technician in turn, asked, "What do you think?"

There was little question that they approved Arturo's plan, but it was Sally who spoke for the group. "All right, Mr. Diggs. We'll get her back, one way or another."

Without another word, they returned to their instruments and began monitoring the *Jana's* progress.

Three uneventful hours passed, only the voice computer broke the monotony with terse messages of deceleration and vehicle system reports. Glancing at the master clock, Arturo announced, "The *Jana* should be at zero velocity by now, but we won't hear for almost an hour."

A few seconds before the scheduled time, they all stopped what they were doing to listen for the computer voice to begin its recount.

"Malfunction. Engagement of the Massafon Engine has malfunctioned..."

They all froze. The message was harrowing, but it was the bland delivery that was insufferable.

"Malfunction of the Posafon mirror..."

"Engine shutdown completed..."

"Posafon mirror has shattered...

"Speed 97,000 kilometers per hour..."

Dashing over to the holographic mirror image, Arturo's heart sank when he saw it was gone. Only the mirror retainer was visible. Deftly punching in the coordinates to enable the hologram image to cover the engine compartment, he watched pieces of the shattered mirror floating around. There was absolutely no chance of restarting the Massafon Engine.

The master clock read 0204 hours.

"Damn, so close," Arturo muttered, expressing aloud what everyone was feeling.

There was no recourse now; the *Jana* was going to be lost. There was no possible way to slow her down. She would continue on into deep space, veering only when acceding to gravitational pull while passing close to another large planet or star somewhere in the far reaches of their own Milky Way galaxy.

The *Jana* would travel forever at 97,000 kilometers per hour, just like a beam of light from a distant star or galaxy, but at a lower speed of almost 27 kilometers per second.

Arturo knew that the chances of hitting a star or planet in the galaxy were less than one in a billion; but even if the ship did impact, little surface damage would be incurred. Still, he was glad he had placed on board her history and other material identifying Earth and civilization.

The computer voice droned on with continuous announcements, but for the little group, there was no interest if recovery was not possible.

The *Jana* was irrevocably lost in space.

Dutifully, but with a heavy heart, Arturo notified Station Control that the *Jana* had malfunctioned and would not be returning to the space station. Brushing aside their questions, he requested a shuttle take him back to San Diego as soon as possible. A cheerless mood hung around the room as Arturo tried in vain to console both himself and the techs for the loss of the *Jana.*

"It was a great job. Thank you for all your help." Individually shaking each hand, he endeavored to keep his voice cheerful. "We'll do it again, after those damn mirrors are fixed."

"Yes sir, Mr. Diggs. We'll build another one and do it again. Just call us, and we'll be there."

Arturo put the data chips in his briefcase, gave a wave, and headed for the shuttle bay.

The following day, an eager group sat around the table in Arturo's study and listened to his

summary of the flight of the *Jana* and to portions of the voice recorder. Jana and Marsh
were exuberant in spite of the loss of the ship.
But the increasingly grim look on Arturo's face
prompted Mohammed Nahal to sense that
something was amiss. Casually he rose and
good-naturedly slapped his trusted friend on
the back, but Arturo didn't even notice.

"History was made yesterday." Mohammed made a slight bow to Jana, "Mrs. Diggs,
your man did it and you never complained during the long hours he devoted to the project.
The ship was honored by having your name
grace it, my dear." Turning, he tapped his forehead in salute, "And Marsh, you never lost
faith. You continued to contribute your vast
knowledge in the calculations and reviewing of
the programs."

Marsh and Jana smiled at their compli-
ments, but Mohammed was saving the choice
praise for Arturo. "And you, my friend, knew
you were right in spite of the naysayers, and
you demonstrated it. The speed of light was
definitely achieved by the *Jana*." Mohammed's
face beamed; even Arturo, in spite of himself,
had to grin back. "What an accomplishment.
Damn me to hell!" Catching himself and
quickly apologizing, "Excuse me, Jana, but I'm
so proud of what you've done, Arturo, I could
just burst."

Jana glanced at her watch, stood up, and
walked over to her husband and kissed him on
the cheek. "I know you three are anxious to
look at the data in more detail. I'd love to listen
in, but I have a book deadline to meet." She

kissed Marsh and Mohammed, and then just before leaving the room, teasingly called over her shoulder, "Now, don't you guys get so involved that you forget we're having a celebration dinner tonight, particularly since I'm personally doing the cooking."

The door had no sooner closed behind Jana than the three men began their detailed review of the recorded data. Inserting the recorder chips into his computer, Arturo flipped on the large view screen. As the immense amount of data began scrolling, he issued voice commands for the various calculations. It didn't take anyone long to verify that the Posafon mirror had a definite burn-through, causing the Massafon Engine to malfunction.

It was the contrast between the space station atomic clock and the *Jana*'s atomic clock of the elapsed time to light speed that caused Marsh to speculate. "The space station atomic clock shows an elapsed time of eight hours, 36 minutes and 45 seconds to light speed, the same as the voice computer and the recorded data. I thought time slowed down as light speed was approached."

"On the one hand," Arturo theorized, "it would appear that Einstein's theory is correct. Time does slow down as one approaches light speed. But when it is achieved, the clocks reset themselves to normal when acceleration ceases. The space station elapsed time and the voice elapsed time agree."

"Which, of course, says," Marsh conjectured, "that time does not slow down at light speed."

252

"Look at the data," Mohammed gestured toward the screen. "You can see the onboard atomic clocks slowing down and finally stopping for a nanosecond, but when c is achieved, they reset themselves to normal, the correct time."

"So acceleration of the vehicle," Marsh absently stroked his beard, "or anything with mass is what makes the data verify Einstein's formula."

"Right!" Arturo agreed. "But, at light speed, and no acceleration, all data returns to normal."

"So I guess if I want to live forever," Marsh laughed heartily, "I should travel at 99.9999% the speed of light."

Both Arturo and Mohammed chuckled at the analogy, but it was the chairman who first spoke, "Not so sure about that, Marsh. Remember it's all relative to who is monitoring what."

"That crossed my mind while we were waiting for the last transmission from the *Jana*," Arturo conceded. "In fact, you both are right. It all depends on your relative position."

"I should have known you'd already have had that figured out," Mohammed grinned.

Arturo opened his mouth to expand his theory further, but Marsh interrupted. "If I may, Arturo. The onboard computer read the clock in the *Jana*'s real time and transmitted what it saw, the elapsed time it observed onboard the ship. The elapsed time telemetered to us, is the difference that we, and our space station instruments, observed and recorded. We, and the instruments, think time slowed. In reality it didn't slowdown onboard the *Jana*. Stated another way, the time difference is relative to the position of who is measuring it, but the actual elapsed times are the same."

Marsh paused, his penetrating eyes boring into Arturo. "I assume you agree, Arturo?"

"Yes, Marsh, your explanation is exactly what I deduced."

Mohammed drummed his fingernails on the desk. "So the theory used by so many 'learned scientists' that if a man traveled for ten years at light speed and returned to Earth, his children would be ten years older, but he may have aged physically only a month or so...is false?" he questioned.

"It's false and also true." Arturo augmented his speculation. "When said voyager returned to Earth, you would see that they both aged equally. However, if the voyager could be seen through a telescope when he was five or 10 light-years from Earth, you would see him as he was five or ten years previously and he would appear to be younger than them by five or ten years."

"Because," Marsh, always the teacher, excitedly interrupted, "it would take that long for the light of his image to reach those on Earth. The speed of light is constant at 300,000 kilometers per second as proved by many, including Einstein. But his equations have been wrongly interpreted," and he slapped his leg with a resounding thud, "as we now know."

Mohammed did not try to get into the two-sided conversation, choosing just to listen as Arturo expounded on Marsh's thoughts. "Einstein himself said that all things in time and space are relative. The time difference is proof of that. He was right, and you hit it right on the head, Marsh, interpretation of what he said...was wrong."

"I'm just a poor struggling young propulsion engineer," Mohammed pathetically whined, "and don't understand all these far-out theories."

"Poor struggling young engineer, my butt!" Arturo snorted.

"Yeah, and with a mind like a steel trap," Marsh guffawed.

"All right, then," Mohammed bounced back, "explain the review of the beryllium bar data."

All were aware that Arturo had placed a ten-centimeter diameter by one-meter long beryllium bar onboard for the purpose of measuring any change in size or mass as the *Jana* approached and achieved light speed. It was to test his theory of whether or not mass became greater and physical size of an object became smaller as the established theories predicted.

Using a computer pointer, Arturo ran through the data diagram on the monitor. "This shows the bar almost vanishing just before the speed of light and the recorder reading the mass of the bar went off scale, but the onboard computer voice said no changes took place. It said everything was normal. The data also shows the bar returning to normal at c."

Marsh rolled his chair closer to the monitor screen, and thrusting his head forward, peered through his half-glasses. "It's the same phenomena as the elapsed travel time measured from two different viewpoints. Again, what is observed in real time aboard the *Jana* while approaching c — versus what we observe is happening to the ship from our perspective — shows up as different measurements."

Mohammed nodded his head in agreement. "In other words, if we could see the *Jana* approaching light speed, she would appear to get smaller and smaller and then vanish as she achieved it. We would also think that its mass would become infinite." He whistled through his teeth at the revelation. "From our perspective of what we would measure, and the accepted theories of Einstein, its mass would become infinite. But the people on board would not see or feel any changes to themselves or the ship."

"I believe that to be the case, Mohammed," Arturo observed.

The men had been so engrossed in their intense discussions and data review that they were unaware of the passing hours. Jana, for some time had been quietly standing at the open door to Arturo's study. When her voice suddenly broke into their conversation, they were caught unawares.

"Excuse me, gentlemen, I think I understand what you're saying, but I don't understand why. The accepted theories say that light speed can't be achieved because of the infinite energy required to push an ever-increasing mass to light speed, yet Arturo, you have achieved it."

"It's all relative, Jana," Marsh responded.

Arturo walked over to his wife and took her hand and led her into the room. "Let me try to explain it this way, darling. If you could see the ship through a powerful telescope as it approached light speed, it would appear to become smaller and smaller. Then if you could have weighted the ship, it would appear to increase its mass greater and greater as the ship became smaller and smaller." He smiled, as if the explanation was all she needed. "On the flip side, if you had been aboard, you would have neither seen nor felt a change."

Jana smiled, "Thank you, Arturo." Then she shook her head. "But, I still don't understand."

"Come here, my dear," and Marsh motioned her to be seated beside him and turned to Arturo. "If I may be so presumptuous, my friend?" he asked.

"Of course, Professor," Arturo gestured for him to take over.

"Jana," Marsh explained, "Einstein's theory is correct when based on the supposition that anything with mass cannot achieve or travel at the speed of light. And he was right. What he didn't know is that photons, which are the only things known to man to be able to travel at light speed, can be split. Neither he nor anyone else ever dreamed of being able to split a dimensionless and zero rest mass particle."

"No one but old Ben," Jana injected, "and you, Arturo. Then she turned apologetically to

Marsh. "I'm sorry, Marsh dear, please go ahead. I'm listening."

Marsh smiled and resumed his explanation. "When the split Posafons and Negafons collide at light speed and in essence create a new and heretofore unknown particle, the Massafon, the previous theory went out the window." He paused, and then seeing a glint of understanding in Jana's eye, pressed forward. "So, my dear, a particle with weight and energy such as the Massafon can travel at light speed, bringing in a whole new set of equations to be pondered over and committed to the written word."

Mohammed, listening intently, volunteered, "Einstein was right, in so far as he knew. Nothing could travel at light speed because of insufficient energy to overcome the presumed ever increasing mass as a vehicle went faster and faster. As Marsh said, 'all previous theory went out the window with Arturo's discovery of the Massafon particle'."

"But how does mass increase and size get smaller?" Jana asked, trying to fully comprehend the phenomenon being described.

At this point, both Marsh and Mohammed yielded the floor to Arturo.

Kneeling beside his wife, Arturo collected his thoughts before beginning the complex explanation. "It's like the clock problem I mentioned to you before, Jana; being relative to one's position when observing the actions of an item approaching light speed and achieving it. To the observer, the theories are right and Einstein's calculations prove it. Mass does increase and size does get smaller. But, and this is a gigantic but, to those on board a vehicle such as the *Jana,* no changes of mass or size are felt or observed."

Jana took a deep breath and asked, "Then what you're telling me is, that without the Massafon being harnessed for propulsive power, mankind would never be able to achieve light speed? And that no source of energy would be available to overcome the increasing mass problem?"

"Exactly, darling," Arturo answered, proud of his wife's grasp of the solution. "Only a particle with mass and the resultant energy that travels the speed of light can be harnessed to obtain enough energy to achieve c." He slowly rose, gesturing to the others, "And we in this room have the secret to the Massafon particle."

"Lover," Jana interceded, "just one more question. What led you to believe that such a particle did exist and that it traveled at the speed of light?"

"You may remember our conversation of over ten years ago, Jana, when we were discussing the ever-expanding universe and..." he could see that Jana was keeping up with him.

"You mean...if it is true that the outer universe is expanding at the speed of light..."

"Yes, as calculated in 2098 by Peri Montabe's revised Hubble's constant..." he injected.

"Then, it becomes reasonable that mass could travel at c. Am I correct?" She looked at him for verification.

"That's right," he encouraged, "go on."

"Well, I remember you theorizing, 'If stars and indeed galaxies at the outer edges of the universe with huge masses could travel away from each other at the speed of light in the ever expanding universe, why couldn't other particles do the same'."

"And I answered, 'It must be because of equations yet to be written, and what better place to look for another particle traveling at light speed than old Ben's prediction of energy from photons. Photons and radio waves, which are the only thing we can definitely measure as traveling at c'."

Satisfied with the explanations, Jana smiled at Mohammed and Marsh, but when she looked back at Arturo she saw a brooding look of misery enveloping his countenance. Jana knew that something monumental was bothering him, which had not yet been addressed. Arturo seemed unaware of the furtive glances that passed between Marsh and Mohammed. They only confirmed Jana's suspicions. Before she could speak, Marsh took charge of the situation.

"Arturo, out with it!" he bellowed in his forthright manner. "What in God's name has you so disturbed?"

Not ready or willing to reveal his agony, Arturo just shrugged his shoulders and turned his back.

Jana moved toward him as if her sympathetic touch could heal whatever was bothering him, but was stopped by the look on Marsh's face.

"My God, boy," Marsh said sharply, "you look like the proverbial kid that had just lost his favorite toy or, worse yet, been denied a sip of his favored drink!"

Arturo whirled around, started to speak, then for lack of a rebuttal, gave a chastened smile. "Marsh, old friend," he finally managed, "is it that obvious?"

"To all of us," Mohammed said with a frown on his face.

There was a long silence as Arturo grappled with his conscience and paced the floor. "Oh hell," he mumbled under his breath, "all of you deserve to know."

Slowly and clearly he described the near disaster of the *Jana's* collision flight path with the Moon. He intentionally ignored the looks of consternation that came over everyone's face, but not a sound or gasp was made until Arturo had finished. He was visibly moved when describing the support of the three-crew members and their vow never to reveal the secret of the near calamity. "Future ships will have multiple engines," Arturo concluded. "Never again will I design a ship with only one engine."

The small-assembled group in the study was silent as each shared the burden of the secret. It was some minutes before Marsh spoke. "Well, we've solved that problem. Now my dear friends, how do we exceed the speed of light and go to the stars and other galaxies in days instead of years and years?"

"Good question, Marsh," and Mohammed spun around, "and how do we do that, Arturo?"

"Beats me." In mock bewilderment, Arturo threw out his palms and shrugged. "Anyway, one step at a time."

"By the way, my friend," Mohammed's voice was low and serious, "everyone still thinks the *Jana* was nothing but a new hotshot personnel shuttle. Not even the station control crew knew its purpose. Only the three techs with you on the space station understood its real objective."

"And they'll keep quiet," Arturo quickly added.

"However, it is a matter of record that you were testing something from the space station." Mohammed raised one eyebrow. "In spite of the security clamp, someone may talk. So be prepared, Arturo."

"I'm more than aware of that," Arturo shifted his weight and then added with concern, "I just hope that you don't have a problem if it does leak."

"Hell, no!" Mohammed said emphatically. "Even if some unauthorized rumor does get out," and he slammed a fist into his other palm with a resounding smack, "I'll take care of my board of directors."

There was a moment of uneasy silence as all contemplated the probability that such a secret could actually be indefinitely maintained. It was Mohammed who broke the tension. "Now for another important point, Arturo. How many copies of your data are there? Equally significant, where are they?"

"Two copies, Mohammed." Arturo pointed to the table. "One for you and one for me."

"I don't need a copy right now," Mohammed averted his eyes from the documents. "You keep both copies in a safe place. If something happens to me, I don't want that particular data lying around where anyone may be able to get their hands on it."

"As you wish, Mohammed. They will be stored in our underground fireproof vault and in a neutral atmosphere."

"The same room where the Diggs' old family Bible is kept." Jana added.

"Fine. And the less said about the data, the better." Mohammed uttered with finality. Then he grinned, "By the way, Arturo, solve the Posafon mirror problem, and we'll build another, and bigger, ship — a ship that will carry people. May as well go whole hog."

"I'll solve it, Mohammed," Arturo replied with conviction, "I just don't know how right now." Returning the smile, he held out his hand, "but I'll solve the problem."

Jana sensed that the conversation was beginning to wane, and took the opportunity to announce when dinner would be served. "Gentlemen and to you in particular, my darling husband, you have my profound gratitude for sending my name to the stars. I can just see it. When some unknown person... or thing... finds my namesake, they'll say, 'What a great honor someone had to have a space ship named after her.' Again I thank you my love." She hugged each man in turn, and gave a special kiss to Arturo. "Dinner will be served in one hour," she called over her shoulder as she left the room.

The following day the electronic news media had headlines.

EXPERIMENTAL SHUTTLE LOST IN SPACE

"A new personnel shuttle designed by Mr. Arturo Diggs for Space Transport, Incorporated, was lost in space because of an unknown malfunction. A Space Transport spokesman had no comment when questioned about the cause of the failure. Mr. Diggs, former Chief Engineer of Space Transport, is the designer of the current generation of transports used by the corporation to carry heavy loads between Mars, the Moon, the Mars-Jupiter Asteroid-Belt and Earth. The first of Mr. Diggs' then new transports blew up, killing all on board. The disaster is believed to have been caused by an error in the computer program designed by Mr. Diggs. Both his parents were on board the Moon-bound transport and among those lost..."

The commentary continued and then concluded with the final sentence:

"A director and board member of Space Transport, who wished not to be named, said that he was unaware of any new personnel shuttle. If so, it was regrettable that such a vehicle malfunctioned during its flight test. The incident would certainly be looked into by the board."

"The first step is completed..."
"Now, he must find..."
"And then perhaps, he will exceed..."
"Nothing before its time..."

A RARE ELEMENT

Arturo had reached the agonizing conclusion that his new engine for light speed would neither be practical or applicable until the problem of the reflective mirrors was solved. Repeated tests of disparate materials had been experimented with, but none had achieved the magic one-centimeter beam diameter without burn-through. On the theory that heat stress was the culprit, he had attempted cooling the mirrors with liquid nitrogen or helium. Although this technique offered increased life, it was not completely successful. Most perplexing to his systematic mind was the fact that identical mirrors, made from the same materials, would disintegrate at different times for no apparent reason.

After almost five years of continuous experimentation, he finally deduced that the incompatibility of the molecular structure of the mirrors and the Posafon beams caused the eventual deterioration. But even this realization brought him no closer to his goals.

As Arturo's air-car descended onto the newly installed circular pad behind his home, he tried to shake both the frustration and fatigue from his bones. Forcing a smile that brightened his still handsome face, he tried to look relaxed, but nothing could conceal the look in his weary eyes.

Jana, clad in a bathing suit, waved a towel in welcome as she ran toward the door of the air-car. She noticed her husband's fatigue, but didn't let her concern show. "Welcome home, my darling."

Instead of taking her in his arms, Arturo placed his hands on her shoulders and held her at arm's length. "My God, Jana," his eyes admiringly roving her body, "You look fifteen years younger than your..." He stopped short of saying "fifty years."

Kissing his neck, Jana whispered, "Marsh is resting, and the nurse is gone for several hours. You don't even need to put on your suit for a swim."

"Mrs. Diggs!" Arturo tried to sound shocked. "What about the neighbors?"

"Since when have you been so modest?" she teasingly shot back.

Sheathed in robes, Jana and Arturo contently lounged beside the pool. She could see the tension shedding from her husband's countenance. "Like something cool to drink, lover?"

"Yes, thanks."

Rising, Jana poured lemonade into a tall iced glass. Handing him the beverage, she bent over, and gently ran her fingers through his wet hair. "Too many long hours, with too little sleep." The statement was rhetorical, and Arturo only nodded.

"Nothing new to report, Jana. None of the materials stood up over a thousand or so microns."

Jana desperately wished she could offer encouragement. Arturo, sensing her hesitation, blurted out his own disappointment. "Damn it all, there has to be an answer." His discouragement belied his hardy conviction. "The worst part is, I don't know how much longer Mohammed can subsidize these tests. We've already received numerous complaints that my `unproductive' tests are tying up the facility."

"Darling, what was it in the late nineteenth century," Jana asked, "that Edison tried for a filament that would allow an electric light bulb to create light, albeit for only a moment?"

Arturo was taken by complete surprise. "It was horsehair. Are you suggesting," and questioned her in an incredulous voice, "I try `horsehair'?"

"Not unless you actually deem it practical," and Jana raised an eyebrow. "It was just meant as an analogy, darling. Even though horsehair was an ineffective material, it was the first time light from electricity had worked, and it gave Edison hope to continue. He did you know, and then he finally found that tungsten gave long life. You have found the horsehair and now you must..."

"Jana, you're wonderful!" For the first time in months Arturo truly laughed. "Simply keep testing until something works."

"My thoughts exactly."

Before she could react, Arturo had bolted from the chair, scooped her up in his arms, and dangled her wriggling body over the pool edge. "I christen thee, Mrs. Wonderful..."

"Arturo," she clung to his neck shrieking, "don't you dare throw me in."

"Then we'll go in together." As their bodies hit the water, her cries of protest were drowned out by the gigantic splash.

"Arturo..." Jana spluttered, coming up for air, "you're a beast. Wait until I get my hands on you." She made a lunge for his shoulders. Laughing, he let her dunk his head under the water. Gripping his hands around her waist and not the least intimidated by her squeals, he lifted her over his head.

There was a sudden distraction as a cushion smacked beside them in the water. "Well, well, well," a loud masculine voice came from the edge of the pool. "I see the kids are still playing."

Arturo had just surfaced after dumping Jana.

"Hi, Dad!" Filip grinned as he pointed to the bubbles rising to the surface of the water. "Better go rescue Mother."

Arturo speechlessly dived down, but Jana had bobbed back to the surface before he could reach her. "Filip," she called out in delighted surprise, "you weren't due back until tomorrow."

Arturo's head popped out of the water, "Jana, are you all right?" But she had already swum to the side of the pool and was being helped out by Filip.

Ignoring her soaked robe, Filip gave his mother a long warm hug.

"Why didn't you let us know you were coming home early?" She asked happily.

"Got a lift on an unscheduled transport and just thought I'd surprise you."

As Arturo began scrambling from the pool, Filip reached down to give him a hand.

"Welcome home, Son." Between hugs, Arturo sheepishly admitted, "Caught us cavorting around again, huh?"

Filip winked. "So. What else is new with you two?"

Before Arturo could respond a frail but familiar voice sounded from the patio. "A man can't get any rest around here with all the noise and frolic going on."

"Uncle Marsh," Filip said as he turned. He flinched when he saw how fragile the ninety-three-year-old man appeared.

Dr. Marsh Bernside dismissed his nurse's assistance and brusquely motioned her to return to the house. He preferred to operate the motorized wheelchair on his own.

"Now come here, my boy, I want to take a good long look at you." Squinting at Filip, Marsh nodded with approval at the muscular young man. "Hmmm, the asteroids seem to agree with you. Now, how long are you going to keep your feet on Earth?"

"As things stand now, just under a week."

"Too short, too short," Marsh growled. Then with a wide grin he added, "Understand you're giving a presentation to your big bosses about the productivity increases you've made in minerals mining."

271

"As the newly appointed manager of Asteroid Geology," Filip proudly broke the news, "I have been requested to meet with the Board."

Marsh reached out to grasp Filip's strong young hand, silently displaying his acclaim.

"Oh, darling," Jana enthusiastically exclaimed, "you didn't mention one word about the promotion."

"Congratulations, Son," Arturo chimed in, slapping Filip on the back. "Now I want to hear about all your work."

"Whoa, Dad," Filip good-naturedly protested. "Age before youth. What's the latest on your progress with the light speed engine?"

Arturo sighed, "Sorry to report, Filip, I'm stymied. It has come down to molecular incompatibility. In a nutshell, the Posafon beams are reacting and are creating new particles that are activated. These set up internal stresses and allow burn-through."

Filip shook his head sympathetically. "So it's still the mirror problem?"

"Afraid so, Son. But enough about my set-backs." Not wanting to spoil Filip's homecoming with any more bad news, he abruptly shifted the conversation. "It's time to relax, celebrate your new promotion, and get a first-hand account of life in the Jupiter-Mars Asteroid-Belt. In fact," he teasingly pointed a finger at Marsh, "I think that Jana will even permit you to have your glass of wine early today."

Sensing his father's reluctance to go into any more detail concerning his own work, Filip forced a grin, "Well, I do have a surprise for all of you tonight. Brought back some new mineral samples to show you after dinner."

"Bring 'em out, boy," Marsh said impatiently. "No time like the present."

"You haven't changed a bit, Uncle Marsh," Filip joshed back, "but you'll just have to wait."

During dinner, Filip discussed his work and the mapping out of new asteroids for possible mining endeavors. Without being boastful, it became clear that he not only had the knack for finding new sources of needed minerals, but the innate sense of how to mine them productively and economically. He related the long hours spent in space suits while on the asteroids' surface and the moving around in low or almost zero gravity. He told how the smaller of the minerals were placed aboard ships and taken to Mars for processing. As Filip talked, it was obvious that he was just as much a businessman as a geologist. He had already evaluated methods for setting up his own company to mine minerals from places already probed and those as yet unexplored.

"Delicious meal, Mother. Nothing can ever replace your home cooking." Jana beamed at the compliment. "Besides all of you, of course," he grinned, "that's what I miss most."

Taking a final sip of his after dinner coffee, Filip set down his cup, "Okay, everyone, show and tell time. Are you ready? Everything's set up in the library."

"You bet, Son," Arturo eagerly rose and moved behind Marsh's wheelchair. "Your permission to steer your chariot, Doctor?"

"Just don't get frisky and try some 'wheelies', young man," Marsh groused back.

Filip took Jana's arm and escorted her down the hallway toward the closed doors of the library. He opened the door, and exposed an array of neatly positioned mineral samples on the antique sideboard. When all had entered the room, Filip explained, "I've arranged each of these in the same sequence that I'm presenting to the headquarters personnel. Actually" and he made a slight bow, "you three are the guinea pigs for my speech."

One by one he explained each of the mineral properties while also describing the mining processes that allowed them to be obtained and readied for transportation to Mars. His narrative included how on Mars they were processed from rough ore to the completed product, depending on the economics and technology involved, and the transportation to Earth for final processing.

"Take this peculiar item." Reaching for a piece of shiny glass that resembled a misshapen diamond, he held it aloft in his open cupped palm. "It's absolutely worthless in its present form because it degrades in an oxygen atmosphere. Bloody stuff hates oxygen in any form, even degrades in water."

Curious, Arturo touched the highly polished piece and asked, "What happens to it?"

"It gets brittle. Though it looks perfectly solid, if I drop it on the floor it will shatter."

"What use is it, then?" Arturo probed.

"On the asteroids, we've been using it on the tips of the digger teeth. It holds up better than cobalt, even the fine grain cobalt found on Mars."

Jana moved in for a closer look, "How did you discover it, Filip?"

"Just one of those brilliant break-throughs, Mother." He gave a chuckle. "A piece lodged between the teeth of one of the robot diggers, but a lot of small particles get snared there. Then when the cobalt teeth had to be re-placed, this particular material showed no wear at all. So, I got the idea of trying it as a tooth. The first teeth shattered on impact. Finally, I tried shaping them in a vacuum, which we have a lot of, and it worked."

"How about keeping it in an inert atmos-phere, such as nitrogen gas?" Marsh's agile mind was still exploring.

"No problem. Best damn...excuse me Mother, best material I ever saw for holding up on the digger teeth. Since there's no oxygen or atmosphere on any of the asteroids, there's no problem."

"How do you machine it?" Arturo's inter-est was aroused.

"With another piece of the same material. To grind it to a mirror finish, I put a powder of the same material between the pieces and lap until it's shiny."

Filip placed the mineral between his fin-gertips, and it caught the light like a glittering diamond.

"This piece was used for almost 92 hours as a digger tooth. Then one of the workers flushed out his life support oxygen system while connecting a new canister. He was standing near the digger, and when we fired it up again to begin work, all the teeth disintegrated except this one."

"Why didn't that break up, too?" Arturo tried to keep his tone casual.

"Apparently it didn't hit any of the rock, since it was on the outside of the digger. We had to replace all the teeth. I saved this one."

"May I hold it?" Arturo asked as he reached for the material.

Filip nonchalantly handed the gem-like stone to his father while continuing his running monologue. "In the space station lab we exposed a few pieces of this material to oxygen, and they disintegrated when hit or impacted by a hammer. Without oxygen exposure, you can't even scratch them, except with another piece of the same material."

"Filip, there isn't a scratch on this tooth." Arturo turned it meticulously between his hands. "It looks like it was never used," he marveled. "How does it hold up over time?"

"It simply wears away over a period of time." Filip shrugged. "Cobalt lasts for about 72 hours of use. This stuff lasts about 500 hours. It doesn't break, doesn't scratch or chip. The surface is as shiny as when it's first polished for installation."

Fascinated by the object in his hands, Arturo persevered further about its merits.

"Has your company tried to use it for other things, Filip?"

"Yes, but so far, the powers that be have termed it too fragile for Earth use. We are using it on Mars, however, in the mining operation there."

"You'll notice, Arturo," Marsh leaned in for a closer look, "one can see right through it without distortion." Then he spoke with canny insight. "What happens if it's placed against something black?"

Arturo smiled as he took the rectangular tooth and positioned it against the black onyx obelisk sitting on the end table. "Good God, Marsh!" he exclaimed in awe, "it looks like a mirror."

"Are you getting the same idea that I am, Arturo?" Marsh's fingers tapped excitedly on the arm of his chair; his aged eyes blazed with excitement.

Suddenly, Filip slapped his head. "My God, Dad, here I've been rambling on about my work and not even thinking about yours. Do you maybe think that this crazy material is what you've been looking for?"

"Maybe, Filip. Maybe." Arturo didn't even try to hide the exhilaration he was feeling, and his hands trembled as he carefully laid the luminous stone on the table. "Can you cut a piece to my specified dimensions and polish it to a 2-rms finish?"

"Sure," Filip agreed, caught up in the excitement of the possible discovery, "and I can ship it to you in an inert pressurized package."

"Good. Get me 10 pieces. I'll draw up a sketch with measurements." Arturo could not contain his eagerness. "How long to make up the pieces?"

"Let's see. By the time I return and we cut and grind the pieces, probably in about two and a half months, you should have the finished items."

"Filip, since you discovered this material," Marsh astutely inquired, "did the company follow established precedent and let you name it?"

"Yes, they did Uncle Marsh, I'm going to name it Diggsanium and register it as such."

Jana took her husband's arm and pulled him aside to whisper in his ear. Arturo nodded agreement. Smiling like a Cheshire cat, she turned to her son. "If you will agree, Filip, your father and I think another name might be appropriate."

"Son, we would like to suggest a name for your consideration," Arturo offered. "How about Bernsidium?"

There was not a moment's hesitation in Filip's heartfelt reply. "I agree. 'Bernsidium' it is."

"No. No. No. That's crazy." Marsh interrupted, "I simply won't have it. The name properly belongs to the Diggs family. And you know it." They could see that although he was flattered to have his name considered, he was serious in his determination to reject the honor.

Before anyone could protest, Marsh dismissed further discussion with a wave of his hand. "Besides, the name of any newly discovered mineral has always gone to the discoverer. Either name it Diggsanium or Filipsanium and no other. Nothing else would be fitting." A devilish twinkle brightened his face, but he was adamant in his decision. "Arturo, Jana, Filip, I'm truly honored, but please, it must be as I say."

All three Diggs recognized that Marsh was truly emotionally touched by the gesture. Jana started to say something, but before she could speak, Filip ended the conversation. "All right, Uncle Marsh. It will be named Diggsanium."

True to Filip's promise, 11 weeks later Arturo received a large container via a Mars-to-Earth transport. Filip had prominent markings plastered all over the outer packaging, stating that the contents were packed in a vacuum within an evacuated canister. The words, printed in red, clearly warned, "DO NOT OPEN CONTAINER IN ATMOSPHERE."

Arturo lost no time in taking the unopened container to the vacuum test chamber at the Space Transport laboratory in San Diego. Once outfitted in the mandatory pressurized apparel and life-support gear, he entered the vacuum chamber with his precious cargo. Opening the sturdy crate, he found inside a round aluminum canister with the same warning, "Do Not Open in Atmosphere," and a handwritten note from Filip.

"Dad, good luck with these. They all meet the specifications you gave me. You only have to send word if you need more. Much love to you, Mother and Uncle Marsh.

Love, Filip."

Removing the vacuum-sealed cap on the canister, Arturo cautiously extracted one of the Diggsanium pieces and held it up for visual examination. It gleamed like a flawless diamond and was as clear as the finest blown glass or crystal. Moving the enlarging microscope inside the chamber into position, he scrutinized the magnified view on a specially built screen. After an hour of intense examination, at magnification powers up to 100,000 x, he could still find no discernable flaws. The first piece was perfect. He repeated the procedure with each of the other nine samples. All were exemplary. With a sigh of relief he replaced the Diggsanium back in the vacuum canister and sealed it. All that was now needed, for each to become a perfect mirror, was to add the proper backing.

Within the capability of his test equipment at the Space Transport lab in San Diego, the reflective efficiency of the new mirrors had come within one billionth of an angstrom. No other material had ever come so close. With the assistance of Todd, the trusted senior technician at the Colorado Laser Test Facility, Arturo had arranged an unprecedented twenty-four hour continuous analysis of the Diggsanium mirrors.

"Mr. Diggs," Todd apologized, "we've been getting a lot of flack about Space Transport's use of the lab." It was obvious that he was uncomfortable about mentioning the problem to Arturo, "There are others wishing test time. But if all possible, we're still going to try for the twenty-four hour uninterrupted test."

"I know you will, old friend." Arturo tried to relieve Todd's embarrassment with a warm pat on the shoulder. "This time though, we're going to change the procedure. I want to install the mirrors while under a vacuum."

Nothing much rattled the senior tech. He was used to acceding, not only to Arturo's requests, but also to some pretty bizarre entreaties of many of the other scientists conducting their experimental tests. "Sure thing, Mr. Diggs. While you put on the pressurized vacuum suit, I'll make the necessary adjustments to the equipment. When you're ready to enter the test chamber, we'll begin vacuum pumpdown on your signal."

Outfitted in the appropriate gear, Arturo carried both his portable recorder and the vacuum canister through the test chamber's double doors. Nodding to Todd that he was ready, he intently watched the vacuum gauge. After a few minutes it read one-millionth torr, or one part in 7,600,000 of an Earth atmosphere. He gestured to Todd that the pressure was correct before beginning to position the Diggsanium mirrors. Satisfied with the installation and the placement of the recorder, he crossed his fingers and retreated to the small vacuum staging room. Closing the test chamber door and energizing the seal, he waited as the room stabilized at atmospheric pressure. He opened the door to the console room and quickly removed the pressurized suit.

"All ready Mr. Diggs?" Todd inquired.

"All ready, Todd." Arturo's heart was racing, but he kept his voice level, "Let her rip."

Todd pressed the switch to start the experiment and had just begun announcing the sequence of events when Arturo suddenly shouted, "Stop the test!"

Shutting down the sequencer as ordered, Todd looked with surprise at Arturo. "What's the problem, Mr. Diggs?"

Arturo's smiling face momentarily stunned the usually unshakable tech; he was at a loss to deduce what had prompted the unorthodox behavior. "Todd," Arturo's voice had a discernable edge of excitement, "while I was installing the mirrors, I was thinking, why creep up on the desired goal? We may as well find out quickly." Then a wry smile crept over his mouth. "Besides, test time at the facility is becoming harder and harder to obtain."

The surprised tech started to object, but Arturo waved any objections aside. "Todd, can you change the beam diameters from 5,000 microns, or one-half centimeter in diameter to a full centimeter in diameter?"

"Sure, Mr. Diggs," the tech hesitantly shook his head, "but you know what's happened in the past. We've always had a burn-through at the 10,000-micron mark. Are you sure you want to do this?"

"Yes, I am, Todd. Can you do it readily?"

"Only take a minute." Giving Arturo one more questioning glance, and receiving a firm nod in reply, Todd began adjusting the fusion reactor and laser gun to produce one-centimeter beams.

"You sure have guts, Mr. Diggs." Placing his hand on the switch, Todd took a deep breath and said, "I'll hold for your signal, sir."

Not even realizing that his eyes were tightly shut, for an agonizing moment Arturo hesitated, as disjointed thoughts charged through his head: Old Newsome, Ben, Jana, Marsh, Mohammed, and Filip. He prayed that Filip's material would work. After all those years of trying, designing, planning, the late hours, and Jana — who never lost her sense of humor nor faith in his quest. His lips moved silently, but no sound was heard, "Oh, Jana, it has to work, it has to!"

"Mr. Diggs?" Todd's voice was ringed with concern, "Are you all right?"

Arturo opened his eyes, "Sorry, Todd. I was saying a small prayer." Then with firmness, he gave the command. "Go!"

Todd nodded and flipped the automatic sequencer to the "on" position. Through the viewing window Arturo saw the fusion reactor beam come on and then the laser beam. Instantly, soft red and black diamonds appeared downstream of the intersection point of the laser and reactor beams. Todd looked through the window with Arturo, the amazement evident on his face. Hypnotized by the continuing diamonds of the Posafon and Negafon beams, the men were riveted to the experiment. The diamonds didn't stop as they had in the past when a mirror burn-through happened.

It was Todd who finally broke the spell. "Mr. Diggs, I don't know what you did, but the Posafon mirror is holding up. It's not burning out like the others did." Glancing at the dials, he all but shouted, "God, in heaven, we're measuring 160 million kilowatts. The energy absorbers can't take anything near that. What did you do, Mr. Diggs?"

Arturo purposely avoided answering, but Todd didn't seem to notice. The tech burst out, "It's working like something...something out of this world. But where does the energy go? How does it dissipate?"

"You're right, Todd." Arturo dodged the question. "It is working like something out of this world." He had already resolved to never reveal what the material was to anyone except Jana, Filip, Marsh and Mohammed Nahal.

"But...Mr. Diggs," Todd persisted, "I still don't understand about..."

"Don't worry about the energy dissipation, Todd," Arturo interrupted. "It's being absorbed without any harm to your equipment."

Todd's face flushed with embarrassment, and he instantly reverted to his trained professionalism. "I understand Mr. Diggs, otherwise the automatic overload would have been energized."

Without comment or expression Arturo simply nodded. He knew full well that data on the Massafons would show up only on his personally designed portable recorder and not the facility recorders.

Six continuous hours of testing passed as both men watched the instruments, fascinated by the Posafon and Negafon beams that never wavered and stayed constant. Todd adjusted his glasses as he glanced up at the precision test clock. "Mr. Diggs, I'm supposed to turn the facility over to the night shift," he began apologetically but then quickly volunteered, "but I'll stay with you, if you wish to make sure all goes as we planned."

"I'd appreciate that, Todd. If you're sure it'll be okay and you won't get into trouble?"

"No sweat, Mr. Diggs. I want to see how long this baby holds up."

Twelve hours had passed. The Diggsanium mirrors continued to reflect the Posafon and Negafon beams without burn-through. Todd looked at Arturo and stifled a yawn. "We can take turns napping on the couch over there. Won't be the first time we've both stayed up to watch a test."

"You've got a deal. I'll take the first watch." Arturo pointed toward the inviting couch, "I'll wake you in about an hour."

Gratefully, Todd stretched out and fell asleep almost as soon as his eyes closed.

Time passed.

Arturo casually glanced up at the clock; it read 4:00 a.m. Engrossed with watching the beams, he thought he heard distant voices but, not wanting to take his eyes off the Posafon and Negafon beams, he half-listened to the faint words.

"Another lock has been opened..."
"More yet to come..."
"Nothing before its time..."

Arturo turned and found there was no one else close-by but Todd. Out of the corner of his eye he saw that the clock now read, 5:30 a.m. Shaking his head he half-mumbled, "That's impossible, I couldn't have been asleep. I just looked a second ago and it was 4:00 a.m." He tried to recall the words of the voices he'd heard; but try as he might, he could only remember one phrase, ***"Nothing before its time."*** Shaking his head, he blinked several times as if there were cobwebs muddling his brain, and an uncontrolled shiver ran through his body. He gasped loudly as he felt a hand touching his shoulder.

"Mr. Diggs," came Todd's familiar voice, "I'll take over for a spell."

Startled, Arturo turned and looked up questionably at the technician's steady face. "What did you mean by ***"Nothing before its time"***, Todd?"

"You must have been dreaming, Mr. Diggs. I didn't say anything. You were muttering in your sleep, but you never left the chair beside the viewing window." Then seeing the bewildered look on Arturo's face, he added, "At least you don't walk in your sleep, Mr. Diggs."

Arturo shrugged and dismissed the event from his mind. As Todd said, it was only a dream. But the memory of those words remained with him.

286

At 7:00 a.m. Todd said, "Well, Mr. Diggs, there's no change in the Posafon and Negafon beams." His voice sounded tired. "The gauges measuring any deformation of the mirrors or any damage, have not moved from their null or zero positions." Almost apologetically he added, "We'll have to shut down at 8:00 a.m. and get ready for the next scheduled test. So, you only have one more hour of testing." Then as if to compensate for the short notice, "But at least you will have the allotted 24 hours of operation at the full one centimeter beam diameters without burn-through."

A touch of irony tinged Arturo's voice, "Unlike those past tests of the other materials."

The tech only shook his head in agreement to the obvious observation.

For several minutes neither man spoke. Arturo turned away from the viewing screen and began pacing the floor. Suddenly he burst out, "Todd, we have less than one hour left on the torus! Right? Then let's make the most of it!"

The tech's face looked puzzled, but before he could speak, Arturo's enthusiastic voice drowned him out. "I know the fusion reactor and laser gun are designed for one centimeter beams — maximum. However, I can bypass the computer-controlled openings to the maximum of 10 centimeters. I'd like to try a test at the maximum beam level possibly available."

"Mr. Diggs, the fusion reactor will handle it, no problem. But the laser gun may be damaged when you use more power," the determined look in Arturo's eyes made him add, "and then again maybe not. It does have a safety margin of almost 2.0." It was his responsibility to offer his best advice, and he tried one more warning. "Though I have to caution you that you do run a risk of damage."

"Let's try it," Arturo stated firmly, "I'll take the risk." Todd cocked his head but said nothing. Without further ado, he made the necessary adjustments for the increased beam diameter test.

Arturo watched in silence as the beams appeared as before, followed by the larger Posafon and Negafon beams.

"Mr. Diggs, we're reading 360 million kilowatts," Todd reported, "steady, with no fluctuations...the mirrors show no deformation or damage."

Arturo was not keeping track of time, just monitoring the successful progress of the test. He was taken unaware when Todd tapped him on the arm and pointed toward the wall clock. "Sorry, Mr. Diggs, we have to shut down now. The next scheduled test group will be here any minute." Then in an unassertive tone, almost an afterthought, "Besides, the temperature of the laser gun coil is almost at the danger point."

"No problem, Todd," Arturo readily agreed, a satisfied glow on his cheeks. "Shut it down."

When the test was concluded Arturo hastily slipped into the pressurized suit, carefully removed the Diggsanium mirrors from their holders, and placed them back in the vacuum canister. After the numerous tests over

the past five years, Todd had stopped questioning the removal of Arturo's personal recorder
from the torus. He so admired and respected
Arturo that he completely trusted his integrity
in this matter.

On the way back to San Diego, Arturo was
bursting with exhilaration. He wanted to call
Jana to let her know the success of the past
twenty-four hours, but held back until he could
unequivocally verify the results.

From the HV1000 train, he went directly
to the Space Trans lab to examine the Diggsanium mirrors. He compared the molecular
structural data he had previously recorded to
the data he had just obtained from the personal recorder. No changes were evident. The
mirrors looked as if they had never been used
or taken out of their protective vacuum canister. It was only then, with a grateful sigh, did
he let Jana know of the triumph.

The following day, Jana, Marsh and Mohammed Nahal sat anxiously in Arturo's study. The
portable data recorder on the table was connected to a flat viewing screen. Marsh, trying to
quell his excitement, tapped his fingers noisily
on the arm of the wheelchair. "My God, Arturo,"
he scolded, "will you stop fiddling with that
machine and just let us see the results."

Mohammed's hardy laugh rang out: "I'll
have to agree with Marsh. What the hell is taking you so long, Arturo?"

"Now, boys," Jana chided, "after nine
years, what's a few more seconds."

"Damn it all," Marsh huskily retorted, starting to wheel his chair toward Arturo, "if you don't know how to work the blasted thing..."

"Marsh, have you no faith?" Arturo laughed as he dimmed the lights. The viewing screen was instantly alive with a soft bluish haze. It appeared denser than in previous tests and the purple sphere surrounding the impact point of the Posafons and Negafons was darker and somewhat larger. The dark purple haze within the enclosed paraboloid was now almost completely black. From the end of the paraboloid a photon beam emitted — the same size as the fusion reactor and laser gun beams.

Arturo broke the silence. "Nothing changed during the test, insofar as the comparison to our previous results. Except..." and he deliberately paused to achieve the full impact of his point, "the mirrors showed absolutely no damage or change of molecular structure. Even when the beam diameters were increased to the maximum available of 10 centimeters, the mirrors held up; burn-through didn't occur."

There were three gasps of surprise as Arturo switched off the screen and turned on the lights.

Marsh softly pummeled his shrunken fists against his wheelchair. "By God, Arturo," he beamed, "you've done it." Swiveling around to face Mohammed, his watery old eyes blazed with zeal, "Here's the answer to the new propulsion system. When do we start on another ship?"

Mohammed slowly rose. His face showed his deep-felt elation. "Congratulations, Arturo." He held out his hands and grasped Arturo's hands. "In fact, why don't you use the almost completed larger ship that we started in 2192?"

"Hell of an idea," Marsh cackled, "with the Diggsanium mirrors you'll be able to utilize the full diameter beam."

Arturo's mind was actively sprinting ahead, "Later we could convert the test ship from prototype status to operational status. As soon as the tests are complete, we could begin construction of a whole new fleet of transports."

Caught up in the fervor of the venture, Mohammed suggested, "Arturo, let's configure the *Jana II* to carry men and..."

"Wait a minute, gentlemen," Jana interceded. "I'm honored, but I think Arturo deserves the honor for the ship to be named after him..." Jana was stumbling for words, "...or maybe you, Mohammed," and gesturing toward Marsh, "or our esteemed Dr. Bernside...and Filip discovered the Diggsanium, so perhaps he should also be considered..."

"Jana," Mohammed resolutely settled the question. "All Space Trans ships are named after various ladies and is a company tradition. Besides," and his voice was tinged with humor, "can you imagine a ship named Mohammed? Hell, some damn fool would nickname it 'The Egyptian Flash'! *Jana II* it is!"

"I second that," Marsh added as loudly as his frail voice would allow.

Jana blushed, and all she could do was give a simple, "Thank you gentlemen. Again,

291

I'm honored." She then rose and gave each man in turn a warm hug and kiss.

Mohammed was touched by Jana's display of affection and appreciation. Clearing his throat, he quickly changed the subject. "As was suggested, Arturo, let's provide the *Jana II* with the capability to carry humans. After the assumed successful unmanned test, we can put a crew aboard and have first hand information on the mass increase as well as size and time decrease issues, visually and otherwise."

"I agree with that," Arturo said. "However, you know it will add another year to outfit her for a manned flight."

"How much longer to just complete the larger ship?" Mohammed questioned.

"I would estimate," Arturo calculated the approximate time in his mind, "probably about ten to twelve months." For a moment he was thoughtful, "But there is another option. We could always go ahead with an unmanned test and retrofit the *Jana II* for manned flight afterwards."

"Okay, done! That's what we'll do," Mohammed nodded. "Take a few days and start when you're ready."

"A few days!" Arturo looked astounded, "Mohammed, I'm ready right now."

Turning to Jana, Marsh asked innocently, "My dear, wouldn't you say that this calls for a celebration?"

Jana gave the elderly patriarch a sly smile before moving over to the liquor cabinet. From a bottle of twenty-five-year-old cognac, she generously filled three glasses. With flair, she removed an equally aged bottle of malt scotch and poured a small amount in Marsh's glass. After she passed out the glasses, all awaited Marsh's standard critique.

"Damn whisky flows like glue around here," Marsh frowned, and comparing his meager portion of malt scotch to that of the others, "and in bloody small portions for some people, I see."

The anticipated remark received the appropriate laughs. Then Mohammed raised his glass for a toast. "To success."

To which all repeated, "To success."

Arturo sipped his cognac before raising his glass for attention. "If I may, another toast." Raising his glass to Marsh, "To my mentor, for all his support and assistance."

A chorus of, "Here! Here!" rang out."

"To Mohammed," Jana injected, "for never loosing the faith."

Not to be outdone, Marsh joined in, "And to Filip for the Diggsanium."

Arturo's voice rang out again, "To old Newsome for starting this quest and Ben for continuing it." He hesitated before turning to his wife and whispered, "To my love, my Jana, the universe awaits us. Without you, none of this..." Overcome by emotion, Arturo stopped his toast to Jana and hugged her tightly.

All sipped at their drinks, each with their own private thoughts and visions.

Mohammed placed his empty glass on the table. "Jana, my dear, I'm so sorry that I can't accept your kind invitation for dinner," he apologized. "The stockholder's meeting tomorrow morning..."

"No apologies necessary, Mohammed," she said, lightly. "I'll walk you to the door."

Even after Mohammed's departure, Arturo, Marsh and Jana lingered in the library, rehashing the test results and the plans to build another ship. They were still engrossed in their animated conversation, when Jana glanced at the time.

"My goodness," sounding abashed, "I told Mary, we'd be in for dinner almost fifteen minutes ago."

"Don't worry, darling," Arturo assured, "Mary's been with us long enough to adjust to our eccentric schedules. If she had everything on the table, we would have been duly summoned."

"Well, then," Jana proposed, "can I refresh anyone's drinks?"

"Please, Madam," over the magnified half glasses perched on his nose, Marsh widened his eyes. With the improvised expression of a pleading child about to be denied the last piece of candy, he implored, "Just a wee thimbleful, if you would be so kind."

Jana vacillated, frowning toward Arturo for an answer.

"I believe," Arturo solemnly replied, "a wee thimbleful would not be a problem, this one time."

Placing their empty glasses on a tray, he went to the bar and poured the drinks. When he handed Marsh his portion, Arturo was puzzled when the old man didn't make the usual comment about the rationed whiskey. Jana also noted the lack of criticism and exchanged a quick look with her husband. But Arturo only shrugged, deciding to disregard the incident.

When no one spoke, Jana was uncomfortable at the silence, so she raised her glass, "Again, everyone, to success."

"Thank you, darling," Arturo rejoined. Then turning to Marsh he was about to offer an additional toast but he stopped short, a perplexed look on his face. Marsh's eyes were staring into space, and he was clutching his glass tightly between his frail hands.

"Marsh?" Jana tentatively began, "Is something..."

Without looking at them, Marsh interrupted, "I have a request to make. Please listen closely."

He had their undivided attention.

"If something happens to me because the Good Lord thinks I've caused enough trouble on this Earth and it's time to leave, I am asking two favors of you both."

Jana gasped. Her shaking hand caused the ice cubes to clink in her glass. Arturo took her drink and set it with his on the tray.

Marsh seemed not to notice or hear as he placed his own drink on the edge of the nearby table. "Please, come sit down beside me." Arturo drew up two chairs in front of the wheelchair and motioned for Jana to be seated in one while he took the other.

Marsh's eyes were steady as he fixed his gaze on Arturo and Jana. It seemed an eternity before he finally spoke. "First, you know I have no heirs. I wish to leave my estate to Filip. The boy wants to start his own business and maybe I can be of some help." Marsh paused, seemingly needing to catch his breath. "The necessary legal documents have already been drawn up. With your permission, of course, I have appointed you both the executors."

Arturo could barely hold back the tears that clouded his eyes. Quickly accepting for both himself and Jana, he simply said, "Thank you, Marsh. It will be our honor."

Marsh then reached out for their hands. "Secondly," he began stiffly, trying to keep his voice from wavering, "since I won't be around when the *Jana II* is successfully tested at the speed of light, I have another request to make."

"Anything, Marsh," Jana's words were barely audible. "You know you only have to ask."

"I wish to be cremated and my ashes placed aboard the *Jana II*. And if possible, Arturo," his aged hand quivered, "at the time of your choosing, would you spread the ashes somewhere around the outer limits of the solar system?" While waiting for Arturo's response, Marsh's dark brown face grew pale.

"You have my word, old friend," Arturo promised. "It will be done."

Nodding, Marsh dropped their hands and lowered his head. "Thank you, my friends."

Jana bit at her lip, unable to say anything. She and Arturo knew that Marsh's time was near and that he had lasted this long out of sheer willpower. He had simply refused to succumb to the stroke of nine years previous until Arturo's success had been achieved.

After a few moments, Arturo grasped his wife's elbow and gently drew her to her feet. Bending over Marsh's wheelchair, she placed her arms around him and buried her head against his neck. Tears streamed down her cheeks.

"Now, now, Jana," Marsh returned the embrace, but there was a note of frivolity in his voice. "It's me who should be sniffling. Always knew that I could never entice you away from that husband of yours."

"Oh Marsh!" Jana wailed as she drew away. Taken aback by the levity, she managed a wan smile and joshed, "You'll never actually know how close you've come."

"My dear Jana," and there was a twinkle in his watery eyes, "with that encouragement, I'll have pleasant dreams tonight." Marsh removed a handkerchief from his breast pocket and quickly dabbed at his eyes. "Now, my friends, if you would ring for the nurse," Marsh turned his chair, "I'm going to skip dinner and just say goodnight."

The next morning, Marsh lay motionless in bed with a smile of contentment on his aged face. He had departed peacefully in his sleep.

The electronic news media carried a detailed broadcast of his life. The announcers began their tribute, "The renowned Dr. Marshall Bernside, famed scientist of sub-sub-atomic particle research, has died at the age of ninety-three and..."

Arturo and Jana commissioned a renowned artist to do a full-size painting of Marsh from an earlier photograph, and an engraved cupro-nickel plaque. Both were installed in the Hall of Honored Scientists in the Chicago branch of the Royal Astronomical Society of London. The plaque read:

Dr. Marshall Bernside
A giant among men
A second father to Jana and Arturo Diggs
A grandfather to Filip Diggs
All he touched was the better for it
His work will endure the passage of time

2198
PRACTICALITY REALIZED

The winter at the remote Space Transport facility, even by Montana standards, had been unseasonably cold. On occasion, temperatures had plummeted to minus 30 degrees. But no mere weather problems had been severe enough to keep Arturo from supervising the completion of the *Jana II*. As agreed with Mohammed Nahal, the ship's ultimate design was geared for use as a personnel transport, capable of carrying a maximum of 200 people and 50 tons of cargo to the Moon, Mars or the asteroids. Also as Arturo had vowed after the loss of the original *Jana*, two Massafon Engines had been installed. At present, the life support systems, seating, escape pods and cargo handling equipment were not installed. They were to be added later after satisfactory completion of the unmanned flight tests.

After enduring such a blustery winter, Arturo and his chief engineer had walked outside the facility to welcome the warm late spring sunshine. Both men had toiled well past midnight and had begun again at daybreak that morning. Their faces were lined with fatigue and their shoulders slumped.

"I'll swear, Mr. Diggs," the young chief engineer remarked, "you seem to be driven by an outside force to get that vehicle into space. You outwork all the technicians. Even those twenty years your junior."

"I guess everyone has something motivating them," Arturo replied while squinting against the bright sunrays. Suddenly his gaze was drawn to a black speck silhouetted against a billowy cloud. "Look up there, Curtis." He pointed toward a large bird circling lazily in the sky. "Watch that hawk. He only has one thing driving him at this minute, and that's where his next meal is coming from."

At that precise moment the hawk, wings folded, dropped like a bullet towards the edge of the facility lawn. At the last minute, when it looked as if he would crash headlong into the tall grass, he spread his wings and with talons open, stretched out his legs. On the fly, the bird swooped into the grass, emerging with a small animal clutched between his claws. The hawk began wildly flapping to gain altitude and finally, satisfied with the height, flew toward the distant horizon.

"I guess," Arturo reflected, "you could compare me to that bird. I circled and circled, searching for the solution to the rocket engine." He gestured towards the lab. "Once I found it, like the hawk spotting his dinner, I have to go at the same speed until I catch it." Arturo hesitated; he was lost in his own analogy. "Like the hawk flying off with his catch, I can hardly wait to get the *Jana II* into space." He was still staring into the sky long after the bird had disappeared from sight; his words sank to a whisper, "...and prove her worthiness."

The chief engineer, one of the handpicked people working on this highly secured and classified project, was sensitive enough to understand his boss did not need any small talk from him at this particular moment.

After a brief and silent interlude, Arturo roused himself, smiling apologetically at the younger engineer. "I'm sorry. I didn't mean to be so philosophic; comparing myself to a hawk."

"No problem, Mr. Diggs. I understand. Whatever support you need, you'll have from the crew. Whatever it is."

"Thanks, Curtis," Arturo nodded in appreciation. As if to change the somber mood, he took a deep breath of the clear Montana air. "Well, shall we go back to the lab and see how the *Jana II* is doing on the final systems checkout?"

To Arturo's complete satisfaction and that of the dedicated team engaged in the project, all vehicle check sheets, computer sequences, data and transmission equipment testing performed flawlessly. The *Jana II* was ready for crating and shipment. She would be put aboard one of Space Transport's large freighter vehicles and taken directly to the space station.

As Arturo settled into the San Diego bound HV1000 train, after thanking everyone profusely for a job well done, he felt drained.

Bidding farewell to the loyal band of engineers and technicians with whom he had spent countless hours, he felt grateful for their combined success and sad that they would not be able, individually, to share in the actual space flight test.

Less than twenty-four hours later, Arturo and Jana were comfortably seated on the spacious deck of Mohammed's La Jolla home overlooking the Pacific Ocean. The afternoon had passed quickly with Arturo's briefing of the readiness of the *Jana II* for flight test. Mohammed had listened with keen interest to the summary of the ship's checkout, only interrupting for minute points of clarification.

"Excellent briefing, Arturo. I can't add anything or see any pitfalls," adding with a wink, "other than the normal worrisome minor issues that always come up on a new venture." Settling back in his chair, he inquired casually, "When do you want to give the magic word for the flight test?"

"Probably the day after tomorrow, Mohammed," Arturo promptly replied. "By the way, I'm using the same *Jana I* technicians. You remember Sally, the senior tech."

"Good. They've never breathed a word about the Moon problem. All are great people." Changing the subject, Mohammed asked, "I take it that you plan to be there at the space station, Arturo?"

Arturo nodded. "And, if you agree, I'd like Jana to go along and see the test. And most important, Mohammed, if you can tear yourself away from your desk for 24 hours, you should also be there."

"Absolutely, Jana should go. She's as much a contributor to your success as anyone. Absolutely, she should go," Mohammed said firmly.

"I accept your invitation without reservation, kind sirs," Jana said with a smile.

"Insofar as my going," Mohammed had already given consideration to the idea, "it may be a good thing for me to be present." Rising, he walked slowly to the edge of the railing. "I can then personally attest to the success of the flight; and there should be no problems at the board meeting when I request approval to retrofit and install the new Massafon Engines on our fleet of transports and personnel carriers."

"What if," Arturo asked, "complications do arise?"

"All the more reason that I'm present," Mohammed countered as he turned to face Arturo. "Then no one can question you about any problems because I'll be in position to back you up on all the details." He gestured with his forefinger to make the point. "But there aren't going to be any mishaps, Arturo. The *Jana II* will revolutionize propulsion technology. Space Transportation, Incorporated, will control space for decades to come." His voice rang with enthusiasm, "Damn right, I'm going to be a part of the first successful demonstration!"

The transport flight, docking and unloading of the *Jana II* was uneventful. The space station itself resembled a child's toy gyroscope. The torus part of the station rotated steadily to create artificial gravity in the inhabited areas. The center tube, connected to the torus through almost frictionless magnetic bearings, did not rotate and therefore didn't have the pull of gravity to contend with when unloading heavy items or equipment. The remote arm holding *Jana II* was connected to the center tube, and thus, like any other freighter or personnel transport, she felt no gravitational pull while docked.

The testing and recording equipment was unloaded through the pressurized dock-way and taken to the reserved control room in the torus. Arturo had personally transported the vacuum canister containing the Diggsanium mirrors.

The normal apprehension, associated with unloading sensitive apparatus in space, was relieved when the equipment was ultimately unpacked and set up in the control room. Arturo, with a sigh of relief, hugged Jana. He seemed oblivious to the three technicians setting up and checking out the provisions.

"Better watch out, Mr. Diggs," one of the techs joked. "You'll forget why we're here."

"No way," Jana laughingly kissed her husband, "he's got a job to do and I'm only here for moral support...and to see that he does it right."

"She's a slave driver," Arturo joked back. "Well, guess we better get at it."

"Welcome aboard, Mrs. Diggs, you'll bring us luck," Sally, the senior tech complimented. "Besides, your namesake, *Jana II*, wouldn't dare cause a problem with you here." She turned back to finish up her duties and then over her shoulder, politely added, "Introduce you to everyone as soon as we stow this gear. Then we'll put you to work, too."

"No thanks," Jana good-naturedly held up her hand in protest, "I'm merely an observer. The safest thing for me to do is stay out of the way and watch."

The techs were unaware that Jana had spent years reading back various results of computer outputs. She had been of incalculable assistance to Arturo by reporting changes that were either successes or potential problems. Mrs. Jana Diggs was no novice either to testing or trouble-shooting.

Outfitted in an External Vehicular Activity suit, Arturo first made an inspection of the maneuvering jets. Then carrying the Diggsanium mirrors, still safely stored in their pressurized canister, he opened the air locks that spanned the space between the space station and the Massafon Engine compartment. Entering the compartment, he began the tedious installation procedure of the mirrors. Returning to the control room, the next step was to run a sequence of the mirror's focal points and angular bearings. After some minor adjustments, he locked in the precise positions, nulling each mirror location to the exact and required angularities.

By 2100 hours, all but two checkouts had been accomplished and it would take less than an hour to complete those inspections. It was a relatively simple matter to sequence the computer flight program, then test the onboard voice computer for relaying real time key events as they occurred.

The technicians, along with both Diggs, had not formally broken for meals; instead, they had snacked on sandwiches and coffee between their chores. Though there had been no mention of stopping until all tests had been fully executed, Arturo arbitrarily decided not to push on for another hour.

"Let's call it a night. We'll finish up in the morning."

"Whatever you say, Mr. Diggs," Sally answered with a note of relief.

Arturo switched on the communications link, "Station Control, this is Jana Control. All checkouts are complete except for two finals. We're going to get some sleep and finish up tomorrow. Does our launch window remain as scheduled?"

"That's a roger, Jana Control. The Chairman said to inform you he would be onboard by 0900 hours if you were still ready as scheduled. Shall we confirm his departure from San Diego?"

"Roger, Station Control. We'll finish up by 0800 hours. If any problems arise we'll let you know in time to notify Mr. Nahal. Launch will be scheduled for 1000 hours." Arturo recited, "Do you affirm?"

"Affirmative, Jana Control. Goodnight and have a good sleep. Station Control out."

In the sparse but comfortable accommodations at the Space Station, Jana and Arturo lost themselves in tender caresses. Through long experience with loving each other in stressful times, their normal tensions began to release. Just before the crest of their rhythmic passion, Jana murmured, "Now, my darling, now."

Jana always jokingly referred to their love making as "their common sleeping pill." Afterwards, they lay contently in each other's arms and were soon fast asleep.

When Jana and Arturo entered the control room the next morning, the technicians were already hard at work.

Sally greeted them and added, "Absolutely on schedule, Mr. Diggs. Just take us another few minutes and the onboard voice computer will be verified."

"What did you do?" Arturo laughingly scolded. "Get up early?"

"Not too far off," Sally conceded. "Just wanted to make sure that everything would be ready when the Chairman arrived."

"Thanks, everyone," Arturo gratefully responded, "I appreciate having a crew like you."

Somewhat embarrassed by the praise, the techs thanked him and continued working. Sally handed Arturo a printout of the completed inspection and then turned to Jana.

"There's hot coffee," she pointed to a small counter, "and fresh sweet rolls, Mrs. Diggs, if you're hungry."

"Thanks, that sounds good, Arturo would you..." But she never finished the question. Her husband was already deeply engrossed in the final test procedures. Food or drink would go unheeded.

At precisely 0900 hours, Mohammed Nahal appeared at the control room door. Entering unnoticed, he quietly placed a fairly large carton and a padded package atop one of the racks and said, "Good morning, everyone."

The technicians bounced to their feet, chorusing a respectful greeting. Mohammed shook hands with each one before turning to Arturo and Jana.

"Perfect timing, Mohammed. All checkouts are on schedule and we begin countdown to launch in 30 minutes." Then with obvious pride Arturo added, "The techs have done a marvelous job."

"We had help, Mr. Chairman," Sally motioned toward Arturo.

Mohammed turned to include Jana. "And you, my dear," he wryly added, "were surely everyone's inspiration."

Jana walked over to Mohammed and kissed him on the cheek. "Absolutely. I kept coffee cups filled, made sure there was an ample supply of sandwiches and cookies, and most importantly, kept out of the way."

"A likely story, Mrs. Diggs," the Chairman teased. Then he gestured to the three technicians, "Regardless of the outcome of the test," he volunteered with a wave of his hand, "there's a considerable bonus for each of you.

But just make sure," he winked, "that you keep that bit of data to yourselves."

"Station Control, this is Jana Control," Arturo called. "We are at T minus 5 minutes and counting."

"Roger, Jana Control. Confirm you are on schedule and counting at T minus 5 minutes for a 1000 hours *Jana II* launch. The area has been evacuated and all incoming traffic has been redirected from your planned flight path for 36 hours." There was a slight pause, "Just make sure you have her clear of the remote arm before engine initiation."

"Roger, Station Control, she'll be clear of the arm," he reassured. "Continuing count-down."

"Good luck Mr. Diggs." There was true sincerity in the otherwise stoic voice. "Station Control out."

As the systematic countdown resumed, Jana quietly watched the proceedings and glanced involuntary out the view port at the *Jana II* as the numerous check-off items were announced.

As Arturo listened to the system review leading to the final stage before launch, his mind began wandering. As before, with the original *Jana*, he recalled both Newsome's and Ben's words. Almost in a vision, their legacies raced through his mind. But it was one part of Newsome's legacy that echoed in his thoughts.

"Trips within our solar system will be child's play com-

> *pared to the conquest of the stars and galaxies of stars which are many light years away, indeed hundreds, thousands, millions and even billions of light years beyond Earth."*

Absently glancing at the clock ticking off the remaining time until the launch, he was surprised that all the reflections about Newsome and Ben had taken only a few seconds. Funny, he mused, how so many thoughts could occur so fast.

"Ten seconds and counting, Mr. Diggs." The senior tech's voice brought Arturo's mind abruptly to the present.

"At T-minus zero," he commanded, "initiate engine sequence! 5156279 alpha omega."

As before, only Arturo knew the latter numbers and words, and it was because of his spoken voice command to the computer that the "initiate" directive was accepted. The actual numbers had been changed, but Arturo had retained the still appropriate "alpha omega," — the beginning and the end.

The remote arm released its grip on the *Jana,* swung out of the way, and left the ship floating free in space. Arturo methodically began vocally verifying the sequence of events of all the operating parameters registering on the monitor screen.

"One tenth power on my mark," he said softly, before issuing the final one word command, "Now!"

310

The "now" command directed the counter rotating wagon-wheels to open slightly and allow one tenth percent of the Negafon beam to pass and collide with the Posafon beam. The Massafon Engine almost instantaneously propelled the *Jana II* away from the space station. There was a sudden burst of applause, then silence. They were all quietly occupied with their own thoughts as they watched the ship from the view ports.

As the *Jana II* traveled out of visual sight and then out of perceivable range, Arturo's mind returned to old Newsome. Why had he signed his legacy, "***Newsome Diggs, ∞ Beginning 1800-1888,***" with "***∞ Beginning***" underlined with a flourish on each end?

Steadily, the onboard voice computer announced speed and mission time. Appointing herself unofficial scorekeeper of the predicted key announcements from the onboard computer, Jana recorded each event on the wall chart as it occurred. Like the previous mission, as the *Jana II* went further and further from Earth, the transmission delay time increased. Five hours after launch, the *Jana II* was approaching the outer limits of the solar system. If the achievement of light speed were successful, it would be accomplished in another three hours and a half, although communication would not reach the control room until an additional four hours and fifteen minutes had elapsed.

The waiting seemed interminable, but there was nothing anyone could do to rush the procedure. To pass the time, Arturo continued to log the key flight announcements, Jana marked on the chart, the techs routinely dozed or busied themselves with trivial progress checks, and Mohammed alternately paced the room and peered at the monitors.

Exactly twelve and three quarter hours after launch, the onboard computer voice announced the first momentous milestone, "Light speed achieved in 8.5 hours. Massafon Engine off. Entering one-hour coast phase. All systems normal..."

"Light speed reached," Jana jubilantly repeated. "Coast period initiated. Check!" With a flourish, she drew a huge bull's-eye beside the anticipated event.

A chorus of cheers echoed through the room as each tried to be the first to congratulate the other.

Two hours later, the computer voice reported, "Coast period over and deceleration begun."

Twelve hours and 45 minutes crawled by before the next message, "Deceleration complete. Vehicle turned around and started for home..."

Trying to control his excitement, Arturo walked around the room, shaking the techs' outstretched hands. "All right, everyone," he cautioned, "we're still four hours and fifteen minutes away from the next communiqué. Let's all take a breather. Stretch your legs, take a nap..."

"My God, Arturo," Mohammed blustered, "how do you expect anyone to relax with every blood vessel in the body about to burst with excitement?"

"Mr. Chairman," Sally politely injected, tongue in cheek, "we can't have anything happen to you on our watch. Please observe your blood pressure, sir, or it'll sure be a black mark on our logs."

Mohammed threw back his head in a burst of laughter. "Well I'm certainly not going to be responsible for sullying your records." Restraining a yawn, he raised an eyebrow, "In fact that couch looks more and more inviting by the second." He moved to the couch and made a show of positioning his large frame in a comfortable position.

Then closing his eyes, he called out, "Oh, just one request, please wake me before the *Jana II* docks."

The calm and almost offhand behavior by the Chairman was a welcome relief from the tension. Whether Mohammed had intentionally or accidentally eased the strain, it was duly appreciated. Broad grins passed among the techs, Arturo and Jana.

Thirty-one hours and 45 minutes had elapsed since launch of the *Jana II*, and then came the next monotone exchange from the onboard commuter voice.

"Return trip coast period completed. Massafon Engine off..."

"Vehicle turned around. Massafon Engine engaged for final deceleration..."

The entire group gave a whooping cheer.

Mohammed placed his hand on Jana's arm. "That means she'll be home in another four hours," he glanced at the precision wall clock, "and exactly fifteen minutes."

Jana anxiously sucked in a breath, her eyes shining with excitement. "The computer messages will be more frequent as she gets closer."

As the minutes ticked by, the number of computer messages gradually began to increase.

The numbers on the atomic wall clock dutifully changed, but to all in the room, it seemed that time was standing still.

Finally, the voice computer began giving an exact recount of the *Jana II*'s forward velocity towards the space station.

"Speed 200,000 kilometers per second and decelerating. All systems normal..."

"Speed 100,000 kilometers per second and decelerating. All systems normal..."

Arturo's brow was bathed in perspiration as he impatiently listened for the next decisive message.

"Speed 5,000 kilometers per hour and decelerating. All systems normal..."

Not waiting for the next report and in a frenzy of elation, Arturo jumped up from the monitors. "That's it!" he roared, grabbing his wife's hand. "The *Jana II* is about to come home."

Like an excited group of children, everyone rushed to join Arturo and Jana at the view ports. As the ship came into view, all eagerly pressed their faces against the glass.

"There she is!" Jana shouted. "Oh, Arturo, you've done it!" Tears ran down her cheeks and she repeated, "You've done it!"

"By Allah," Mohammed said emotionally, "you have done it Arturo, you sure have. She worked perfectly."

In the background the onboard computer voice droned that the Massafon Engine was now pulsing on and off, but the group's attention was riveted on the maneuvering jets flawlessly guiding the *Jana II* to the space station's remote arm.

Slightly over 36 strenuous hours had passed since the *Jana II* had left on her historic maiden journey.

The computer voice issued one last unemotional report.

"Massafon Engine off. Docking complete. All systems normal."

Still grasping Jana's hand, Arturo walked over to the console. "Station Control, this is Jana Control. The *Jana II* is secured in the remote arm. All mission objectives were met."

"That's a big, big roger, Jana Control. Congratulations Mr. Diggs and Mr. Nahal."

"Thank you, Station Control. Jana Control out." Without waiting for any reply, he switched off the communication and turned to Mohammed. The two men shook hands firmly and then fell into each other's arms. Arturo pulled Jana into the embrace; and, in a reflexive action of sheer joy, they all hugged one another, congratulating, and talking all at once.

In the midst of the excitement, no one noticed Mohammed walk over and open the box

he had many hours before placed on the rack.
From the insulated container, he removed a
vintage bottle of champagne. Then he took it,
and a second padded package back to the glee-
ful group. "May I interest anyone in a toast?"
He handed the bottle to Arturo. "Don't worry,"
he advised, motioning toward the box still sitting on the rack, "there's more, and it's all
properly chilled."

Jana immediately started toward a cabinet for glasses, but Mohammed stopped her. "I
think these are more appropriate for the occasion, my dear," and with a flourish, he opened
the padded case. Brilliantly gleaming against
the red satin lining, was a matched set of eight
beautifully cut crystal champagne glasses.

"Oh, Mohammed," Jana's eyes widened
in surprise and admiration. "They're antiques
and absolutely exquisite."

"Jana, will you please read aloud the in-
scription on the foot of each glass," Mohammed
requested.

Peering down at the three lines of etched
writing, her mouth fell open. Finally she read:

*"Jana II—Successful Demonstration
Flight—Sept 10, 2198."*

She passed the glasses around, and
Arturo popped the champagne cork. All raised
their filled glasses as Mohammed offered the
first toast.

"To the *Jana II*," and he turned toward
the view port, where the ship loomed in silhou-
ette.

"To the *Jana II*..." all solemnly repeated
in unison.

Mohammed drained his glass, and then with a chuckle said, "Thank God we don't have a fireplace here in the space station."

The junior of the techs was puzzled. "A fireplace, sir?"

"An old, old custom, son," Mohammed gently explained, "of throwing your glass in the fireplace after celebrating a special toast and event." Twirling the glass in his hand to catch the brilliant hues of the cutting, "It would be a shame to see these beauties smashed. Jana was correct, they're truly antique." He added, "They were made in the late 19th century by T. J. Hawkes in Corning, New York. He named the pattern, 'Constellation'. Appropriate, don't you think."

Stunned looks crossed the faces of the three techs and they automatically tightened their grasp on the rare glasses.

As the toasts continued, a neat row of empty champagne bottles had appeared on the table. As often happens in an atmosphere filled with exhilaration, the revelers did not seem to feel the normal effects of the bubbly spirits; they only became more mellow and friendly. Arturo took the last bottle from the box and divided it equally between each person.

A serious look crossed his face as he raised his glass for the last toast. "To old Newsome and his foresight. To Ben, for his beliefs and life's work. To Marsh for his trust and help. To Mohammed for his never ending friendship and support. To Sally and her crew for their meticulous work. And last, to my

Jana, who never stopped believing and was always there."

In a gesture of camaraderie, each downed their champagne in a single gulp.

It was a month later, when Arturo was requested to present the data from the *Jana II's* successful flight to the Space Transport, Inc., board of directors.

Mohammed Nahal, as Chairman of STI, pounded the gavel to begin the meeting. "Gentlemen, I believe all of you know Mr. Arturo Diggs, and so I'll dispense with any further introductions." Pausing for full effect, "A month ago, I personally witnessed the successful test of a space vehicle powered by a new engine designed by Mr. Diggs," he looked around the room at each director, "which will revolutionize space travel. I'm happy to report that the vehicle, named the *Jana II,*" with a slight nod to Arturo, "after his beautiful wife I might add, achieved the speed of light at 300,000 kilometers per second. I'm sure each of you..."

There were loud gasps around the large table. One of the board members sputtered in disbelief, "The speed of light?" Then he added emphatically, "That's impossible. I've heard of Mr. Diggs' work, but..."

"Take my word for it, gentlemen," Mohammed brusquely overrode, "I was there. I saw it happen." There was an unabashed rash of murmurs as the directors skeptically shook their heads.

Undaunted, Mohammed controlled the rising commotion with a sharp bang of the gavel. "The speed of light was achieved by a propulsion system Mr. Diggs has named the Massafon Engine." Before anyone could break in, Mohammed rose and switched off the overhead lights and illuminated the individual monitors in front of each director. "Now, if you'll permit, I'd like Mr. Diggs to present the data from the flight."

For the next hour Arturo presented the flight data and emphasized the relevant planetary travel times with the Massafon Engine. He defined the shrinking size and time paradox at the speed of light and the increasing mass theorem. He was also careful to explain why Einstein's work was still valid, even with the discovery of the Massafon.

Arturo concluded his presentation with a summary of potential flight profiles to other planets. "I draw your attention to the chart with which we began the presentation."

MASSAFON ENGINE PLANETARY TRAVEL TIMES VERSUS DISTANCE - ONE WAY

(Including acceleration and deceleration of 1,000 g's, the maximum where human protection is possible)

PLANET	MEAN DISTANCE KILOMETERS	FLIGHT TIME	VELOCITY KM/SEC	% SPEED OF LIGHT	CURRENT FLIGHT TIMES*
MOON	384,000	7 minutes	971	0.32%	1.5 hours
MERCURY	93,000,000	1.7 hours	15,110	5.0%	7 days
VENUS	42,800,000	1.1 hours	10,251	3.4%	3 days
MARS	76,000,000	1.5 hours	13,360	5.5%	5 days
ASTEROID BELT	199,000,000	2.5 hours	22,100	7.4%	14 days
JUPITER	778,340,000	5.0 hours	43,426	14.5%	54 days
SATURN	1,427,010,000	6.8 hours	118,378	19.8%	98 days
URANUS	2,869,600,000	9.6 hours	167,867	28.0%	199 days
Neptune	4,496,670,000	12.0 hours	210,136	35.3%	311 days

*Current flight times are based on maximum velocity attainable by Space Transport, Inc. vehicles in operation today.

Even in the dimly lit room, Arturo could see that a majority of the directors still had dumbfounded expressions on their faces. "Perhaps," he diplomatically suggested, "for those of you who have forgotten some of your Physics I classes, a brief, and non-technical review would be in order."

A rotund board member jovially injected, "Especially for some of us dimwits who never even got past algebra."

"That's hard to believe, Harold," Mohammed smoothly countered, "coming from a man who founded, and heads, one of the largest financial institutions in the country."

"Hell, Nahal," Harold shot back, "I hire experts smart enough to do the bean-counting and grunt work."

There was a hearty round of laughter at the interchange. When the diversion had settled, Arturo lightly tapped the table. "Then with your permission, ladies and gentlemen," he waited a moment as the heads slowly turned toward him, "back to the basics." He ignored the sighs from the small handful of directors who believed themselves well above a primer explanation. "The flight times outlined on the graph before you depend solely on how much acceleration, technically called "g's," a human can withstand. Based on today's technology, our current electromagnetic fields can only protect a human against a maximum of a 1,000 g force, or an acceleration of 1,000 times Earth's gravitational pull of 9.82 meters per-second."

Satisfied when he saw a few heads nod in comprehension, he continued, "Without that protection, a human weighing 80 kilograms on Earth, would weigh 80 times 1,000 g's, or 80,000 kilograms due to the acceleration. Of course, he'd be crushed and never survive the trip. And that's the limiting factor of speed achieved versus the trip time to planets. All trip times are based on the maximum g force against which we can protect the crew and passengers."

A sharp cough from the end of the room obliged Arturo to look in that direction. A board member, who was a renowned physicist, raised her hand for the floor.

"Yes, Dr. Meirs?" Arturo courteously asked.

"Do you foresee ever being able to exceed our current limit of 1,000 g's acceleration and thus be able to shorten the times even further?"

"Possibly. But as you know, the vehicle itself must also be able to withstand the increased forces of acceleration. At some point there is a diminishing return of increased g's, versus vehicle weight and, finally, versus payload. For the present, 1,000 g's appears to be the practical limit." The uncomplicated explanation appeared to suffice and Arturo proceeded with his discourse.

"If I can direct your attention back to your monitors," he gave the directors a moment, "you will notice that the Massafon Engine's full capability is never used. In other words, space travel in our solar system will never fully utilize full light speed."

Harold, the stout director again cut in, "Excuse me Mr. Diggs, but if the potential is there, why not use it?"

"As an example, sir," Arturo explained, "Pluto is some 5,900,220,000 kilometers away. To reach the speed of light of 300,000 kilometers per second at 1,000 g's acceleration, the distance covered by a space vehicle would be 4,580,000,000 kilometers in an elapsed time of 8.5 hours. By the time you slowed down to zero speed, the vehicle would have covered 9,160,000,000 kilometers, or beyond Pluto by about 3.3 billion miles..."

One of the other directors, who was prone to outbursts, and obviously had not been listening closely, interrupted, "If the vehicle, at the speed of light, would reach Pluto in less than fourteen hours, what's the necessity of slowing down to zero speed?"

From the rear of the room, Dr. Meirs' voice sounded sarcastic, "Because, damn it, the vehicle has to slow down to keep from over-shooting the planet."

"Thank you, Dr. Meirs," Arturo acknowledged. "Let me attempt to clarify. Since the vehicle is limited to 1,000 g's, flight profiles are based on 1,000 g acceleration half way to the target planet. Otherwise, as Dr. Meirs aptly pointed out, if the vehicle's speed were not reduced, it would pass the planet." He paused, but no one spoke. "When the vehicle is turned around, at the half way point, it slows down at the same rate of 1,000 g deceleration, because the Massafon Engine fires backwards during this deceleration. Now let me repeat in a different way, if we did not slow down while exceeding 1,000 g's, the passengers would be crushed from the force of the deceleration, the same as they would if we exceeded the initial acceleration g's."

Arturo was careful to speak concisely and slowly, so as not to insult any director's capacity to grasp his explanation, but to avoid confusing those not technically inclined. "The distances on the chart to our solar system planets are based on their average distances from Earth. For example, Mars mean distance is approximately 76,000,000 kilometers from Earth. Flight times will vary, longer or shorter, depending on where the particular planet is at any given time."

He was pleased to note the nodding of heads and the director's attention to the monitors. "You'll also notice the round trip time to Pluto is just over a day. The current round trip time on one of our unmanned exploratory vehicles is over two years. Round trip to Jupiter or its moons is now over 30 weeks, versus 10 hours for the Massafon Engine vehicle. Mars by comparison is now a round trip time of just over 3.0 hours, versus a little over ten days with the current vehicles. Again, please remember the trip times projected are for the mean, or average, distances from Earth..."

Some of the board members simply accepted his summary and were mentally projecting what the new Massafon Engine would do for the Space Transport Corporation. A few still struggled with the complex scientific breakthrough.

"Mr. Diggs, may I call you Arturo?" Dr. Meirs waited for a response.

"Certainly, it would be my honor."

"Arturo, the law of conservation of energy states that energy can neither be created or destroyed. We know that photons have an energy that's not unlike radio or communication signals, except the wavelengths are much shorter. But the measurable energy is very, very small compared to what your Massafon Engine has achieved. Where does the energy come from?"

"An excellent question, Dr. Meirs," Arturo complimented. "The energy of a concentrated density of photons has always been there. It only remained to demonstrate how to release it." He turned to include all the board members. "You see, a photon is thought to be massless, without any physical and measurable dimensions. In point of fact, a photon doesn't have either of those. Further, its rest mass is zero."

All eyes in the room were now focused on Arturo. "But, when a photon is split, positive and negatively charged particles are formed. When the particles are made to collide at the speed of light, they combine to form another new particle, the one I named Massafon..." his slight hesitation was deliberate, "...which has mass and huge amounts of energy. I didn't create these particles of mass and size, nor were the Posafon and Negafon particles created. They were there all the time but in a different form which necessitated a method of release. I realize that the Massafon particles go against all accepted scientific theorems, but they do exist."

"That's good enough for me, Mr. Chairman," Harold emphatically stated, reassured by the looks of endorsement from the board members. "I don't pretend to grasp all the technical data, but I leave that understanding to Mr. Diggs and other more learned colleagues." He gave a slight bow of his head in the direction of Dr. Meirs.

"Excellent," Mohammed projected, not waiting for discussion. "Now, ladies and gentlemen, with your approval, I propose to immediately begin plans to retrofit all our ships, including transports, personnel carriers and remote vehicles with this new Massafon Engine."

Switching on the overhead lights, Mohammed took his place at the head of the conference table. "I believe you have all come to the same conclusion about what this new engine will achieve for our company." In concise terms, he began outlining the merits. "First of all, the cost of operations will be significantly reduced. Secondly, the travel times, wherever we choose to go, will be reduced by 60 to 700 times, depending on current speeds of the vehicles."

Then a wide smile brightened his face, and he purposefully lowered his voice. "Thirdly, a trip to the nearest star, Alpha Centauri, is now in the realm of possibility, possibly a new civilization, with a round trip time of about 8.7 years."

Caught up by the possibilities, one of the board members excitedly said, "Hell, it used to take a quarter of that time to Pluto and back. Now it's under 14 hours away or a round trip time of about a full day."

There was no doubt. The entire board saw the business potential of the new engine. They continued to question Arturo about the lead-time to retrofit the entire fleet and how long to construct new and bigger ships. It was evident they were particularly intrigued with an Alpha Centauri vehicle.

"To retrofit the existing fleet of Space Transport vehicles," Arturo began answering the flurry of inquiries, "will require the use of higher strength materials, even better than lithium-aluminum."

"Would you go over the increasing mass and shrinking time and dimensions issues again," one board member requested, tapping his brow, "I can't seem to get it straight in my thick skull."

Trying to be as exact as possible, without confusing the issue, Arturo again covered the findings of the *Jana II*'s flight and his rationale concerning what really happens as the speed of light is approached and finally achieved. When he finished, he summarized with a singular statement. "Einstein was not wrong. He simply was unaware of the Massafon particle and its ability to travel the speed of light. Without that particle, his theories are valid to observers watching something such as a manned space ship approach the speed of light. Remember, however, the people on the space ship and the space ship itself, are not aware of the presumed changes. Only the people on Earth observing think they see a change in mass, time and dimensions."

A board member who had not previously spoken asked, "But I've been told that calculations say it would take the total energy produced by all Earth's power plants to accelerate a metric ton to 99.9999% of the speed of light and still never achieve light speed. How do you rationalize that?"

Arturo smiled and looked the questioner in the eye. "Two ways. First, discovery of the Massafon particle, which has been proved to have mass, size and travels at the speed of light. Secondly, the flight of the *Jana II*. She did travel at 300,000 kilometers per second. Our data proves it."

"But how," the board member persisted, "do you answer the question of two and a half centuries of accepted theorems regarding the impossibility of achieving light speed?"

"Again, the accepted theorems are based on, 'nothing can travel at the speed of light', and therefore infinite energy was required. And nothing on which all the theorems were based could, until recently. Now we have a particle that travels only at light speed, as far as we know. The 'book' will have to be rewritten."

"Thank you, Arturo." Dr. Meirs astutely brought the questioning to a halt. "You've answered our queries, appropriately and in depth. Now, Mr. Chairman, I think it's time we consider your approach."

"Thank you, Doctor." Mohammed rose, turning to Arturo and shaking his hand. "And thank you, Mr. Diggs, for an excellent presentation." He spoke formally but with a warm smile and a twinkle in his eye.

Equally reserved, Arturo replied, "You're welcome, Mr. Chairman." Realizing it was his cue to leave the meeting, he walked around the table to shake hands with each board member.

The door had hardly shut behind Arturo when Mohammed launched into his well-rehearsed presentation. "Ladies and gentlemen, if you will please take out the documents sequestered in your individual coffers."

Each of the twelve directors pushed a hidden button, which opened a recessed panel concealed in the conference table. Instantly, a leather-bound book appeared in front of each member.

"Before you is my proposal, compiled with the help of Arturo Diggs and my staff. If you wish, I'll give you a few minutes to glance through the contents."

Leaning back in his chair, his corpulent belly almost touching the edge of the table, Harold impatiently admonished, "Let's not fool around with protocol but get right down to how much cash you project we'll need for the new engines and to retrofit the entire Space Transport fleet."

Mohammed could always count on this particular board member to bypass time-consuming amenities. When there was no further comment, the Chairman flipped open his own text. "Agreed! I would like to call your attention to section five, the financial pages."

While the directors noisily flicked the pages to the designated section, Mohammed launched into his brief opening statement. "As per the financial projections, you can clearly see that we generate enough cash to achieve complete retrofit in about five years." He only hesitated long enough to underscore his next declaration: "We still would have considerable cash left for stock dividends to the shareholders. The chair is open for a motion to proceed."

The positive mood of the directors was visible in their expressions. Round after round of questions were presented by the board, whether trivial or not, Mohammed answered in precise and concrete terms. His recurring theme being Space Transport's ability to control transportation within the solar system, to open up further planets for possible new or continuing sources of minerals, and to establish colonies on receptive planets or moons.

"It seems to me," Harold summed up, "we have the needed capital and now, the Massafon Engine, to do the job. There isn't a single planet in the solar system which wouldn't need the same supplies and transportation as the current colonies."

Recognizing that any further discussion would be irrelevant, Mohammed promptly emphasized his most marketable point. "With the advent of the new ships, no one can compete with us, either in transportation time or payload. No one!"

"Mr. Chairman," Dr. Meirs candidly picked up the reins, "without additional discussion, I move to accept the proposal to retrofit the entire fleet with the Massafon Engine."

The words had barely been spoken, when Harold spoke, "I second the motion."

"All in favor," Mohammed leapt in, "Say aye."

An overwhelming chorus of "ayes" echoed in the room.

"Any nays?" but Mohammed had asked only out of convention and then banged down the gavel, "Seconded and passed, thank you, ladies and gentlemen."

There was an expression of satisfaction on Mohammed's face, and he allowed a few minutes of quiet conversation between the board members before politely tapping his pencil on the table for order. "There is an important detail that I wish to bring to your attention. There are two keys to the success of the Massafon Engine, each of which are known only to Arturo and myself. For security reasons, the details of these will remain only with the two of us."

Frowns appeared on several of the directors' faces, but Mohammed held up his hand for patience. "If anything were to happen to both of us," he clarified to allay any fears, "our lawyers have been instructed to reveal the details to the new chairman of Space Trans."

"Do you propose," one of the attorney board members asked, "registering the engine with the international patent office?"

"Absolutely not!" Mohammed thundered. "That would only give our competition proprietary information with which they could possibly copy it and, along with slight changes, be able to break the patent."

331

"Besides," Dr. Meirs interjected, to stop any further discussion, "as long as the two keys are kept secret, why bother."

The female attorney board member who had originally posed the question emphatically nodded in accord. "I agree. The fewer people that know the particulars, the better off the company is to protect its assets. One other question, though, what does Mr. Diggs receive for all his work, other than his agreed-upon consultant's salary?"

This was exactly the question that Mohammed wanted the board to ask, but before he could reply, Dr. Meirs' voice sounded from the rear of the room, "I move that Mr. Diggs be given a proper reward for his work." She paused to assess the other board members' reactions. Pleased by the positive nods, she added, "That amount should be increased as each of the new engines is proved successful."

"I second that motion," the attorney promptly replied.

Not even waiting for the Chairman's call for vote, the board unanimously affirmed the motion.

"And you certainly have my agreement," Mohammed smiled. "Harold," turning to the heavy-set director on his right, "as chairman of the board's compensation commission, would you and your committee please give us a recommendation for Mr. Diggs' additional benefits?"

The five-committee members stood and followed Harold into an adjoining room. Behind closed doors, the caucus lasted but a few minutes. When they returned, Harold presented the committee's recommendation, which was then seconded and approved by all board members.

"Thank you, ladies and gentlemen, that completes the agenda." Bringing the meeting to a close Mohammed asked, "Do I hear a motion to adjourn?"

After the board members had left, Mohammed called Arturo to join him.

"Well, Arturo," he beamed, "you'll never have to worry where your next meal is coming from. The board was most generous, whereas normally they're skinflints," and he couldn't help chuckling, "except where their own fees are concerned."

"It wasn't possible without your help, Mohammed," Arturo gratefully responded.

"Come on, don't be so modest. It was well deserved and are purely just dues." Then abruptly turning to the task at hand, "In any event, you've got your work cut out for you. I want the entire fleet retrofitted with the Massa-fon Engine as soon as possible..." and shaking his finger at Arturo, "...before I retire in seven years at the ancient old age of seventy."

Arturo started to object to the reference of being aged, but Mohammed, embarrassed by his own sentimentality, all but pushed his friend toward the door. "Now get out of here. Go home and share the good news with your beautiful Jana."

2199
THE ASTEROID

Filip Newsome Diggs had two momentous concerns on his mind. He had enjoyed the mining
and geology work in the Asteroid-Belt but was
anxious to embark on launching his own company. The enforced long stays in the space stations had become monotonous. In the scant
free time he had, there were only so many
books he could read and so many exercises to
speed away the hours. But what was most
troubling was that none of the women on the
stations appealed to him as a wife. It certainly
wasn't the lack of love affairs with beautiful
and exciting partners, but each time there was
always something missing. What he really
yearned for was to embark on his own business
with a life partner by his side, just like his dad
and mother.

The compensation he had received over
the past six years and Marsh's inheritance had
been carefully saved, with much of it invested
in the spiraling Space Transport stock. His
contract year was up, and if he chose, he would
be allowed to spend a month on Earth before
having to decide whether to renew an agreement for another one-year term. At twenty-

eight, Filip made the key decision of his life. He resigned his position with the mining company and decided to be his own boss to bring his dreams into reality.

Jana and Arturo could not help but observe the excitement in Filip's face and amplified in his voice. Since arriving in San Diego two weeks before, he had listened intently to Arturo's success with the *Jana II.* He guaranteed his father that the Diggsanium material was readily available and there would be no problem in obtaining it.

It was the Diggsanium that was the basis for Filip's venture. From the mining corporation for which he had worked, he already had obtained a contract to purchase the entire and obscure medium-sized asteroid where Diggsanium was found. His former employer was indifferent to the mineral, since their primary interest was raw material, not finished goods. They had no manufacturing facilities and thus the massive debts to finance the conversion equipment. Aside from the Diggsanium, Filip intended to set up a modern manufacturing facility to produce other mined products. Filip's plan included living quarters for himself and technicians he'd hire. He also foresaw being able to machine these minerals in quantity on his airless asteroid, where a complete vacuum existed and raw materials would not be destroyed by oxygen contact.

"Dad, Mother, if I can finance it, the damn thing is a gold mine. Besides, it would also give Space Transport a guaranteed lock on

Diggsanium since I'd control all of the available supply."

"What did the banks or the Planetary Investment Corporation have to say, Filip?" Arturo asked with interest. "You've spent most all the past two weeks talking to them about the investment."

"Most of the banks will loan 50% of the initial funds required if I put up the remaining 50% as equity. With my savings, and the generous inheritance from Uncle Marsh, I can swing that, but it doesn't leave anything for expansion, working capital..."

"Or emergencies," Jana injected, but the pained expression on her son's face made her recant. "I'm sorry, dear, I spoke before thinking."

"That point, lack of adequate capital, has been brought to my attention more than once, Mother."

"Then," Jana looked upset, "you certainly didn't need my thoughtless input."

"You're forgiven," Filip countered, then with a twinkle. "Isn't that what moms are for, to remind over zealous offspring of their limitations."

"Oh, darling, I didn't mean..."

"Just kidding," and he gave her a warm hug. "Anyway, PIC, the Planetary Investment Corp., based on my putting up the same aforementioned amount of equity, will invest any of the additional monies needed so I won't be undercapitalized."

"Well, Filip, that's wonderful news," Arturo said enthusiastically.

"But, and there always seems to be a 'but', for that, they want 80% of the company." Filip's face was set in firm conviction, "Dad, I don't mind giving up some ownership, but not 80%."

"I agree, Son," Arturo shook his head thoughtfully. "After all, you're the only one that knows how to design the machines to shape the Diggsanium."

These were the financial problems that had faced entrepreneurs since the dawn of time — money to realize their dreams and hoped for successes.

"Filip, you know the stock and bonuses we get from Space Trans will be more than your mother and I will ever need."

Jana nodded in agreement, but before she could speak, Filip almost shouted, "Now wait a minute, you two! I didn't tell you all this in the hope you'd finance me. No way! I'll find the money without having to use your funds." Like his parents, Filip was a proud man and did not look for or anticipate handouts.

"Just a minute, my hotheaded tycoon," Arturo laughed, "any financing we discuss is purely on a business basis."

"That's right, Filip." Jana stood staunchly with her husband. "Your father and I only want to be silent partners. For our investment, we two will each acquire 25% ownership of the company. You receive the remaining 50%."

Filip pursed his lips, vehemently shaking his head back and forth.

"It's up to you to operate and manage the business," Arturo paused, and deftly added, "and make it successful. I won't have time to help because of my involvement in building the new transports. You'll have to go it alone...and you can."

"No! I appreciate your offer, but that's too much to ask and..."

"Filip, your father is right," Jana sternly overrode his objections. "Of course, we want you to succeed in whatever you choose to do." Her face softened into a smile. "And what better way than for our own family to work together. You'll make money, and we'll share in your success." She could see that Filip was weakening and so to hasten his decision, urged, "Then it's settled. Unless you disagree, as of this moment, the three of us will become partners in a new business, with you running it."

For a prolonged moment, Filip turned away from his parents, stifling an impassioned sigh. Unsure of their son's reaction to their generous offer, Jana and Arturo glanced uneasily at each other. The young man pivoted around with an affectionate grin on his face. His voice was filled with emotion as he extended his hands to his parents. "To my co-partners, the best colleagues and most important, friends, a son could ever hope to have."

As Jana grasped her son's outstretched hand, her dark eyes filled with tears. Clasping Filip's other hand, Arturo could only murmur, "Thank you Son." Then befitting the magic moment, that only those so intimate could ever share, Arturo gathered his family into his arms.

The spell was finally broken when Filip summed up his feelings. "In a few years, we'll buy our own ship, which I already christen...the *Jana III.*"

A throaty laugh exploded from Jana, "For heaven's sake, what in the world would my family have done if I'd been named Clementine?"

"Oh, my darling, oh my darling..." Arturo burst into song, "Oh my darling, Clementine, by any name you'd still be mine!"

Not to be outdone, Filip picked up with his own version. "Oh my darling, oh my darling, Janatine, you're a mother who is so sublime..."

"...so pristine..." Arturo crooned in harmony.

"...so diamondtine..." Filip intoned.

"...my favorite valentine..." came Arturo's deep baritone.

"...and your shoes are number nine..." Filip echoed.

Holding her hands over her ears, Jana wailed, "Now, both of you, stop it this instant."

"Really, my dear," Arturo admonished, "don't you enjoy being serenaded by two handsome men?"

"And I was just getting warmed up, Mother...your hair the color of sabelline..."

"No more, no more," Jana giggled and covered her face. "You're embarrassing me to death." Then in desperation, "Anyway, we're out of time and rhyme." She began to laugh at her own unintentional paraphrase and pun. "Did I really say that?"

Arturo chuckled and glanced at the wall clock. "Your mother's right. We're due at Mohammed's for dinner in less than an hour."

"Good grief," Filip started for the door. "I've got to change." Over his shoulder he commented, "Haven't seen little Jamille in years. Does she still wear pigtails?"

Jana's mouth fell open in astonishment, but Arturo smugly motioned her not to respond.

Dinner that evening was excellent. The servants and cooks had outdone themselves, but unfortunately the fine cuisine had been wasted on Filip. If his life had depended upon it, he could not have accounted for a bite or taste of food he had eaten.

While the small group discussed various subjects, Filip found himself transfixed by Mohammed's twenty-one-year-old daughter, Jamille. Her name, Filip reminded himself, was an adaptation of the old Arabic word for "beautiful." He tried to recount how many years had passed since he had actually seen her, at least six, maybe eight or nine. Their paths never crossed when he had been home on vacation because she had either been traveling or attending college at her father's alma mater in London. Although they had grown up together, and been playmates on occasion, she was certainly not the chubby little pig-tailed youngster he remembered. The baby fat had disappeared. She now had a willowy, tall, curvaceous slim body, crowned with flowing blond hair falling to her waist. Glancing at Mohammed, with his dark brown hair, he recalled that Jamille's mother also had lovely blond tresses. A twinge of remorse passed through him at the thought of being unable to attend Mrs. Nahal's funeral several years ago when he was stationed in the asteroid belt.

Filip tried to remember what his parents had told him about Jamille, either in letters or conversation. He knew of her high IQ, which even as a youngster had been well over 160, and he had always respected her brilliance. Unlike many of the other younger girls of his acquaintance, Jamille had always been an excellent conversationalist. The only details he could actually recall were that she had started college at fifteen and had obtained a master's degree in business management. The most important fact that no one had informed him of was that the "little pig-tailed" girl had blossomed into a ravishing beauty.

When Jamille caught him staring at her, Filip blushed and averted his eyes. When he finally plucked up the courage to look at her again, their eyes locked. A beguiling smile parted her full lips and revealed the most perfect teeth he had even seen. Deep in his soul, Filip knew she was the most beautiful woman he had ever met.

To Filip, Jamille's voice sounded like a choir of angelic harps when she melodiously said, "I'm so anxious to hear, first hand about your last six years in the asteroids."

The three elder diners placed their napkins on the table and retired silently to the library. Filip and Jamille remained seated. Over an hour had passed before they realized that they had been left alone.

Filip and Jamille were married barely a month later. She wholeheartedly shared his dreams and plans, and had no reservations about leaving Earth to build a home and business on a distant asteroid. To each other they were one entity — destined to be together.

Over the next several months, Arturo surpassed himself — the *Jana II* had been upgraded to a manned vehicle. Life support, navigation, control, and escape pod systems had been installed. Although the vehicle had been outfitted in Earth's atmosphere, the Massafon Engine compartment with the sensitive Posafon and Negafon mirrors would be free of oxygen as long as the engine was operating. But if the engine were accidentally turned off, air would rush in and damage the mirrors. Arturo solved this problem by designing an automatic partition to operate like a camera diaphragm, which when closed, would leave an airtight vacuum in the engine compartment. The diaphragm was sequenced to operate just before air was able to surge inside to the sensitive equipment, thus keeping the mirrors free from damage by oxygen.

Arturo was to accompany the captain and the copilot on the first manned flight. He had chosen the flight path of the original *Jana*, taking the *Jana II* past the planet Pluto by almost 4.4 billion miles. The round trip was 36 hours for a total distance of 20.5 billion kilometers at an average speed of 158,200 kilometers per second. Two hours of the flight would be at light speed of 300,000 kilometers per second.

There was no vibration or noise as with rocket engines that employed the chemicals of beryllium-hydrogen or deuterium-tritium, which were vaporized by a fusion reactor. In fact, the crew felt no sensation of movement, except during the initial acceleration phase.

When the Massafon Engine was shut down after achieving light speed, the electrostatic magnetic field in the crew cabin was reduced from 1,000 g's to one g, and the occupants could move around freely. The vehicle was capable of proceeding almost indefinitely at c because there was no pull of gravity or atmosphere to slow it down.

As the *Jana II* coasted, Arturo picked up the canister he had brought with him and motioned for the copilot to energize the small jettison port he had designed into the side of the vehicle. He removed the cover and carefully inserted the canister into the awaiting port.

"Goodbye old friend. You will travel at the speed of light throughout the galaxy for all time. Your last wish has been fulfilled." Tears streamed down Arturo's face as he pushed a switch that propelled the sacred canister containing Dr. Marshall Bernside's ashes to the eternal vacuum of deep space.

As Arturo had predicted, neither he nor the crew noticed any change in themselves, the

344

elapsed time, or size of the vehicle and its component parts.

Six months after other successful manned test flights, the *Jana II* was declared operational and began regular shuttles of personnel to-and-from Mars and the Asteroid-Belt.

2202
WORLD COURT JUDGEMENT

During the past three years Arturo had at his disposal the entire engineering staff of Space Transport, Inc., for designing the retrofit packages for the freighters and personnel carriers. Work on the transport vehicles was conducted two at a time, with the huge freighters given priority. Retrofit of the vehicles required complete replacement of the electrical controls, crew and passenger pod electrostatic g fields, and the computer and navigational systems. All vehicles were strengthened to withstand the forces of acceleration while achieving light speed. New parts for the freighters were assembled on Earth, and then taken into orbit for final assembly in space. Personnel carriers were retrofitted on Earth with the Diggsanium mirrors for the Massafon Engines being installed under vacuum while the diaphragm was closed and the compartment evacuated of all air.

Arturo had made the decision to use the original Massafon Engine design, as opposed to installing a larger fusion reactor and rubyionium laser gun for increased thrust. The latter necessitated multiple engines to handle the huge payloads the transports were capable of carrying. The engine compartments and engines were removed and replaced by 48 bundled Massafon Engines. Each was housed in 10-meter diameter by 40-meter long tubes at the extreme rear of the vehicle. The old fuel tanks were duly converted into cargo space, which doubled the payload from the original 50,000 metric tons capacity.

The newly conceived control system allowed all or only a pair of opposed engines to operate as required by the particular destination versus the desired transition time. Four additional Massafon Engines were placed perpendicularly to the aft end of the freighter at 90° to each other for directional control.

Smaller personnel and equipment carriers, along with planetary exploration vehicles, carried two, three or five Massafon Engines, depending on the vehicle size and payload requirements. Directional control was achieved through gimbaling or moving the engine tubes at angles from the vehicle line of thrust.

As each newly retrofitted freighter was completed and flight-tested, it had gone into service. Customers were hungry for this new short-time flight service. They increased their orders for additional raw materials and finished goods from space stations, Mars, the Asteroid-Belt and the Moon. The larger Massafon transports were kept busy. Smaller vehicles were also in constant demand to explore for new sources of materials on other planets such as Mercury and the moons of Jupiter and Saturn. The continual additions of recreation and permanent living quarters on the Moon and Mars resulted in small multi-domed cities. Supplies were always in demand; in spite of the flourishing hypo gardens of vegetables, flowers and plants, the new residents requested more.

Jana and Arturo watched through the viewport of the Space Transport orbiting space station as the last vehicle to be retrofitted was released from its docking arm and turned towards the Moon. As the 100-meter diameter x 500-meter length freighter slowly began to move away from the station, they watched as it suddenly accelerated and disappeared from view. Only the pencil-like light from the photon beam emanating from the Massafon Engine remained; it also disappeared as the flight path was corrected to the programmed heading. Arturo and Mohammed insisted that Jana be present when the last vehicle, named "San Diego Lady", was deemed operational.

"That's the last one, lover. Now, maybe you and I can take a trip to South America...or Egypt...or the Moon...or at least somewhere away from constant work and schedules," Jana said eagerly.

"Hell of an idea, hon. Where would you like to go? Perhaps we could visit Filip, Jamille and the kids in the asteroid belt. It's been sometime since they were here and..."

Jana interrupted with, "No! I love them all dearly, but I know what will happen if you two get together. Nothing but talk about work and new projects, and it will be anything but relaxing. And I want you to relax for a while before the next venture, whatever that is."

Encircling his wife in an embrace, Arturo agreed, "Okay, you win. Where to and when?"

"My love, my Arturo," and she gave an excited sigh, "Mohammed has arranged for his personal shuttle to drop us off at a little resort in the Ural Mountains of United North Asia. There are no visi-phones, electronic news media, or communications of any kind with the outside world there." Jana gently pushed aside, waiting for a reaction.

"And just how long will we stay at this Garden of Eden you and Mohammed have arranged?" Arturo asked, putting his arm around her waist.

"A month."

"A month? Good lord, what do we do when we're not in bed making love?"

"Wonderful skiing in the mountains, hiking, swimming, fishing, horseback riding, golf, and just plain relaxing with no schedules or deadlines to meet. No worries, no pressures and no work. And most of all, just you and I together. How does that sound, lover?"

"Guess I don't have a choice," Arturo said, ducking Jana's playful punch.

"Mohammed guaranteed that no matter what happens, you won't be called for any reason. And further, we are to stay there the full 30 days before even considering leaving. Oh, Arturo, let's do it."

"When do we leave? By the way, what about clothes, skis, golf clubs and so on?"

Jana took his hand and pulled him towards the door leading to the shuttle, saying, "It's all arranged. New clothes, skis, clubs and whatever else we'll need has been provided by Mohammed — using my list, of course."

True to her word, the shuttle took them to the resort, and Arturo quickly shed his pressures and worries. Jana kept him busy with the various activities and the pure pleasure of their just being together without schedules or meetings to attend. He gradually let go of his continuous thoughts for future light speed research; but in the back of his mind was the question, "How can the speed of light be exceeded." In an idle moment, the ending of old Newsome's legacy randomly crossed his mind and he wondered what "∞ *Beginning*" meant. Arturo felt that he had accomplished the beginning with Grandfather Ben's help, but he still wondered about the symbol for infinity—∞.

As Mohammed Nahal prepared for the board meeting that afternoon, prior to the stockholders meeting the following day, he saw that freighter payload had doubled during the last six months. This was no surprise, since the Space Transport Corporation was the only company with the large Massafon transports. A few companies had smaller vehicles, but world customers had used them only when Space Trans was solidly booked. But now, the new Massafon freighters had even taken that business. Why not? The travel time was considerably less, plus the payload per freighter was double the previous capabilities. Mohammed even had offered to sell the old chemical-nuclear engines at twenty cents on the dollar to anyone wishing to buy them. Two companies had bought engines, but even then couldn't compete. As a result, profits from the increased payload would pay off the investment in the new Massafon vehicles in less than three years. Preparation for board members and stockholders was a pleasure when everything was going right and money was being made.

As he walked down the hall to the boardroom for the enjoyable meeting he anticipated, a tall man got out of the elevator and strode towards him, closely followed by a company security guard. "Mr. Mohammed Nahal," the stranger said and stuck out his hand, "a moment please."

The security guard, quickly and apologetically responded, "Mr. Nahal, I tried to tell him you were unavailable, but his credentials were in order and..."

Taken aback at the sudden confrontation, Mohammed answered after a moment, "Yes, I'm Mohammed Nahal. And who are you, may I ask?"

Holding up his credentials the stranger said politely, "I'm from the Council of World Governments, who have requested that you be given this letter. Now that it's delivered, I'll leave and not take up any more of your time. Thank you, sir. It has been most pleasant meeting you."

With that, the stranger immediately reentered the waiting elevator, with the security guard following, leaving Mohammed wondering what that was all about. On his way to the board room, he glanced at the letter and saw it was correctly addressed to him as Chairman & Chief Executive Officer of Space Transport, Incorporated in San Diego, California. The return address was listed as World Governments Resources Committee, New York, New York, USA. Clearly printed in red were the words, HAND DELIVER. He thought, "More important things were at hand than a probable solicitation for some charitable fund of the Committee." Not that Mohammed wasn't sensitive to charity drives. Space Transport gave generous amounts each year to a vast array of Committee sponsored charities. Absently sticking the envelope into his portfolio, along with his report to the board and agenda, he dismissed it from his mind.

The secretary's report was waived, the old business quickly dispensed with and the awaited for new business report was given by Mohammed to the board. Unmanned exploration trips to unexplored planets were reviewed, along with results of the findings. Payload reports, sales and profit statements, future projections and, overall status of the company was covered in minute detail. The board, overjoyed with the results, showed its approval in the few questions asked.

"In summary, ladies and gentlemen," Mohammed concluded, "we now completely control space. No competitor can touch us in pricing per kilogram of payload transported. We're down to ten cents per kilo, including the

30-year depreciation of the vehicles and equipment. Also, no one can even approach us in trip time, with exception of Geo Transport's Moon trips; even now they only have a few vehicles — and damned few at that — mostly personnel carriers, small supplies and equipment."

"Mr. Chairman, what about the possibility of exploring our nearest neighbor, the star, Alpha Centauri. Might there be planets circling it?" the physicist board member queried.

"Good question. Months ago I took the liberty of asking the staff and Arturo Diggs to begin plans for an unmanned vehicle to explore a new solar system. And Alpha Centauri it is. If there's anything there, we'll find it."

"When do you expect to launch such a vehicle, Mohammed."

"In approximately three to four years."

The board members approved of Mohammed's actions, with one member commenting, "We never get ahead of you, Mohammed. I still remember how you handled all that work of Mr. Diggs. Thank God you did. We probably would still be debating whether or not to approve money for such a 'hair-brained idea'." Everyone chuckled, but each knew the statement to be true.

After the laughter subsided, the senior member of the board stood and solemnly offered a toast with a cup of coffee. "To our Chairman, Mohammed Nahal. It's men like him that make corporations great." Mohammed started to object but wasn't given a chance. "I repeat, it's men like him that are not afraid to take calculated risks to make companies like Space Transport the leaders in their industry."

After the "hear, hears" and other congratulatory comments, Mohammed offered his own toast. "To Arturo Newsome Diggs, without whom, we would not be patting ourselves on the back today! It was his vision and his ancestors' vision that made all this possible." A couple of the board members wondered what he meant by "his ancestors," but in their elation, they let it pass and raised their cups to Arturo Diggs.

"Do I hear a motion to adjourn, before we bust our shirts with praise," Mohammed asked as he started to close his portfolio. His eye caught the envelope the stranger had given him just before the board meeting. "Just a minute, there may be some more new business." While describing the events in the hall, he began to open the letter.

Most board members had gotten up and were only waiting for a seconded motion to adjourn. "Probably more requests for money. God, if we gave to every request, we'd have to sell Space Trans to cover the donations," one member grumbled.

"I motion for adjournment," another said.

Before a second could be made, Mohammed frowned and said, "This letter says, all Space Transport board members and Space Transport, Incorporated and I, have been sued by the World Governments Resource Committee with charges filed in the World Court as of 1300 hours today. Ladies and gentlemen, please take your seats. I will read their charges aloud."

The elation of the board members evaporated and with sober expressions, they sat down again. As Mohammed scanned the letter, one member finally couldn't stand the suspense and spoke up. "Mohammed, what do you mean sued? For what? And what the hell does the World Governments Resources Committee have to do with it?"

Mohammed finished reading the letter, laid it beside his portfolio, and with a grim look on his face, said, "Simply stated, ladies and gentlemen, we're being sued for restraint of competition."

A more vociferous member slammed the table with his fist and thundered, "Restraint of competition. What in billy blue blazes does that mean?"

Mohammed summarized the letter; "The Committee is 'claiming' that we have locked out all competition with our new vehicle propulsion engines. They further charge that this lack of competition results in our prices not being fair to customers throughout the world. The last charge is that I, and the board, have conspired 'illegally' to drive all our competitors out of business for our own benefit. They are asking that Space Transport be broken up into separate corporations with specified space routes into space and then sold to the highest bidders."

As Mohammed finished the summary the board members began disavowing the claim.

"God damn it we put our company's money up to make Space Trans what it is today. What did these other bastards put up? Nothing, that's what!"

"What risks did they take 50 years ago when everyone wanted better space transports?"

"None. All they did was cry for more help from their governments."

"Space Trans was built with private money, and without any damn government help."

"Conspiracy, my ass. With who? With what? They're crazy!"

"Hell, we cut the prices last year because of lower operational costs per kilo transported. What else do they want."

The anger continued unabated until Mohammed finally rapped on the table for attention. "Ladies and gentlemen, we have no choice but to assume the Committee means business. First, I suggest we get our legal firm to find out just what they really want. Second, I suggest we'd better find out who, or what, is really behind this letter. The Committee has for years stuck to political issues and pretty much stayed out of industrial company affairs. They do have the power to regulate trade where necessary, but it takes a three quarters majority vote to regulate an international company such as ours."

"Where the hell were our three representatives to the Committee? Why didn't we know about this?" a board member asked.

"An excellent question, good sir. Let's find out!"

Mohammed again spoke up. "We have to reveal this letter to the stockholders tomorrow. It will probably be in the news tonight — so we'd better be prepared to answer any questions."

With that, the motion to adjourn was seconded, and the members left the boardroom.

At the stockholders meeting the following day, Mohammed knew that his prepared speech and operating results would not be the main issue. At the podium, with live transmissions to stockholders throughout the world, he gave a brief recount of company profitability and goals, and concentrated on how Space Transport had been built to its present greatness without any government help. He also stressed the huge investments in the company made by private enterprise. After completion of the remarks, the letter from the World Governments Resources Committee was put on screen for all to read. He summarized the letter and after waiting a short period to allow the stockholders to read the charges in detail, he opened the meeting for questions. Inquiries from the stockholders were ones of concern, all of which he answered straightforwardly. It was the often-loaded questions from the news media that he dreaded.

"Isn't it true that you, Chairman Nahal, and other major investors own over 50% of the stock?"

"Why did you and the board conspire to drive others from business?"

"How much would you reduce prices if Space Transport had competition?"

"How are you going to respond to the charges?"

"Why don't you allow others to buy your vehicles and provide fair competition?"

"Did Space Transport have political help to get such a monopoly and were payoffs made?"

"Are you sure that no government money was used to finance Space Transport's research and development?"

"Were any government facilities used for Mr. Diggs' research on the new engine?"

"How do you feel about the possibility of the corporation being broken up?"

Mohammed answered most questions with a simple yes or no. Others were answered quickly and without emotion. The questioning continued until finally the allotted time was exhausted and the meeting was adjourned.

That evening the electronic news media covered the stockholders meeting in detail, including releasing a copy of the letter from the World Governments Resources Committee. The inquiries by the reporters and the answers by Mohammed were repeated. Some of them castigated Space Transport for not allowing competition. After a long dissertation, one commentator concluded his remarks by saying,

"In spite of what the Chairman of Space Transport says, there is no doubt in this commentator's mind the world would be much better off if Space Transport were broken up and others given a chance to compete. It's a shame that all space travel is completely monopolized by one company, Space Transport. They should be forced to share their good fortune with other companies and this commentator urges our government to support the World Governments' lawsuit and request the breakup of Space Transport."

As Mohammed watched the news in his home study, he suddenly stood up, slammed his clenched fist into his other hand and bellowed, "Now I know what the bastards want! But which bastards in particular?!"

Long after many in the news media had dropped the story, three commentators continued the same harangue and commented on every detail they could dig up. Politicians from all countries were interviewed. Many smelled blood, and a chance to perhaps gain a space transportation system for their own nations. It was obvious to all that political and public opinion was going against Space Transport.

Arturo and Jana returned from their vacation after spending close to five weeks in almost isolated relaxation. Even Mohammed's message to contact him as soon as they returned did not seem ominous.

"Arturo, how was the vacation?"

"It was great, Mohammed. You should try it sometime. Your recommendation of a resort was absolutely excellent. The Ural Mountains are beautiful. The peace and quiet of being completely out of contact with the outside world was great. First time we'd been there, but it won't be the last."

After more small talk about the vacation, Mohammed's face suddenly became grave on the visi-phone.

"What's wrong, Mohammed?" Arturo asked with concern in his voice, "You look tired."

"I am, Arturo. I am." Mohammed then outlined in detail the letter and the events that had transpired since Jana and Arturo left for the Urals.

"God Almighty, Mohammed. What can I do to help?"

"Nothing Arturo. Nothing. The best assistance you can give me is to concentrate on getting a ship ready for an unmanned trip to Alpha Centauri. We need to know if life exists there, no matter what happens in the World Court. Also, there may be new minerals worth mining and perhaps a place for a new colony."

"But, there must be something more I can do?"

"No, Arturo. This is a political ball game and I'll handle it. Please bear with me and spend your time on the new AC vehicle. Besides, you'd lose patience with all the legal issues and politicians. Allah knows, I have a hard enough time myself with these stupid ass questions and all the vultures hovering around. No, you spend your time on things you can control and not on things that possibly no one can control."

"Can you beat this suit, Mohammed?"

"Inshállah, Arturo, Inshállah," Mohammed answered, using the language of his ancestors.

Six months later, Mohammed, the Space Transport board and their lawyers sat in conference in Zurich, Switzerland, the day before the trial was to take place. Each detail was again reviewed. The profiles on each person from the World Governments Resources Committee were gone over one more time. The briefs filed by both sides were given a final evaluation. The Space Transport lawyers had done all they could possibly do in preparation for the trial.

Mohammed asked the lead attorney representing Space Transport his opinion of the outcome. "It all depends on the testimony of the members who have been chosen to represent the entire Committee. If they can convince the seven judges that there has been conspiracy or restraint of competition, then the game's over. I give it a 50/50 chance of going either way. The problem is that the facts of the case are not the issue. The real issue is purely political. Space Transport does have a monopoly and there are those, as we found out, who want a part of the action. Some are from the North

American States and some from other countries. One in particular is Geo Transport. It has the most to gain, since it is still in business and has the infrastructure to handle the technology."

"Well for sure, they, among others have been hurt, but they're such a lousy outfit. Lowe squandered resources that should have gone into research and development. Some of his mining ventures were absolute disasters and almost broke the company," Mohammed commented, an angry look on his face.

"For a change, I wish the World Court system was like the days of the twenty-first century," the lawyer commented.

"You mean when appeal after appeal could be filed and a case could go on almost forever?"

"Well, yes. Now every one has one shot, and the decision of the court is final. No more never-ending appeals."

"I, for one, would not wish to go back to that ridiculous system, in spite of our position," Mohammed stated emphatically. "In any event, it's late and unless there is more to discuss, I'm going to bed."

Everyone agreed that all had been reviewed and they were as ready as they'd ever be.

The trial lasted for a week. Each side presented its case, and the seven judges asked many pertinent questions. Neither side could read the judges reactions, but each thought their arguments had the edge. The topic of free enterprise was discussed and reexamined. It became apparent that the charge of conspiracy was not going to be a central point. The only issue was whether or not the monopoly and resulting lack of competition constituted a violation of world law.

The Chief Judge said that a verdict would be rendered the following day. The attorneys knew that a fast decision could be either good or bad for their side and would not venture an opinion as to whether or not they'd win.

The following day Mohammed, the board members and his attorneys, along with the World Governments Resources Committee Chairman, lawyers and representatives, gathered in the courtroom to hear the judges' decision. The Chief Judge thanked everyone for their cooperation and began his summary of the court's determination.

"In the matter of the World Governments Resources Committee versus the Space Transport Corporation, the key component is whether or not world law has been broken regarding the monopolizing of an industry. In so doing, the court must take into account the political aspects of its decision. The intent of the law was to prevent a monopoly from damaging the citizenry of the world through excess charges or other issues. The intent was also to prevent any one country or company from gaining such power that the political balance of the world would be negatively influenced by that country or company and result in that power being used for personal gain or reward." The judge stopped and looked at both parties before continuing.

"At the same time, the intent of the law was not to restrain a company from pursuing better products and services than its competitors through research, development and good management. It is clear that the Space Transport Corporation has had not only outstanding research but outstanding management, which led to their current position as the leader in their field." Again the judge paused.

"Referring to the charge of conspiracy by the chairman and board of directors for personal gain, it is obvious to the court that was not the intent of the Space Transport Corporation, nor did the management or board of directors engage in such endeavors. Therefore, the court finds in favor of Space Transport, its chairman and board members. That charge is dismissed."

Mohammed was elated at the finding, but he knew that more was to come regarding the other two charges. He, like the others, waited with apprehension for the judge to continue.

"With regards to the charge that Space Transport Corporation conspired to lockout all competition, it is evident that any good businessman would attempt to lockout his competitor or competitors from his marketplace of business if at all possible. This competition to win creates better products, better quality and better value for the consumer. It was not the fault of Space Transport that the competition couldn't keep up with it or couldn't finance the proper research for better space vehicles. It was the fault of the individual companies." The judge again stopped and looked around the room.

"Therefore the court has no choice but to find in favor of Space Transport. This charge is also dismissed."

Mohammed's pulse quickened and he waited patiently while the judge drank a glass of water before ruling on the remaining charge. When he had drained the glass, the judge began again.

"With respect to the charge that the monopoly of space transportation by Space Transport is not fair to the users of their services and the consumers of the users products, it is an issue relating to the desires of the world's nations. It is evident to this court that Space Transport has not taken advantage of its monopoly and overcharged the users. The evidence presented bears this out. Indeed, the work of Space Transport has resulted in charges for cargo being reduced by over 200% during the last 30 years — a feat no other competitor could match. Thus, the competition went out of business or was severely curtailed in its activities. For the latter, Space Transport cannot be criticized but complimented. If criticism is due, it should be leveled at the competing companies." Again the judge stopped.

Mohammed's spirits rose, but he had been through too many battles to celebrate prematurely.

"However," the judge continued, "it is true that a monopoly does exist, and competition is nonexistent for all practical purposes.

The law doesn't cover a situation wherein the monopoly that made the world a better place was gained through the honest efforts of honest businessmen and honest scientists, engineers and technicians — particularly when no government funding is involved."

The judge refilled and then sipped from his glass of water, and Mohammed felt a rising sense of doom in his chest. It was obvious the judge did not relish the task of explaining the last charge and wanted to ensure that a clear understanding of the decision was made available to all present and to the world. He again continued.

"Without such a precedent, the court is obligated to attempt to fulfill the wishes of the various world governments as to the best situation for all concerned. Thus, the issue becomes a political one. It is political in the sense that a decision in this case is not a point of law — for no law has been broken — but a political decision affecting the future of the world."

It was even more apparent that the judge was not happy with the yet to be revealed resolution.

"If the Space Transport Corporation could guarantee that future management would conduct itself as the current management has in the past in the performance of their duties, then the decision as to whether or not a monopoly exists would not be a political issue. Of course, Space Transport Corporation cannot make such a guarantee; and thus, a political issue, along with a social issue exists. Those issues must be resolved."

Mohammed had a sinking feeling, but he stared straight at the judge.

"The World Governments Resources Committee members have responsibilities to their respective governments. These governments approved of the suit against Space Transport. With that in mind, it becomes apparent that the desire of the various governments is to have competition with Space Transport, because of the fear of the power of the monopoly at some future time in our society. Regretfully, the court must find in favor of the World Governments Resources Committee on this charge." A loud cheer was heard. The judge held up his hand for silence.

"Although the decision is in favor of the Committee regarding the charge of a monopoly, the court has latitude as to how it will be implemented. And I might add, implemented fairly to all concerned, in particular, Space Transport." He nodded toward Mohammed and then resumed talking.

"The court is mindful of the outstanding management, research and vehicle expenditures of Space Transport to achieve its current position of dominance. Therefore, the request that the company be broken up and the pieces sold to those wishing to invest is denied."

Mohammed's spirits rose somewhat, but he instinctively knew the judge was not finished with the subject of the monopoly.

The judge shuffled his papers and brought out a single piece, which he scanned. Mohammed waited impatiently until the judge finally looked up and began again. "In the matter of the monopoly of space travel by Space Transport, it is the order of this court that the following be carried out immediately." He momentarily stopped, glancing again at the verdict.

"First, Space Transport must allow those qualified investors or companies who wish to compete, full access to their design of the new propulsion engines, since they are the key to any success a new venture may possibly achieve.

"Secondly, those investors or companies must pay to Space Transportation a sum equivalent to 150 billion dollars for the rights to the design. The amount is high because of the worth of the design rights and to ensure only serious investors will participate. Those without staying power to build a truly competitive firm will think twice before committing their funds.

"Thirdly, if an investor wishes to buy a fully completed ship from Space Transport, he may, and Space Transport must construct and deliver such ship or ships. Its net profit may not exceed 15% of the cost of construction. Investors have eight years to place orders.

"Fourthly, each who buys the design rights or a completed ship must pay a royalty of 5.0% of their dollar volume gross sales to Space Transport for a period of eight years.

"Fifth, wherein government contracts are sealed bids and since the new competitor must pay a 5.0% royalty, all government contracts officers throughout the world shall add 5.0% to the bids of Space Transport to equalize the

369

evaluation purposes. This ruling shall last for a period of three years from the time a company has started bidding and operating space vehicles — but in no event exceed 10 years from this date. As regarding private enterprise, the court does not wish to interfere and leaves the pricing of contracts to Space Transport and its new competitors. Private enterprise customers will decide the best value for their money.

"Lastly, the court's decision was not reached without considerable thought as to what was equitable to all concerned. It is hoped that new companies do come into being. It is further hoped they become as solid as Space Transport. Strong space companies will lead the world to greater heights, resulting in better products for all people on Earth and those in space. It is also hoped the management of Space Transport will support the court's decisions in the spirit with which they are intended."

Again the judge stopped and looked Mohammed directly in the eye. "The court could have ordered the company broken up, the same as a court did in the late 1900's when American Telephone and Telegraph had an almost monopoly. Because of Space Transport's contributions to space travel and a different way of looking at things in our century, it would not have been in the best interests of the world to disassemble the company. And this court will not allow it to be disassembled in spite of pressure from any quarter — political or otherwise."

The lawyer for the Committee tried to question the court's decisions and finally interrupted, "It's not fair. You're distorting the intent of world law and the wishes of the people. I wish to register an official objection for the record."

"The improper request for registering an objection is denied. The gentleman will kindly restrain himself, or I'll have him removed. The judgment of this court is inviolate and must be carried out. Those opposing or circumventing this judgement will be severely dealt with. I remind everyone, by world law of which every country is signatory, there is no appeal to this judgement." The judge looked directly at the Committee lawyer as he spoke.

Mohammed visibly slumped in his chair, a multitude of thoughts running through his head. "It is not as bad as I thought it would be. This judgement I can live with, and competition be damned. Space Transport is far ahead and we'll stay ahead. By God, the judge was fair." He understood the dilemma the judges had and decided they handled the case commendably. He shuddered to think what could have happened if the Committee politicians had their way. "No, the court handled it well." He then personally thanked the court and complimented the judges on their wisdom and foresight.

Then he remembered Arturo — God in heaven. How could he tell him the outcome? How could Arturo ever accept revealing the pulse rate of the laser gun and the Massafon Engine mirror material — both keys to successful operation. Mohammed wondered if Arturo would accept the decision of the World Court and allow his work to be used by anyone other than Space Transport. Mohammed knew that if Arturo refused to divulge the close-kept secrets and if he defended him, Space Transport ran the risk of incurring the wrath of the court. He made his decision. It would be Arturo's call and if he refused to release the pulse rate and material, Mohammed would stand beside him — come what may.

Jana and Arturo were in the study when the electronic media presented the results and blasted the World Court's decision. The announcer read the decision in detail and concluded with the usual closing summary.

"This commentator wonders at the wisdom of the court's decision and directions. It would seem the court gave the Space Transport Corporation a reward for being a monopoly instead of punishment for having unfairly driven almost all their competitors out of business. How can anyone compete against such a giant? It doesn't seem fair. We can only hope that the court's orders will result in competition for space travel and the world is better off for it."

The latter portion was phrased with a frown and a woebegone look on his face.

Jana was beside herself with anger. "How can they do that? It means your development of the Massafon Engine can be used by anyone with the money to buy it."

"Calm down, love. Don't worry about me — us. I worry about Mohammed's reaction. He's a tough nut, you know."

"Mohammed has no choice but to comply with the order, Arturo. But how can the court order you to comply? The two keys to the engine are the result of your work, not Space Transport's," Jana said with rising anger.

"Simple, Jana. Space Trans funded my work and I received compensation from them. Technically the work and the two keys of pulse rate and the mirrors belong to them. In any event, that's the way the court would look at it."

Jana forced herself to compose her emotions while she stared pensively at the ceiling. After a few seconds she smiled and looked at Arturo. "You know, Arturo, maybe it's not so bad after all. It will take years for a competitor to become viable and really compete with Space Trans. And in the meantime your research can continue."

"I know, love. Frankly, it doesn't bother me to release the two keys and the Massafon Engine design. That job is finished. Now, I want to work on how to exceed the speed of light," Arturo replied.

"What approaches to the problem does your fertile mind have now?"

"None worth commenting on, I'm afraid. A couple of ideas looked good for a while, but while we were at the Urals, I discarded them and..." Arturo stopped and smiled sheepishly at Jana.

"I knew it. You didn't completely forget your work. Shame on you. Here I thought your thoughts were only on me while we were there"

"They were, hon. But sometimes a few strays crept in. Now let's forget about the court's decision, and just think about us."

Arturo got up from his chair and walked swiftly across the room. As he leaned over to kiss her, she said, "That's my boy, and don't you ever stop."

Mohammed had returned to his office the following day and immediately reached Arturo by visi-phone. "If you're free, old friend, can you come down to the office today?"

"Of course. I've just been waiting for your call."

"Great! I'll send my air-car to pick you up. See you here." The screen went blank.

Mohammed and Arturo faced each other while sitting comfortably on the couch in the office. Arturo had received a blow-by-blow description of the World Court proceedings and the judges' orders. He had given his opinion to Mohammed regarding the actions that had to be taken by Space Transport.

"You really mean it don't you, about releasing the two Massafon keys for successful engines?" Mohammed stated rather than questioned.

"Yes, I do. My only concern is for you and Space Trans and the effect it would have."

"Hell, Arturo, we'll survive this and maybe even be stronger. A little competition will be good for us, and I'll tell you a little secret. I've missed it. Keeps us sharp and the company in better shape for the future."

"I agree, but it still bothers me the way it was done. What triggered the Committee to file suit?"

"I've had the best available snoops trying to find out, to no avail. Like you, I still wonder who the sons-of-a-bitches were that started this," Mohammed said grimly and continued, "Our committee reps and attorneys said, 'they were blind sided'."

"As you said before, it had nothing to do with being a monopoly," Arturo added.

Mohammed banged the wall with his fist. "Damn right it didn't and the judges saw through that. It had to do with someone wanting our engines, vehicles and route structure without having to pay for them."

"Any idea who?" Arturo asked.

"None! None what so ever!" Mohammed thundered.

"I saw the Chief Executive of the Ground Orbit Transfer Corporation and he thought it was a travesty. He was worried the Committee might come after his company. No, it wasn't him."

"If I ever find out who it was..." Mohammed began vehemently, "I'll..." Regaining his composure, his sense of humor took over. "I'll pat him on the back and say, 'good luck, you bastardly son of Satan'."

The two men continued talking and planning how to implement the judges' orders properly. After exhausting the subject, Arturo took his leave and started for the door.

"By the way Arturo, I'm recommending to the board that you be given 20% of the 5.0% royalty we'll receive from the new competitors, whoever they are."

"You don't need to do that, Mohammed. You funded my research, and it properly belongs to Space Transport."

"It will be proper and legal. You and I have never had formal legal papers for our activities together, but this one will necessitate legality. The 20% will be for all rights to the Massafon Engine, including design, the pulse rate and mirrors." Mohammed's face had a determined look.

"Mohammed, I know that Space Trans owns the rights to all that anyway. I'm not in the habit of turning down money, but..."

The Chairman interrupted Arturo. "I know all that and so will the board, but I believe in reward where reward is due and our friendship has nothing to do with it. I'm not an altruist, and you know it, Arturo. You deserve it and besides, I want you to continue working on improvements to stay ahead of the new competitors. Agreed?" and Mohammed stuck out his hand.

"Agreed, and thank you," Arturo said softly as he shook his hand.

As the private visi-phone line beeped to indicate an incoming call, Joal Lowe saw a familiar face on the view screen. Since the caller couldn't see him until he pushed the receive button, Lowe decided to wait a bit longer before answering. Besides, he liked having people wait until he was ready to acknowledge them. After ten seconds, Lowe engaged the receive symbol. The gray-haired man on the screen did not seem the least perturbed about having to wait for Lowe to take his call. He was used to Lowe and his eccentricities.

"Meet me at the alternate location in one hour," Lowe commanded.

"As you wish," the man said as the screen went blank.

"Bastard," Lowe thought as he got up and went to the waiting auto-car. Lowe voiced the coordinates into central traffic control and the auto-car began to follow the silver line stretching ahead. As the car sped along at 150 kilometers per hour, Lowe fumed to himself. His anger almost consumed him and his usually cherubic face was replaced by one of hateful grimaces. The auto-car entered an underground parking lot serving a large shopping complex and went to the lower floor where it stopped beside another car. The occupant of the other car got out and approached Lowe's car. Getting in, he turned to Lowe, his eyes never leaving his face.

"You failed! Your plan didn't work," Lowe stated indignantly to the other.

"I did not fail. Everything went exactly as planned, down to the last detail," the other countered in a level voice.

Lowe's smile disappeared and he almost screamed, "God damn it, you failed. The court didn't approve of the breakup of Space Transport. The money paid to all those fucking politicians, world reps and ministers was wasted."

"Herr Lowe, you knew that the seven judges on the court were unapproachable, and we agreed to that before the job was undertaken. No, I did not fail."

"You should have found a way to get to them. Everyone has a price! You should have found a way." By this time Lowe's face had the grimace the other was so familiar with.

"I will tell you for the last time, everything went as planned. The targeted Committee representatives did their jobs. The key ministers did their jobs. The key politicians did their jobs. I did my job. Space Transport now has to sell the rights to their space engines." The short-cropped haired man stopped talking, but his steely eyes focused intently on Lowe's face.

"Yes, they have to sell the rights for 150 billion dollars and a royalty of 5.0%. If you'd succeeded, I'd have gotten them for free." Lowe stared with hate at the other man and finally stated firmly, "I'm not going to pay you the remaining fee!"

"You will pay, Herr Lowe, you will pay or you will die."

Lowe fumbled for a small laser weapon, but the other man was quicker. He grasped Lowe's left arm in a grip of steel. Lowe felt a pinprick on the underside of his wrist and he dropped the laser on the seat.

"What have you done, you double-crossing prick?"

"Given you an unknown poison that is slow acting. Unless you have the antidote within eight hours a fatal heart attack will occur. As I said, Herr Lowe, 'you will pay or you will die'."

"You bastard!" Lowe was silent for a few seconds and then whined, "How do I know the poison's real, and how do I know if it is real, the antidote will work?"

"You don't. You only have my word."

"Your word. What good is that? You could take the money and run."

"I'm a professional, Herr Lowe. The antidote will work." He opened his other hand and a small tablet lay in his palm. "This is the antidote. Where is the money?"

Lowe had stopped struggling, but the steel grip never loosened. "You win. Take this down." He gave the location of a public lock-box and the combination for opening.

"Give me the antidote." The other complied and placed the tablet in Lowe's mouth. Within a minute his eyes drooped and he began to slump in his seat.

"What did you give me, you son-of-a...!" His eyes closed, and he sagged unconscious down into the seat.

Horst got out of the auto-car, taking care to darken the windows of Lowe's car to prevent anyone from seeing Lowe sleeping. The antidote was a sleeping pill, good for 24 hours. That gave Horst plenty of time to check the lock-box. If the money was there, Horst would return in time to administer the real antidote to Joal Lowe and he would awaken with nothing more than a slight headache. If he didn't, Lowe would never wake up. He had decided that this was the last job he would ever do for Lowe. The man was becoming too irrational and that could be dangerous for Horst — he knew when to drop a client who couldn't be trusted.

Horst was careful to leave his auto-car a few blocks from the building where the locker containing his payment was located. Leisurely, he walked the distance to the building; and once inside, he quickly found the locker. Having memorized the code, he methodically punched in the numbers. A green light appeared signifying the combination was correct, and he opened the door with anticipation. As the door of the locker was opened wide, he peered into its depths. Suddenly he jumped back, but it was too late. A sudden blast of vapor hit him in the face; and as he began to crumple to the floor, his last thought was, "Herr Lowe, you too will die." He sank into unconsciousness — never to regain his ebbing life.

Horst's death certificate read, "Numerous simultaneous ruptured blood vessels in the brain, resulting in corresponding multiple strokes and death."

Joal Lowe's death certificate read, "Massive coronary induced by complete rupture of the aorta."

The electronic news media carried the news about Lowe's death with a final summary.

"Mr. Lowe was under a lot of stress as a result of continued loss of business to Space Transport, Inc., although the world court had provided an opportunity for upgrading the Geo Transport fleet with light speed ships. He had encountered problems in raising the required financing..."

"Mr. Lowe is survived by his wife, who has been confined in a mental institution the past 15 years and his son, Ronal, an employee of Geo Transport, Inc."

2207
A DREAM COME TRUE

Man's innate desire to seek additional knowledge had initially paved the way for exploration to every corner of the solar system. But it was the acute awareness that Earth's once vast supply of valuable minerals was being rapidly depleted that spurred the quest to find new sources on other planets. There was urgent demand for, among others, tungsten, vanadium, niobium, manganese and molybdenum. Many of the asteroids, along with Mars, had these needed minerals, both in abundance and in virgin state.

Even cloud covered Venus boasted a small domed colony for its new mining venture. Though the gravity was 91% of Earth's, it was far better than Mar's 38%. But cooling down the Venus torrid 487° C temperature to the required 22° C inside the dome for human comfort was not only difficult but costly. By comparison, heating the Mars domed colonies — from -43° C outside to +22° C inside — seemed like child's play. Work on Venus, outside the dome, was impossible except in specially constructed and protected vehicles. Even ground travel over the planet was unacceptable because of the erratic volcanic activities and Venusquakes, which unfortunately struck without warning. The Venus colonists faced a confining and harsh existence, accomplishing most of their mining activities by remotely operated machinery.

On one of the Jupiter moons, Ganymede, another modest domed colony was being built atop a tall mountain for mineral mining. Other Jupiter moons were still under evaluation, but Callisto had already been rejected, either for domed habitation or mining because of its thick, impenetrable ice crust. Io was also ruled out because of its incessant and violent volcanic eruptions.

Saturn's moons were the subject of considerable interest, though none had yet proved to be practical for exploitation. Cloud cloaked Titan was at one time thought to be habitable, but at -180° C below zero, it was for all intent nothing but a body of hydrocarbon oceans. The few scattered landmasses that did emerge through the seas were little more than frozen hydro-carbonic clumps. Although the same was true for Uranus and Neptune, the study continued.

The exploration to Pluto had been an undisputed failure. It was discovered that the surface temperature was -260° C, only -13° C from absolute zero, close to the point where all molecular activity ceases. Solidly frozen methane encased the planet; and even Pluto's moon, Charon, was also uninhabitable. There was talk of the possibility of mining methane ice, but analysis promptly proved such a venture to be financially impractical. Earth's exploration companies unequivocally wrote off Pluto and its moon.

Gigantic telescopes continually orbited Earth and Mars, and half a dozen more made planetary orbits around the sun. The high precision 'scopes were capable of assimilating data from the Milky Way and a myriad of galaxies of which twentieth and twenty-first century astronomers could have only dreamed.

Space Transport's construction of an unmanned vehicle, destined to be sent to the three Alpha Centauri stars in Rigel Kent — the closest solar systems to Earth — had been underway for years. A round trip time of approximately 8.8 years at the speed of light placed these stars within the realm of definite possibility for exploration by unmanned and, ultimately, manned ships. Research data by astronomers led to the belief that over a half dozen planets were possibly orbiting Alpha Centauri A, not to mention Alpha Centauri B and C. All agreed that an unmanned vehicle should first determine whether or not planets did indeed orbit the stars. If planets did exist, their atmospheres and physical makeup — most important of all — any life forms, would dictate a manned trip.

Two years earlier, Mohammed Nahal's intended retirement as Chairman, at age 70, had been deferred. The Space Transport board had convinced him to continue until the unmanned probe to Alpha Centauri had been built, launched and returned to Earth. Arturo's contribution to the company had been invaluable, both as a consultant to the advanced technology group and as designer of the improved support systems of the new vehicles using the Massafon Engines.

During the previous five years, Mohammed and Space Transport had carried out the World Court's orders to the letter. Surprisingly, the rulings had not been as complicated to implement as originally thought. Only three companies had actually come forward with the 150 billion dollars for rights to the Massafon Engine. One had already tragically gone out of business. Their vehicle, on a flight to Ganymede, collided with a small three-kilometer asteroid. The disastrous explosion obliterated the ship and everyone onboard. Cause of the accident was never definitely proved, but it apparently resulted from inaccurate programming by their company technicians. Space Transport was duly exonerated of any possible fault or responsibility.

A second of the three new companies was still struggling to compete, but it was at least making progress with two ships in operation. The remaining corporation, Geo Transport, had a fleet of three ships in service; all purchased from Space Transport, with five additional ones under construction by other firms.

Space Transport had competition, but the inevitable price war had subsided and business had returned to an even keel. Geo Transport would bid at cost on occasion, when it appeared that its other new competitor was close to winning the job, but it knew better than to engage Space Trans in a price war. Space Transport's cash flow allowed them to bid successfully on any contract they felt was important to their route structure. Unlike their competitors, however, they were in business to make a profit and not simply to increase business volume.

On a late August afternoon, the entire Diggs family, along with Mohammed, was on the patio enjoying San Diego's favored weather. Jamille and Filip, with their seven year-old identical twins, had returned to Earth for a long overdue vacation. The active youngsters were making so much commotion that the three grandparents and their parents looked up in concern, but the twins gave not the slightest hint of slowing down.

"Jamille," Mohammed shook his head in wonderment at his daughter, "you and Filip have your hands full with those two." Then laughingly, amused at the children's antics, "Both of them remind me of myself when I was that age, full of energy and anxious to see how I could drive my parents crazy."

"Oh Daddy, this is nothing," Jamille laughed. "You ought to see them in zero or half gravity."

"Allah, spare me!" he pleaded, raising his eyes skyward.

"Well, Dad Nahal," Filip came to the rescue, "they'll be out of your hair all afternoon. We're taking them to the animal zoo." But he couldn't resist a last tease, "Want to join us?"

Mohammed looked aghast at the thought. "No thank you. Just wear them out, bring them back home when they're exhausted, and give us grandparents a chance to spoil them completely rotten."

"And then we parents," Jamille groused back, "get the pleasure of trying to straighten out the two little insufferable monsters?"

"Of course," Mohammed laughed.

"Wait a minute, Filip and Jamille," Arturo cut in, "I think you'd better read the fine print in your grandparent's contract."

"Our what?" Filip played along.

"Your father's right, dear," Jana chimed in, tongue in cheek, "it clearly states that the sole assignment charged to grandparents is the duty to humor, indulge, pamper and cater to each and everyone of them until..."

Arturo couldn't resist, "...they are absolutely putrefied!"

"Hear! Hear!" Mohammed and Jana echoed in unison.

Filip and Jamille exchanged horrified glances; and, speaking for both of them, Jamille wailed, "We've been had."

"Tell you what," Jana volunteered, "if you promise not to walk my legs off, I'll go along with you. I haven't been to the zoo in years. Besides it'll be fun seeing it through Webb and Marna's eyes."

"That's right," Arturo acknowledged, "the twins have never had a chance to see live wild animals."

"Our asteroid dome is hardly the place to harbor a zoo." Filip quipped.

"I have a kitty, Grandfather," Marna piped in as she ran to Arturo, and bounced into his lap.

Not to be outdone, Webb plopped himself atop Mohammed. "She does not. It's our kitty, and I named him Jasper."

Sibling rivalry immediately ensued over who had exclusive ownership of the unfortunate feline and who had actually chosen its name.

Tactfully, as grandmothers are prone to do, Jana deliberately shifted their focus. "I don't know about anyone else, but I'm going to go into the kitchen and fortify my tummy with some cookies and milk." As she started walking toward the house, she called over her shoulder, "Do I have any other takers?"

The children scrambled to her side.

"I get first choice," Webb squealed.

"You do not," Marna screeched back. "Girls go before boys."

The twins continued their one-upmanship as they disappeared into the house.

The grandfathers exchanged bemused glances, but Arturo had a perturbed look on his face. "After seven years on the Mars-Jupiter Asteroid-Belt," he seriously inquired, "how are you finding conditions up there?'

"At first, I'll admit," Jamille smiled at her husband, "even though we were still newlyweds, our pressurized quarters were pretty cramped."

Filip raised a teasing eyebrow that prompted Jamille to reach over and pat his hand. "Anyway, once Filip got the Diggsanium business in full swing, and we were able to expand our quarters and construct a dome," she smiled affectionately at her husband, "it's been just like home."

"Refresh my memory," Mohammed inquired. "How many people occupy your space colony now, Filip?"

Doing a quick calculation, "About eighty-five, including children, and one couple is expecting to make another addition any time now."

"That will make a total of eight 'space children' born on our asteroid," and Jamille's voice sounded wistful. "Webb and Marna were the first, and after we'd set the precedent..."

"...the conception just got out of control." Filip quipped.

"Oh, darling," Jamille grimaced, "terrible pun."

Everyone laughed loudly at the play on words.

"Thanks, Dad Nahal," Filip quickly changed the subject, "for making sure that your freighters bring in our weekly stock of food and supplies."

"One of these days," Mohammed theorized, "all the asteroids and planets will be self-contained." He shook a finger at the group, "Mark my words."

"In the meantime," Arturo added, "keep the freighters flying."

"Webb Newsome Diggs," Marna's shrill childish voice rang out, "you come back here with my cookie."

"And with that note of exchange," Filip stood up and grabbed his wife's hand, "I think it's time to throw the kids to the lions."

The twins gave a noisy farewell to Arturo and Mohammed.

"See ya later, alligator..." Webb squealed to his grandfathers.

"Half an hour, dinosaur..." Marna retorted.

As they disappeared behind the high shrubbery, Arturo looked quizzically at Mohammed.

"Where in the hell," he said astounded, "did they learn that jargon?"

"Beats me," Mohammed shook his head in bewilderment. "Must be some newfangled space slang."

They settled back in their respective chairs, contentedly propping their feet on the table. A few moments of contemplative silence ensued, before thoughts turned to their favorite subject — space travel.

"How soon will we launch the unmanned vehicle to Alpha Centauri A?" Mohammed asked, resting his hands on the chair arms.

Arturo removed his feet from the table, and leaned forward. "It's ready now," and it was said so quietly that Mohammed turned his head to see if he had heard correctly.

Arturo gave a wide grin, "The flight tests and a simulated ten year trip for accelerated aging testing of the components has been successfully performed. All we're waiting on are the completion of the data tapes and the programming of the remote landing probes. Should be receiving the stats any time."

Mohammed folded his arms over his chest. "If it hadn't been for having to build those four ships for the other companies," he muttered, "we could have launched two years ago. But, we didn't have a choice," he sighed. "We had to comply with the court orders."

"Come on now, Mohammed," Arturo needled, "you and I both know we could have found excuses." Then he corrected himself. "I should say, found reasons for not putting their ships ahead of our own Alpha Centauri vehicle in the production process. We complied for the sole purpose of making sure we honored your personal commitment to the Chief Justice of the court. I saw the hologram of you saying, 'Sir, I will honor the court's direction. On that you have my word'. Then the two of you shook hands on it."

"And I meant it," the Chairman said softly. With a sigh, he unfolded his arms and, placing his feet on the ground, sat up straight. "Now back to my question, when will you launch for Alpha Centauri?"

"Current schedule says in six weeks. And I'd like to launch from the Space Transport orbiting station."

Mohammed nodded agreement. "I know you and the astronomers in the space science division spent a great deal of time studying which of the three stars of Rigel Kent to investigate. Did you ever come to any conclusions as to which might have the best chance of having orbiting planets containing life — whether humanoid, animals, bugs, lichen or microorganisms?"

"I'm betting on Alpha Centauri A." Arturo's eyes had a distant look. Gazing past Mohammed, his voice took on a faraway tone. "Its diameter is only twenty-three per cent larger than our sun, but its mass is ten per cent greater. This particular star has a spectra class of G2 and a luminosity classification of V, the same as our sun."

"Is the effective black body temperature comparison the same?"

"Almost, if the spectra class is correct." Arturo rattled off the figures. "Our measurements show the black body temperature to be only 300° Kelvin less than the sun's 6,000 K. Of course the real temperature is over a 1,000,000 K at the corona."

"I thought that Proxima Centauri, or Alpha Centauri C was the closest star to our solar system," Mohammed observed.

"It is, but it's only one tenth of a light year less than Alpha Centauri's 4.37 light years distance," Arturo affirmed.

"I see what you mean. At the speed of light, it's only..." Mohammed hesitated, "...it's only longer by thirty-five to thirty-six days. Do you still have the other two stars as secondary exploration targets?"

"That we do. The ship will go to Alpha Centauri A first, then to Alpha Centauri B and to Alpha Centauri C on the way back. I think our best chance of finding planets with life is on Alpha A."

Although Arturo answered with authority, even he knew that with all the data that had accumulated, no one could actually predict what would be found.

"What about planets and life forms on the other two stars?" Mohammed persisted, reluctant to drop the subject.

"Their spectra class indicates lower temperatures of 3800° K and 2200° K. For example, Alpha Centauri C," he explained, "also known as, Proxima Centauri, only has a mass of one tenth of our sun and a temperature of 2200° K. There may be planets, but the chances for life are relatively slim."

Mohammed raised an eyebrow, prompting Arturo to expand his theory further. "There's just too much difference from our own solar system for life, as we know it, to evolve as it did here on Earth."

"In other words, the 2200° K of Alpha C is among the cooler stars, but it evolved differently than our sun, and because of that," the chairman probed, "probably wouldn't support life forms."

"Seems that way," Arturo shrugged, "but who knows for sure? We'll investigate all three and find out."

"How long do you estimate the trip will take; including exploration?"

"I estimate anywhere from nine to ten years, depending on what the remote probes detect."

"Hope I'm around when she returns," Mohammed sighed.

"You old war horse." Arturo laughed, rising just enough to slap his old friend on the back. "You'll live to be a 120 years old."

Mohammed didn't jump to the bait; instead, he shifted the emphasis. "In any event, I intend to be there for this launch. I remember the last time we were at the space station together." As if to remind Arturo of the historic event, he added, "It was the *Jana II*'s first flight."

"What a couple of days those were." Arturo grinned, and each man silently recollected that momentous occasion.

"By the way, Mohammed," Arturo abruptly shifted to another topic, "I've been meaning to ask, where did Geo get the money to buy our technology and new ships? Have you ever found out?" When the Chairman didn't immediately respond, Arturo was sorry he'd inquired. Attempting not to put his friend on the spot, he added, "Not that it actually makes any difference."

"No. No. You have the right to know, my friend." Mohammed took a deep breath. "It isn't exactly a secret." But his voice was uncharacteristically halting as he launched into the explanation. "As best as we can tell, the money was provided by a blind trust fund out of the Unified Asiatic States. My understanding is, this particular group is comprised of a majority of investors who had generated their wealth from profitable mining contracts on Mars."

Mohammed's face hardened, as if he was searching for the right words. "We have no reason to believe that the trust is anything but, shall we say, derived from legitimate money. Being a singular trust fund, the investors took the company private." He gave a short laugh. "A damn smart move on their part. Thus for all intent and purpose, it is not now possible to estimate the actual financial soundness of Geo."

"Well, I'll tell you one thing, Mohammed, if the current Geo operates the way the former Geo Transport did under Joal Lowe, those investors are going to be out a lot of money."

"I wouldn't be so sure about that," Mohammed cautioned, taking his friend by surprise. "Perhaps you've been too preoccupied to keep up on the present affairs of Geo."

Arturo frowned. "Maybe you'd better bring me up to date."

"It was not too long after Joal Lowe's death, that his son, Ronal, at the young age of 33, was made president and chief operating officer. Almost immediately after Ronal assumed that position, considerable progress was made in securing financing. It would appear, at least on the surface, that Ronal Lowe has been very good for Geo. Anyway, the young man seems to have good business sense."

Sensing that Mohammed would prefer the subject of Geo be dropped, Arturo changed the topic.

As only close friends can enjoy each other's company, the two men bantered back and forth, oblivious to the passing hours. Mellowed by the warm sun and soothing dialogue, Mohammed suddenly burst out, "Did I ever tell you how proud I am of that son-in-law of mine?" A flush of pride reddened his bronze face. "Filip has done an outstanding job in building up the Diggsanium business."

Arturo beamed in appreciation and repaid the compliment in kind. "And that daughter-in-law of mine is the best thing that ever happened to the Diggs family."

Mohammed closed his eyelids contentedly. "I relish the weekly voice letters from Jamille, giving me all the news and the updates on shipments and orders. I especially enjoy plugging it into the holographic system; then it's just like she was in the room." Suddenly a sheepish grin tugged at the corners of his mouth, and he added, "Oh yes, Jamille says she sends you and Jana the same letters."

"Thank God she does!" Arturo responded. "Filip sure as hell never takes the time. If it weren't for Jamille, we'd never hear anything." Then he confided, "But you're right, Mohammed, Filip has done a good job. Did I tell you that he's even paid back the loan we made him to start the business? Both Jana and I wanted them to save the money for expansion, but no, he and Jamille paid it back right then and there."

"We certainly have reason to be proud of our kids." Suddenly he was interrupted by the babble of young voices, "Speaking of our brood, here they come."

The twins came running around the corner with armfuls of stuffed toys. In their enthusiasm they drowned out each other to describe the wild animals to their attentive grandfathers. Mohammed and Arturo gave in to the inevitable and realized that further adult conversation was impossible; but their faces showed their delight with the children's animated description of what they had done and seen at the zoo.

The executive offices at Geo headquarters were opulent. But to the president and CEO of the firm, the Persian rugs, priceless paintings and the antique furniture were merely the furnishings that befitted his position.

Ronal Lowe, indifferent to his surroundings, paced moodily behind his desk. He was an imposing figure of slightly over two meters tall, and quite well proportioned. He stood out in any group. In contrast to the porcine face and body of his father, the son had inherited the angular features of his forbearers. Only his small close-set eyes — continually darting as if to seek out an unseen enemy — were reminiscent of Joal. He was not handsome but he could marshal a facade of concern or even tranquility with those he wished to impress. But today his countenance had assumed its normal petulant self-centered look.

Startled by a knock at the door, his head jerked around at the intrusion.

"Enter!" he irritably commanded.

An assistant appeared at the open door; her face and voice reflected her experience with Ronal's moods. "I have the latest progress reports you requested, Mr. Lowe."

Ronal just curtly pointed to his desk. She placed the sheaf of papers as instructed and hurriedly left the office.

Ronal flipped through the reports, stopping when he came to the particular section detailing the five additional freighters under contract for construction.

"Good!" he murmured as a satisfied grin spread over his thin lips. "The stupid fuckers have slipped the schedule again by another three months."

Commanding on the view screen, he demanded, "Get me the Orbital Manufacturing CEO on the phone."

Waiting for the call to appear on the screen, Ronal sat down in his leather-covered swivel chair and rocked back and forth while he reviewed the status report. After a minute, his assistant's mask-like face again appeared on the screen.

"Mr. Lowe, the CEO of Orbital is in a meeting and left instructions to hold all calls."

"Damn it," Ronal blasted, "tell that son-of-a-bitch I want to speak to him right now. I don't care what he's doing. Now! Do you hear? Now!"

Within a few minutes a man's haggard face appeared on the screen. "I'm sorry, Mr. Lowe," and his voice shook slightly. "We were discussing how to make up your schedule. That's why I didn't take your call."

Ronal began a tirade against the contractor's company and personal character. He threatened to sue for lost revenue if the ships were not completed on schedule and concluded with the threat, "I'm withholding progress payments until you make up the lost time on the two remaining ships."

The gaunt face on the screen winced and the voice pleaded, "If you do that, delivery will slip even further."

"You mean to tell me that you're short of cash and that my payments are all that's keeping you going?" Ronal retorted, as if surprised by the admission. Shaking his head in a pretense of disbelief, he proposed, "According to our contract, I suggest that you either make up the schedule or borrow money to keep going." The man on the screen closed his eyes in resignation.

Ronal was fully aware that the Orbital Manufacturing Company had exhausted its line of credit with lending institutions. He also knew that for some time it had depended solely on his payments to stay afloat during the construction phases. His intention was not to drive the company from business; at least not until his five ships were completed. Ronal had a preconceived agenda, and the delays in production had played conveniently into his hands.

"Tell you what," Ronal sighed, feigning compassion, "I'll give you the name of a lending institution that will advance you the money to continue. But in no way will I continue progress payments until the ships are back on schedule."

Plunging into the trap, the CEO gratefully asked for the lender's name. Ronal had his fish hooked and could afford to toy with his catch before landing him. Canceling off the screen, he absently rubbed the diamond birthmark on his left arm. Assured that his prey would be contacting the proposed lender, Ronal laughed aloud, gloating over his conquest.

He was busily perusing the latest financial reports on Geo, when, unannounced, a slight Asian man entered the room, bowed slightly, and sat down on the plush couch. This was a wordless signal that Ronal should leave his desk and join him. Though angry at the interruption, Ronal concealed it behind a perfunctory smile. He rose and cordially performed the necessary pleasantry. "How nice to see you Mr. Yenta. How was your trip?"

It inevitably galled him when this particular Geo board member came into his office as if he owned it, which in truth he did. Mr. Yenta was the primary force behind the blind trust that kept Geo in business.

With an enigmatic grin, Mr. Yenta went straight to the point of his visit, "How are you doing with the Orbital Company?"

"The CEO at Orbital," Ronal boasted, "is going to call your Asian trust fund for the loan. And as we planned, once he's committed, we'll own his company."

"Are you sure he can't make up the schedules?"

"Positive," Ronal answered unequivocally. "He didn't believe the fine print in the contract that allows small changes at no charge." Eager to crow, he mistook the bloodless smile on Yenta's face as permission to proceed. "A little change here, a little change there and bingo, schedule slippage. And then, we've got him by the balls. If he slips, we don't pay. If we don't pay, he borrows more money. And each time he borrows, he uses more of his company as collateral. Finally, we have collateral equivalent to controlling interest of Orbital. Your loan company forecloses and we have a transport manufacturing company. Simple?"

"It sounds good, Mr. Lowe," there was a note of warning in his words, "but, if you fail, the board's wishes will not be carried out."

"I won't fail," Ronal bragged. "You may quote me to the board."

"Very well." Yenta steepled his fingers together just below his chin, a gesture that Ronal detested. "Now, onto another subject. What about the possibility of Space Transport launching a vehicle to Alpha Centauri?"

Ronal did not hesitate in his answer. "Our informants tell us that Space Transport is indeed going to launch an unmanned ship to Alpha Centauri. Their objective is to see if the planets there have life or new minerals that can be mined productively."

Mr. Yenta's eyes narrowed, fixing Ronal with an expressionless stare. Not sure of Yenta's thinking, Ronal quickly added, "Of course, if we had dropped everything else we could have beaten them there. And..." but he was rudely interrupted.

"Let them go." Yenta dismissed any further explanation with a curt wave of his hand. "If anything there is worth having, we'll send a manned ship, using their data and findings. Let them pay for the first trip. We'll go on building Geo until it's as big as Space Trans."

Ronal knew Yenta's statement was a direct order, not idle conversation. Even though he agreed with the strategy, he felt a knot in his stomach at being so pointedly commanded. Ever since the takeover by the Asian trust, he had not been brought into the inner circle for consultation or discussion.

Mr. Yenta, without another word, got up from the couch, bowed ever so slightly in Ronal's direction to indicate that the unscheduled meeting was over and left the room.

Ronal had always resented Yenta's attitude of superiority, but he was also fully aware that without him and the other Asian board members, Geo would never have been able to finance the speed-of-light transport ships. He was certain that Yenta was not the man's real name; in fact, he suspected that all of the board members had aliases. "They all look so much alike, I wouldn't recognize them anywhere else." In Ronal's thinking, cultural stereotyping was alive and flourishing.

There was also no question in Ronal's mind that as long as Joal Lowe had lived, he would never have been more than an errand boy for his father. The two men had never gotten along; and like all his direct ancestors, he had despised his paternal parent. It had always been father against son and son against father. Each Lowe had unknowingly followed the same pattern as his predecessors. Woes betide anyone that crossed them, especially the Diggs. Ronal was ignorant of the justification for detesting the Diggs, but he had been so thoroughly indoctrinated with the hatred that he, in turn, had instilled it in his own young son and daughter.

His left arm itched, as it always did when he thought of the Diggs family. "Yes", he mused aloud, rubbing the diamond birthmark, "I need that fuckin' Yenta and the rest of them — for now."

In the age old tradition of designating an appropriate name for the first unmanned ship for Alpha Centauri, the Space Transport board of directors met in private discussion. Unbeknown to either Mohammed Nahal or Arturo Diggs, they unanimously agreed to name the ship after Mohammed and Arturo's only granddaughter. Both men were thrilled with the recommondation and honored by the choice. With much pomp and ceremony the new unmanned Alpha Centauri ship was formally christened the *Marna.*

The media described the ship as being of a completely different configuration from any other Space Transport vehicle. One reporter, taken with the *Marna's* round cylindrical center body, portrayed the ship as, "...surrounded by six spheres at her amidships section, she looked like a stubby finger with a ring of six large pearls at the second joint." A more scientific author explained that in front of the spheres was a shield attached to the center body at 45° for protection from space debris. Still another journalist went so far as to comment that "...the shield looks like a short skirt that failed to cover the vehicle's nudity." But all agreed that the *Marna's* gleaming beauty lay in her simple lines. The only things that kept her from looking like a solid and continuous piece of metal were the almost indistinguishable lines for doors and access panels. No other protrusions were visible; even the normal viewing windows were absent.

The official christening of the new ship was in an open-air ceremony at the Space Transport's San Diego facility. The Diggs family, the entire compliment of Space Transport management, the board of directors and all employees participating in the *Marna's* design and construction were in attendance. The press corps, invited to broadcast a live coverage throughout the world of the momentous occasion, almost outnumbered the other spectators and officials.

When Mohammed Nahal stepped to the podium to dedicate the ship, instead of a speech, he chose to use a time-honored tradition. As the legendary champagne bottle shattered against the hull, he said simply, "May she fly a broom on her mast antenna as she returns from space trials."

A young reporter, standing near the dais, asked, "Mr. Nahal, what does flying a broom back from space trials mean?" There were chuckles from a few old-time space technicians who then teased the young man for being "wet behind his ears!"

Mohammed quelled the digression with a wave of his hand. "If I may have your attention, please. As my father used to tell me, there's a reason for everything — except Grape Nuts."

A ripple of laughter rumbled through the crowd, and Mohammed began a dignified explanation directed to the young, but embarrassed, reporter. "Dating back to the 17th century, a popular phrase was 'a new broom sweeps clean.' During the war between the Dutch and the British in 1652, a Dutch admiral ordered a broom tied to the masts of all his ships to signify that he would make a clean sweep of the British from the seas." He then grinned. "Of course, he didn't meet that commitment. But in the centuries since, ships of many nations have flown brooms as signs of outstanding success of sea trials or missions accomplished. The most famous use was by American submarines during the 1940s in World War II. When they had used all their torpedoes against enemy ships, many skippers chose to fly a broom from the conning tower on return to port to symbolize a clean sweep. Since then, many nations have used the broom to signify successful checkouts of new sea going ships. For almost two centuries now, the symbolic phrase, 'she flew a broom' has meant the space ship checked out satisfactorily."

Another member of the press held up his hand for recognition. "Chairman Nahal, since this ship is of such a different configuration from all of Space Transport's other vehicles, could you tell us something about the *Marna*? I have your handout of the particulars, but it would be appreciated if we could hear a description in your own words."

Mohammed turned to Arturo and motioned him to the podium. "Mr. Arturo Diggs, the ships designer, and father of the Massafon Engine, should be the one to make the response. Arturo, if you will, please give a general description of the *Marna*."

Mohammed moved aside to relinquish the podium to Arturo. "Thank you, Mr. Chairman. First of all, ladies and gentlemen, if there are questions during this review, please don't hesitate to ask." He glanced around and saw appreciative nods from several of the media. Reciting from memory, he began the technical summary. "The 50 meters diameter by 100 meters in length core of the mother ship houses seven Massafon Engines, navigational equipment, the data recording and the data transmission systems. The six 20 meter spherical shaped ships attached in a circle around the mother ship are landing probes. Each probe has its own Massafon Engine for landing, exploring, and then returning to the mothership."

Arturo paused for a question.

"Mr. Diggs, what is the purpose of their globular contour?"

"The spherical shape of the probes was chosen to allow rapid spinning through any type atmosphere on any possible planets we hope to discover. Also, it gives the probes the ability to move easily for small distances over a planet's surface without having to go airborne."

The reporter nodded in acknowledgement. Seeing there were no further questions, Arturo continued his discourse. "On board each of the probes are various pieces of equipment for visual transmission, soil analysis, atmospheric analysis, and communication with any intelligent life forms."

Another of the media corps held up his hand to interject a question. "What will you do if life is found, particularly if it's humanoid?"

"Our sensors and scanning 'scopes will detect any humanoid or animal life forms before the probes are released from the mother ship. If any humanoid forms are present, an evaluation of their evolutionary cycle and civilization status will be made. We've prepared various messages and communication methodologies for any contact that we could possibly imagine."

"Such as?" the questioner continued.

"Such as mathematics, the Arabic numbering system, physics equations, a map of our solar system and star maps, among many other items," Arturo replied and then added, "along with photos and sketches of people trading goods, working and relaxing with families."

"What if the civilization is considerably ahead of our own? What messages will you communicate?" the same questioner persisted.

"The identical way as if they were in the same evolutionary period as ours. The only changes will be if their evolution is a thousand or more years behind ours. Then we have to be careful that we don't scare the hell out of someone and become a legend before our time," Arturo responded with a broad smile.

"But what," the zealous reporter persisted, "if they are more advanced than us and try to capture a probe or the mother ship?"

"We don't worry about the probe." Arturo patiently explained. "All its data will be transmitted back to the ship anyway. However, we could lose plant samples, if there are any or other miscellaneous items the probe may choose to bring back. You see, each probe is programmed with artificial intelligence computers to evaluate whatever it finds. If anything other than the probes approach the *Marna*, she'll immediately leave. Assuming the presumed life forms had the capability to travel at the speed of light, they probably would have visited us by now. Since they haven't, we assume the *Marna* can outrun anything someone there could send after her."

"What if the initial indications are that the presumed planets are too hot or too cold or have nothing to offer for the future?"

"In that case, I guess we will know there is nothing worthwhile pursuing around the three stars in Rigel Kent. But, we will at least have learned that. We'll still send the probes down to the surface, and if possible bring them back to the mother ship and back to Earth."

The youthful reporter, who had queried Mohammed about the broom, hesitantly raised his hand. "What are the chances of finding life forms, either humanoid or microorganisms?"

Before Arturo could answer, Mohammed fielded the question. "Good question. If one considers that there are billions of stars, then the odds are very low that any form of life exists on planets around the three Alpha Centauri stars."

The youthful reporter's voice wavered slightly, but he continued. "But, you're assuming life as we know it. What about life in different forms from our own experience?"

"Another good question," Mohammed answered, making the young man feel more at ease. "All our scientific research indicates that for life to survive in any form, it must be based on carbon — although, there are those who believe a silicon based life form can exist. Who knows for sure? We intend to find out, however, about the possibility of life on any planets surrounding our nearest neighboring stars."

"Mr. Chairman," another questioner challenged, "any odds you wish to quote on finding life?"

"No. Because, you see, the evolution of life is almost an 'accident' when one considers all the various events that must take place to allow life forms to come into being. I hasten to add though — with the trillions of stars in the universe — that millions or even maybe billions of accidents may have happened and that mankind is not alone in this vast universe."

There was a hush as the crowd meditated on his words. Although Mohammed could clearly see some skeptical frowns on a few faces, he elected to continue his philosophy. "Accidents," and he emphasized the word, "I truly believe, are by design of whoever or whatever engineered our vast universe."

It was at that moment that the mood was shattered by a loud voice. "Jeff Mitchell, World News Analysis, speaking."

This was the commentator who had harshly criticized the World Court for its decision not to break up Space Transport. All heads turned and the camera crews focused on him as he began to speak. "Mr. Chairman, re-

THE QUEST

garding this mission of yours to Alpha Centauri, wouldn't it be more productive to use the
money for setting up new colonies on Mars and
open up new opportunities and jobs for our
multitudes of people?" He seemed to have no
intention of asking a question. "It seems to me
that this major expenditure is not in the best
interest of the people of Earth and that the
money could be better spent elsewhere, particularly since the trip is only for the glory of
Space Transport and not for the average man. I
submit that the real reason is for..."

Before the commentator could finish,
Mohammed thundered, "Are you making a political statement or asking a question? If a political statement, make it elsewhere, but not
here. If you're asking a question, I'll answer it if
it is properly phrased without political implica-
tions."

The commentator glared at Mohammed.
"Of course, Mr. Chairman." He then smiled for
the cameras. "To rephrase my question. Is this
trip only for future Space Transport profits and
its monopoly of trade with our nearest
neighbors on Alpha Centauri? Will you share
any data you record about planets around Alpha Centauri A, B and C?"

It was all Mohammed could do to speak
without rancor. "As Chairman of Space Transport, I can assure you that all data will be
shared with everyone throughout the world. Insofar as profit is concerned, of course we expect
to make a profit, but..."

"So it is just for profit," the commentator
interrupted, "instead of improving life for the

411

world's population. I thought so. How can you..."

Mohammed lost his patience. "You are completely out of line, sir! I suggest you address your remarks to the evening newscast and keep your thoughts to yourself while on Space Transport property." He then regained his dignity and control of his voice, "I repeat, Mr. Mitchell, this is not a political forum! It is an occasion of import to the entire world — an experience to remember. Mankind's first attempt to visit another solar system will long be remembered, long after you, sir, have gone to your just reward." In a gesture that the confrontation was now past history, Mohammed smiled and said, "Now, for those wishing a tour of the *Marna*, please follow the guides to the elevators, and..."

"Just a moment, Mr. Nahal, if you please." This was the voice of one of the most respected and revered newscasters of the last several decades.

Mohammed raised both his hands to stop the exodus towards the elevators. "Will everyone please stay where you are."

"Thank you, Mr. Nahal." To Mohammed's astonishment, the elderly newscaster mounted the stairs to the podium. "As one of the more senior commentators here, may I offer apologies from all of us in the media for the seemingly rude questions and assertions by one of our associates." Though he looked directly at the Chairman while speaking, everyone distinctly heard his voice. "Not all of us contend that industry has only profit in mind when embarking on a new venture. The majority of us know that Space Trans' contributions to the world are unparalleled. Again, I hope Space Trans management, all the people here today, and those watching this momentous event at home accept our apologies for the discourteous remarks by one of our colleagues. We all wish nothing but the best for the *Marna* and Space Transport."

Extending his hand, first to Mohammed, then to Arturo, the venerable and distinguished commentator shook hands. The applause from the group was thunderous. With the exception of the flushed-faced Jeff Mitchell who left in a huff with his crew.

A week later, the final checkout flight of the *Marna* was completed, and true to Mohammed's prophesies, everything went according to plan.

Proudly attached to Arturo's detailed summary of the computer records sent to Mohammed was a decal of a broom. The accompanying note read, "The broom is aloft, captain. We launch for Alpha Centauri A one week from today. Your presence at the space station for the launch is requested." It was signed, "Arturo".

Mohammed insisted that the entire Diggs family be included at the space station to witness the launch of the *Marna*. The twins were exemplary angels during the final preparations. They watched with interest as the various dials, gauges and readout screens displayed varying types of data. Webb was particularly captivated by the hologram of the solar system. Alongside, was the flight path of the *Marna* to Rigel Kent, represented by another hologram of the three stars. Simulations of the flight path by the master computer in the two holograms were, to the youngster, like watching an electronic game. Webb learned about distance, g's, velocity and most of all, time requirements for space travel.

As the small family group watched in expectation, Arturo and the technicians completed the checkouts. When they finished with the checks and sequencing, Arturo gave a required summary of the flight, phrasing some of his comments so the children would have a clearer understanding of the procedures.

"Time to light speed at 1,000 g's acceleration is 8.5 hours, while traveling a distance of approximately 4.6 billion kilometers..."

"Remember, the data transmissions will take longer and longer to receive as the ship goes farther and farther..."

"We should be able to see the *Marna* for about 15 seconds after the engines are energized, or about 27 kilometers before she goes out of visual range..."

"And now, we're ready for the command to launch..."

"Station Control, this is Marna Control. We are on schedule for launch in exactly two minutes."

"Ah, Roger, Marna control. You're cleared for launch. Good luck Mr. Nahal and Mr. Diggs."

Jana walked over to Arturo and took his hand. He leaned over and kissed her on the cheek.

Turning back to the control panel, Arturo gave the final commands. "Initiate engine sequence 879241 alpha omega," using the same code format as the previous *Jana* launches. Almost as if in repeated fantasy, phrases of old Newsome's legacy ran through his mind.

"Trips within our solar system...child's play...compared to the conquest of the stars...legacy for his descendants ...beyond the speed of light...infinity...the universe."

When the remote arm had released the *Marna* and she was floating free, Arturo looked out the view port, sucked in his breath, and gave the order, "Now!"

The counter rotating wagon-wheels opened slowly on all seven engines and the seven photon beams, emitting from the back of the *Marna,* could be seen by everyone on the space station. Accelerating slowly, the ship only covered a kilometer in five seconds. Continuing to pick up speed as power was increased, the *Marna* disappeared into space in just under 15 seconds. The group, gazing through the view ports, remained at the glass for another minute, unwilling to leave. It was only then that congratulations were offered to Arturo, Mohammed and the crew of technicians.

Twelve and three-quarter hours later, the computer voice announced, "Speed 300,000 kilometers per second. All systems normal. Massafon Engine shut off. Entering coast period..."

Mohammed brought out champagne for the adults and fruited sparkling water for the twins. Numerous toasts and presentations were made, including unique drawings and a special poem written by Webb and Marna for the occasion.

To the delight of those present, Mohammed presented everyone with a sterling silver model of the *Marna*, beautifully engraved with:

The *Marna*
Earth's first mission to the stars
Alpha Centauri A, B & C in Rigel Kent
Designed by Arturo Newsome Diggs
Built by the Space Transport Corporation
"A Dream Come True"

2217
DISAPPOINTMENT

Ronal Lowe had been successful in taking over the Orbital Manufacturing Corporation as a result of his financial backers advancing money to allow the company to complete his three freighters. As he had anticipated, Orbital couldn't repay the loan per the schedule, and within two years Geo Transport had control of the company. The following year he acquired the remaining stock and now had 100% control. Because he had few scruples about people and business, at forty-two, he had become a ruthless businessman. Orbital now was producing ships for the Geo Transport fleet at a rapid rate, and the company's fleet was almost 50% of Space Transport's fleet. The company had not shown a profit until the past year because of the huge cash outlays for the new ships. The increase in space transportation requirements had served Geo well. Although their market share had grown significantly, they were still far behind Space Transport. The other competitor was still in business, but they only had small portions of the market — now dominated by Geo and Space Transport.

Ronal gathered up the reports intended for the board meeting and made a final cursory review. Satisfied that he was well versed with the details of the events over the past two months, Ronal left his office for the boardroom. He knew all the Asian members and the few domestic members were waiting for the latest results from Geo Transport. Ronal entered the boardroom and shook hands with the assembled group. After the social amenities were performed, he called the meeting to order, dispensed with the minutes of the last meeting, and went directly to Geo Transport's status report. He reviewed Geo's progress, answered questions, and then summarized.

"Ladies and gentlemen, our sales for last year grew by 20%. For the first time since we began the expansion program with the new freighters, we're showing a profit. At our current schedule of new freighters coming on line, we should have a fleet equal to Space Transport in about ten years. Until then we'll continue to press the competition with Space Trans."

The board members nodded. They were used to long term planning and were not afraid to wait for many years to achieve their goals. One board member spoke up after the new business was dispensed with and asked, "Any word on the unmanned probe sent to Rigel Kent by Space Transport?"

"Yes. Our contact at Space Transport, who shall remain anonymous says that messages came in a couple of weeks ago and no life forms of any kind were discovered — most important — the planets may prove to be impractical for commercial ventures." Ronal stopped, then added, "Just as well, since it means we don't have to invest in ships for manned exploration and mining. The formal announcement is expected any day now."

The board members nodded again and the meeting was adjourned. This was the first time Ronal had felt in charge of a board meeting. Heretofore, he had been a mere flunkey making a report.

Arturo and the Space Transport planetary research group had studied the final messages sent by the unmanned probe two weeks previously, and had come to the conclusion that in spite of their wishes and the world's hopes, absolutely no life forms were found — not even microorganisms. Worse yet, the planets that had been discovered were not unlike the planets of their own solar system. Most were gas balls like Saturn and Uranus. A few were rocky and inhospitable like Mercury. None even approached the physical properties of Mars. No new minerals were found that would make commercial exploitation practical. When the messages had first come through a year and a half ago, they were elated at finding a few undiscovered planets around the three stars. The messages continued with each new discovery and their elation slowly diminished, as it became more and more evident that financially the trip had been in vain. All knew, however, that astronomers would be overjoyed at the data, in spite of the commercial disappointment. As the data was summarized for release to the news media, Arturo, Mohammed, and the research group, could not hide their disappointment.

"Well, Arturo, I guess we now know about our closest neighbors. Nothing there is worth pursuing. Sure cost us a lot of money to find that out."

"At least Mohammed, we now know what's there. I do find it notable that what we did discover was much like our own solar system, except for the planets orbiting around the twin stars, Alpha Centauri A and B."

"That is interesting, the twelve planets orbit around and between the two stars in a figure eight," Mohammed said — with emphasis on 'is'.

"At least it'll give the astronomers something to chew on for years to come. Imagine that! When the planets are in the middle of the figure eight, light from the two stars means no night. And the gaseous surfaces of seven of the planets vaporize from the terrific heat, and recondense as the planets continue their orbit," Arturo added in an effort to point out something of scientific interest and show that the effort was not in vain.

"I guess you're right, but damn it, I'd hoped..." Mohammed stopped and stared into space with a glum look. His good natured humor finally took over, and he laughed as he said, "Can you also imagine the other five planets of mostly rocky mineral, boiling as they pass between the stars, then solidifying as they move away and cool off. No way we could ever have a manned dome on one of them or the others, for that matter. Talk about hell in action!"

Arturo laughed with him and added, "Couldn't be much worse than all that debris around Alpha C, no large planets, just a jumble of rocky asteroids ranging in size from grains of sand to 5,000 kilometers in diameter. None of which, I might add, had anything worth pursuing. Good thing the ship sensed them and went in slowly, or we might have lost the whole mission."

"Alpha C is a small star, but an old one. The debris may have come from the other two stars when they were formed and wound up around Alpha C. We'll leave that for the astronomers to figure out. Too bad none of the asteroids weren't made of gold, silver or pure palladium — or at least something worthwhile." Mohammed had relaxed and was sitting back contemplating the long awaited results.

"The *Marna* is on the way home now and should arrive in a year and a half, the middle of 2219. I doubt that anything additional will be learned from her trip, other than some of the smaller asteroids she picked up, along with samples of the rocky and gaseous planets around the twin stars. You know, we didn't realize just how close Alpha Centauri A and B were."

"Yeah. Five hundred million miles seems a long distance until one considers that the twins are closer to each other than we are to Jupiter. Amazing how they exist without crashing into each other," Mohammed mused, his gaze far away.

"I must say Mohammed, all was not lost on this trip. Look at the data we've accumulated. As far as I'm concerned, the trip was a success, whether or not we found anything of value for use on Earth."

"I couldn't agree more, Arturo. But enough of this! Finish the summary release, and let's go to the interview," Mohammed requested while walking to his office.

Space Transport's press secretary had handed out the fact sheet release an hour before Mohammed came into the conference room to take questions about the results of the *Marna's* amazing trip. During the interview, Mohammed was careful to stress the value of the mission to science, never giving any indication of the voyage not being a success. The press was jubilant about the results and congratulated both Mohammed and Space Transport. All questions answered, Mohammed and Arturo were about to leave the briefing when one last question was asked.

"When do you plan on retiring, Mr. Nahal? Not that you should retire, that is, but you previously said, 'after the mission was completed' — no offense, sir."

"None taken young man," Mohammed said with a smile. "I'm 82 now and I think I'll turn over the reins to someone else. About time, don't you think?" Mohammed added.

"And you Mr. Diggs. Will you continue as the top consultant to Space Transport or will you hang it up also?"

Arturo started to answer, but Mohammed interrupted him and said, "I'll answer that. Mr. Diggs can stay at Space Transport as long as he wishes, but I'm going to do my level best to convince him to 'hang it up' as you said. About time both of us relaxed from the daily grind."

"How do you feel about that, Mr. Diggs? Do you agree with Mr. Nahal?"

Arturo looked over to where Jana was seated, listening to all that was said. "Yes, I agree with Mr. Nahal. It's time to retire. Besides I have personal projects to work on." He looked directly into Jana's eyes during the last sentence.

The reporters saw Arturo's steady gaze and all looked at Jana, who at sixty-nine — three years younger than Arturo — was still beautiful and most attractive. She almost blushed but arose instead and purposefully strode toward Arturo and Mohammed. Taking each by the hand she raised them high into the air to salute their great achievements. "I give you the two men who made history in space transportation. My husband and his boss, who is the father of our daughter-in-law, but most of all, our friend."

Everyone present stood up and clapped. Jana hugged Arturo and Mohammed in turn and when the applause finally stopped, she led them from the room.

On the way to the waiting air-car with Jana and Mohammed, Arturo's mind was on further stars and solar systems yet to be explored.

Again, old Newsome's legacy ran through his mind.

"...beyond the speed of light...infinity...the universe."

"But how...?" he asked himself.

2225
GREED

Propping his elbow on the desk, Arturo wearily let his forehead rest on his bent knuckles. As his eyes closed, he involuntarily sighed. The pressure over the past eight years to find how to exceed the speed of light had gradually taken its toll. Frustration at the inability to achieve his goal had almost driven him to distraction, and he found himself repeating theories over and over again on the slight chance that an avenue had been overlooked — but time and again, it had proven a futile exercise.

When a burst of bright sunlight flooded the artificially lighted study, Arturo blinked his eyes in annoyance.

"Arturo, my love, look who's come to say hello!" There was a happy tone to Jana's voice. "And most important he wants to give you a breather from your work."

Looking up, it took a moment for Arturo to focus his eyes. He could make out the form of his wife and only a slight outline of another tall figure against the open patio door. He almost knocked over the chair as he hurriedly rose. His fatigue vanished.

425

"Mohammed!" His face broke into a warm smile. "Well, if you aren't a sight for sore eyes."

"And you too, my friend." With an agility that belied his almost ninety years, Mohammed strode across the room to grasp Arturo in the customary hug and then bestow the two traditional kisses on each cheek.

"What a wonderful surprise!" Arturo reciprocated the greeting in kind.

"Come on outside you two," Jana said while gently propelling the two men out to the sunny patio. "Enough of this stuffy room. Time to smell the flowers."

"I hope I'm not intruding," but Mohammed was not apologizing. "On impulse I decided that a cup of Jana's special blend of coffee..."

"Coffee, hell," Arturo said sharply, not even glancing at his watch. "It's happy hour."

"I just happen to have a vintage bottle of champagne on ice, gentlemen," and Jana pointed, "right here in the cooler."

"I take it that we were actually expecting company?" Arturo teasingly raised an eyebrow at his wife. "Or had you something else in mind?"

"Why, darling," she quipped back, "always."

"As I said before," Mohammed joshed, comfortably settling himself in a lounge chair, "if I'm intruding..."

Arturo lifted the champagne from the ice bucket, appreciatively glanced at the label, and then tested the bottle between his hands for the correct coldness. "Needs another fifteen minutes to be at the precise drinking temperature. So, Mohammed, if you'll excuse us..." Arturo placed his arm around Jana's waist and pulled her to him.

Not the least daunted by this display of affection, Mohammed casually surveyed the beautifully landscaped garden. "Jana, my dear, your roses this year are truly some of the most magnificent specimens I've ever had the pleasure to behold." Without pausing for breath he went on to a completely different subject. "Oh, by the way, Arturo, I stopped by Space Transport today and they told me everything was going just fine. In fact, 165 transports are on line and in continual operation."

Still enveloped in Arturo's embrace, a loud chortle erupted from Jana's throat.

"What did you say, my dear?" Mohammed innocently asked.

"You two never fail me." She shook her head. "Both of you have been retired from the company for over seven years, and when you're together, it only takes about two minutes before Space Trans leaps into the conversation."

"Guilty as charged," and Mohammed sheepishly grinned at Arturo. "And, if one of us hadn't brought up the subject," tenderly taking Jana's slim hand and lightly brushing it against his lips, "you would have thought we were becoming senile and brought it up yourself to remind us."

Jana burst out in another laugh. "You're right, you know." Seating herself next to Mohammed, she excitedly asked, "Tell me, what else is happening out there in the business world of space travel."

"Since you inquire," and he instantly warmed to the issue, "Geo Transport now has 97 freighters in operation, but Space Trans is still holding to their normal profit margins."

Not about to be left out of the conversation, Arturo questioned, "Is Geo profitable yet?"

"No one really knows. Although they appear to be thriving, their actual financial condition is still kept confidential." Mohammed hesitated, and then waved his forefinger at Arturo, "Ah, and one other thing you might find interesting. Space Trans had to replace the Diggsanium mirrors on one of the freighters."

"Oh, really?" Arturo said with surprise and interest. "Do you recall which freighter?"

"Yes. It was the first one that we retrofitted with the Massafon Engine back in 2202."

Arturo pulled up a chair next to Mohammed, sat down, and leaned forward. "How many hours were on the mirrors at replacement?"

"Just a minute, I took some notes." Mohammed reached into his pocket and removed a small electronic recorder. "Exactly 23,186 hours, to be exact."

"What was the evidence of failure?"

"According to our lab crew, it simply disintegrated." Seeing the concerned frown on Arturo's face, he quickly added, "But you always predicted that we couldn't expect the mirrors to last forever, and you were right."

Arturo reclined against the overstuffed cushions and placed his entwined fingers behind his head. He was deep in thought. It was some moments before he spoke. "Has there been any progress in finding another material that works as well as Diggsanium?"

Mohammed did not even attempt to sound optimistic. "None. None whatsoever. And the only source of Diggsanium to be found is on Filip's asteroid."

The only sound was the breeze rustling the trees, and the intermittent chirps of the birds. Eventually Jana broke the silence. "Filip has calculated that, like Earth's oil situation in the twentieth and twenty-first centuries, there is even a limit to the supply of Diggsanium."

"However," Arturo added, "he also believes that if only five per cent of his asteroid is mined of minerals, the Diggsanium yields will last for over 5,000 years, at least at the current rate of consumption."

A soft chuckle caused the two men to look at Jana. "Jamille and Filip always say they're the only ones they know who are slowly digging and processing themselves out of house and home."

"True, true." Mohammed reflected, then laughed, "Actually, as an analogy, their asteroid actually looks sort of like a potato, only about 60 kilometers long and 40 in diameter, but they're moving and shipping a lot of ore."

"Of course they only get about a pound of Diggsanium for every five tons of ore processed," Arturo pointed out.

"I think I remember Filip mentioning," Jana injected, "that the digger teeth replacement is a much larger market than the mirror market."

"That's right." Mohammed agreed. "The teeth only last about 500 hours before they wear away to the point of being unusable."

"If I might," Arturo had a serious tone to his voice, "get back to the mirror failure. This means that an automatic replacement of mirrors will have to be scheduled for the future."

"That's correct, Arturo. Space Trans has currently set automatic replacement every 20,000 hours. Since the transports have 48 engines, that should give adequate safety margins. If not, they'll lower the replacement times."

Arturo nodded, "Good, that's good."

Jana motioned toward the chilling champagne, "Do you think we could have a sample now?"

With a chagrined expression Arturo jumped up, exclaiming "Oh, my God, I forgot all about it."

As Arturo made a flourish of removing the cork with his thumbs in a loud pop and then pouring the bubbly liquid into the glasses, Mohammed and Jana politely clapped approval.

After a toast Mohammed launched into the purpose for his visit. "Now tell me, Arturo, what have you been up to since we last saw each other?"

"Not a heck of a lot, Mohammed. Jana keeps me busy with her galley proofs, her literary parties, and her book signings. I'm the chauffeur, you know."

Mohammed gave a hearty guffaw. "Yeah, I'll bet. Getting you away from your quest for exceeding light speed is a chore I wouldn't relish, but if anyone can do it, Jana can."

"Thank you kind sir, but..." Jana frowned as she paused and glanced at her husband.

"I think my dear bride is trying to tell you that only an angel from heaven could have tolerated the discouraging progress I've encountered with my research."

"You mean you've had absolutely no progress on how to exceed the speed of light?" Mohammed's concern was obvious. "But I thought you ran a test at the Colorado facility and made a breakthrough which would lead to a possible solution."

"I thought so, also," Arturo shook his head dejectedly, "when we discussed it last month by visi-phone. Again, it was a blind alley. Everything I've calculated or tried hasn't worked. Frankly, I'm out of ideas."

Jana placed her glass on the table and walked over to Arturo to massage his neck and shoulders. "That'll be the day when my Arturo is out of ideas. What he really means, Mohammed, is that he's out of ideas — "today." Tomorrow or the next day, he'll begin pursuing a new path. I know how he thinks and how he works. You'll see."

"As I said, it takes an angel to..."

Arturo was interrupted by a beep from the extension visi-phone that an incoming message was being transmitted. Automatically he asked, "From whom?"

The visi-phone's monotone voice replied, "Filip and family."

With a beaming face, Arturo gave the command to have the message received in holographic image. Instantly, three-dimensional images of Filip, Jamille and the twins, Marna and Webb, appeared in the center of the patio. Presented in full color and half-life size, the family group was seated in the atrium on their asteroid. All waved and smiled, then they turned to Jamille as their spokesperson.

"Hello, one and all. We're sending the same message to my dad as to you, Mother Jana and Father Arturo. We want you three to come to our asteroid for my Dad's 90th birthday next month. The twins have completed their masters' degrees at Mars College, and will be with us to attend the party. While you're here, Filip wants everyone to see the new eruption of the volcano, Pele, on Jupiter's satellite, Io. All four of us went to see it recently, and its beauty is beyond description. Amazing how that little moon can have such a huge volcano. It's only slightly over 3600 kilometers in diameter, but the lava shoots up over 50 kilometers and falls back down like a huge flaming geyser. Besides, it would be fun to have the entire family here all at one time. Please come."

After Jamille, each of the twins took turns imploring their grandparents to come to the asteroid to celebrate Mohammed's birthday.

When they had finished, Filip put in his entreaty. "We really want to see you here and show you all the things we've accomplished since your last visit. Besides, as Jamille said, we've never had the entire family here at the same time and what better occasion than Father Mohammed's birthday. Also, Dad, Mother, I want to discuss the business with you. Let us know as soon as you can. Please come."

The invitations to the family gathering over, each began relating their latest activities. Marna, always a beautiful young girl, had matured into a striking woman. Webb, taller than his father and equally as handsome, still retained his impish personality. The twins gave detailed accounts of how they envisioned using their acquired expertise to enhance life on the Diggs asteroid. Already holding a degree in Progressive Psychologic, Marna was completing her residency in Space Medicine. Webb's interest had always been in Geological Engineering, and his advanced studies had proved beneficial to the mining industry on the asteroid. Much to Jamille's delight, the twins proudly gave a detailed tour of the flower garden that their mother had so carefully nurtured in the domed community. After almost half an hour of family chatter, Filip and Jamille again repeated the invitation and concluded with, "We'll plan on it." The message ended with unison shouts of, "See you next month."

When the holographic images faded, Arturo, Jana and Mohammed were momentarily silent, and then, all began talking at once.

"With Marna and Webb's college responsibilities, we haven't seen them in person for several months..."Jana began.

"I just can't believe the twins are twenty-five years old now..." Arturo added.

"Jamille and Filip look wonderful, even if it was only a holographic..."

"In other words," Jana cut through the rambling discussion with the decisive comment, "we're all going for a visit next month."

"But, of course," Arturo and Mohammed roared in unison.

The first order of business for the trip was to select the quickest route. Mohammed quickly solved the problem of transportation. "I don't want to go by freighter. Takes too long. By the time we stop at Mars and go on to the asteroid, it'll take 12 to 15 hours because of taking on new cargo. Tell you what, I'm still on the board of Space Trans. I'll commandeer a fast shuttle for us. We can be there in, let's see, where is the asteroid in relation to Earth right now?"

Arturo motioned them to follow him into the study. He turned on the new work computer and commanded, "Bring up data on planetary travel times." A second passed before the green light flashed. "What is the direct flight time 18 days from today, from Earth to the Diggs asteroid located between Mars and Jupiter?"

Straightaway the computer responded, "Two hours and thirty minutes at a halfway point maximum velocity of 7.43% C. The Diggs asteroid will be 199,000,000 kilometers from Earth 18 days from today."

Mohammed walked to the visi-phone. "No problem, my fellow travelers. I'll call and reserve the hotshot shuttle right now. These old bones can take that short flight — don't relish a flight to Mars and then on to the asteroid. I become dehydrated and get a headache when I'm aboard a freighter too long." He laughingly turned to Jana and shook his finger, "And don't you dare say, it 'comes with age'."

The new Chief Executive of Space Transport arranged for the shuttle to be available for the following month, pleased that he could be of such assistance. He also stressed that the vehicle would be theirs to use as long as they wished and as they saw fit.

Knowing it would take approximately twenty-two minutes for Filip, Jamille and the twins to receive their confirming arrival time, the three grandparents sent their acceptance and like enthusiastic kids, began making plans for the trip.

Word of Mohammed's 90th birthday fete had spread quickly throughout the close-knit domed community of Diggs asteroid. For two weeks, everyone had pitched in to make this a gala occasion by helping Jamille prepare menus of favored dishes, polishing silver, shining crystal, and cleaning the guesthouses. The small space jitneys used for flying over the Lilliputian asteroid had been scrubbed clean and methodically checked for mechanical perfection. Families loaned precious personal holographic tapes of preferred operas, music and sports for the visitor's enjoyment. Dinner invitations and offers to entertain were so abundant that Jamille and Filip found it impossible to accept all of them. The entire community wanted to be involved in making this a memorable visit, not only for the three guests, but also for Jamille and Filip.

There was a unique relationship between the two owners of the Diggs asteroid and their employees, built on respect and loyalty of all concerned. Much of the profit made by the company over the years had been shared with the workers and management. Many had made millions and could have grandly retired to a life of luxury on Earth, but like Jamille and Filip, preferred to call the asteroid "home" and continued working with those they adopted as extended "family."

The five hundred men, women and children living on the asteroid had long since outgrown the original dome. It had been replaced with one that had a hundred times larger footprint, plus the addition of many smaller satellite domes for the unmarried or single workers. Since the twins were in Mars College, Jamille had taken over the infrastructure management of the domed community. There were always the inescapable breakdown problems of the environmental equipment that made the domes habitable — the worst being the artificial gravity. When it wasn't working and until the auxiliary systems activated, anything that wasn't firmly anchored would levitate, including the inhabitants. Though the condition only lasted for a short time, it was still maddening. In spite of that and the restriction of movement outside the dome, few left because of the problems.

Settling the inevitable problems or misunderstandings that were bound to arise among the human residents fell under Jamille and Filip's jurisdiction. But it was absolutely vital to the existence of the populace that such disruption be handled with fairness and harmony to all concerned. To their credit, only twice had employees been expelled from the asteroid and then only for just and documented cause.

It was barely dawn, but Filip, sitting at the kitchen table, was already on his second pot of darkly brewed coffee. He frowned at a minute computer chip that lay on his open palm and was absorbed in listening to the voice of his computer. When the replay of his message ended, he inserted the chip and quietly ordered, "Duplicate."

When the task was completed, he removed the chip, carefully placed it in a protective container, and then sealed it securely. For a long moment he contemplated the receptacle, focusing on the familiar name and address. His sense of foreboding had increased over the past few months. This morning when he awoke, he knew that the message must be sent to Arturo in San Diego. For a reason that he did not even attempt to comprehend, it was important that his words be dictated and waiting for his father and mother when they returned to Earth. Turning back to the computer, he gave a final command, "Erase entirely. No copies or duplicate are to remain in memory."

In less than a second, the routine voice of the computer acknowledged the directive, "Memory erased, no backup remains in system."

Filip switched off the machine and was in the process of refilling his coffee cup when he heard a rustle at the door. Jamille, still sleepy, was attempting to slip into a peignoir while trying to smother a wide yawn at the same time.

"Why did you let me sleep so late, darling?"

"You looked too beautiful and content to wake, my love." Filip gallantly countered.

"That's never stopped you before." Though said lovingly, it did not hold the usual wide-awake conviction that the words usually implied. Trying to rouse herself, she stretched her arms over her head. "What time is it, anyway?"

"Exactly seven hours before our guests arrive for the big party."

At the prophetic commentary, Jamille became fully alert. "Oh, Filip," she moaned in dismay, "there's still so much to do!"

Just as she turned to dash from the room, he reached out and caught her arm. "Not until you sit down and have a cup of coffee."

"Not now, darling, I have to..."

Gently pushing his wife into a chair, he chided, "All the arrangements have been completed down to the last detail." The dismayed look on his wife's face induced him to add, "Remember you showed me your lists, and every item had been checked off with a big red 'okay'."

Jamille nodded in agreement, but her uneasy expression showed she was not completely convinced. Reaching over to take a sip of Filip's coffee, her face screwed up in distaste. "Ugh, this coffee's bitter. I'll make a fresh pot."

"Personally, my love, I prefer it strong."

438

"Filip," she groaned, "don't tell me you reprogrammed the coffee replicator again?"

He could not contain his laugh. "No, my love. I know better, but how I did it is my secret." When he didn't receive a response, he took her hand in his and gravely added, "but most important, I'm concerned about all your fretting about the folks' visit — they've been here on numerous occasions."

"Yes, but not the entire family at the same time," she countered. "Oh, Filip, this trip..." then almost to the point of tears, "it's so important that everything is just right. I can't explain it, but..." she looked at him, pleading for understanding.

He stood — reached down and pulled her to her feet — and gently took her trembling body in his arms. " My love, it's been in my thoughts, too. Perhaps we'll never again have the opportunity to have everyone together on the asteroid."

She gave an involuntary cry of pain, "Please don't say that."

"I didn't mean we wouldn't ever see them again, darling. Please don't misunderstand. When we're on Earth, we can still have gatherings at our home in San Diego."

Jamille's eyes clouded with tears as she gazed up at her husband. "I know our San Diego house is beautiful, but Filip, the asteroid is our real home."

Trying to console his wife, Filip tried another approach. "Then let's plan a yearly celebration up here. We'll tell them that it's part of the 'grandparents' contract' that they attend."

439

When he saw Jamille's smile he knew he was on the right track. "Let's see, my mom's birthday is next, so 2226 we'll commemorate her party. Then the following year will be my dad's..."

But before he could finish, Jamille kissed him. "Thank you, darling. I'm sorry I've been in such a lousy 'funk', but it's all over now."

"Then you're not going to be mad at me," he teased. "When I tell you what I really did to the coffee programmer?" Anticipating her reaction, he darted out of her reach.

Chasing him around the table, Jamille grabbed for his robe but missed. "You didn't..."

Throwing his hands in the air as a gesture of surrender, Filip whooped, "Time out." Picking up the small sealed container in which he'd placed the computer chip, he tucked it under his arm. "Have to get this to the outgoing freighter." Then he spoke almost too casually, "Do you have anything that needs to be sent today?"

Jamille was sensitive to her husband's mannerisms and suspected that something was bothering him. "No, darling," she shrugged, "nothing that can't wait."

Filip nodded and without replying, turned and left the room.

When the small Space Transport hotshot shuttle landed on the Diggs asteroid pad, an egress tube snaked its way to the door to attach itself firmly. It was only moments until the ready signal flashed, indicating the tube was pressurized and the occupants could leave the ship.

"We're all clear, Mr. Nahal, Mr. and Mrs. Diggs," the shuttle captain announced as he opened the exit door for his passengers.

To their genuine surprise, almost the entire colony had come to greet them, waving welcome banners and birthday balloons. At the front Filip, Jamille, Marna and Webb stood with arms outstretched.

"I'm overwhelmed," Mohammed declared in a loud voice.

Jana and Arturo were momentarily speechless, dazed by the warmhearted outpouring. "My goodness," Jana finally was able to gasp, "what a magnificent greeting."

Marna and Webb were the first to reach their three grandparents, closely followed by their parents. So as not to infringe on the privacy of the family group, the rest of the gathered community discreetly began to disperse.

"Thank you, everyone, for a most wonderful reception to Diggs asteroid," Arturo called out to the crowd.

"Believe me, Dad," Filip hugged Arturo, "this is only the beginning of what we all have planned for your visit."

"I hope you brought big appetites," Marna's bright blue eyes widened, "'cause Mom and everyone have prepared enough food to feed all the people on at least twenty asteroids."

"Now that's not true. Don't exaggerate," Webb contradicted his twin. "It's only about eighteen asteroids." The elder adults could not help but laugh at their grandchildren's banter.

"We'll certainly try to do justice to each and every feast," Mohammed affectionately patted his tall grandson on the shoulder, "and if not, I'll send for extra hotshot shuttles to take the leftovers back to Earth."

"Come on Mom," Filip took Jana's arm, "wait until you see your social schedule, but first we'll give you a fifteen-minute reprieve to get your space legs."

As predicted, the dining room table was laden with enough delicious edibles to feed a small army. The asteroid managers, as well as their wives and families, had joined in the gathering; and after the meal, the adults eagerly adjourned to Jamille's beautiful atrium to hear firsthand news of the events on Earth. The discussion would have continued until well after midnight, if Mohammed's yawn had not proclaimed the late hour. After the guests had departed and Jana, Jamille, and the twins had retired, Filip and Arturo tarried in the domed atrium.

"Son, something's bothering you." Watching Filip's brooding eyes during the evening, Arturo saw through his son's mask of cheerfulness. "Would you like to talk about it?" The question posed, he leaned back, not pushing for an answer.

"I don't know Dad," Filip truthfully answered. "It's almost like everything here on the asteroid is just too good and it just seems..."

"Like anything this good can't last forever?" Arturo finished the unspoken sentence. "I know the sensation. But do you have anything on which to base these feelings, whatever they are?"

"That's just it, Dad. I don't." He turned away from his father, involuntarily clenching his hands into frustrated fists. "Let's forget it. Everything is okay...really."

"If you say so," Arturo replied in a level tone, "but remember your mother and I are always there if you need to talk." Sensing that no more was to be discussed, Arturo slowly rose from his chair.

Filip turned, smiled, and walked over to hug his father. "Thanks, Dad. I know you and Mom are always there for the family and me. If I figure it out, I'll give you a call."

Without a word, Arturo clasped his son by the shoulders and then said, "Goodnight, Son. And thank you again for a most wonderful evening." He was about to turn and leave, when some sense of import made him hesitate.

"By the way, Dad," Filip offhandedly commented, his gaze focused on some distant object, "I sent you a chip today with some of my thoughts on it and a history of our activities on the asteroid." Still looking past his father, as if further explanation was necessary, he added, "I thought it would be a good addition to the family Bible."

Arturo's initial response was to question why the chip had been mailed to him instead of just being given while he was here, but he forced himself to repress the question with a slight smile.

"That's great Filip. I'll make sure it gets in. But, Son, since the Bible will be passed on to you, wouldn't you rather do it yourself?"

Attempting to brush off the question, Filip was only able to come up with a flimsy excuse. "Well, you know how you want to do something for a long time? Well, this morning I sat down and did it. I hope you don't mind."

There was no doubt in Arturo's mind that Filip was troubled in spite of his son's attempt to sidestep the actual problem. There was an obvious strain, and to put Filip at ease, he gently replied, "Of course I don't mind. Your mother and I will see that the chip is placed in the Bible. But you must update it when the Bible is in your possession."

"I promise, Dad. I promise."

There was nothing more that Arturo could add to alleviate Filip's uneasiness, and so he just nodded.

"Well, Dad," and it was said with too much joviality, "guess we'd better turn in. Tomorrow's the big day to visit the volcano on Jupiter's moon."

"Yes, Son," Arturo really tried to be enthusiastic. "We're all really looking forward to the trip."

Over breakfast next morning, the three grandparents discussed with Marna and Webb the exciting tour that the family would be taking to Jupiter and its moon Io. Spread out on the table were a series of exquisite holograms the grandchildren had taken on their previous trip.

"The only problem," Marna was explaining, "is that the sight is so spectacular and your full attention so focused, you almost forget to take the holograms."

444

"That's because," and Webb gave his twin a brotherly nudge, "you forgot your camera and had to keep borrowing mine."

"I could have gone all day," she indignantly shot back, "without that friendly reminder."

Ignoring her, Webb blithely went on. "Anyway, we should get some even more striking holograms using our new holographic equipment."

"Of course," Marna triumphantly interrupted, "once I coached Webb in the correct procedure..."

"After you'd hidden the instructions from me in the first place, what did you expect?"

Even though the twins were adults in every other respect, they still reveled in good-natured sibling rivalry and one-upmanship. Neither actually took it seriously, but Jana laughingly held up her hand, "Whoa, slow down, you two. Why don't you show your grandfathers the new gear and see if they can figure it out," winking at the grandchildren, "without the instructions."

"Right on!" Webb shouted.

Marna jumped up from the table. "Beat you to it."

In their hurry, they didn't notice their parents coming through the open door. "Just a minute," Filip cautioned, "before you knock us down."

"Oh, sorry, Dad, Mom, didn't see you," Webb apologized.

Jamille threw up her hands in mock despair. "For the life of me, I don't know what happens to you two sometimes. Normally you both are models of decorum, then it's like you're still seven years old."

"Actually, Mother," Marna recited in her most cultivated and clinical tone, "it's an expression of the everlasting love that we have always shared. Even fraternal twins have bonding that is not found between ordinary siblings."

"Thank you, Marna." Webb employed his bass voice to full effect. "I couldn't have expressed it better." Holding his arm chivalrously toward his sister, "Ma'am, it would be my pleasure to escort you from the room."

Marna daintily laid her hand on his arm. "Oh no, kind sir, it is truly my pleasure."

Their faces were masks of gentility as they strode out the door, and it was a full moment before their giggles echoed down the hallway.

Mohammed could no longer hold back a loud howl of laughter. "You're right, Jamille, I truly believe that those two, regardless of how old they are, will always be seven years old to each other."

"It's hopeless, Dad," Jamille conceded, "once they get on a roll," she raised her eyes skyward, "and I think it's just wonderful."

"Well, for what it's worth," Jana confided, "I've never known a brother and sister, twins or not, who were more loyal to each other."

"Of that there's no doubt," Filip enjoined. "And it's marvelous that they'll always be there for each other..." He started to add something more but ended the sentence midway.

Arturo could almost read his unspoken words but instead of elaborating, gave a hearty, "Hear! Hear!"

Jana noted a momentary silence and abruptly changed the subject. "We missed you at breakfast, dears, what have you been up to this morning?"

Jamille and Filip furtively exchanged glances. "Actually, Mother," Filip cleared his throat, "we have good news and bad news. The good news is that you all will have more room on the hotshot shuttle..."

When her husband hesitated, Jamille filled in the lapse: "The bad news is that we won't be able to take the trip with you."

"Oh no," Jana's face vividly portrayed the disappointment. "Really it's not that cramped. The shuttle has room for ten people, and if you came along, there would still be three seats left."

"That's not the real problem," Jamille vigorously shook her head. "It's the day of final exam for the student class in biophysics, and the instructor is occupied having a premature baby."

"Is she all right?" Jana asked with immediate concern.

"She has the best of medical care, Mother Jana," Jamille assured. "The chief of obstetrics flew over from Mars this morning."

"Perhaps the students," Jana tentatively suggested, "could take their exam at a later date?"

"Not possible, Mom," Filip explained, "Jamille will have to give the test, grade the pa-

447

pers, and tell those with the four highest grades that they are eligible for a space expedition."

The three visitors looked puzzled.

"The scores," Jamille elaborated, "must be submitted no later than 2400 hours today." Apologetically, she added, "These kids have worked so hard for this opportunity, I just can't let them down."

"And you shouldn't, my dear," Mohammed ended any further debate. "Though we wish you were coming with us, of course." Then he turned his head toward Filip, a raised eyebrow asking the unspoken question.

"As the old saying goes, when it rains, it pours." But no one seemed to appreciate the overworked simile. "Anyway," Filip started again, "the delivery supervisor just informed me that we have a pressing problem in delivering some ore shipments and processing additional Diggsanium."

Both Arturo and Mohammed started to say something, but Filip waved off their obvious concern. "It's nothing that can't be solved by tomorrow, but it will take my involvement to stave off a major penalty hit."

"Then by all means," Mohammed recommended, "we'll just postpone the trip for another time."

"We won't hear of it, Dad. Every hour of next week is scheduled with parties that members of our community have planned in your honor," Jamille said with finality. "Besides, Filip and I saw the eruption last month." Greeted by the trio of skeptical looks, she was forced to take a parting shot, "This will be Marna and Webb's time with their grandparents. And you certainly wouldn't want to disappoint your only grandchildren, would you?"

"I don't know about you, Arturo," Mohammed gave a resigned sigh, "but I've never stood a chance against a woman's logic."

"Nor I."

"Oh" and Jana glared at the two men. "After all these years, that's wonderful to finally find out."

A look of relief crossed Jamille and Filip's faces. "Well, I'm glad you all understand," he volunteered. "Now that it's settled, let's get you headed for the shuttle."

"And we'll see you back here in about nine or ten hours." Jamille smiled confidently.

As the hotshot shuttle lifted off, Filip and Jamille watched until it disappeared from sight. "I hope they weren't too upset about our change of plans," Jamille lamented.

"Of course they were. But they looked pretty excited once they had reconciled themselves to the facts. Anyway, I guarantee, it'll be a trip and experience that they'll always remember."

"I love you, my darling," and she pulled her husband close and startled him with a kiss and embrace.

"My love, if you didn't have those kids waiting to take their exam..."

Jamille gave a low laugh. "Until tonight..." she brushed his mouth again with her lips and pulled away.

With a sigh, Filip turned and headed for the ore processing facility. Once there, he began inspecting the huge containers of ore and the vacuum-packed containers of Diggsanium that had initiated the late order problem. After a thorough discussion with the foreman, they concluded that the shipments were not as critical as first imagined and the formidable penalty charge could be avoided. Filip was about to leave the facility when he noticed a large quantity of Diggsanium pressurized containers neatly stacked in the corner awaiting shipment. After walking over and reading the shipping labels, he was surprised to see that all were addressed to businesses he had never heard of before. All were clearly marked, "paid in advance." He shrugged, still wondering as he left the dock, who were these unfamiliar names and companies; he made a mental note to inquire — tomorrow.

The hotshot shuttle had almost completed the two hours and thirty minute trip to Jupiter. The captain had scheduled two to three hours more for viewing the volcanic eruption of Pele on Jupiter's moon, Io. Portable recorders, seismic activity analyzers, and hologram-cameras were at the ready, as Jupiter loomed huge in their view.

Though the occupants onboard could barely see Io as yet, their anticipation was mounting. Suddenly a hulking red spot, like an evil eye, glared through clouds, as if to warn of impending disaster for all that dared approach the gigantic planet. In spite of the advanced technology of Space Transport and even Geo, no manned ship had set down on Jupiter's gaseous and liquid surface. Its tornado-like winds were unpredictable and could easily destroy a manned landing craft. Even if a landing on the surface was desirable, there was no hard surface because the planet was covered with liquid hydrogen in a metallic conductive state. The unmanned probes sent into the surface had indicated the impossibility of establishing a manned colony.

"That red spot gives me chills." Jana said, her face pressed to the view port. "But it is beautiful," she said in wonderment. "Although it never seems to change."

The shuttle captain reduced the Massafon Engine thrust to zero and prepared to use the small guidance engines to maneuver closer.

"Look, Grandma!" Webb pointed. "I can see Io clearly. There's Pele."

When they were within 100 kilometers of the erupting volcano, the surface of Io showed the reddish brown sulfur and sulfur dioxide covering the surface. Pele indeed looked like a flaming orange giant geyser. From the geyser, clouds of orange brown sulfur gas drifted into the depths of space, forming figures, which if one had the imagination of a child, looked like faces, animals, trees and flowers. The small group gazed in awe at the colossal "red flower," and recorded in their mind the once-in-a-lifetime spectacle.

They had in fact exceeded their allotted time when the captain suggested that they might enjoy a flyby of the moons, Ganymede

and Europa, while returning to the Diggs asteroid.

The refreshments from the well-stocked picnic
basket had been devoured by the time they
were within half an hour of reaching their destined asteroid.

"There's an unaccountable pinpoint flash
in the far distance, Mr. Nahal," the captain
calmly reported over the intercom. He had
barely finished his announcement, when the
shuttle was struck by a slight tremor.

"What seems to be the problem, Captain?" Arturo immediately asked, taking control
of the communication.

"I'm not sure, Mr. Diggs, give me a moment to check all systems."

To not worry his family, Arturo nodded
confidently. "Just one of what we call, 'space
twitches'; nothing to be alarmed about, but I'd
feel more comfortable if you tightened your re-
straints."

Within minutes all systems had been
checked, and the captain verified that operation was normal. "Perhaps, Mr. Diggs, you'd
like to join me up forward." There was no hint
of alarm in his voice; on the contrary, he added
with a chuckle, "Always appreciate a good copilot."

"Sure you can cope with that, Captain
Breen?" Arturo jested, and released his re-
straints. "You know I have the reputation of always wanting to be the captain."

"No problem, sir," Breen smiled back. "You'll always be the true skipper of any ship in space."

Arturo laughed, winked at Jana and the twins, and slapped Mohammed on the shoulder. "How can I resist that invitation?"

Slipping into the right seat of the forward compartment, Arturo observed Breen had unobtrusively turned off the intercom to the rest of the shuttle.

"Mr. Diggs," Breen began, "I didn't want to alarm anyone, but there's some trouble with the primary and backup navigational system. I haven't been able to pick up the Diggs asteroid homing signal."

Arturo gave a quick scan of the control board and was unable to see a problem. "Let the computer follow the location coordinates and it will bring us in on target."

"Sir," the captain said matter-of-factly, "we are running on the computer. We're at the exact location of the asteroid, yet there's nothing here."

"Are you sure the navigational system is functioning properly?"

"Yes Sir, and as you can see, the homing signal beacons from domes on other asteroids, along with the Mars signals, are coming in loud and clear."

"You're right, captain," Arturo affirmed. "There's nothing wrong with the navigation system or homing system. The asteroid simply isn't here. Scanners are picking up a lot of dust and particles but no asteroid."

"Then you confirm — that it's simply gone?"

"That's impossible! It simply can't just disappear. Let's check the instruments and re-calibrate, using all the locator signals available."

"I've done that three times Mr. Diggs, and we are precisely at the intended destination."

"Check with Mars as to our exact placement. Have them verify our location on priority status."

"I've already sent a request for emergency coordinates ten minutes ago, Mr. Diggs. Accounting for signal transmission times, we should be receiving a reply in about five to seven minutes."

Feeling a burden heavier than he had ever felt, Arturo returned to the cabin to tell everyone what he knew of the implausible to believe situation. The group waited for the Mars message in agonized silence, while Arturo and the Captain continued to examine the instruments and re-calibrate with other known homing signals.

The Mars message verified that the shuttle was in the exact position where the Diggs asteroid should have been. In vain, each searched the view ports for the asteroid or any sign of it ever having been there. Nothing was seen but a flurry of minuscule dust particles.

The inevitable had to be accepted. Although it seemed impossible, the asteroid, along with Filip, Jamille and 500 men, women and children had mysteriously and irrevocably vanished from the solar system.

Kant Adams, a seasoned commentator and a trusted friend of Mohammed Nahal and the Diggs family, was solicited to broadcast the worldwide announcement of the asteroid disaster. His resonant voice strained, paused and almost broke as he gave his address.

"Four days ago this commentator reported on what seemed to be an impossible situation...the disappearance of a manned asteroid in the belt between Mars and Jupiter. As all of you know, the Diggs asteroid disappeared with seemingly no explanation. Investigators from Mars and Earth have found that various space stations around the sun, Earth and Mars, monitoring the flow of traffic, comets and meteors, recorded an unknown object traveling at the speed of light in the solar system. Latest calculations indicate it was headed toward the asteroid belt where the Diggs asteroid was located. No one knows what the object actually was or whether or not it could have collided with the asteroid. The investigators do know its trace evidence disappeared in the asteroid belt. Is it possible it struck the Diggs asteroid? If so, what was it? Investigators are searching for any clues in space. All transportation companies have verified the location of their ships, and none has accounted for any missing vehicle."

Watching the anguished face of the commentator as he gave his report, Ronal Lowe propped his feet up on his desk and leaned comfortably back in his swivel chair. A gleam of triumph shown in his small eyes, but he stopped smiling as the announcement went on.

"Among those missing from the community of five hundred people are the owners of the asteroid, Jamille and Filip Diggs. Jamille was..." and his voice broke here, "the daughter of Mohammed Nahal, the former Chairman of Space Transport, and Filip was the son of Jana and Arturo Diggs. As most of our viewers are aware, Mr. Arturo Diggs was the discoverer of the light speed Massafon Engine. It is my sad duty to relate that Mr. Nahal and Mr. and Mrs. Arturo Diggs, along with their grown grandchildren, Marna and Webb, discovered the disaster while on their way back from Jupiter and Io ...

Ronal angrily flipped off the news media broadcast in mid-sentence. "Shit," he spat out the word between his teeth, "the whole fuckin' lot of them should have been blown up."

Years of careful planning had gone into formulating Ronal's plan. The cunning strategy had been devised so as not to draw any undue attention. Five years previously, both Ronal and Mr. Yenta, agreed that the secret of the Massafon Engine lay in the material from which the mirrors were composed. Those who controlled the supply dominated space transportation. But even if Geo had been able to purchase the Diggs asteroid from Filip — an unlikely scenario — the World Court would never condone Diggsanium to become a monopoly exclusively for one transportation company. That had been previously proved with any viable company being given the right to purchase the design rights to the Massafon Engine. Thus, Geo would have been forced to make the material available to any company desiring it even its archrival, Space Transport.

It was Ronal's idea that Geo stockpile Diggsanium in vast quantities, enough to last their expanding fleet of freighters for hundreds of years. Mr. Yenta surreptitiously provided the funds, utilizing front companies for the Asiatic-Geo combine that legitimately participated in mining, tooling and machinery. So as not to cause suspicion, Geo continued its normal purchases of Diggsanium. It was by such a scheme that over 250 metric tons had now been secreted in an underground sealed vault on the Moon.

Stockpiling was only a part of the scheme that Ronal had devised. Several years ago, he had scheduled a small, unmanned vehicle retrofitted with a Massafon Engine, to be sent in orbit around Pluto, ostensibly for scientific purposes. It was reported as having crashed on Pluto during its initial approach and being totally destroyed. But unmanned ships had been demolished before, and this incident did not incite much media coverage. Since Pluto had been declared not commercially viable for exploitation, rarely did ships go near the planet, nor was it under continuous traffic monitoring.

The diamond shaped birthmark on Ronal's arm seemed to pulsate as if it had a life of its own. He gave a sadistic laugh as he recalled the chain of events that led up to the annihilation of the Diggs asteroid. There was no remorse or even a thought for the five hundred human beings. When his agents had informed him that the entire Diggs family would be assembled on the asteroid for Mohammed Nahal's 90th birthday, it seemed the ideal opportunity to achieve two goals with a single blow.

All he had done was send a simple coded message to a remote mining asteroid in the Mars belt. The message was relayed and the "lost" unmanned vehicle on the far side of Pluto was awakened from its dormant two-year sleep. The little ship's computers were promptly activated to full operation. Preprogrammed guidance thrusters dutifully began spitting on and off until the vehicle was directed toward its computer-plotted course. The Massafon Engine energized at one-tenth percent power, and the vehicle left Pluto's orbit to head into deep space.

The guidance thrusters maneuvered the vehicle in a large parabolic loop, covering over five billion kilometers away from Pluto and the solar system, until it had obtained a heading back towards the sun. Correcting until the desired course was obtained, the Massafon Engine wagon-wheels were opened to full power. Eight and one half hours later, the vehicle had obtained the speed of light. The Massafon Engine continued to operate, enabling the guidance thrusters to continually update the flight path by using the homing signal to which it had been locked. As the vehicle drew near its destination, a final correction to the flight path was made, and the guidance computers transferred any further modification to the input from the asteroid homing signal.

When the 200,000-kilogram vehicle hit its destined target at the speed of light, it was with the force of 50,000 fifty-megaton hydrogen bombs. The Diggs asteroid — and everything on it — vaporized on impact. Only dust remained in the vast reaches of space.

Ronal roused himself from his reverie, and spoke aloud to himself, "Earth's seemingly infinite supply of irreplaceable Diggsanium was lost for all time, except for Geo's stockpile. But I possess enough mirror material to last for hundreds of years. Now we'll see who controls the destiny of space."

"Too bad Arturo Diggs is still alive!" He gave a ruthless laugh,"...but losing his son and daughter-in-law — and before that, his father and mother — maybe that's rightful justice and even better..."

2243
THE WORLD'S LOSS

Grief knows no bounds with the loss of a child. Mohammed Nahal never recovered from the catastrophe that had claimed his cherished daughter and beloved son-in-law. He had unconditionally withdrawn from any involvement with Space Transport and exhibited no curiosity in the Diggsanium mirror problem, or anything connected with space. Mohammed died in his sleep — just before his 108th birthday — one hand holding a photograph of the entire family taken on the Diggs asteroid on their last and fateful visit in 2225. At his memorial service, tribute poured in from all over the world — a fitting homage to one of the pioneers of space travel.

Even after the passage of eighteen years, Jana and Arturo still mourned for Filip and Jamille, never forgetting to include in their prayers the hundreds of souls of the entire lost community.

Sorrow had been softened by the frequent presence of their grandchildren, Webb and Marna. Attempting to ease the pain by their nearness, the twins had undertaken supportive roles for Jana and Arturo. Aside from their careers, Marna and Webb had, for all intent, placed their social and personal lives on hold for a number of years. Both were now happily married, but they still paid daily visits to their grandparents.

Arturo's concentrated drive to discover how to exceed the speed of light had entirely ceased. His energies centered solely on a replacement material for the lost supply of Diggsanium. The quest not only eluded him — but the entire world of space engineers, metallurgists and physicists. Whatever material was tried, nothing could be relied upon to perform for more than a few hours, sometimes only minutes. Space Transport had developed a system of rotating materials along with conserving their scant supply of Diggsanium mirrors, but even that would allow operation for only a few hours before burnout. Although Space Trans continued to operate, it was at much less efficiency and with only one quarter of their fleet. It was only a matter of time before they would no longer be able to compete in transporting heavy loads at light speed.

Geo Transport, dominating the space market with 150 vehicles in full operation and with a seemingly endless supply of Diggsanium mirrors, boasted of attaining almost total market control and, with that, significantly increased prices.

Comfortably propped on a high kitchen stool in her grandparent's kitchen, Marna put the last daintily rolled tea-sandwich on a silver platter.

Not quite satisfied that the artistic composition was flawless, she began rearranging the placement.

"Even the ancient Chinese didn't strive for perfection in their works of art, my darling," Jana laughingly admonished. "To do so would have meant they were immortal."

"Saintly, I'm not, Grandmother," Marna facetiously rebutted, "just following your example. "

Jana raised an eyebrow. "My example?"

"Of course. You spend hours on your exquisite flower creations and arrangements. Every bloom, leaf, and twig has to be just in the precise position to meet your exacting eye for beauty and configuration."

"Oh, Marna," the matriarch blushed, "I just try to make the bouquet look pretty."

"And after all the work you put into making these delicious sandwiches, the least I can do is present them with flair." She popped one of the morsels into her mouth and closed her eyes in ecstasy, "Oh, Grandmother, these are delicious."

"Thank you, dear," Jana graciously accepted the compliment, "I remembered that they were one of your favorites."

A wicked twinkle pursed Marna's face. "Let's not share them with Grandfather and Webb," and she reached for another diminutive sandwich, "and eat them all up now."

"Both your brother and your grandfather would skin you alive," Jana teased, laughingly pushing the platter out of her reach.

"All right, if you insist on putting their interests above mine." She slipped down from the stool and started to pick up the tray of glasses filled with iced refreshments.

"OK, Grandmother, you win," Marna said cheerfully. "Let's go share the goodies with the men-folk."

Arturo and Webb were preoccupied in conversation when Marna and Jana entered the study. "One would think that another material would be found somewhere in our solar system which would replace Diggsanium, Grandfather. I simply cannot believe that, on all the asteroids and planets that have been explored, no trace of this specific material has been found."

"Nothing. Absolutely nothing has been found that even remotely duplicates Diggsanium."

"What about the substitute materials and the rotating system of replacement mirrors," Webb persisted. "Can't that system be used to keep the vehicles going?"

"To a point, but only to a point. The problem is that their failure rate varies all over the map."

Unobtrusively, Marna placed the tray of glasses on a side table, then took the platter of sandwiches from her grandmother, and entered into the conversation. "Exactly what does that mean, Grandfather?"

Arturo looked up, startled at the unexpected voice. "My goodness, I didn't hear you come in. Can we help you carry anything?"

"No, thanks," and she set the platter on the coffee table for all to reach and then settled herself on the couch next to her brother. "Please continue your discussion about the failure rate that's being encountered."

"Well, the best material that so far has been found is pure silicon-30 glass, but the failure rate varies from a few minutes to a few hours. Not being able to predict its functional time makes it impossible to guarantee the safety of a flight crew."

"Like what happened to the flight of the first unmanned *Jana*?" Marna questioned.

"Exactly." Arturo smiled, pleased at his granddaughter's immediate perception. "Without the Massafon Engine operating, a ship with a mirror malfunction will continue at the speed it was operating at the point of mirror burnout. No one will pilot such a ship unless we can guarantee they will not be lost in space."

"Like the original *Jana* was over 50 years ago, back in 2192," Webb somberly added, expressing everyone's unspoken thoughts.

"Grandfather," Marna inquired, "don't the ships sometimes have up to 48 engines, with numerous mirror replacement systems? By adding more spare mirrors and for that matter, more engines, wouldn't that be enough to guarantee safety of the flight crew?"

Arturo reached for a sandwich. "There is a practical limit to how many more engines can be added and how many replacement mirrors can be installed. But even doing that, the chances of losing a vehicle and crew is still probably one in a thousand."

"And I can guarantee," Webb rose, walking to the side table to bring the refreshment tray closer, "that no one wants to be that one in a thousand."

"Astonishing as it may seem," Arturo gave a cynical laugh, "for enough money, there are those who will accept a contract to pilot a vehicle with substitute mirrors. But neither Space Transport, nor I have taken part in that type of agreement. We would never consider the possibility of losing a crew, not to mention a ship loaded with valuable cargo."

Jana started passing out the filled glasses. "Don't those space vehicles with substitute mirrors have to pay exorbitant insurance rates, Arturo?"

"To put it in one word, astronomical. Aside from the safety of the crew and ship, it's money that Space Transport doesn't have. That's why we're no longer competitive with Geo."

Webb thoughtfully looked into his drink. "Which brings up a probing question. How is Geo continuing to operate all their ships and even add to the fleet?" He looked up suspiciously. "They must be facing the same Diggsanium scarcity as Space Transport."

"That, Webb, is a mystery. Obviously Geo has a stockpile of mirrors, but how much, they won't say. One thing is for sure though, the way they're going, they'll drive Space Trans out of business in a very few years."

"Thank God, Mohammed isn't alive to see that," Jana whispered aloud.

As each in the small group averted their eyes, a sudden silence engulfed the room. It was Marna who broke the somber mood.

"Grandfather," she cheerily announced, "I promised to stop by and see Webb's new offspring this afternoon." Picking up the almost empty tray of sandwiches, she turned to Jana. "You don't mind if I leave now do you, Grandmother.

"Yes, darling, I do mind." Jana's unexpected reply took everyone by surprise, and the stunned looks she received caused her to laugh. "I only meant that I want to visit our new great-grandchild also. Let's go together."

"Oh, Grandmother, you're too much. Of course you can go with me to see, Vaughn Newsome." Marna began nibbling at the few remaining tea sandwiches and followed Jana to the kitchen.

Arturo and Webb shook their heads in amusement. When the two women were out of earshot, Arturo reflected for a moment before speaking. "Those damn mirrors. Webb, it seems all I can think about is the loss of light speed ships for Space Transport and what will happen when Geo's supply runs out."

"Don't let it prey on you, Grandfather. Another material will be discovered someday. Never give up that hope."

As he had done for almost twenty years, Arne Harland maneuvered the large transport rack loaded with empty canisters into the freight elevator. Fitted with hydraulic wheels and a small motor, the sturdy metal structure was designed so that, even when fully loaded, one person could manipulate it with ease. Pressing the coded button, Arne routinely watched the elevator monitor display as he and the cargo gradually descended down the solid rock abyss below the surface of the Moon. When it reached one hundred meters, there was a slight thump, and in the one-sixth gravity it was difficult to maintain perfect balance, causing his heavy oxygen pack to shift slightly on his shoulders. Irritably, Arne pulled at the straps to tighten them. Satisfied that the load was distributed evenly on his back, he released the latch on the elevator door. Turning, he backed out of the elevator and grasped the handle on the transport rack to propel it slowly down a wide passageway.

It only took a few moments for him to reach the end of the corridor and stop in front of a thick vault door. Before giving the cryphograph that would automatically unseal the door, he methodically checked to see if any stray molecules of oxygen were present. Reassured with the analyzer reading, he conscientiously began punching in the signal. This was only one of many steps in his job process that demanded concentration. If he made a mistake, the combination would spontaneously reset, and it would take precious time to request the new one. That had happened to him once, fifteen years ago. He had not only caught hell but was almost fired over the error, a blunder he had vowed never to make again.

The thick, steel reinforced circular door swung open, flooding the cave-like storage facility with light. As Arne pulled the cargo rack into the chamber, he could see himself reflected in the luminous brightness of flawless Diggsanium mirrors. Row upon row of sturdy shelves held Geo Transport's entire stock of the priceless material, which had been concealed and protected for near twenty years in this underground Moon vault. Originally each mirror had been packed in a separate vacuum canister, but the bulky containers took up too much valuable space, and so the mirrors were laid upon shelves and packaged as needed.

This was Arne Harland's sole occupation: to place a single mirror inside a vacuum canister, seal the lid, and deliver the amount required to the loading dock. Today's order was for forty-eight mirrors, enough to fill one freighter. It was late in the day — near his quitting time when this requisition had arrived — and he'd been ordered to process the entire shipment immediately.

As he unloaded the triple-jacketed canisters from the cargo rack, he systematically checked each one to ensure they contained no oxygen or air. The actual procedure of placing the mirrors inside and sealing the vacuum containers was a routine chore, and the technician's thoughts began wandering to his long awaited vacation on Earth. His was a lonely job, and the visions of Hawaii and scantily clad women on the beach danced through his mind. He had saved a lot of money from his well-paid job, and his dream of early retirement had been gnawing at him for some time. Why not he thought? He'd been keeper of the vault — almost a prisoner of his vocation for twenty years — "he deserved to retire."

Working in the low gravity atmosphere, he tried to move slowly and deliberately; but given the edict to expedite the transfer, he ignored the carefully thought out procedures and began carrying two filled canisters at a time to the cargo rack. Though the round canisters did not weigh their normal forty-five kilograms in the Moon's gravity, Arne could feel the trickle of sweat building up inside his pressurized suit and oozing throughout his body.

He stopped for a moment and adjusted the moisture collector to maximum. In his haste to pick up the last two canisters, he stretched out both arms and bent down in a too abrupt motion. In the low gravity, his feet came off the floor and, in slow motion, he helplessly spun in a circle. The oxygen pack on his back struck a blunt corner of a shelf, causing the spin to stop so suddenly that his head crashed against his helmet. Dazed, he instinctively reached for the regulator to increase the flow of life-giving oxygen. It took a few minutes for his senses to clear, and he cursed himself for the foolish mistake. Gingerly picking up the two remaining canisters, he placed them on the transport rack and pushed it out of the vault. He methodically checked to see that everything in the vault was in order and closed the heavy round door. Returning to the elevator with his precious cargo, he was still bothered by his reckless action. It could have not only cost him his job but perhaps, his life. He angrily closed the door and pushed the "up" button.

During the ascent to the disembarkation area, Arne decided not to mention the accident to anyone. Normally, the first thing he did before unloading the elevator was to take off his pressurized suit. Following standard practice, he carried the suit to the vacuum hose that would draw out any moisture. Connecting the hose to the moisture collector, he tried to open the valve on his suit, but it was slightly bent. Applying more force on the small valve handle, he finally heard the hissing sound of moisture being drained into the vacuum hose. When the tube automatically shut off, very little water had been removed. "That's funny," he mused, "I didn't sweat as much as I thought."

Dismissing the incident, Arne hung the suit on a peg, reached for a tag labeled "need replacement," and carefully dangled it on the faulty suit valve.

As he began to unload the canisters from the transport cart, his daydreaming took precedent. "Maybe, I should just go ahead and retire after this vacation," he pondered. Then with resolve, "The hell with it, I'll just retire. I've had enough of this place."

True to his decision, Arne Harland never returned from Hawaii. He sent word to Geo Transport that he had opted for early retirement. His assistant was promptly promoted; and on his first day, an order came in for one hundred and forty-four mirrors that, as Arne had duly instructed him, were painstakingly loaded and shipped to Mars for retrofit of three freighters.

Ronal Lowe sat at his place in the Geo board-room, a tight smile curling his thin lips. He had been ignored during most of the meeting as if his presence was of no import.

Finally the Chairman of the Board pointed a finger in his direction. "Mr. Lowe," and all heads dutifully turned toward Ronal, "please give us the latest income statements."

"Thank you, Mr. Yenta," and he rose, starting to hand out individual reports.

Mr. Yenta curtly waved off the papers. "That will not be necessary, Mr. Lowe. We are all familiar with the actual results. All we want from you is a brief summary."

Ronal's anger over the obvious slight almost boiled to the surface, but he clenched his jaw and spoke evenly. "Our income from two months ago is up by 20% and sales are up by 12% as a result of the latest price increase and new orders taken from Space Transport." Then he sat down.

As if to keep his attention, a board member asked, "How much longer can Space Trans hold out?"

"Probably only another few years, at which time their fleet of transports will be down to zero. The freighters are coming off line from lack of replacement mirrors at the rate of about six a year. They may have a few small personnel carriers left, but that's about all. At that time we'll have complete control of all space activities, from holiday cruises and freight hauling to continued exploration of the solar system."

"Are you sure our supply of the Digg-sanium will last for the hundreds of years you predicted?" another member asked.

"Absolutely. We stockpiled over 250 metric tons, and assuming we don't increase our freighter fleet over our present 150 vehicles, the usage for the entire fleet is less than 16 metric tons every 20 years."

Mr. Yenta folded his slender fingers together in the familiar steeple fashion and slightly bent his head. "We have enough mirrors — ground and ready to install to last for over 300 years — at the current fleet level."

"By that time," a board member squinted through his thick glasses, "another material should be found, but Geo Transport will have such control of space that we will continue to dominate for many more centuries."

"I assume, Mr. Lowe," Mr. Yenta's guileless voice belied his testy words, "you still can assure us that the World Court will not direct Geo to divulge its supply of mirrors and to share the supply with Space Trans or any other competitor?"

"We are perfectly within the rules of fair competition. The Court realizes that if we share our supply, the world will exhaust the supply at twice the rate. Besides, a replacement has been sought for these past 18 years, but to no avail. The Court understands the world's scientists need as much time as possible to find a new material. You have my assurance," Ronal stated with certainty, "the World Court will be no problem."

"And the security around the stockpile of mirrors, Mr. Lowe?" Mr. Yenta's eyes narrowed as he critically appraised Ronal.

"Full security at all times." Ronal felt on firm ground again, and his tone was confident. "Only myself and you actually know the location of the mirrors, Mr. Yenta."

A smile barely parted Yenta's taunt lips. "And the two technicians that have access to the stockpile."

"They're well paid to keep their mouths shut," Ronal answered. "In fact their bonuses and retirement pay are predicated upon the location remaining secret."

Ignoring Ronal, Yenta turned away, "Of course, if anything happens to Mr. Lowe, or myself, other designated board members will receive the location via a coded micro-chip from our security people."

With a dismissing wave of his hand, Yenta motioned toward Ronal. "That will be all, Mr. Lowe. The board has private matters to discuss."

Seething inside, but presenting a controlled exterior, Ronal rose from his chair, bowed slightly, and strode from the room.

Back in his office, he poured a tumbler of whiskey, quaffing it down in a single gulp. Ronal didn't display his anger openly, as had his father and forefathers; rather, he carefully kept it in check when others were present. He was justly proud of his emotional control, having observed how Joal had permitted his emotions to overrule his business judgment. After all, it was he, not Joal, who had put together the Asian combine. And it was he who had worked out the plan for destroying the Diggs asteroid and using a stockpile of Diggsanium to control space transportation. That other people had suffered as a result was of no concern. He had done what no other ancestor had been able to accomplish — "the hated Diggs family was finished."

Looking up at the oil canvas of his father that still hung on the wall, Ronal began talking to it as if Joal were actually in the room.

"You old fool, you almost lost Geo Transport because of Arturo Diggs' new light speed engine. And you would have gone under if it hadn't been for the World Court decision to allow the Massafon Engine to be used by other competitors."

He rested his feet atop the desk, and a note of loathing crept into his voice. "I succeeded where you and your father, and his father and his father and all their fathers before couldn't accomplish. Finally the damn Diggs are getting a taste of their own medicine. I did it. Me! Not you, or any of your forefathers. How's that, you fuckin' old man?"

Tilting the whiskey bottle toward his glass, he splashed the remaining liquor into the tumbler. Suddenly he jumped from the chair and, with glass in hand walked over to Joal's full-length portrait. "They're finished, old fart. I did what you and your ancestors only dreamed of."

The eyes in the painting seemed to glare back at him, and he shook his fist. Then in fury he threw the whiskey at the painting while repeating over and over, "I did it you fucker! You didn't!"

The molecule floated around the enclosed vault, seemingly with a mind of its own, but it was not alone. By molecule standards, their numbers were few, and all could have been contained in less than a cubic millimeter. Like its comrades, the molecule soon found an inviting place and stopped its search. It knew nothing, for it had no consciousness. It only had an attraction to other molecules with which it could join, not knowing or caring about the havoc it was causing. It colonized and began to perform its function.

"Jana, are you all right?" Arturo shouted anxiously as he saw his wife stumble in her beloved flower garden.

"Yes, love. I'm fine," she cheerfully called back, "just a little woozy from stooping over."

She hadn't told Arturo that the dizziness she had experienced had grown much more frequent during the last month. Her doctor had informed her that the lack of equilibrium would increase and there was nothing that medical science could do to correct it. At ninety-five, she was simply wearing out. Jana accepted the verdict and admonished her trusted doctor not to tell Arturo.

"Come over here, lover," Jana beckoned, slowly bending down into a sitting position. "The new hybrid just opened."

Arturo walked down to the garden and kneeled beside his wife.

"Isn't that a beauty?" And her hand reached out to touch the gigantic fiery red blossom.

"Not as vibrant and beautiful as you are, my love."

A demure smile brightened her still lovely face, and her eyes shone with adoration. "I love you, my Arturo. What a life we've had, my darling. I wouldn't change one minute of it. I love you."

Jana leaned her head on his shoulder, and Arturo cradled her in his arms, softly rocking her body against his. Kissing her hair, he could feel that her breathing was barely perceptible.

"I'll take you in for a nap, my darling."

She made no reply.

Salty tears came into his eyes as he felt her breath became shallower and her slight body slump heavily against his.

With tears streaming freely down his face, he took both her hands and continued gripping them tightly as if to will her back to life. "Wait for me, my darling. Wait for me."

After Jana's death, Webb and Marna spent every possible minute with Arturo, but their grandfather's only pursuit was to put his affairs in order. He knew that time was short and that his legacy and bequest for the Bible, as all his ancestors had done, must be completed.

This day, he had requested to be left alone. Sitting in his study, he was again listening to the microchip, which Filip had left almost two decades ago, as his contribution to the Bible. The chip contained a voice recording of the history of his work and setting up the Diggsanium business on the asteroid, the recounting of his marriage and the birth and growing up of the twins. All but one small segment Arturo had never told anyone about, with the exception of Jana.

It was with anguish in his heart that today he intently listened to that particular part.

"Dad, please don't upset anyone with what I'm about to say. I hope we can laugh about it and erase this part of the chip. Anyway, as a small kid I remember Grandmother Margarite Diggs used to say that she sometimes had clairvoyance about certain subjects. Mother also had occasions of telepathy. Maybe I inherited the way I've felt for the last few months from them. For some reason, I've felt an impending sense of something like a disaster or an unexpected event," there was a short chuckle, "an unwanted one. In any event, I've shipped 50 Diggsanium mirrors to you, Dad, two per vacuum canister. The canisters are in a large vacuum container, disguised to look like a safe. Since the whole thing weighs about two tons, I don't think anyone will try to abscond with the safe. Use it as you will and hopefully you'll never need it. Why I did this, I suppose I'll never know, but it was something I just had to do, along with getting my input to our family Bible. Please don't worry about my presumed premonition. Everything will be fine. I love you and Mother."

With brimming tears, Arturo copied the part to which he had just listened in his own handwriting and signed Filip's name. Carefully, he placed the document in Filip's safe containing the hidden Diggsanium mirrors. Once done with the task, he erased that part from Filip's chip. Only then did he begin to write.

The hidden legacy would be in his own handwriting, as would his open family bequest, the same as Ben and Newsome had done. All his work on the Massafon Engine and exceeding the speed-of-light had been carefully transferred to a microchip and resided in the drawer of his desk. The Bible lay on a small table beside his desk. He continued carefully in his most legible handwriting. As he wrote, he could feel his time approaching and he tried to go faster.

Finishing his bequest, he laid it aside for later inclusion in the Bible. He then picked up Filip's historical chip and inserted it in the Bible with the previous bequests of other Diggs ancestors. His own microchip was placed in a small sealed container and put into Filip's safe. Picking up the Bible and laying it on his desk, he carefully removed the leather laces on the back cover and inserted his handwritten legacy. He wasn't sure why it had to be hidden from future Diggs descendants, but he followed in the tradition of old Newsome and Ben. To do as they had done was right; that he knew for sure, and to do otherwise was unthinkable. Somewhere, someday, somehow, another Diggs would find the legacy and continue the pursuit of light speed — and beyond — when the time was right.

While Arturo Diggs was writing his bequest and legacy, Ronal Lowe was receiving the most disturbing news of his life. These were tidings that would eventually change the character of the world. He listened horrified as the Operations Vice-President of Geo Transport gave his hurried report.

"Mr. Lowe, all we know for sure was that when freighter 0023 started the Massafon Engine, the mirrors shattered immediately. That's all we know for sure," he repeated. "We had just installed new mirrors at the 20,000 hour change-out requirement, but they completely disintegrated when the engine was fired up."

"Were all procedures followed during change-out of the mirrors?"

"Yes sir, they were. Another set of replacement mirrors was due to arrive just over three hours ago and installation should be complete." The Ops Manager glanced at his watch and continued, "Should be ready just about now."

"How long until the Massafon Engine is engaged?"

"Another 30 minutes. Shouldn't be any further trouble. The other problem was probably a fluke."

"We'll see about that. Okay, let me know the outcome of the start-up." With a curt gesture he dismissed the Ops Manager.

Ronal knew something was terribly wrong. He could feel it coursing through his veins. Every fiber of his being seemed to be screaming in apprehension. Refusing all incoming calls, he impatiently stalked around his office. Only one thing was on his mind. What was happening? For him the seconds were minutes and the minutes seemed hours while he waited for the report of the second mirror installation.

Finally, the allotted time had passed and he couldn't stand the suspense. He left his office and went to the Ops Manager's control site. As he entered he heard the Moon-base manager's voice on the visi-phone and was not encouraged by his grim expression.

"All mirrors shattered on impact of the Posafon and Negafon beams. When I say shattered, it looks as if they had been hit with a sledgehammer. We've ordered replacements, but I think we've got a serious problem of some sort."

Ronal's blood seemed frozen in his veins — like small water pipes in sub-zero weather. If the mirrors were shattering on impact of the beams and the stockpile of mirrors was useless, his grip on space travel would vanish. In fact, all high-speed space travel would be a thing of the past. There was no more Diggsanium to be had. He had destroyed the source.

One week later, over 20 tons of mirrors from Geo's stockpile had been tested under vacuum conditions in their laboratories. All had shattered. The mirrors were worthless for use in a Massafon Engine. Ronal Lowe knew that it was only a matter of time until his fleet of transports would be grounded for lack of mirrors. He decided to keep the disastrous news to himself. Those in Geo, privy to the information, were ordered to keep quiet. Immediately he initiated a program to find an alternate material, as had Space Transport and all the other competitors and researchers throughout the world.

It only took a few days for the story to gradually leak to the electronic news media and a reporter to relay to the world a startling story.

"This commentator has learned that Geo Transport has had problems with their transport engines. This is the engine that was developed by Mr. Arturo Newsome Diggs for travel at the speed-of-light. Since the unexplained disintegration of the asteroid where the key element of the engine was mined, a suitable substitute has not been found. Geo Transport continued operation as a result of a seemingly large stockpile, much to the detriment of Space Transport, who has seen its fleet of transports dwindle to one quarter of the original size for lack of the rare material. It seems that over 50 tons from Geo's stockpile have been tested under laboratory conditions, but all disintegrated and were useless. Further, it is reported from reliable sources that 20 sets of this material have shattered during freighter engine start-up. If the reports are accurate, the future of space travel as we now know it is in serious jeopardy."

The commentator went on with descriptions of the Massafon Engine and the unexplained explosion of the asteroid where Diggsanium was mined.

Ronal Lowe ordered an immediate investigation to determine the cause of failure of the Diggsanium material. The inquiry centered around the storage area on the Moon. The technician, Arne Harland, who had retired to Hawaii, was interviewed, but the investigators learned nothing conclusive. Arne was ordered to return to the Moon to retrace his steps during his last, and final, loading of the Diggsanium mirrors.

Numerous times Arne painstakingly reviewed his every motion. Over and over he answered questions about the elevator ride to the vault, his procedure to ensure a complete vacuum existed before opening the vault door to the Diggsanium storage, and the checking of each container for leakage. Then he showed how he placed the mirrors one by one in the vacuum canisters, loaded the transportation trolley in the elevator to the embarkation point, then removed his suit and shipped the material.

In his desire to place blame somewhere, one persistent investigator requested that the technician's vacuum suit and the records of maintenance be analyzed. Finding that the moisture collector drain valve had been replaced, the investigator began to question how and when it was damaged.

After hours of grueling questioning Arne reluctantly admitted that he had accidentally fallen and that perhaps the suit valve could have been damaged. The replaced valve was located in the refuse center, and when tested, it was found to have a slight leak. Continued testing of the retrieved valve revealed that four cubic centimeters of human sweat could have possibly seeped through in approximately twenty minutes. It was further determined that Arne had remained in the vault for approximately ten to fifteen minutes after his fall.

The conclusion was that approximately two cubic centimeters of human moisture had leaked into the Diggsanium vacuum vault. One of the inspectors, in exasperation, began picking mirrors at random and throwing them against the steel walls of the vault. All shattered on impact.

There was now no doubt about the inquiry's results and the cause of the resulting disaster. The oxygen molecules in the technician's human sweat had attacked the entire supply of Diggsanium mirrors — making all the mirrors worthless for use in the Massafon Engine — mirrors which held the key to transportation in space up to the speed of light at 300,000 kilometers per second.

Earth was again dependent on space vehicle engines, which could travel only at maximum speeds of 170 kilometers per second. The greed of a few people had robbed Earth's population of high-speed space travel and the possibility of ultimately sending mankind to other solar systems in the Milky Way.

The greatest benefit to mankind since the formation of the Arabic numbering system, utilizing zero, which allowed numeric ranges from negative infinity to positive infinity, was now useless.

As Ronal Lowe walked into the boardroom at Geo Transport, the all Asian board members greeted him with grimly impassive faces.

Mr. Yenta did not mince words. "Mr. Lowe, have you definitely determined that all the Diggsanium in our stockpile is useless?"

"Yes!" Ronal answered without any explanation, knowing that each and every member had a complete report on what had happened, who was responsible, and the disastrous results.

"Mr. Lowe," Yenta commanded, "you will leave the room while we discuss your disposition."

"Gentlemen, as Chief Executive Officer," Ronal objected, "I protest to..."

Mr. Yenta interrupted. "Mr. Lowe. You have no choice." Ronal knew his objection was being ignored and he felt depredation of his inner self.

Only three minutes passed before Ronal was ordered back in the boardroom. Though he restrained his outward emotion, he experienced the same sense of foreboding he felt when initially notified of the first failure of the Diggsanium mirrors. The board members' expressions were unreadable. Try as he might, he could not detect any emotion or feeling on any of the twelve faces.

"Mr. Lowe, it is the unanimous decision of the board," Mr. Yenta announced, "that you shall be relieved as CEO of Geo Transport, effective immediately. Your office has been secured by our security people, and you are to leave the premises of Geo Transport without delay."

Before Ronal could object, the door to the boardroom opened and two uniformed security officers he had never seen before seized his arms. Realizing that any form of protest was useless, he allowed them to lead him from the room.

Once in the hallway, he vainly tried to shake off the vise-like grips. "I can walk, God damn it." Then he demanded, "Take your fuckin' hands off me."

The guards simply tightened the pressure. Instead of using the private elevator that went directly to the restricted roof area, which housed his air-car, the guards steered him down office corridors. As he was being escorted through the building, Ronal had glimpses of employees peering at him from doorways and he heard the excited whispers behind his back. It was the most humiliating experience that Ronal Lowe had ever endured.

When the three men eventually reached the transport pad, Ronal was physically shoved into his air-car. The guards turned on their heels, returned to the building and locked the door behind them.

Ronal's fury overcame coherent thought. Consumed with the intensity of his rage, he failed to input the coordinates for an automatic flight path. Instead, he overrode the computer and switched to an emergency mode. The voice of Central Traffic Control computer promptly inquired as to the nature of the emergency. Inflamed by the intrusive voice, he reduced the volume down to indistinguishable levels and commanded the air-car into flight at maximum acceleration.

It was only after he was away from Geo headquarters that he calmed down enough to order the air-car to proceed directly to his home, but he did not decrease the speed.

Ronal's state of mind compelled him to vindicate himself and assign blame elsewhere for his removal as CEO. "It was those damn Diggs," he shouted, as he banged his clenched fists against the padded console. "They caused this. If they hadn't had all the Diggsanium mirrors to themselves, this would never have happened. I'll get them. I'll get them if it's the last thing I ever do."

With uncontrollable fury, Ronal switched on the holographic computer and began a tirade of incoherent abuse against the Diggs family. When he finally wore down, he directed that his dictation be transferred to his home holographic computer.

Engrossed by his own self-indulgent interpretations, he was at first unmindful of the slight vibration that rocked the air-car. As the vibrations increased, he began to panic. His fear was not that he would be a hazard to others in his flight path but that they might endanger him. He had forgotten about the built-in safety system, which would not allow an out-of-control air-car to jeopardize others in the same path.

A shrill alarm sounded as Ronal's air-car began violent maneuvers to avoid impact with other vehicles or with anything else in its route. Too late he grasped for the control that he had overridden — the safety restraint — which kept one securely in the air-car's seat. An unexpected sharp turn of over 10 g's, threw Ronal with such force, that his head hit the roof of the air-car like a ripe grapefruit thrown against a brick wall. It made no difference to Ronal that the impact made a large dent in the overhead metal. His skull was cracked open and his brain had already begun oozing. He died without knowing what happened.

The foolproof air-car safety system automatically decelerated and directed itself to an open lot. When the car landed, all power was turned off except for the emergency signal giving its location to Central Traffic.

Inside, Ronal Lowe lay like a rag doll with arms and legs akimbo, as if some mischievous child had thrown it across the room.

That evening the electronic news carried a brief recount of his demise and a brief summary of his tenure at Geo Transport and recent dismissal as CEO. The impassive commentator concluded with a footnote.

"Mr. Lowe is survived by his

wife and two sons, both of whom are in politics and were recently elected to committees in the World Government. Ronal Lowe was 74."

Arturo took no pleasure from the news concerning Ronal Lowe's death. He had never personally met the man that unbeknown to him, had caused so much pain and anguish to him and his family. But the announcement that Geo's entire Diggsanium mirror stockpile had been damaged was of keen interest.

Geo, like Space Transport, would have to begin relying on the same old nuclear-chemical engines that he had developed over sixty-three years ago. Since the Massafon Engine retrofit of all space vehicles, no later developments had come forth and Arturo's original engine was the only one available.

One day he hoped his light speed re-search would be of use to those on Earth, but it would not be in his remaining lifetime. He could only presume that a future Diggs de-scendant would carry on and expand upon the work he had begun. Exploration of other aster-oids for Diggsanium would be severely curtailed without the Massafon Engine; and without any real progress during the last eighteen years, the development of a substitute material looked bleak. The Diggsanium in Filip's safe was not enough to make any difference to the world's current problem, so Arturo decided to not re-veal its existence. He knew that it would be needed by one of his descendants in some fu-ture time.

Summoning his grandchildren, Webb and Marna, he re-emphasized the importance of the underground vault containing the Bible and family history — and especially the large safe from Filip. Arturo was careful not to inform them of the contents in Filip's safe; he said only that it contained a vital part of the Diggs heritage and would open at the right time for some future Diggs.

After the family briefing, Webb and Marna watched their grandfather walk out to the garden and begin to pick a bouquet of roses. They were touched by the slow and methodical manner with which he cut each long stem. He seemed to derive so much serenity from the simple chore.

Coming back to the house, Arturo, as Jana had always done, started placing the beautiful roses in the vase he and Jana had bought over 70 years ago. It took him some time before he was satisfied with the arrangement, but he finally stepped back and nodded approval. Turning to Webb and Marna, he had a look of serenity on his face. "If you'll excuse me for awhile, I'm a bit tired." He straightened his shoulders and started walking down the hall.

"Is there anything we can get you, Grandfather?" Webb asked.

"No. Thank you, anyway." Then he stopped and turned to look directly at his two grandchildren. "Yes! I almost forgot. On my desk is a piece of paper. Would you be so kind and put it in the Bible for me right now. I meant to do it earlier, but I neglected to do so. Thank you."

Marna's loving smile bespoke her devotion to the elderly patriarch. "Of course, Grandfather. And we'll still be here when you wake up from your nap."

Arturo gave a slight wave of his hand and then turned and disappeared down the long hallway.

A mystified look passed between Marna and Webb. It was an unusual request that Arturo had made of them, and they were curious about the importance of placing the paper in the old family Bible immediately.

Webb walked into Arturo's study and began to scan the handwriting as soon as he picked up the paper; as he handed it to Marna his tone was solemn. "It's Grandfather's bequest to his descendants. All Diggs have done this since old Newsome. Each has left something for the future."

The twins had been fascinated by the written bequests in the Bible since they were children, and they wondered about Arturo's urgent request that his bequest be placed in the Bible today.

"Oh my God!" Marna exclaimed, as the date at the end of the hand written page seemed to jump out at her. Tears began streaming down her cheeks.

Webb put his arm around his sister, not even trying to control his own sorrow. His voice cracked in grief. "We should be with him."

Brushing away the wet stains on her face, Marna could only nod her assent.

When Marna and Webb entered the bedroom, Arturo lay peacefully on the bed with a serene smile still on his lips. At ninety-eight, he had gone to sleep, never to awaken. He had died with the vision of his beloved Jana coming down the aisle to join him on their wedding day.

Still holding her grandfather's final bequest in her hand, Marna knelt beside the bed. For a few moments she and Webb prayed silently in his memory.

"It's time, Marna." Webb gently pulled his sister to her feet, and linked her arm in his. They slowly walked together to the vault, which held the family Bible. Webb recited the numbers of the multi-combination to unlock the heavy door; then he removed the aged Bible and carried it to a nearby table.

Marna lovingly opened the leather cover, and turned the pages carefully. "Dear, dear Grandfather, your bequest should be read aloud before we place it in the Bible."

In a surprisingly strong voice, Marna began reading.

> With the belief in my work by my dear and beloved wife, Jana, who was always there to encourage me, even during the darkest of times; the financial support of my close friend Mohammed Nahal; the scientific help of my second father, Dr. Marshall Bernside; the discovery of Diggsanium by our son Filip; and my pursuit of Grandfather

Ben's thoughts, I solved the problem of a space ship traveling at the speed of light. Our ancestor, Newsome Diggs, would have been proud. Unfortunately, the solution for travel by humans to distant stars and other galaxies in practical time periods was not solved. Someone in the Diggs family will pick up the work and go far beyond my achievements. When the right person comes along, he or she will know they were chosen as I was chosen. All others are to pursue the life and dreams of their choice, the same as all Diggs who descended from Grandfather Newsome. My love is always with you.

Arturo Newsome Diggs
2145-2243

Webb frowned as he reread Arturo's bequest. "I wonder what Grandfather meant by, 'Newsome Diggs would have been proud'."

"I don't understand it either, Webb," Marna replied. "Old Newsome Diggs' bequest didn't mention traveling to other stars or anywhere in the universe."

> *"He found the keys much quicker than..."*
> *"The work was brilliant..."*
> *"The right family was chosen..."*

"One final step..."
"It's a shame that..."
"So many hurt by so very few..."
"The dark-side of man..."
"It will still evolve..."
"But how...?"
"Nothing before its time, Newsome..."
"Nothing before its time..."

THE QUEST